Praise for

A MARKED MAN

"Intriguing . . . Rich in period detail . . . A successful novel appealing to those who enjoy Revolutionary War historical mystery." —*Historical Novels Review*

"The story line is fast paced and the investigation super, but it is meeting the prime real persona and fictional characters representing the divided times in Boston in 1774 that makes *A Marked Man* a strong late-eighteenth-century thriller." —*Midwest Book Review*

"Hamilton breathes vivid life into her historical characters . . . A satisfying read for mystery lovers and American history buffs alike." —*Kirkus Reviews*

"Well crafted . . . Hamilton once again brings to life colonial Boston on the brink of revolution, vividly portraying such noted patriots as Sam Adams, leader of the Sons of Liberty; silversmith Paul Revere; and Dr. Joseph Warren." —*Publishers Weekly*

Praise for

THE NINTH DAUGHTER

"An exciting new mystery series set in revolutionary Boston. Abigail Adams could become my favorite historical sleuth." —Sharon Kay Penman, author of *Devil's Brood*

"Barbara Hamilton plunges us into colonial Boston, where we walk beside the legendary Abigail Adams as she tries to find justice for a murdered young woman while also helping with the birthing pangs of a new nation." —Victoria Thompson, author of *Murder on Sisters' Row*

continued . . .

"[An] exceptional debut . . . While bringing to life such historical figures as Sam Adams and Paul Revere, Hamilton transports the reader to another time and place with close attention to matters like dress, menus, and the monumental task of doing laundry. Historical fans will eagerly look forward to the next in this promising series." —*Publishers Weekly*

"Hamilton . . . has just the right touch to guide the intelligent Abigail through the dangerous shoals of being a patriot while seeing the good side of the colonies' English rulers. There are no missteps here in what should prove to be a captivating series for all historical fans." —*Library Journal*

"The wry repartee between Abigail and John, together with the fact that this clandestine investigation of the murder of loose women would never have made the official record, make Hamilton's debut believable and gripping." —*Kirkus Reviews*

"A deep historical mystery. Based on true activities of that time, Ms. Hamilton weaves a tale that could have actually taken place . . . A finely written first in a new series story with a surprise ending. I am eager to see what comes next." —*The Romance Readers Connection*

"A super Revolutionary War–era . . . amateur sleuth." —*Midwest Book Review*

"The story line provides a deep look at Boston as rebellion is in the air. Fans will want to join the tea party hosted by Ms. Hamilton with guests being a who's who of colonial Massachusetts." —*The Mystery Gazette*

Berkley Prime Crime titles by Barbara Hamilton

THE NINTH DAUGHTER

A MARKED MAN

SUP WITH THE DEVIL

SUP WITH THE DEVIL

Barbara Hamilton

BERKLEY PRIME CRIME, NEW YORK

THE BERKLEY PUBLISHING GROUP
Published by the Penguin Group
Penguin Group (USA) Inc.
375 Hudson Street, New York, New York 10014, USA
Penguin Group (Canada), 90 Eglinton Avenue East, Suite 700, Toronto, Ontario M4P 2Y3, Canada
(a division of Pearson Penguin Canada Inc.)
Penguin Books Ltd., 80 Strand, London WC2R 0RL, England
Penguin Group Ireland, 25 St. Stephen's Green, Dublin 2, Ireland (a division of Penguin Books Ltd.)
Penguin Group (Australia), 250 Camberwell Road, Camberwell, Victoria 3124, Australia
(a division of Pearson Australia Group Pty. Ltd.)
Penguin Books India Pvt. Ltd., 11 Community Centre, Panchsheel Park, New Delhi—110 017, India
Penguin Group (NZ), 67 Apollo Drive, Rosedale, Auckland 0632, New Zealand
(a division of Pearson New Zealand Ltd.)
Penguin Books (South Africa) (Pty.) Ltd., 24 Sturdee Avenue, Rosebank, Johannesburg 2196,
South Africa

Penguin Books Ltd., Registered Offices: 80 Strand, London WC2R 0RL, England

This book is an original publication of The Berkley Publishing Group.

This is a work of fiction. Names, characters, places, and incidents either are the product of the author's imagination or are used fictitiously, and any resemblance to actual persons, living or dead, business establishments, events, or locales is entirely coincidental. The publisher does not have any control over and does not assume any responsibility for author or third-party websites or their content.

FIRST EDITION: October 2011

Library of Congress Cataloging-in-Publication Data

Hamilton, Barbara, 1951–
    Sup with the devil / Barbara Hamilton.—1st ed.
        p. cm.
    ISBN 978-0-425-24320-6
    1. Adams, Abigail, 1744–1818—Fiction.   2. Murder—Investigation—Fiction.
3. Massachusetts—History—Colonial period, ca. 1600–1775—Fiction.   I. Title.
    PS3558.A4215S87 2011
    813'.54—dc22

                                                              2011006678

PRINTED IN THE UNITED STATES OF AMERICA

10 9 8 7 6 5 4 3 2 1

For Brandy & Joey

SUP WITH THE DEVIL

One

Horace Thaxter
Cambridge, Massachusetts

23 April 1774

Abigail Adams
Queen Street, Boston

Dear Aunt Abigail,

John (my cousin, not your esteemed husband) has told me upon many occasions of your extraordinary acuity in seeing through the riddles of criminal conduct, a veritable Alexander (if one may so term a member of your sex) cutting the nodum Gordium *of both puzzling circumstance and the* obstructio deliberi *of evildoers.*

Therefore, I write to you in a state of mental perturbation regarding events that befell me this week, which I am at a loss to interpret.

The events were made the more troubling because I was introduced to them by a letter from Mr. Adams (your esteemed husband, not his notorious cousin), which induced me to believe myself safe in entering a situation at best equivocal, and at worst giving rise to fears that I might have been—and may still be—in danger of my life.

Might I beg the pleasure of calling upon you on the 30th, when Mr. Adams will be returned from the circuit courts and propriety will permit you to receive a male caller? This is a matter that troubles and—though others have said it is the merest exiguum—*frightens me. I look forward to the favor of your reply.*

Your ob't h'bl svt,
Horace Thaxter

Propriety indeed. Abigail Adams, perched on the back of Uzziah Begbie's delivery wagon as it jolted its way along the extremely narrow streets of Boston's North End, reread her nephew's letter with mixed amusement and exasperation. *You'd think the boy was forty instead of barely seventeen.*

You'd think I was a sixteen-year-old village maid instead of a woman of twenty-nine with a husband—off at the Maine Assizes or not—*and four children.*

And you'd think we were in London instead of Massachusetts, where women have been going about their business in perfect freedom and safety since the Indians left. Does he think the neighbors are going to suspect him of an assault on my virtue?

Or suspect me of an assault on his?

On second thought, reflected Abigail, tucking the letter back into her smallest marketing basket, *considering some of my neighbors . . .*

In addition to Horace's letter, which had arrived late yesterday afternoon, the basket was stocked with apples, carrots, corn-bread (wheaten flour of any kind gave Horace migraines), a small crock of honey, and ten hard-boiled eggs, and rested beside her on the narrow bench that served as a wagon-seat. On her other side, the carter Uzziah Begbie clucked to his horse as the wagon made its careful way among the carts and barrows that cluttered the cobblestones of Prince's Street. To their right loomed the piled-up rooflines of Copp's Hill, a maze of steep alleyways and small yards; to their left, through a break in the roof-lines, Abigail could glimpse the placid green water of the Mill Pond. Wind from the river flicked her face, caught a strand of her black hair that had escaped her neat white cap. She smoothed it primly into its place again. Were she on the farm in Braintree, she reflected—the land that her "esteemed husband" (as Horace Thaxter described him) and his family had farmed for three generations—she would have pulled her cap off altogether, run to the top of Prospect Hill to let the wind of the bay have its way with her hair . . . would have revelled in the sweetness of May after so harsh and unsettling a winter.

But this was Boston, and people did talk.

Indeed, as they rounded the last of the brick and timber houses and came to Gee's Shipyard on the rocky nose of North Boston, people were doing nothing but talking. The boundaries of the street itself dissolved into a roughly defined apron of gravel and mud around the end of the hill, beyond which lay the hard blackish sapphire waters of the bay. Sailors, roustabouts, stevedores, and the lady who sold hot pies stood in knots among the piled timber and coiled cables, gesturing out toward the British warship that patrolled the bay and half shouting over the clattering symphony of shipyard hammers.

I hear the King's going to close the port . . .

He can't do that, can he?

They say in Salem there's a royal commission on its way to inquire . . .

Royal commission my backside, my cousin says they'll send troops from Halifax and hang the rebels that did it . . .

Sam Adams'll never let that happen.

Don't be a fool, Adams is the first man they'll hang. The King won't put up with rebellion . . .

No, agreed Abigail silently. *The King won't put up with rebellion.*

And she wondered for the dozenth time since leaving the house if she had any business going out of Boston even for an afternoon.

Her common sense told her that even if the King sent a Royal Commissioner to investigate the circumstances of last December that had resulted in over three hundred crates of East India Company tea being dumped into Boston Harbor, trouble wasn't going to erupt on the first day. For one thing, the Sons of Liberty—the semi-secret organization devoted to defiance of the King's arbitrary commands—would have to take the measure of the commission's mandate and decide what to do. And these days, Sam Adams—her husband's wily cousin—kept a tight rein on the Sons, cooling violence in one place, puffing it up in another, simplifying the issues at stake, and playing upon the angers and fears of men like a virtuoso playing upon a pianoforte.

A journey out to Cambridge for the afternoon would likely do no harm.

She hoped.

Begbie drew rein to let a half-dozen men pass, bearing on their shoulders the massive beam of what would be a ship's keel. Some of them called out greetings to him, asked after wife, children, that keg of nails they were waiting for . . .

Abigail returned her thoughts to the note she had received.

To what "troubling" events did John introduce Horace by letter? As far as Abigail knew, her esteemed husband—stout, peppery, brilliant, and maddening—hadn't had anything to do with any of the Thaxters other than John Thaxter, his young law clerk and Horace's cousin (*second cousin? Uncle? That was the trouble with being related to half the colony . . .*) for over a year, one whole branch of that well-off merchant clan having decided that she—Abigail—had stepped down in the world by marrying a farmer's son even if he *was* related to the extremely respectable (*back then, anyway*) Deacon Adams of Old South Church . . .

And into what earthly situation could John have pitchforked the boy that would have put him—so he believed—in danger of his life?

A man in the leather apron of a ship's carpenter emerged from a chandler's shop, crossed the gravel, and spoke to the deliveryman, quiet beneath the din of hammering. Abigail didn't hear his exact words, but she knew what they were.

Any news . . . ?

Begbie shook his head.

Only a few clouds spotted the bright April sky, but Abigail felt a chill and pulled her shawl close about her.

No news yet.

Six weeks for the news of the so-called Tea Party to reach England. Then whatever Parliament was going to decide to do about the rebellion growing in the colony. Then six weeks back.

Which meant that whatever was going to happen, was going to happen soon.

"Half a mo', Mrs. Adams." Begbie sprang down from his seat, darted down the split-log steps to the shipyard. From where she sat Abigail could see the broad, flat shape of the ferry scow and no sign of its captain or crew. A carter, a country minister in a black coat, and two stout farm-women in wide-brimmed straw hats clustered by the ferry landing, talking eagerly with a couple of men in sailors' slops.

Even the gulls that wheeled above the dumped remains of some fisherman's unsold catch seemed to be yammering rumors to one another.

Men came and unloaded an immense coil of ship's cable from the goods-wagon; Begbie took the horse's bridle, led the animal down to the ferry just as Obed Pusey and his crew reappeared and began collecting sixpences for the voyage. Abigail climbed down before they crossed the wet black wood of the wharf, and sought out the bench farthest aft and as close to the mast as she could get without interfering with the crew's work. Crossing through the confluence of the Charles River and the bay itself, the ferry would roll like a home-going drunkard and—a disgrace to her merchant heritage—Abigail knew she invariably became seasick in even the half-mile voyage from Boston to Charles Town across the harbor.

The sharp spring wind filled the sails as the men poled the scow off the wharf: Abigail resolutely fixed her eyes on the tidy cluster of brown houses, of orchards and farmlands, on the feet of the mainland hills. Like Boston, Charles Town stood on a peninsula, connected to the mainland by a neck of land, but from Charles Town you didn't have to wind around rivers and over bridges to get to the town of Cambridge, where young Horace Thaxter was presently in college.

A letter from Mr. Adams . . . which induced me to believe myself safe in entering a situation at best equivocal . . .

Of course, Horace always believed himself in danger of his life. Abigail recalled more than one conversation with the weedy boy devoted entirely to his recital of his latest symptoms, which ranged from *tremor cordis* to sanguineous congestion of the lungs. At the time of their last meeting he had been, she estimated, fifteen and "grinding" with a tutor to prepare himself for Harvard College. Horace was tall, thin, and filled to the hairline with Aristotle and medical quackery. That had been on a visit to Salem where his parents (as well as Abigail's sister) lived, shortly after Abigail's son Charley's first birthday.

Now Charley was three.

This is a matter which frightens me.

After long and complex circumlocutions in Latin, it came down to that. *This is a matter which frightens me . . .* Simple words in English.

And it was true—Abigail admitted it to herself—that she took a deal of pleasure in chopping through the Gordian knot of puzzling circumstance and the deliberate obstructions of evildoers.

It was also true that it was May, after a winter remarkable for the bitterness of its cold, and that once Mr. Begbie's goods-wagon was off the rocking waters of the bay and onto the road that ran along the feet of Breeds and Bunker Hills, the sweet-smelling quiet of the countryside made a blessed change from Boston's fishy reek and the stinks of sewage and backyard cows, the twitter of birds a delight after the rattle of carts and the shouting of boys playing in Queen Street and the clatter of hammers in Mr. Butler's cooperage next door . . .

The peaceful air a relief from that dread that seemed to have settled over the town like a pillow pressed to an uneasy sleeper's face.

What will we do if . . . ?

It should be any day we'll hear . . .

Massachusetts in the spring.

The countryside that lay between Charles Town and Cambridge was prosperously settled, orchard trees parting now and then to show Abigail tidy farmhouses, and fields of corn already shoulder-high. Cows chewed mildly in their pastures;

gray stone walls lined the road. In patches of woodland, finches and robins sang. Abigail dearly enjoyed the noise and excitement and conveniences of Boston—the ability to simply go down to the wharves for Spanish lemons or to a mercer's on the next street if she happened to decide her daughter Nabby needed a new dress. The ability to go to a bookstore and purchase the newest works of Goldsmith or Smollett, or the fact that John could bring in newspapers printed that day. The fact that in winter, snow did not mean utter isolation. Yet she had been raised in the parsonage of a very small village, and in her heart, she sorely missed the scents of deep grass and woodland in May.

As Mr. Begbie had a number of deliveries in Cambridge and was likely to pursue his second vocation—that of collecting and disseminating news and rumor—when they reached the outskirts of the village, Abigail bid him good-by with thanks. "I shall finish up at the Golden Stair, on the Common," said the carter—a neighbor of hers on Queen Street—shaking her hand in farewell. "You'll find me there in three or four hours—time enough to locate your nephew—and we'll still be back at the ferry long before the sun's down. Good luck, m'am!"

Good luck indeed, reflected Abigail good-humoredly, as she set off with her marketing basket in the direction of the College, whose cluster of brick halls she glimpsed through orchard trees, for she hadn't the faintest idea in which of its several buildings Horace was lodged. The open-sided quadrangle of Harvard College faced the town common, across a lane and a four-foot wall. A young man in a freshman's short gown emerged from the gate as Abigail drew near. He bore a wig box and walked swiftly, as if pursued or in fear of pursuit, and hesitated for an instant when she waved him over. "Are you acquainted with Mr. Horace Thaxter? Would you know—?"

"I say, I say—!" Another scholar in the longer gown of a more senior student strolled over from a group of his friends. "You there, Yeovil—"

The freshman gave Abigail a harassed look and turned.

"What are you up to, Yeovil?"

"I was speaking with this lady, sir," said the boy. He looked about fifteen—Horace had been sixteen and a half when he'd entered the college the previous September, but they took boys younger even than this one—with linen spotlessly white against the blue of his academic gown and a beautifully curled pigeon-wing wig, powdered like marble.

"Now, Yeovil," chided the newcomer, who looked rather like a ferret in a scarlet gown, "a *freshman*? Address a *lady*?"

"And so beautiful a lady," added another of the group, coming over and making Abigail a handsome leg as he bowed. *"Che il crin s'è un Tago e son due Soli i lume/Prodigio tal non rimirò Natura . . ."* Between a crumpled neckcloth and an elaborately curled wig, his face was plump and unshaven, and his eyes, set in little cushions of fat discolored by sleeplessness, had the twinkling and rather dangerous intelligence of a pig. The effect was of a dissipated baby who had been spending far too many nights in a tavern. "How may your humble servant be of use to you, fair stranger? You, Yeovil, run along . . . Where *were* you off to?"

In a taut voice that showed an unfortunate tendency to crack, the boy said, "I was taking this wig to be curled, sir." He held up the box.

The fat student viewed it through a quizzing-glass; his companion in the red gown, suppressing a grin, exclaimed, "Why, so you were! And whose wig is that, Yeovil?"

"Mr. Lechmere's, sir."

"Lechmere, Lechmere . . ." The older men—and the other

two of their group who had joined them—all made a great show of trying to remember who Lechmere was.

"Egad, isn't he a sophomore?"

"Disgraceful . . . !"

"For shame!"

"Tell you what," said Red Gown, and produced from his voluminous sleeve two pewter pitchers, "why don't you be a good chap and, while you're in town, just hop on over to the Crowned Pig and fill these up with our good host's best?"

John had told Abigail about the customs of the college: Yeovil, a lowly fresher, was obliged to do the bidding of his seniors. She also guessed that Red Gown was probably a junior and thus able to preempt the boy's services (*How was he going to carry both pitchers full of ale and also Mr. Lechmere the Sophomore's wig box . . . ? Which of course was the point, the wretched boys . . .*).

Thus she wasn't at all surprised when Yeovil had been dispatched on his errand and the fat student—whose lush yellow gown gave him the general appearance of a gargantuan squash—made another bow, to find her request for Horace's direction interrupted yet again . . .

"Excuse me, my very dear madame, I beg of you—Yeovil!" the fat man yelled. "Yo, Yeovil, come back here, blister it!"

He was the senior, then, reflected Abigail with a sigh. Or a bachelor-fellow, by the look of him. And privileged to preempt the junior's request for ale, which had preempted the sophomore's demand for his wig to be taken to be curled . . .

The fat student's companions were stamping and slapping each other and smothering with laughter to such an extent that none of them saw another man—crimson-gowned and a few years older than they—until he had crossed the yard from the gate and reached Abigail's side. "Pugh, aren't you getting a little old for this kind of trick?" he asked in a quiet voice.

Pugh turned, piggy eyes sparkling in their pouches of fat. "*Dulce est disipere in loco*, my dear Ryland . . . Have you a quarrel with educating the wealthy in the arts of humility?"

"When it involves rudeness to a stranger," replied his dear Ryland, "yes, I have. How may I serve you, m'am? My name is Joseph Ryland— Are you here in search of someone?" With a gesture he led her away from the group and farther into the quadrangle.

"I'm looking for Mr. Horace Thaxter, yes, thank you. I am Mrs. Adams, his aunt."

"I've heard him speak of you, m'am. Did Mr. Fairfield write to you, then, about Thaxter's illness?" Mended red gown billowing, Mr. Ryland led Abigail cattycorner across the yard to the old brick building that enclosed its southern end. "I'm sure it isn't as serious as Fairfield thinks it—"

"What happened?" asked Abigail, startled.

Ryland made a gesture of frustration. Unlike the refulgent Mr. Pugh and his friends, the young man—she guessed his age at nearly thirty, her own age . . . *A tutor, then, or a bachelor-fellow waiting for an appointment somewhere*—wore his own hair, long and only lightly powdered; he spoke with the accents of Pennsylvania. "To be honest, Mrs. Adams, I think it was the food in the Hall. Do what they will, the Governors cannot keep the kitchen staff from buying the cheapest slops they can come by and pocketing the difference, and I know Horace's constitution is a delicate one. I was going to let the matter go another day—I am the Fellow in charge of Massachusetts Hall—and then write his parents . . ."

They entered the building by the most westerly of its several doors, and Mr. Ryland led her down a wide hall and then

up one of the residential staircases. "He'll be in Captain
Fairfield's room—he fags for Fairfield, a noxious custom . . ."

As they reached the first landing, a young man stepped
from the room on the right, his dusky face and black Indian
braids startling against the white of his neckcloth and shirt,
and the sober darkness of waistcoat, breeches, and stockings.
Ryland said, "Weyountah, how is Thaxter? Mrs. Adams, this
is Weyountah—Mr. Enoch Wylie—one of our best men in
the sciences. Weyountah, Mrs. Adams of Boston, Thaxter's
aunt."

"Good Lord, get that woman out of here!" called a voice
from the left-hand room, and the door opened to reveal a
fair-haired, cheerful young man with a weather-burned com-
plexion and a gray coat rather heavily laced with gold on the
sleeves. "I knew it—Ryland's trying to get the lot of us sent
down for bringing a female in here . . . Diomede!" he called
back into the room behind him. "Get on out here and bring
a rope—tie up Mr. Ryland and throw him into the river—"

"Don't be a fool, Fairfield, this is Thaxter's aunt come to
see him."

"Doesn't matter," said Mr. Fairfield, in the slurry drawl of
a Virginian. "The Governors will never believe a gang of
towsers and tosspots like us . . ."

Spots of color appeared on Mr. Ryland's cheekbones, and
he stepped back—with rigid reserve—as Fairfield led the
way briskly into the left-hand chamber. The Indian Weyountah bowed to Abigail and gestured her to precede him, then
followed her in, leaving Mr. Ryland upon the landing and the
door open behind them.

Horace got quickly to his feet from the desk where he sat
by the window. The chamber was the usual one for the College: small, very tidy, furnished with a desk by the window, a

couple of chairs that young Mr. Fairfield had obviously brought
with him from Virginia, a small fireplace, and a little table.
On a neat sideboard were ranged a coffee-roaster, pot, and a
lacquered Chinese canister, presumably for coffee beans; there
was a smaller caddy for tea, spouted blue-and-white pots for
tea and water, and tidily arranged cups and saucers, not all of
them matching.

Horace Thaxter hadn't changed much in two years, Abigail reflected; she didn't think his weight had increased by so
much as an ounce, though he'd grown a good five inches, and
he had not been short when last she'd seen him at fifteen. All
elbows, knees, and spectacles, he wore an extremely shabby
suit of faded black coat and breeches, clearly handed down
from someone both shorter and more robust. He said, "Aunt
Abigail—!" and held out a bony, ink-stained hand.

From the doorway, Ryland said, "I'm glad to see you on
your feet, Thaxter," a small crease of worry between his brows.
"Captain Fairfield, if I may remind you—"

"I know, I know, dash it! That hell-begotten Greek class,
may they all descend unto Avernus together—"

"Hades, actually," put in Horace, stepping aside as an
elderly black man—who'd been arranging wood and kindling
in the hearth—gathered his hearth-brush and ashes and slipped
from the rather overcrowded room . . . Presumably Diomede,
Abigail guessed. And presumably the one responsible for the
room's spotless order. There was a chest in the corner that,
by what John had told her of the Virginia and Carolina men
when he had studied here, would contain the slave's blanket,
upon which he would sleep on the floor . . .

"Avernus being the Latin . . . Aunt Abigail, you truly
shouldn't have—"

"Horry, I shall smite you with the poker if you tell me

once more the difference between Latin and Greek . . . Yes, yes, Ryland, take your duty to the Muses as given, and I'll be along as soon as I've done my duty to decent manners."

"I shouldn't want you to be—"

"It's my business if I'm sent down or not," Fairfield snapped. "You're not my dry nurse. Dash it," he added, as Ryland disappeared into the shadows of the rather gloomy staircase, "now I've offended him again. If it's not one thing, it's another. Diomede"—he thrust open the door to the inner chamber— "go fetch some water for Mrs. Adams for tea—or would you be of the Rebel persuasion, m'am, like all the rest of the Adamses I've heard of, not to speak of every other scholar in this curst school? Or is the issue of *tea* now considered settled once and for all?" And he raised his brows in a quirky jest.

"Coffee," said Weyountah, "is I believe the proper alternative. Or cocoa." And he guided Abigail to one of the chairs beside the cold hearth.

"You sounded as if a visit would do you good." Abigail took Horace's hand with a smile and set her basket on the corner of the table. "You know your mother would never forgive me, were you left to languish without someone at least making sure you were still alive."

"Cocoa, then," said Fairfield, snapping his fingers as Diomede appeared in the doorway. "And sink me if that dashed Beaverbrook hasn't stolen my cocoa . . . Go upstairs and get it, would you? And thrash the little maggot if he's there. Shall we take ourselves off, Horace, while you visit with your aunt? I daresay Ryland only showed her up to make sure I came along to his Greek class and didn't get sent down, which old Hogden promised he would, if I'm late again. When class is done, m'am," he added with a bow, "I trust you'll join us for dinner at the Golden Stair? Diomede"—he leaned through the staircase door to call after the ascending slave—"after you've provided cocoa for Mrs. Adams, run along to the Golden Stair and bespeak a dinner for five. Oh, and fetch me my—"

Patiently, the servant reappeared, took from the seat of the other chair the red gown and four-square cap of scholarship—Abigail could see Horace's hanging on a peg on the wall—and held them out to his master.

"You're a wonder, Diomede . . ." Fairfield called back over his shoulder as he dove through the door. "And if you don't save me some of whatever's in that basket, Thaxter"—his voice trailed back up the stairs—"I shall tell Mr. Pugh you've been tupping his mistress—"

Weyountah said, "I'll be in the laboratory should you need me, Thaxter," and with a bow to Abigail, departed.

The room seemed suddenly, echoingly quiet.

Horace's breath blew out in a sigh. "Aunt Abigail, I beg a thousand pardons for having written. No consideration in the world would have induced me to do so, had I thought you would put yourself to the inconvenience—"

"Don't be silly." Abigail fetched her basket from the table and held it out to him; his pale face flushed slightly with pleasure when he saw what it contained. He moved the table closer to the hearth, which was cold, the afternoon being far too fine to need a fire. "And tell me, please," she went on, "what troubling events befell you and why you think John had anything to do with them?"

"That's just it, Aunt Abigail." Horace made a move toward the door as if he would have closed it, then hesitated—no doubt recalling the extreme strictures the College set upon its students having women in their rooms—and settled himself awkwardly in the chair opposite her. "I think Uncle John had something to do with it because Mrs. Lake had a letter of introduction from him—and from Uncle Mercer in

Connecticut—recommending her in the highest terms. But I suspect that she poisoned me—and I very much fear that she will try to do so again."

"Good Heavens, why?"

The boy shook his head helplessly. "I haven't the slightest idea."

Two

John Adams
Boston

16 April 1774

My dear Horace,

Let this serve as an introduction to Mrs. Lake, a woman of the highest probity, and as urging that you oblige her in her researches. She is a member in good standing in the Brattle Street Congregation, and in that capacity, I have known her for many years, and can vouch for both her character and her intentions.

Yrs obt'ly,
John Adams

"This is nothing like Mr. Adams's hand." Abigail set the letter down among the cocoa cups. "And I can assure you at once that there is no Mrs. Lake in the Brattle Street Congregation."

Silently, Horace held out the other letter.

It purported to be from Justice Mercer Euston—Abigail identified him as a connection on the other side of the Thaxter family and well-known across the border in Connecticut—but even to her inexperienced eye, the smudgy, spidery handwriting looked suspiciously similar. The paper, so far as she could tell, was identical.

"And who," asked Abigail, "is Mrs. Lake?"

"That's just it." Horace propped his thick-lensed spectacles more firmly onto the bridge of his nose. "I have no idea. We seem to be moving *per nocte ad tenebris*, unless she is some relation to Henry Morgan . . ."

"Henry Morgan the pirate?" Abigail experienced the momentary sensation that she and her nephew were not engaged in the same conversation.

An inexplicable pink flush crept up Horace's cheekbones. "He was Governor—and later Lieutenant Governor—of Jamaica . . ."

"Yes," said Abigail, "I know. Why would this Mrs. Lake's relationship to him cause her to poison you—if poison you she did . . . ?"

"I think she did," said Horace earnestly. "Though my symptoms bore a certain resemblance to my previous attacks of gastritis and the symptoms that sometimes accompany my headaches, in other respects they were such as to frighten me. Please believe me, Aunt Abigail. I have spoken of this to no one—not to Weyountah, who has been a brother to me here; not to George Fairfield, who has been so good as to take me under his wing . . . No one." He pressed his hands together, palm to palm as if praying, and rested his lips against them, an attitude Abigail remembered from his boyhood. For a moment she was prey to the curious sensation of seeing in the young man the reflection of an infant she had held—herself a fragile and studious girl of eleven—in her arms.

"I will believe you," she assured him. "But tell me everything, from the beginning, and leave no detail out. One cannot reconstruct the sense of a disputed text," she added, with a glance at the contents of the desk beside the window—a mountain of books in Greek, in Hebrew, and in tongues stranger still whose very writing was alien to her—"if one is given only fragments to work with."

"That's true," agreed Horace. "And it started with those texts."

Horace Thaxter—for all his youth—was virtually the only scholar at Harvard who made a study of Oriental Languages, by which was meant (Abigail gathered) Arabic, Persian, Russian, and Biblical Aramaic, there being no one in the colony (and probably not in Britain, either) who could understand Chinese. Horace had begun his fascination with these tongues as a child, getting his merchant father (baffled but indulgent and impressed in spite of himself) to arrange for him to be tutored in the first three by sailors who had come through the port of Boston at various times, and had continued a stubborn quest for further knowledge ever since. By the age of twelve he had begun correspondence with members of the Royal Societies in both London and Paris, and had amassed a small quantity of books in each of those languages, as well as lexicons treasured as if they were chests of gold. Abigail well remembered Horace's childhood reputation in the family: the boy had always been regarded as strange, but she now saw him, in his own element, as the man he would be, a pathfinding scholar on a road that no one she knew or knew of had traveled before.

He must somehow get to Oxford, she thought, listening to his brief preamble. *Here, we can do nothing for him, and 'twere shame to waste so mighty—if odd—a gift.*

"I have something of a reputation here in Cambridge," he continued shyly. "I can only attribute it to that, that Mrs. Lake sent me up a message last Tuesday—the nineteenth—asking me to meet her at the Crowned Pig on the Waterford Road and enclosing these letters from Mr. Adams and Uncle Mercer."

"Why the clandestine meeting?" asked Abigail. "Didn't that seem amiss to you?"

"Not really." The boy blushed redder. "Perhaps it should have, but one can be fined, you know, quite severely, for having anything to do with a woman—not yourself, of course, m'am, being family . . . But it's not unusual for care to be taken even in quite innocent meetings. I didn't think anything of it."

Remind me to keep you locked in your room if ever the Navy press gang comes to town.

The Crowned Pig was a tavern about a half mile beyond the last of the handsome mansions of the town, mansions built by the wealthy merchant families who—by staying in the good graces of the Governors and obtaining the best political appointments—ruled Massachusetts. Mrs. Lake proved to be a beautiful woman a few years older than Abigail herself—Horace estimated—who asked him, was it true he could read Arabic? Horace said that he could, whereupon the lady offered him twenty pounds to come with her in her carriage and do a job of translation from that language.

"What did she look like?" asked Abigail, adding—when her nephew merely looked confused by the question—"Other than *beautiful*. What color was her hair?"

"Dark. Brown, I think, not black like a Spaniard's."

"Eyes?" *Of course he didn't look her in the eyes . . .* "Nose large or small? How was she dressed?"

"Like a lady," said the boy promptly, but that was the best he could do—not unusual, reflected Abigail. Most men she knew—with the exception of John and her friend the silversmith Paul Revere—could attest to whether a woman was naked or clothed, but were left blank by distinctions between a round gown or a jacket and skirt. Much less could they say whether the said garments were blue or green, wool or calico, English-cut or sacque like the French. At least "like a lady" could be interpreted to mean not, for instance, in the bodice-and-skirt of a tavern-wench or a farm-girl's faded linsey-woolsey hand-me-downs.

Something a woman couldn't get into without the assistance of her maid.

And Mrs. Lake had a carriage, a closed post chaise driven by a groom, in which she and Horace rode for some two hours before descending to what—by Horace's rather sketchy description—sounded like a well-to-do farmstead, a brown wooden house of two storeys set some half mile back from the road.

"The groom took the team around to the stable in the rear of the house when we descended," said Horace. "I noticed him particularly, because his face was scarred—" With two fingers he touched his hairline and drew them down across his left eyelid, until they converged at a point an inch or so above the right-hand corner of his mouth. "And his eyes were so light, a very pale blue under extremely dark brows. He looked like a rough man—a veritable beast—and I found myself hoping Mrs. Lake would accompany me back as far as Cambridge. Perhaps I should have been more cautious," he added unhappily, "but twenty pounds is a great deal of money—enough to pay for my board and room here for next year."

"*Clausum possidet arca Iovem,*" sympathized Abigail. "And did she indeed have a document in Arabic, of all things, which needed translation?"

For some reason Horace's blush flared again, and he answered—his voice a little stifled—"Yes. And it was curious," he added, puzzlement returning him to some of his composure, "because it had clearly been copied by someone who didn't know Arabic—by someone who didn't even know that Arabic is written right-to-left, not left-to-right. I could tell by the way the letters were drawn. Even at first glance I asked where she had copied this from—because I'm always looking out for Arabic texts, you understand, and she said, 'Never you mind.' She sat me down with the text—it was about two pages long—and pen and ink, at the table in the study of this house, where the light was good, and the whole time I worked, she sat in a corner, watching me and playing patience—"

"Playing *patience?*" The solitary card game was an interesting choice, Abigail thought, for a lady—though of course there were plenty of ladies of the highest degree who hadn't the wits to read nor the domestic virtue to sew . . . a task that Abigail herself hated.

"Yes, m'am."

"And you translated this document?"

"Yes, m'am." His cheekbones had now gone a fiery pink. "Her message asked me to bring my Arabic lexicon, which I had."

"And what on earth was it, to put you so to the blush?"

Horace avoided meeting her eyes. "It was an account—quite—er—Petronian—of an . . . an encounter between Governor Morgan and a female pirate named Jezebel Pitts, which was supposed to have taken place in May of 1688 in Port Royal. It was written not in Arabic, but in English using

Arabic characters, as a sort of code-writing, and contained passages that would have been better suited to have been translated into Latin . . ."

"Good grief!"

"The tenor of the account would lead one to believe that the writer had been present, for it included a mix of veritable pornography and quite treasonous and conspiratorial assertions on the part of Governor Morgan—a plot to raid the colony's treasury with the assistance of—er—Mistress Pitts and her men, though there was no mention of where the bullion so acquired was to have been bestowed, nor of course any indication of whether the plan proceeded to—er—consummation."

"Consummation indeed," murmured Abigail, her eyebrows raised nearly to her hairline. "When was Port Royal destroyed?"

"Sixteen ninety-two, m'am."

"And lies full-fathom five, with nobody to miss the pilfered gold. How long did it take you to translate this remarkable document?"

"About three hours, Aunt Abigail. Mrs. Lake read it through without so much as a blush, and by her expression seemed most vexed that it had nothing to say about the whereabouts of the treasure . . . She asked me, two or three times, if I had translated it all, and I swore to her that I had. In the end she brought me a cup of coffee and some bread and meat, and went to summon her coachman, it being quite dark by then. I will say I was extremely hungry and rather vexed that all I might eat was a little bit of the meat, which is poisonous to my digestion but which would not bring on a migraine like the bread would. And coffee, I believe, is a pernicious drink, not suited to human consumption, so I poured it out after a few sips. To this abstention—for being of dyspeptic habit I depend upon regular meals—and to the exhaustion of concentration, I attributed the sleepiness that overwhelmed me.

Mrs. Lake and her coachman had to assist me into the chaise, and I so misliked the man's appearance that I struggled to remain awake and to observe if I could the countryside we traversed."

Abigail did a moment's mental calculation. "With no moon that night you're fortunate he didn't have you in the ditch."

"Yes, m'am. Yet I found the countryside wholly unfamiliar, as one does by starlight, and despite the fact that I was shivering violently, I kept nodding off. At last I woke to find the chaise standing still in what appeared to be a stand of woods. I called out to the coachman and had no reply. I tried to open the door of the chaise and for some reason could not—it was very dark within, since we were in the woods, and in my befuddled state I couldn't find the door handle. At last, convinced that something terrible was about to happen, I used my Arabic lexicon to break the window-glass and put my hand through to open the door from the outside—"

"Reasoning that Mrs. Lake could scarcely have you up for vandalism if her coachman had abandoned you in the wilderness?"

The young man's black eyebrows pulled together behind those thick lenses. "Aunt Abigail, at that point I know not what I was thinking. I staggered when I came down from the chaise, and it seemed to me that I could hear someone or something approaching me through the woods. It came to me, I know not why, that the whole of the events of the evening might have been orchestrated by one of the senior classmen—'tis precisely the sort of thing Black Dog Pugh likes to do—for my discomfiture . . . An' 'twere not that, I had not liked the coachman's face nor his mien. It may seem cowardly of me," he added in a stifled voice, "and foolish, too, but I fled into the woods."

His long, slender fingers toyed with the corn-bread on the

plate; he was caught between the shame of being teased the whole of his short life and the memory of very genuine terror.

"Have you any idea where you were?"

Horace shook his head. "Weyountah says that a farmer from Concord brought me here in his wagon, having deduced—in quite your style, m'am," he added with a faint grin, "that I was from the College by the circumstance of me clutching my Arabic lexicon to my breast when I was found in a ditch at the side of the Concord Road, raving of pirates and gold. I did not come to my right senses 'til nearly evening and then was vilely sick all the next day. I begged Weyountah and George not to breathe a word of my absence—George is the dearest of good fellows but a complete, er, rattlepate—for fear that I might be sent down for having to do with a woman and for getting drunk, though George has told me that had I been drunk my symptoms would have been quite different."

"Do Weyountah and Mr. Fairfield know—" She paused as a discreet tap sounded at the door, and Diomede put his head in to ask after the state of the cocoa pot. "Do Weyountah and Mr.—or is it Captain?—Fairfield—"

"Mr. Ryland calls him Captain because that's his rank in the militia troop he formed."

"Did he, indeed? Do they know about Mrs. Lake?"

"No, m'am. Weyountah says he thinks that I was poisoned—he has made a study of plants and says there's something called mad apple or Jamestown-weed that produces such effects—and I said I had gone to visit friends and had eaten of sallet at an inn. Such accidents do happen, he says, and naturally an innkeeper would have sent me on my way when I began to rave. In the light of Mr. Adams's letter, and Uncle Mercer's, I had almost convinced myself that something of the sort had indeed taken place—that it was an accident on the part of Mrs. Lake, and there was an innocent explanation. Then, four days ago it must have been, St-John Pugh—a most arrogant bullyboy . . ."

"Black hair, green eyes, and a nose like a suffused potato? Wears a yellow gown?"

"Even so, m'am—the Black Dog, he's called. I condole you to have made his acquaintance," added the boy, with his donnish smile. "He has been a senior here at least three years, they say, and has made my stay at this college a calvary. 'Tis only because George took me in as his fag that I've had some protection, though George doesn't truly need a fag the way other seniors have them: I mean, he has Diomede to keep his rooms for him and run his errands. But he lets me study here in his rooms—Pugh used to come looking for me in my own, to send me on made-up errands to the farthest end of town . . ."

"Does he not have a fag of his own?" John had always been philosophical about the fagging system in effect at Harvard— the freshmen attaching themselves to seniors as partial protection against hazing; it was something one simply had to endure in order to get an education. Abigail, aware that it was almost certain that her sons would one day be freshmen here, regarded it in a less sanguine light.

"He does, m'am. And slaves as well, two of them. But he likes to bully and is a positive *diabolos* for spiteful vengeances. As I was saying, Pugh caught me on Friday and sent me on an errand into the far end of the town, to the Pig; and when I came out of the inn, I saw Mrs. Lake's coachman across the road."

"Did you so?"

"I knew him, m'am. The scar on his face is like the mark of Cain. There were two men with him, one tall and powerful with a shaven head that poked forward like a turtle's, the other a man of medium size with an ear missing and his nose most horribly scarred. All three were swarthy, and the mutilated man wore his hair in a long queue, smeared with tar as sailors do.

They were looking about them, and as I knew no one at the Pig, I asked no questions but simply made haste to leave by the kitchen door. It was then—Friday evening—that I sent to you."

"As well you did," murmured Abigail. "We seem to have stumbled into a broadside ballad here—all we need is an endangered maiden who is true heiress to the treasure, though I reckon Mistress Pitts was very well able to take care of herself. How much do your friends know, or guess?"

Horace shook his head. "What they know is only that I went to visit friends and was found unconscious in a ditch the following morn. What they guess . . ."

His brow furrowed, and for a moment the boyish face with its pasty adolescent spots and its too-large nose seemed, suddenly, that of the man he would be. "Weyountah has taxed me, two or three times, with questions. He guesses I wasn't telling the truth, and he's seen that I'm afraid. George . . ." He grinned affectionately. "I'm sure George took him aside and told him that if I'd had the red blood in me to go off—er—drabbing, and ended up drunk in a ditch, I'd be the better not to have some praying Indian chasing after me for the details. They put it about that I was sick—"

"'Tis what Mr. Ryland seems to have thought."

"Well, he's the Fellow in charge of this hall, so if word of any of this reached his ears, he'd have to report it, you see. And he'd really rather not know."

Abigail raised her brows. "He seems to me a most honest man—"

"Oh, he is! *Amicus humani generis.* He does most of the work in George's troop—the King's Own Volunteers—if the truth be known. But by the same token, he knows that if George gets sent down, that's the end of the Volunteers. *Quod verum est* and all that, of course . . . but what Dr. Langdon doesn't know won't harm him."

Three

When George Fairfield returned after his Greek lecture ("Lord, how am I supposed to know the difference between Ajax son of Telamon and Ajax son of that other fellow?"), Abigail could easily understand the glow of hero worship in her nephew's eyes when he spoke his friend's name. Long-limbed and handsome, the young Virginian had the instinctive air of command that came—Abigail guessed—from ordering black slaves around for most of his life, and the exquisite manners acquired in a society where impressing landowners more wealthy than oneself (or their relatives) was the only way to advance one's family's fortunes.

Yet he had great kindness and an instinctive sense of justice. Over dinner at the Golden Stair Tavern on the Common ("Madame, God would send me to Hell if I obliged you to eat the food they serve in the Hall!") during a lively argument about how far democracy ought to be permitted in the government of each colony, he argued not from Locke or Rousseau ("Good Lord, m'am, I couldn't tell the one from t'other if

they were both to offer me a hundred pounds!") but from the
men he'd met in the backcountry beyond his father's plantation. "You can't put men like that in charge of making the
laws of the colony, m'am! First thing they'd rule is that it's
perfectly fine for them to close off the lands the Indians hunt
on and chop them up into farms to sell to new immigrants,
and then to shoot any Indian who tries to stop them."

Since Abigail had met hundreds of such men in Boston—
particularly since the beginning of John's involvement with
the Sons of Liberty—she was hard put to find an argument
against this. "Just because a man owns no property doesn't
mean he's a self-seeking savage . . ."

"No, m'am. But in my experience, it means he's *likelier* to
be than a man who's had an education—"

Yet when Uzziah Begbie—as democratic a soul as one was
likely to meet in all of Massachusetts Colony—came in seeking her, Fairfield beckoned him to the table and bade the
innkeeper's wife bring beer and another plate, and asked him
all about his carrier business and were the roads as terrible
when one went west as they were in Virginia?

"He acted as protector to me when first I came to Harvard," said Weyountah to Abigail, under cover of this dialogue,
"though he was only a year before me. No one wanted an
Indian to fag for him, as you might expect, so I was very
much on my own. He made sure I knew all the rules, like not
wearing a hat in the Yard and not swapping gowns with anyone, so I wouldn't be boxed—"

"And telling us which seniors to watch out for," added
Horace, with a glance across the tavern at Black Dog Pugh
and his minions, who had gathered near the windows to drink
and flirt with the innkeeper's spritely niece. "Pugh or his
boys—the thin one is Jasmine Blossom, I think his real name
is Jessamy, and the one in the blue coat is Lowth—will send

freshmen into town for punch, knowing it's against the rules, and when they're caught by the provosts, will deny having done so. Then the fresher gets fined four shillings, which is a great deal, especially in winter with candles to buy."

"The rumor runs," contributed Weyountah, "that the neighbors of Pugh's father back on Barbados all take up a collection, once a year, to keep the Black Dog in Harvard and in the interest of maintaining good order on the island."

"And the—er—virtue of their daughters. Heaven only knows how he's remained here long enough to become a junior bachelor—"

"Well, he's not stupid," said the Indian, "and I understand he's made better use of his time here visiting merchants in town and learning of their business than he ever has studying his Latin. Perhaps he only courts their daughters."

"*Vincant divitiae*," concluded Horace with a grin, and then coughed violently in a drifting cloud of pipe-smoke from the direction of Pugh and his friends.

When Begbie had gone—with Fairfield's assurances that he would send Mrs. Adams home in his own chaise—Abigail and Horace told the other two young men of the true course of Horace's adventure last week: of the assignation with Mrs. Lake, the letters of introduction, the scandalous document, and the carriage-ride that was almost certainly intended to end in Horace's death. "Can you write out what you recall of the document?" suggested Weyountah at once.

"I think so," said Horace. "My memory is very good, and because I translated it, I paid particular attention to every word. It wasn't a treasure-map or anything."

"Not an obvious one," said the Indian. "But it might have contained clues—every third word, every fourth word . . ."

"Yes, but unless he can recall every single word that's of no use," protested Fairfield.

"No," agreed Abigail. "Yet 'tis a good idea, and once Horace writes as much of the document as he can recall, some pattern may emerge that strikes one of us that was not evident to him at the time. Take a look at these." She held out to the others the two mendacious letters, and Weyountah held them where the westering window-light could fall on them most brightly. "They're complete fabrications, of course, but does anything about them suggest anything to either of you?"

"Good quality ink," said the Indian at once. "And expensive paper."

"Moreover, a writer who knew how to cut quills and keep the flow of words going," pointed out Abigail. "The hand is a confident one, without hesitations or blots. Further, the writer is accustomed to forming complex words: *intentions*, *probity*, *researches*. He knows how to *sound* like a lawyer or a judge."

"He certainly convinced our Horace," said Fairfield with a grin and a gentle nudge at his friend's shoulder. "What do they say about the pure not seeing anything but purity?"

"With your permission," interpolated Abigail, "I shall take these two letters back to town with me. John's away, *naturally*," she added, unable to keep exasperation from her voice—*When WASN'T John away when you needed him?*—"but my friend Mr. Revere—the silversmith, you know—has a most acute eye for the details of handwriting and other telltale signs. He may very well see things in these that are hidden from us."

She half expected the young Virginian to object at the mention of Paul Revere's name, but he'd clearly never heard of the man in his life. Like most people outside of Boston, George Fairfield's knowledge of the Sons of Liberty was limited to Sam Adams and James Otis (who hadn't been able to be active among them for years, poor man) and some of their more spectacular exploits, like sacking the Governor's house, destroying shops, and dumping $92,000 worth of tea into the harbor.

Instead he declared, "And *I* am going to do the obvious and have a look around the ladies of the surrounding country-side to see who might be Mrs. Lake."

To which Weyountah laughed, "Why does it not surprise me that George is going to look around among the ladies?"

"Dash it, man, the woman wasn't just made up out of mud for the occasion. She has to have come from someplace, chaise, coachman, and all."

"For that matter," said Weyountah thoughtfully, "where would this Mrs. Lake—or whoever she really is—have gotten a text in Arabic, or Arabic lettering, to copy from? The only scholar in Harvard who had any Arabic texts at all was old Reverend Seckar, and Horace got all of his when he died."

"And lucky thing he did," said Fairfield. "Poisonous old screw was going to leave them all to the College and stick his poor wife and sister without a bean. You got a few too out of that lot, didn't you, Weyountah?"

"Are you also a scholar of Oriental languages?" inquired Abigail—though why a young man who'd been born in a two-room wigwam in the woods of Rhode Island shouldn't have as much of an interest in the wisdom from another por-tion of the world as one who'd been born thirty miles away in a two-room farmhouse in the woods of Massachusetts, she didn't know, once she thought of it.

The Narraganset shook his head. "No, natural science," he said. "Astronomy, chiefly, but really anything I can get my hands on. The books Mrs. Seckar was selling off were ruin-ously old and of little use, given the advances that have been made in the studies of things like atmospheric vapors and air and water pressure. I've begun correspondence with Mr. Franklin," he added, naming a little shyly the foremost scien-

tist and philosopher in the colonies. "He's been good enough
to recommend me to the Royal Society in England, which
has been of enormous assistance. There's so *little* over here."

"So little of anything," sighed Horace wistfully.

"Which brings us back," declared Fairfield firmly, "to where
we started. Where would that Arabic text have been copied
from? Who would have written a document like that in *Arabic*, for the Lord's sake—"

"Obviously," said Abigail, "someone who knew Arabic
writing and was using it as a code to keep a record of a disgraceful encounter—I assume for purposes of blackmail."

"Would Henry Morgan *care* if everybody on the Spanish
Main knew he was having a—um—Latin lesson"—Fairfield
hastily interpolated a euphemism, having clearly, for the
moment, forgotten that Abigail was a respectable matron and
his friend's aunt to boot—"with someone by the name of
Jezebel Pitts? I don't imagine Mistress Pitts would mind.
Besides," he added, "they've both been dead for years."

"The principal activity *Governor* Morgan was practicing
with Mistress Pitts," Abigail reminded him starchily, "is called,
without going into Latin, *conspiracy to commit embezzlement* . . .
and given the fact that it involved assistance from pirates, it
probably would be considered treason as well by an Admiralty Court. Reason enough to justify hush-money to someone, I'm sure, even if they did not manage to lift any actual
gold. But as Mr. Fairfield so justly points out, both parties
have been in their dishonored graves for decades. Sam might
know . . ."

"Sam—Adams?"

Abigail remembered too late—just as Fairfield had forgotten that she was an aunt and a respectable goodwife from
Boston—that her listener was a Loyalist to whom the name
of her husband's notorious cousin was anathema.

"No, Sam Brooke," she extemporized hastily. "A neighbor of mine on Queen Street. An elderly gentleman who once—I suspect—had a great deal to do with the smuggling trade and may very well have known Mistress Pitts in her old age." She felt like kicking herself, because of course Sam Adams was precisely whom she meant. Three-quarters of the Sons of Liberty were mixed up in smuggling to one degree or another. Why put yourself in danger of an Admiralty noose, if it weren't to avoid paying the King's taxes on this, that, and the other, every time the King decided one of his friends needed a job as a special revenue collector?

Abigail had frequently deplored the fact that wily Cousin Sam seemed to be on a first-name basis with half the wharf-rats in Boston Harbor. *But on this occasion*, she thought, *he might as well do some good* . . .

If he wasn't packing to get himself out of Boston, she reflected grimly, before the King's vengeance—whatever it was going to be—for the tea came ashore.

Whatever it was going to be, it was almost certainly going to involve a warrant for Sam Adams's arrest.

What broke her sleep every night for weeks—and had caused her to warn her fourteen-year-old servant-girl, Pattie, and John's clerk, Thaxter (not Horace but his—and Abigail's—esteemed cousin), to stand ready to take the children to Uncle Isaac's house at the first sign of trouble—was not knowing how far beyond Sam the arrests would spread.

And what the Sons of Liberty would choose to do about the situation.

She picked up the two letters again and realized that the window light had faded to the point where they were difficult to read. "Good Heavens, it must be getting close to sun-down," she said in alarm. "If I'm to be back to Boston—"

"Aunt Abigail, mea culpa—"

"Dash it, where's that lazy buck Diomede?" Fairfield sprang to his feet, strode toward the kitchen. "He'll have the chaise harnessed for you before a fly can wash his little hands, m'am—"

In fifteen minutes Abigail was being assisted into an extremely elegant English chaise outside the Golden Stair, with bows and thanks and assurances that Horace would be permitted neither food, drink, nor sleep that night until he'd finished a verbatim copy of Mrs. Lake's disgraceful document. In twenty, she was clinging to the brass rail of the vehicle as it bowled sharply along through the slanted evening sunlight on the road to Charles Town. Like most Virginians, young Mr. Fairfield favored spirited horseflesh, but Diomede—a big-shouldered man in his fifties—was a skilled and careful driver: Abigail was disconcerted and exhilarated by the speed, but never frightened.

When Diomede apologized for the pace—"But for a fact, m'am, we'll be fortunate to make the ferry before it closes down"—she felt encouraged to ask him, was he himself familiar with the countryside hereabouts?

"Not like a native, m'am," he said, in a deep velvet bass. "I came up with Mr. Fairfield in '70, and he's a personable young gentleman, as I'm sure you've observed. The year before last, when there was such a to-do about that revenue ship that went aground in Rhode Island and was burned by smugglers claiming to be against taxation, Mr. Fairfield formed up a company of gentlemen loyal to the King—the King's Own Volunteers, they call themselves—and so he's widely known from here to Medford and always being invited to stay at this house or that. Mr. Charles Fairfield—Mr. George's father—gave me instructions to make sure that he kept to his book."

The valet smiled as he reined in to let an oncoming wagon

pass in the narrow road where it swung around the base of Prospect Hill. "But it's true also that so far as I can see, the reason a young gentleman goes to college is to meet men of property and consideration, and to make friendships that will be of use to him later in life. So I guess one could say, I've seen as much of the countryside as a man can, traipsing behind a very popular young gentleman with his baggage."

Abigail laughed. "You have my sympathies," she said. "Do you happen to know the name of the farmer who brought Mr. Horace back to Cambridge on Wednesday? I think Weyountah said he was from Concord."

"From that direction," agreed Diomede. "Mr. Rutherford has a farm just this side of Lexington, on the Concord Road. He said he found poor Mr. Thaxter by the road near Pierce's Hill."

Abigail mentally placed the location, a wooded country of old farmsteads and stone field-walls. A two-hour drive from Cambridge would indeed put Mrs. Lake's "brown house of two storeys" somewhere between Menotomy and Lexington, particularly if the woman had taken the precaution of not driving straight there. *John would know.* And if John weren't yet home from the Maine Assizes, Revere—when she showed him the bogus letters—would very likely be able to tell her: the Sons of Liberty made it their business to know everyone in the countryside around Boston, if for no other reason than to know were they adherents to the Crown's policies and power, or in favor of colonial rights?

Yet for all its superficial resemblance to the little towns of the Massachusetts countryside—her family's village of Weymouth, or Braintree where John's mother and brothers lived—Harvard was different. In Weymouth or Braintree, everyone had known one another since childhood, and a strange face was instantly noted and commented upon. Hers certainly had been when nine years ago John had brought her to that little brown farmhouse as a bride, although everyone knew Parson Smith's three daughters and his gadabout son . . .

People came and went from Harvard all the time. Praying Indians like Weyountah from converted villages in Rhode Island. Gaudy exotics like St-John Pugh. She reflected uneasily on the openness of the buildings of Harvard College, the ease with which anyone could ascend any of those staircases . . .

"Whoa!" Diomede drew rein. "M'am, your pardon, I beg you, but it looks like Sassy's picked up a stone."

And indeed, even as the little mare slowed her pace, Abigail could see she was favoring her off fore.

It crossed her mind very briefly that the delay would cost her her return, but she said at once, "No, of course—"

She took the reins as the servant sprang down and hastened to the mare's head. She was carrying it low, Abigail observed worriedly, and holding her hoof from the ground— *She must really be hurt* . . .

Diomede worked gingerly, testing and probing in the woodland twilight. When he came back to the chaise, even in the gloom, she read consternation on his face.

"Is she all right?"

"She'll *be* all right, m'am," said the servant. "But she's cut the frog of her hoof—there must have been a nail or something in the road—"

Abigail sprang down from the chaise at once. "Poor little lady," she said. "And such a nuisance—but you know, I think I rather pushed my luck talking to those boys as late as I did, and having to walk back to Cambridge is no more than I deserve. Will she be all right to be led? I suppose we could leave the chaise here for a short time . . ."

The man relaxed—as a slave, reflected Abigail, he had

probably witnessed the human limits of bad manners and pet-
ulance among those who considered a) that their convenience
ranked higher than an injured animal's pain and b) that if they
missed the ferry, it must be the fault of the driver. "I don't
think there's call for that, m'am." He looked around him at the
darkening woods. "It goes without saying that Mr. Fairfield
will pay for a bed for you at the Golden Stair. I hope it's no
inconvenience——"

"The only inconvenience," replied Abigail grandly, falling
into step with Diomede as he turned the mare's head back
toward Cambridge, "will be to my aunt and uncle, who will
be obliged to look after my children tonight." In the shadowy
trees, wrens and thrushes, mockingbirds and starlings all
twittered and whistled as if to make sure of their territories
before they settled down for the night. A breeze riffled the
leaves, filled the world with the soft green scent of hay. "Of
course I shall sleeplessly weep the whole night through at
spending the hours apart from them," she added with a blithe-
ness that made the servant grin, "yet I trust that somehow I
shall survive the experience of not separating Johnny and
Charley from killing one another when Charley hides Johnny's toys, and not being woken up twice and three times by
Tommy wanting a story or a drink of water——"

"Oh, m'am," said Diomede, and clasped his hands to his
heart, "please don't go on——I'm afraid I shall weep."

"I do beg your pardon," said Abigail.

They led the limping Sassy the two miles back to Cambridge in perfect amity.

Diomede left Abigail in one of the college parlors while he
took Sassy back to the stables; in a few moments George Fairfield came running in, green robe billowing and Horace at
his heels. "M'am, I am covered with shame——!"

"Nonsense! I was telling Diomede, I look upon the whole business as an excellent opportunity to get a complete night's rest, something one doesn't, you know, if one has three sons under the age of seven."

"Well, you'll have rest at the Golden Stair on my account—or rather my Pa's, since he's the one who settles them all," added the young man with a grin. "Poor old Sassy! Thank the Lord, Diomede saw her falter as quick as he did. She's taken no hurt—the man's a wonder with horses. With just about everything, come to that . . . I could have taken a whip to that brute Pugh for telling me only yesterday that I'd best sell him off cheap because he pilfers my liquor now and then. Lord, I'd trust Diomede with a bottle a lot sooner than I'd trust Pugh or either of those so-called grooms of his—wild savages straight off the boat from Africa! Diomede was born in Williamsburg and raised a gentleman, *and* his father before him!" He tucked Abigail's cloak around her shoulders and sprang to open the parlor door for her, seeming blithely unaware of any incongruity in the fact that he could describe a man old enough to be his father as a *gentleman* and yet possess the legal right to sell him off like a mule. "His manners are a sight better than Pugh's, anyway—though I suppose the same could be said about Sassy."

Mrs. Squills at the Golden Stair didn't appear a bit surprised at Abigail's reappearance with the two scholars: "The way those boys were talking to you, I knew you'd never get to the ferry in time," she said, her smile as she curtseyed making her look much older—she was missing several of her teeth. "Mr. Horace's aunt, I think Diomede said? Now, go along with you," she added briskly, flapping her apron at Abigail's escort. "Before you're fined for being out of your rooms after dark, *and* in a tavern—"

"They wouldn't fine me for being with my *aunt*," protested Horace, and the tiny innwife's face flexed into an exaggerated expression of astonishment.

"There's another college here in Cambridge that you've been going to all this time without telling me?" she demanded. "Because the Dean of *Harvard* would fine you for being out with your own *mother*, let alone an aunt . . . *And* I know full-well about the little minx *you've* got waiting for you out behind the stables," she added, with a glare at Fairfield.

"I——?" Fairfield pressed his hand to his heart and raised his eyebrows in innocent bafflement.

"Run along with you!" She shook her head as Fairfield made a dancing-master's leg to Abigail and saluted her hand before he strode off, laughing, across the dark of the Common, Horace trotting loyally at his heels. "They're good boys," she added, leading Abigail toward the stair. "For all they drive an honest woman mad with their, 'I'll pay you next quarter for a batter-cake today.' I don't know which is worse, George with his lady friends or Horace with his nose forever in a book!" She collected a couple of abandoned beer mugs from the table, as she passed it, to add to her tray. "Well, 'tis the peskiest kitten that grows to the best mouser, you know. I wouldn't give tuppence for a lad that didn't run about the town seeing what he can get himself into, would you?"

Abigail smiled, thinking of her own too-serious Johnny's hair-raising experiments with building mousetraps and measuring the current of the tides in the Mill Pond. "Nobody's ever shown me a lad that didn't," she responded, "so I wouldn't know."

Her mind returned to Johnny as she made ready for bed ("Now I've a clean hairbrush that I keep for those who're taken by circumstance unexpectedly . . . And let me lend you a shift for tomorrow, Mrs. Adams—I've one just laun-

dered, and I know you'll want a clean one in the morning . . .
No, no, just send it back when you're home . . ."). Unfair, of
course, to abandon her children to Pattie and Aunt Eliza—to
whom Pattie would unfailingly take them, once it was clear
that their mother had missed the ferry. Six-year-old Johnny
had an instinctive dislike of change, and little Tommy—at
eighteen months—was of an age to want things to remain
the same . . . and Nabby would worry. Abigail wished, as she
brushed out the raven cloak of hair that fell to her hips and
braided it for the night, that there was a way that she could
have sent them a note, at least, reassuring them, though it
would be obvious what had happened . . .

In time, she hoped, Johnny would be coming to Harvard,
as his father had. Abigail hopped quickly between the spotless sheets, blew out the candle . . .

But in ten years, she could not keep herself from asking,
would the college still be in existence? A year ago, or two, the
question would have been unthinkable. Harvard College was
the best and oldest school in the colonies. Yet in throwing the
King's tea into the harbor, the Sons of Liberty had effectively
declared their rebellion against the King's authority. Only a
fool or a child would talk himself into believing that the
retribution for this behavior wouldn't be severe . . .

And her acquaintance with the Sons of Liberty convinced
her that whatever the King did, their reaction would be
equally violent.

As she drifted toward sleep, she heard again, on the edges
of her dreams, the angry shouting of mobs that had at various
times attacked the shops and businesses of men who'd
denounced the Sons. Remembered the sparkle in Sam's eyes
when he'd related to her how he'd egged on a mob to even
sack the house of the Governor: the building had been gutted,
and the collected records of the first years of the colony,

painstakingly collected by that scholarly gentleman in order to write the first comprehensive history of Massachusetts, had been torn and trampled in the gutters . . .

Remembered, too, the crack of guns in King Street, the black pools of blood in the blue evening snow. It was too easy to picture in her mind the college buildings in flame or occupied by troops . . .

Though she had knelt by the bed to say her prayers before undressing, Abigail propped herself on the pillows a little and again folded her hands. *Whatever paths they tread*, she prayed, *ten years from this night or with the coming of this night's dawn, You have already laid out for them, for their good and Your best purposes. But as their mother, I beg of You, keep them safe, hold their hands in Yours . . .*

She must have fallen asleep in midprayer—as she almost invariably did when she prayed in bed with the featherbed up to her chin—because the next thing she knew, it was morning, and Mrs. Squills was knocking on the door of her room with the news that George Fairfield had been murdered in the night.

Four

T hey're saying Diomede did it." Horace's face was white as paper, save his eyes, which were swollen and red—he had been weeping for his friend when Abigail had come into the Golden Stair's private parlor.

"Who's saying?" She took the chair on the other side of the small fire. Beyond the window, mist still lay on the Common, and the birds she'd heard twittering themselves to sleep last night when George was alive were waking in every tree and shrub.

"The Dean, and Dr. Langdon—the President of the College—and the sheriff, Mr. Congreve. He was drunk— Diomede was—but just because a man's had a dram or two . . ." Horace broke off in some confusion, with an expression of helpless guilt, remembering no doubt the numerous family discussions in which the consumption of alcohol was roundly denounced as the root of considerably more evil than grew from the greed for money.

"Of course not!" It said much, in Abigail's opinion, that

Horace's tolerance for the foibles of others had widened to that extent. Two years ago the boy had been an unconscionable prig on the subject. *One gift of a Harvard education . . .*

"Diomede would never have raised his hand against George." These last words came out as a whisper, and Horace sank into the chair in which he'd been sitting when Abigail—hastily dressed and tying a fresh, clean, and borrowed cap of Mrs. Squills's over her hair—had hastened into the room.

With astonishing good sense, the landlady—who must have been nearly as upset over the murder as Horace was—brought in a tray of coffee things. Abigail poured a cup for herself and hot water for her nephew, to which she added a little honey. "Drink that." When Mrs. Squills went out, through the open door of the ordinary blew the voices of men discussing the crime: *murdering nigger—drunk as David's sow—knife still in his hand . . .*

"What happened? You'll feel better. Who's there now?"

"Weyountah," whispered the boy. "He waked to the sound of George shouting at someone—not shouting, really, just raised voices . . . His room is across the landing. Mine is above Weyountah's—Mr. Beaverbrook from New York is above George, and you couldn't wake Beaver if you set his rooms on fire. But George often shouts at Diomede, you know . . ." He put his hand quickly to his mouth as if to catch back the present tense.

"What time was that?"

Horace shook his head. "When the bell rang for chapel this morning, Weyountah went across and knocked at the door—We all have to work to make sure George gets to chapel. It's Diomede's job, but the last two times Dio had a few drinks, George was fined, and Dr. Langdon warned him . . . So either Weyountah or I will check. When Diomede didn't answer, Weyountah went in and found him asleep—"

"In the study?" She remembered the small leather chest in the corner of George's little study, which contained the slave's pallet and, no doubt, every other item the man owned. In Virginia, she had been told, the house-slaves often slept on the floor of their masters' rooms, like dogs.

Horace nodded, struggling to speak in something resembling normal tones. "There was blood on his hand, and on the sheet—" His voice cracked, and he raised the cup to his lips, needing two hands to hold it steady. "Weyountah ran into the bedroom. George was lying in his bed, in his nightshirt. He'd been stabbed—there was blood all over the bed—"

Abigail put both of her hands over the boy's cold one. "Was there a knife?" She knew better than to believe what the men in the next room were yelling to one another.

Horace nodded. After a moment he recovered himself enough to reply, "On the floor next to Diomede's pallet, covered with blood." Then, when she came around to kneel beside his chair, he threw his arms around her shoulders and held her desperately, his body trembling with the impact of the first great grief, the first blow of loss and violence in his life.

Abigail held him, stroked his back as she did Tommy's when the little boy had a nightmare, saying nothing. But her mind raced. Her grief at the young man's death seemed to run in tandem with her shock at the manner of it, and totally separated from the thousand questions that formed themselves up, sharp and clear as if she saw them written down on a paper before her. *What kind of knife? Was it one of George's, or strange to the establishment? Diomede would know that—probably Weyountah also, he seems an observant young man . . . Was there anything missing from the room? When did George come in last night? Was Diomede dressed?*

Was there anything in the bedroom that seemed out of place?

But Horace was barely seventeen years old and had just

taken a wound as agonizing as the one that had killed his friend, and for a time she did nothing but hold him, letting him know that there was someone to hold.

He took a deep breath, let it go. Let go of George, as if he had been clinging to his friend's hand. He began to say, "I'm sorry—"

"Shush. Can you take me back there now? Are you able for it?"

Horace nodded, pushed his steamed and tear-blotted spectacles back into place, then removed them, and fumbled to clean them on the end of his neckcloth. "Diomede would never have done it," he said.

"Was he drunk? George said he drank . . ."

"Never to the point that he didn't know what he was doing!"

"But to the point that he wouldn't wake up if someone else put a bloodied knife into his hand? What is it Lady Macbeth says? *I'll gild the faces of the grooms withal . . .*"

"But no one *would*!" protested Horace. "George hadn't an enemy in the world!" He got awkwardly to his feet and gallantly helped Abigail to rise.

Not even the man George kept at his beck and call for four years, away from family and friends, only for his convenience in a foreign town? An American born and bred, gentlemanly and intelligent and kind, who had to sleep on the floor and live out of a chest the size of a breadbox, so that he was there to 'make him mind his book,' keep him away from unsuitable ladies, and wake him up in time for chapel?

It was the first thing the Middlesex County sheriff was going to say.

"It doesn't take a plot, or a lifelong foe, to do murder," she said quietly. "Only a moment's rage. Let us go and see what we can learn."

* * *

The entire student body of Harvard—some two hundred young men and boys between the ages of fifteen and twenty-five—were either milling around the westernmost hallway of Massachusetts Hall or pushing their way up and down Horace's staircase. Horace bleated, "Here, let me through— I have rooms up here— Please let me through . . ." to absolutely no effect.

Abigail caught the first brightly colored sleeve that came her way, yanked it purposefully, and said in a voice honed by six years of dealing with young Johnny at home, "Excuse me, sir, I am Mr. Fairfield's aunt— I beg your pardon, sir, but I am a member of the family— Please let us pass—" in so firm a tone that the young men so addressed either backed down out of the staircase or, farther up, squashed themselves flat against the wall. Abigail's normal conversational tones were brisk but soft, yet at need she could call up a particular timbre of voice that could cut flint. "I beg your pardon, we must get through— Please excuse us, sir, but we're members of the family—"

In Fairfield's study, men were packed tight, all of them shouting at the slumped form of Diomede, who huddled in a chair in the corner with a harassed-looking man in a blue coat before him, whom Abigail recognized—from years of association with John's legal practice—as Seth Congreve, sheriff of Middlesex County. Diomede was shaking his head, saying, "I don't remember, sir! I don't know—" He raised his hands, sticky now with drying blood that blotched and boltered the white sleeves of his shirt. "I swear I didn't—drunk or sober, I'd never have touched a hair of his head!"

His clothing stank of blood and rum, and tears of shock ran down his face.

"So you're saying you're so drunk you didn't even hear— Can you gentlemen please be silent!— So you didn't hear your master arguing with some other man—someone whom you weren't even aware was in the room?"

"He could have been," barked St-John Pugh. "I warned George about that nigger's drinking . . ."

And the weasel-like sophomore Jasmine Blossom demanded sarcastically, "You were so drunk you didn't even wake for a man walking in bold as paint and stabbing your master after a quarrel loud enough to wake the Injun? Oh, let me have another story, Papa, it's not nearly bedtime yet!"

"Mr. Pugh," said Abigail briskly, "would you and your friends be so good as to assist Mr. Congreve in clearing the room a little? One can scarcely do justice if one isn't able to hear oneself think. Mr. Ryland, just the man I wished to see—Might you detail some of the King's Own Volunteers to eject anyone not immediately connected with the investigation? Thank you—Mr. Pugh is also assisting me . . . Deputize whom you will—"

"Yes!" Congreve swung around with a gesture of a man with a sack of corn beset by pigeons. "All of you, out of here— Mrs. Adams!" he added in surprise. "What on earth—?"

"I was working with Mr. Fairfield," she said, "on a strange little puzzle that involved him and his friends; I am horrified to hear of this. And of course Mr. Adams will undertake to defend poor Diomede, who quite obviously had no more to do with the killing than Mr. Ryland or Mr. Pugh—You there, Mr. Yeovil, are you associated with the sheriff? No? Then please take yourself out—"

"What puzzle?" asked the sheriff, as Ryland pushed past him into the bedroom—even more crowded—beyond. "And why 'obviously'?"

"A man who's drunk so much that he doesn't know what

he's doing is unlikely to win a hand-to-hand fight with a sober one," she retorted briskly, though she was not, in fact, at all certain that this was true. "Certainly not as swiftly as this battle proceeded, in any case. Mr. Ryland, could you ask Mr. Beaverbrook to remain, and of course Mr. Wylie——" It took her a moment to remember Weyountah's baptismal name. "Is there a physician here?"

"Mr. Perry." Congreve nodded toward the bedroom door, then turned toward the task of ejecting the last of the stragglers. "Mr. Perry teaches medicine here at the college."

"Mr. Pugh," called Abigail, "might I prevail upon you to keep guard at the bottom of the staircase with your men? Thank you," she added, not giving the bachelor-fellow a chance to say yes or no. "You have been of inestimable assistance——" She caught him by the sleeve and thrust him through the door and into the faces of Lowth and Jasmine, just reascending after pushing the last of their fellow classmates out at the bottom of the stair. She closed the door on him, reopened it long enough for Ryland and another young man whom she vaguely recognized as one of the younger members of the Oliver family—relatives of the Governor—to push out the last few observers, then closed it behind them all.

Harvard men—and raised in the best traditions of good manners—they clearly had been taught that one doesn't push back against a lady, and weren't quite sure how to deal with one who summarily ordered them out the door.

"There," she said, and walked back to the corner where Sheriff Congreve still stood—looking rather amused—beside Diomede. "It wants but a little firmness—and getting the right people to think they're going to receive more than their due. Might I speak with the prisoner, Mr. Congreve? I truly cannot imagine the man would turn against his master— and Mr. Adams will want to know every detail I can glean."

"And Mr. Adams sent you out here?" He sounded doubtful about that, as well he might. Being a lawyer's clerk required an education, something Abigail was sharply conscious that neither she nor any other woman was allowed to obtain. Nor would she or any other woman have been permitted to exercise the skills of a lawyer if she somehow acquired them. And a lawyer who sent out a woman—much less his wife!—to do a man's work would have been, quite simply, committing professional suicide.

Abigail lowered her voice, though the little study was now empty except for themselves, Diomede, Horace, and a pale and rather wizened-looking young man who was probably Mr. Beaverbrook, who lived immediately above this room. "The matter upon which Mr. Fairfield asked to see me," she explained—*And it isn't QUITE a lie*, she reasoned, *as the poor young man really did consult me for my opinion once he knew what was taking place*—"was, we had thought, a family matter concerning my nephew Mr. Thaxter, and for this reason I hesitate to speak of it without consulting Mr. Adams. Whether it has any bearing upon this shocking turn of events or not, I have no idea, but Mr. Adams will certainly undertake to defend Diomede, whom we both know would never have done such a thing."

On the other side of the table, the servant raised his head, the first flash of life returning to his eyes that Abigail had seen since she had come into the room. The first flash of hope.

She went on as if it were the most natural thing in the world, "The family side of the business not being completed, Mr. Fairfield paid to have me stay in Cambridge last night, at the Golden Stair. I will of course write at once to Mr. Adams, who is at the Maine Assizes this week, and to his clerk in Boston, Mr. John Thaxter, who graduated from here last year. But I know Mr. Adams will want to know the precise details of the scene, as they were before the rooms were disturbed, and will also want to know everything that can be recollected by both the witnesses and the accused—which as you know yourself can become very quickly distorted with the passage of time."

Congreve nodded and scratched at the edge of his wig— horsehair, Abigail guessed, and probably vastly uncomfortable: she could see the little rim of reddened flesh all around its edge where it irritated the skin. He said, "I see. And that's perfectly all right, Mrs. Adams—a very respectable gentleman, your husband is, and a fine lawyer. Mr. Langdon—"

He turned to the waspish, red-faced gentleman— resplendent in a red doctor's gown barred with black velvet and a startling full-bottomed wig—who appeared in the door of the bedchamber.

"Might Mr. Perry be spared for a few moments to describe to Mrs. Adams—here acting as her husband's amanuensis— the condition of the body and the room when you were summoned?"

"Actually," said Abigail, "what Mr. Adams would ask me to do—and on those occasions when I have acted in his name before this, he has been most emphatic in his instructions— would be to enter the chamber myself and compare my own observations with those of"—she could see President Langdon bristling up like a porcupine and the stooped, graying gentleman in black behind him who had to be Dr. Perry radiating disapproval at this display of womanish inquisitiveness—"of observers trained to analyze the smallest details. Mr. Adams has a horror"—here she could at least put the genuine ring of truth into her voice—"of information coming at third-hand, as you gentlemen"—she divided her deprecating smile among the three men—"must also abhor for its potential for mistakes. He has quite trained me to describe matters exactly as I see them, without the addition or subtraction of thoughts of my own."

John had done nothing of the sort, of course. But she knew he had always admired that quality in her, which she had possessed long before that sturdy, brilliant, opinionated, and passionate—not to say maddening—little gentleman had come into her life when she was fifteen.

Langdon and Perry looked mollified.

Horace—with singular and, to Abigail, surprising presence of mind—produced a memorandum-book from his pocket and said with the air of one deputized to stand ready on the fringes of events, "Your notes, m'am."

Abigail said, "Thank you, Mr. Thaxter," with her most serene air, and preceded the doctor and the college president into the chamber where George Fairfield's body lay.

Five

D r. Perry stepped quickly across to the bed and drew the sheet over George Fairfield's face. Perry would have pulled the counterpane up to cover the splotches where the blood—turning dark now as it dried—had stained through the linen, but Abigail held up her hand and asked, "How was Mr. Fairfield lying when you came in, doctor? It's one of the things my husband will wish to know." Her words stayed him long enough for her to note that there seemed to be three or four sources of blood—wounds that had bled. *Plenty*, she thought, *for the killer to 'gild the faces of the grooms' and, like the wily and wicked Lady Macbeth, transfer the blame with the blood.*

"He lay on his back," said Perry. "His limbs were composed and the sheet drawn up to his waist, for as you recall, 'twas a mild night. There was no evidence of struggle." With a sharp twitch of his wrist he flung the counterpane into place. Despite herself, Abigail felt relieved.

"Where was he stabbed?" she asked.

The man's upper lip seemed to lengthen at the idea of a woman wishing to know such things, even to pass the word on to her husband. "Thrice in the breast, two of the blows penetrating the heart. Once in the side, up under the ribs—"

Left side, Abigail noted. That's where the blood had flowed out, anyway.

Abigail had seen dead men before. There were families, she knew, who didn't believe in having their girl-children assist in the laying-out of the dead—grannies, uncles, younger children who didn't make it through sickly winters or the endless barrage of ailments that hammered the very young before their tenth year—but hers had not been one of these. And after one has prepared for burial the body of one's own child—poor tiny Susanna, who had barely passed her first year—no other death hits quite so hard.

She recalled going with her mother and her sister Mary to help one of her aunts lay out a cousin when she, Abigail, was barely seven: Mary was ten, and the dead child was Abigail's own age. It was Abigail who had helped her mother braid the little girl's hair. She remembered asking, Would Annie be angry that it was Abigail who was alive today and Annie who was dead? and getting an hour and a half on the subject of how much luckier and happier Annie was to be dead and with Jesus . . .

Probably true, she reflected, looking down at the worn linen where it lay over George Fairfield's face: the little mount of nose and chin, the silky tousle of blonde hair just visible at the top. Certainly true, in fact, and what she had told Nabby—only with greater brevity and, she hoped, greater tenderness—a few months ago when little Jemmy Butler next door had died. But she had thought at the time, *Will Annie miss her doll Penelope? Or her baby sisters? Or the way the sunlight makes crazy patterns of elongated diamonds on the plaster of the bedroom wall first thing in the morning? Or the first sweet strength of that first sweet spoonful of molasses on hot corn-pudding first thing on a cold morning?*

Would George miss driving Sassy full tilt along the roads to visit his friends, when he was *invited to stay at this house or that . . . widely known from here to Medford* as he was? Would he miss riding with his Volunteers in preparation for a rebellion they all guessed was coming but that he would not see?

She raised her eyes to meet those of Weyountah, who sat in such stillness as to be almost invisible on the room's single chair at the foot of the bed.

Would he miss his friends?

From the door, President Langdon commented, "Given the attitude of the body, and Mr. Wylie's testimony"—he nodded toward Weyountah—"as to raised voices and harsh words spoken to a man already laboring under the intolerable resentment of his servile condition, and given the presence of Mr. Fairfield's rum-bottle in the study and its contents all over the slave's clothing, it seems clear that Diomede drank himself into a state of rage while his master slept, and entering the room, stabbed him as he lay in his bed. Deplorable, of course, but no more than can be expected when a man practices the injustices of slavery upon his fellow creature—"

"But that gives no explanation for the blood on the floor of this room," said Abigail.

"I beg your pardon?" Dr. Langdon was clearly not used to having his diatribes against slavery interrupted by anyone, let alone a woman, for mere practicalities.

"There is blood on the floor," said Abigail, pointing. "It's been tracked and trampled about, but you see where the main stain of it lay, here, beside the desk by the window. Was the window open?"

President and doctor looked at each other.

"It was not." Weyountah got to his feet. A step—the

bedchamber was a tiny one—took him to the place; Abigail fetched the branch of candles from the little work-desk beneath the window, searched her pocket for flint and steel—which of course she'd left back at the inn . . . She caught up flint and striker from the bedside table. The room looked north onto the quadrangle of grass that lay between the college buildings and at this hour of the morning was gloomy. No wonder the poor boy had trouble waking up.

She knelt, holding the lights close to the floor. The main portion of the stain was clear to see. Not quite the diameter of a cider-mug, it was clearly outlined on the scuffed oak, as if it had lain there half the night. By comparison, the blots and tracks where the crowding students—and Dr. Perry himself, belike—had stepped in it were superficial. Her handkerchief, wet with a little discreetly applied spit, cleaned one of them up at once, but the original stain—which had lain hours longer—it could not touch.

There were two others, between that stain and the bed, in direct line. Round drips, and set, as if they, too, had lain there for many hours.

"He was stabbed here, by the desk," said Weyountah softly, "and dragged or carried to the bed. The wound under the ribs—"

"Which I cannot see how it could have been made," said Abigail, "by a man standing over him on the room side of the bed. You can see how the bed lies against the wall, with the head pointing south, the feet north toward the window. The left side, where the stab-wound is, would be away from a man standing in the room. But if he were stabbed here, standing up, of course the attacker would stab him in the left side—"

"And carry him to the bed and stab him thrice more, to make sure of him."

Abigail turned, frowning, back toward Perry and Langdon in the doorway. "And then proceed back to his pallet in the study and go to sleep? Without even washing the blood from his hands? When all the college was sleeping, and he could easily have fled—"

"The man was drunk," pointed out Langdon, in a tone of disgust. "I—and others—remonstrated with the boy about retaining a drunkard in his service, but he would not listen. Preferring, I suppose, the prestige—if one can call it that—of owning a Negro to the drudgery of making up his own bed."

"If your honor will pardon me for speaking," said Weyountah, "in my experience of the man, Diomede was not a habitual drunkard. He would go on an occasional spree for an evening if he thought Mr. Fairfield was not going to return to his rooms until late, as was the case, I believe, last night. But this is not the same thing as a man who punishes the bottle night after night."

"'Tis but a step, and a short one," replied the president coldly, "from the 'occasional spree,' as you call it, to greater and greater frequency as the demon takes hold. Surely *you* of all people do not deny the pattern?"

"No, sir." Weyountah's voice held level, despite the reference—which Abigail considered tactless in the extreme—to the notorious effect that white man's liquor had on many of the Indians who used it. "I speak only of my observation as to where Diomede stood in regard to that pattern."

"With what was he stabbed?" Abigail wondered if Perry would let her get a look at the wounds themselves and decided that a request to do so would only exacerbate a futile situation.

"The paper knife from Mr. Fairfield's desk was in Diomede's hand, m'am," said Weyountah.

"Would a paper knife be sharp enough to kill a man?" *And do I need to worry about Johnny getting his hands on John's from the study desk and murdering Charley while I'm away?*

The Indian edged between doctor and president—neither

of whom looked as if they would have made way for him, had either been able to find a good reason for standing on his dignity to that extent—and returned from the outer study a moment later with the bloodied weapon in his hand. "The edge is no sharper than it has to be to cut paper," he said. "But the point would surely be a deadly weapon in a strong man's hand."

A bit gingerly, Abigail took the hilt and touched the point with her fingertip. Aside from the smallness of the guard and the narrow blade, it would have almost served as an actual weapon: English-made, steel, with ivory plates on the hilt and a blade about seven inches long. Long enough and strong enough to reach the heart.

"And is there anything missing from the room? Where did Mr. Fairfield keep his money, for instance?"

"In his pockets, if he had any," replied Weyountah with a sigh. "Or in a desk-drawer or lying on the corner of the desk. Every excursion involved George searching for money—" A slight break flawed his voice as he remembered a hundred or a thousand tiny, trivial scenes. "And he never had a penny."

"I thought his father was rich!"

"He is, m'am. And George had credit all over town. But actual money in his pockets—"

"The boy was a gamester." Langdon's voice reeked with disgust. "And worse," he added darkly, meaning, Abigail guessed from Mrs. Squills's remarks at the Stair, given to wenching. Weyountah laid the paper knife on the corner of the desk and looked over the untidy papers there.

More than untidy, thought Abigail. Shuffled up together into loose bundles, the way Sam's were when he had been looking for something in his overcrowded study.

It could just mean that George Fairfield had mislaid his money and had searched his own desk. Still . . .

Two Spanish doubloons and a couple of Pennsylvania pound notes lay on the floor, as if they'd fallen when the desk was opened. A dozen or so books—the *Iliad* and the *Aeneid*, lexicons of Greek and Latin, Hoole's *Catonis Disticha de Moribus* and Ezekiel Cheever's *A Short Introduction, to the Latin Tongue, for the use of the lower forms in the Latin School, Being the Accidence abridged and compiled in that most easy and accurate method wherein the famous Mr. Ezekiel Cheever taught*, were piled on a chair higgledy-piggledy.

She remembered the tidiness of the front chamber. Looking around her, every portion of the bedroom save the vicinity of the desk attested to Diomede's housekeeping skills.

The stain on the floor was exactly between the desk—which stood beneath the window—and the bed.

She asked, "Does it look to you as if George had done any work at this desk? As if he'd been *able* to do work at it as it is?"

The Indian frowned and reconsidered the papers—the fact that no single paper lay in the center, that the inkstand and standish had been moved to the windowsill . . . the fact that, in effect, the desk looked as if someone had taken everything off it, then piled it back on . . .

"He did keep up with his work," said Abigail, standing at Weyountah's side. "He spoke of it last night . . . See, there's been wax dripped on the surface of the desk, fresh, it looks like, and *under* these papers . . . When did George come in last night, do you know?"

"The curfew is nine o'clock," pointed out Dr. Perry, rather severely, from the door.

Weyountah said nothing, but the glance he gave Abigail spoke clearly enough.

"Mrs. Squills spoke yesterevening of George meeting *a friend* out by the stables," she went on, turning toward Horace, who now stood a little behind the physician and the college president in the doorway. "Horace, you walked with George from the inn after he so very kindly saw to my lodging . . ."

In a stifled voice, Horace said, "We—George and I—parted between Massachusetts Hall and the brewhouse. I-I did warn him 'twas nearly nine, and he said he'd not be late."

And quietly, Weyountah added, with a warning glance toward Perry and President Langdon, "George had many *friends*. If he . . ."

Voices raised in the staircase outside, followed immediately by a thumping on the outer door. "Dr. Perry, sir—!"

At the same moment, Abigail became aware of voices in the quadrangle below.

Going to the window, she saw Pugh's tall, skinny follower Lowth slumped unconscious beside the door of the staircase, with two of his companions bending over him. Another young man lay on the ground, surrounded by his friends, a short distance away. She turned back as the excited young Mr. Yeovil burst into the study, crying, "Dr. Perry, Dr. Perry, they've been poisoned!"

Mr. Ryland, hard on his heels, added, "Dr. Perry, there's something very strange going on . . ."

Sheriff Congreve led Diomede away to the town jail while everyone piled and crowded after the stricken scholars as they were carried into the parlor of Massachusetts Hall. Since one of them was Mr. Lowth, Pugh and Jasmine Blossom had apparently lost any interest in guarding the staircase; even as she turned from the window, Abigail heard some of them coming up the stairs. *They'll trample over the room like cattle . . .*

She dropped behind as Langdon and Perry followed everyone out, then quickly turned down counterpane and sheet—she'd heard both John and her friend Joseph Warren speak of doing this with the victims of murder, and it made good sense to her—and caught up the paper knife, intending to compare the width of its blade with the size of the wounds. But as she turned back, she stopped, stood for a moment, and looked down into George's face: that young man she'd met but yesterday, that *personable young gentleman*, as Diomede had called him, who had talked of men as he'd found them, who'd never been able to tell Ajax son of Telamon from Ajax son of the other fellow, who'd come running from an assignation with a willing wench to make sure she, Abigail, was housed in the best inn of the town . . .

Someone killed him, she thought, and her throat tightened suddenly, her eyes flooded with tears. The slight changes of mortality had already taken hold, so that his face was not so disturbing as a man's new-dead. Her uneasy horror was gone, leaving only memory and pity.

Someone stabbed him, ended his life at the age of—what? Twenty-one? Twenty-two? With all the world before him . . .

Feet in the stairway; voices in the chamber.

What was it the Romans said? *Ultio prima, secundae lacrimae.* Vengeance first, then tears . . .

No, she corrected herself, as she laid the blade against that strangely ivory-colored flesh. *'Tis not vengeance I seek but salvation for the man who didn't do this crime . . .*

All four of the wounds looked a good half-inch wider than the width of the blade.

Swiftly, Abigail pulled down the young man's nightshirt, drew up the coverlet, even as she heard the doctor's voice cry angrily in the staircase, "Here, this won't do!" She dunked her handkerchief in the water-pitcher and was wiping the last traces of blood from her fingers when Joseph Ryland came in.

"Are you finished here, Mrs. Adams? Dr. Perry has sent for a litter to carry poor George's body to the infirmary—"

"What happened out there?"

The bachelor-fellow shook his head. "Lowth was suddenly taken queer, he said, and slumped down as if he'd been shot. In the next second Mosson went down, too—Waller and Blossom said they were feeling queer . . ."

Abigail stared at him for a moment, then said, "Oh, those wretches!" and dashed past him and out into the study.

The cut-glass rum-bottle that had stood next to Diomede's bloodstained pallet had been tucked unobtrusively behind a chair. It was empty.

"And it serves them right!" she exclaimed. "Only now of course there's no way of proving it—"

"Poison?" Ryland followed her, brow drawn down half in consternation, half in disbelief. "How could—?"

"*I have drugged their possets*, Lady Macbeth says." Abigail sniffed at the carafe, but could smell only the overwhelming reek of rum. "More likely laudanum than poison—"

"Meant for George?"

"Those idiots," said Weyountah, going to the window—meaning, Abigail guessed, Lowth and Jasmine and Waller and Mosson who'd thought it was so clever to sneak an extra drink while everyone was milling about . . . "'Twould serve them well if it *were* poison."

Ryland and Abigail—carafe in hand—were already hurrying down the stairs.

In the parlor where Abigail had waited last night for young Fairfield, dark little Mr. Blossom was being plied with hot coffee while half-a-dozen masters and students were trying to revive Lowth and Mosson. The smell of burnt feathers and panic filled the air. "They've been poisoned!" cried Mr. Yeovil again, and Pugh shouted to a little freshman named Pinkstone—presumably, thought Abigail, his own luckless "fag"—to run fetch coffee from his own room, which was on the staircase of the new hall directly across the quadrangle from that of Fairfield, Weyountah, and Horace.

"They have not," retorted Abigail, entering hard upon this line. "Mr. Blossom, did you drink the rum in the carafe in George's room? I thought so. Mr. Waller?" A tall young man with a long, horsey face—sitting with his head between his knees in a circle of frightened acquaintances—jerked upright shakily and gazed at her with pupils narrowed to pinpricks, even in the gloom of the parlor.

"I did, too—" gasped another young man in a green robe. "I-I feel so queer . . ."

"I'm sure you do," returned Abigail briskly. "There was laudanum in the rum, which would amply account for poor Diomede not waking up—"

"And for poor George—" cried someone else.

"The blackguard!" exclaimed another young gentleman. "To poison his master, then drink himself stupid in celebration—"

"Nonsense!" snapped Abigail, taken aback this interpretation of her evidence. "Fairfield was stabbed, for one thing, and for another, a killer would have to be stupid to take a drug like that before even getting out of the room—"

"It's exactly what that nigger of mine would do," remarked Pugh, straightening up from beside the pile of coats where Lowth lay. "Only he'd probably drink off half the rum before drugging it, to give himself a little Dutch courage—" He put his hands on his hips, regarded Abigail's openmouthed indignation with some amusement. "They don't think the way white people do, m'am," he said. "You ask any man who's grown up among 'em as I have. They don't look ahead—not two minutes, not two feet. Like dealing with a lot of four-year-olds."

"That's ridiculous!"

Pugh raised one eyebrow. "Got a lot of 'em in Boston, have you, m'am, to know 'em so well?"

And a man with the accent of the Carolinas affirmed, "Ours sure don't think before they act."

As she looked from face to face, Abigail was shocked to observe how many of these young men were nodding—some of them unwillingly, but accepting the judgment as it stood. Someone said, "Poor old George!" and someone else, "My Aunt Caro was killed by a nigger maid—"

"And what do you expect," demanded Dr. Langdon, rising from beside Dr. Perry where both men had knelt beside the vaguely stirring Mr. Mosson, "when you have grown up in an atmosphere envenomed by the vice of slavery? When a poor Negro is driven to desperation by the ill-treatment of a vicious master—"

"Aunt Abigail—"

She was opening her mouth, breathless with anger at these assumptions about Diomede and anyone else of African descent, when Horace quietly touched her elbow.

"Aunt Abigail, I'm sorry, but . . . there is something missing from George's room. Two books," he said.

Six

I'm afraid they were not terribly edifying volumes." Horace shyly pushed up his spectacles more firmly onto the bridge of his nose. "I only took note of them because—"

"You needn't explain," said Abigail kindly. The poor boy was only barely seventeen, and she recalled what her brother William had been like at . . . well, considerably younger than that. "And if they were as unedifying as all that, they might very well have gone the way of the rum." She glanced back over her shoulder as they emerged from the parlor into the open quadrangle and reentered the hallway to mount Horace's staircase. Even in here, Dr. Langdon's thundering peroration on why Diomede must have done murder because of his degradation under slavery could be heard with damning clarity. "What were they?"

"Aretino's *I Modi*, with the—er—illustrations by Raimondi," stammered Horace. "And Brantôme's *Les Vies des Dames Galantes*. Also illustrated." His blush went from his hairline down under his neckcloth. Abigail thought his ears were going to catch fire. He must have looked over Fairfield's shoulder at the illustrations, if no more. "And I don't think they could have been sneaked out of the room by anyone in the crowd this morning. Weyountah was in the bedchamber with George the whole time."

"Did he keep them in there?"

Horace nodded. "The desk has a false bottom in it," he said simply.

And Weyountah explained, "There are no locks on the doors of the chambers, so people are always pilfering things. Nothing big—there's not a man among us who would steal his neighbor's money—but if a man has tea, or coffee beans, or has just had a package from home with something sweet in it, he's likely to come back to his room and find less of it than there was when he went out. Of course no one is permitted spirits, so no one can report it if he comes back and finds his rum has been watered—"

"It's one reason, I think, that seniors let us fags study in their rooms," put in Horace. "So someone will be there, should they have something they'd rather didn't disappear—though in truth, Aunt Abigail, it isn't the nest of thieves we must sound like. For one thing, most of us are in the same lectures at the same times—"

"And for another," added Weyountah, as they approached the staircase, "everybody gets to know everything, pretty much, and if someone goes about pocketing coffee beans, it doesn't remain a secret for long."

They stopped at the foot of the staircase door to let a small procession descend. Mr. Ryland, his faded crimson gown giving him the archaic look of a priest, walked ahead; behind him, four college servants in rough tweeds carried a stretcher covered with the blankets that Abigail recognized from George Fairfield's bed. She moved to put her arm around Horace's waist in comfort, then restrained herself, recalling that Ryland was the Fellow in charge of the Hall. No sense having the poor boy fined four shillings on top of everything else.

"Will Dr. Langdon write to George's father?" she asked softly.

Horace nodded, unable to speak, and Weyountah said, "I imagine so, yes."

"Do either of you know the man? Or does Mr. Ryland?"

They looked at one another, shook their heads. "Only from hearing George speak of him," said the Indian. "He'll be coming, I'm sure, to—to take George home . . ."

"And to deal with Diomede?"

She could tell by their faces that this aspect of the situation had only begun to surface through shock and grief.

Horace said, "Oh, dear—"

And Weyountah, "Oh, Christ."

"*Dear Mr. Fairfield,*" said Abigail drily. "*I regret to inform you that your son's valet has murdered your son in a fit of drunken rage over his enslaved condition, which is no more than is to be expected. Shame on you for transforming him into a man so degraded as to do the deed, and it serves you right that he did. Please come and have him picked up for trial before the Virginia courts.* What is the penalty for a slave who kills his master, in Virginia? Hanging? And how likely is it that he'll receive even a hearing, let alone a trial?"

"Negligible," said Weyountah softly. "And no, it's not hanging. It's burning at the stake. When will Mr. Adams return from Maine?"

"Friday," said Abigail. "Possibly Saturday, though there's talk of him going down to Providence next week. I expect they'll hold Diomede here for Mr. Fairfield's arrival, rather than try him under Massachusetts law, which means that no matter how many affidavits we can collect attesting his innocence, he shall still face judgment entirely at the hands of a father mourning the loss of his only son and men who have spent the whole of their lives watching for the slightest signs of defiance and murder in their slaves."

"Can Mr. Adams have the trial moved here?" With a swift and rather guilty glance about them, to make sure that Mr. Ryland and his party were out of the hall, Weyountah led the way up the staircase again. "How would one go about that? Petition the Governor?"

"'Tis what I'll try," said Abigail grimly. "John hates the man, but the one time I've met him, His Excellency seemed kindly and well-disposed. I've heard nothing personal against him, save that he's a self-serving blockhead who gives all colonial offices and perquisites to his family and friends, and any man might do that. Even one who has written to the King advising that the harshest measures be taken against the colony for our disobedient persistence in wanting to have the rights accorded to the meanest ditchdigger in a British parish.

"The problem is," she added, as they slipped through the oak door and stood in the tiny study again, the stink of blood and rum very strong now in the close room. "The problem is, 'twill be difficult to convince His Excellency or anyone that murder—sufficiently premeditated to entail the drugging of a servant—was done for a couple of pornographic books. It seems a small matter to be the worth of a man's life."

"Think you so, m'am?" Weyountah, kneeling beside the rumpled and blood-smudged pallet that still lay along one wall of the study, looked up, his dark eyes somber. "My grandparents were killed, and three of my aunts, because a band of Massachusetts militiamen took the wrong path in the woods one day on their way to avenge the killing of four cows and a herdsman by the men of a Pocasset village that they couldn't manage to locate. Such was their desire for vengeance, however, that they followed the path, *knowing them-selves to be lost*, and burned the village that they found at the end of it, though they *knew* that they'd come upon Narragan-setts rather than Pocassets. About twenty people were killed—men, women, and children who had no more to do with the original cow-killing than had the islanders of Oata-hite. My mother only escaped because she was down at the creek catching fish that afternoon. She was ten."

Abigail was silent, looking down at that young man, in his faded blue scholar's gown and his trim, dark, threadbare suit. The blood on the sheets nearby seemed to mutter and whisper of the violence done in the room beyond: that some-one had considered something worth not only the life of George Fairfield but of his slave also . . .

But ten years of talking over John's cases with him had told her—if a childhood listening to the sins and enormities of an isolated New England village had not—that men walked the earth to whom the avoidance of inconvenience or embarrassment was sufficient justification for taking another man's life.

"Would a student caught breaking into another man's room stand in danger of being sent down?" she asked. "Par-ticularly at night—"

"Absolutely."

"*Sine dubium.* The thing is," went on Horace diffidently, as he followed Abigail and Weyountah—rather white-faced but resolute—into the bedchamber beyond. "The thing is, George had only just gotten those books . . . what was it, Weyountah? Two weeks ago?"

"Exactly two weeks." Weyountah removed the stacked papers from the desk, handed them to Horace, his move-ments swift as if the two of them worked underwater, with only limited time available in the room that stank of their friend's lifeblood soaked into the mattress of the bed. "The twelfth of April. He kept them in here."

He opened the desk, revealing the shallow compartment inside empty of everything save a few sheets of paper and some broken quills.

"Was there usually more in here?" Abigail inquired. It looked nothing like John's neat desk at home, but then, Fairfield had not impressed her as a scholar.

"I think so," said Horace, his arms filled with papers, books, and Greek and Latin lexicons. "But I usually worked in the front room, not in here. The college provosts will sometimes search the rooms—I know Pugh pays the ones over in Harvard Hall and the Fellow in charge of the hall as well not to touch his—and last term Jasmine tried to blackmail George over some love-letters a girl had written to him . . . that's when he started keeping everything hidden in this desk."

Weyountah hooked his finger into an almost-invisible hole at one side of the desk's interior and lifted out the false bottom to reveal a second compartment beneath. This contained a vast rummage of disordered papers: bills—from tailors, bootmakers, the college stables for feed—mixed with letters and notes. Abigail picked one up, *Deerst Geo Ill bee back of the brewhous tonight dreemin of you ellie . . .* There was also a small sack of coffee beans and a flask of rum. "He kept the books in there," said Horace. "I know, because I came in yesterday morning earlier than he'd counted on, and he had the desk open and was looking at them—" Color crept up into his face again and faded almost at once, as he remembered not the pictures in the book, but the nearness of his friend who would never ogle questionable pictures again. After a moment he swallowed hard and went on, "And the same woman who sold them to him, sold me four books in Arabic."

* * *

Her name, said Horace—over a breakfast of Mrs. Squills's sausage and corn-cakes at the Golden Stair some half hour later—was Mrs. Seckar. "Her husband held the Vassall Professorship of Religion for about a hundred years," explained the boy. "He was very much a disciple of John Calvin and would hear of no innovation in the teaching of his master—"

"He was a pride-sick old bigot." Weyountah poured out coffee for himself and Abigail from a yellow pottery pitcher, while Horace sipped the mild tisane of honey, mint, and water that was all his fragile digestion would tolerate. "Cruel, too. He led his poor wife a frightful life, then left the house and bulk of his estate to fund a position here at Harvard. She was selling the books—which were hers—in order to have a little money to take with her when she went to live with her cousins in Medfield."

"The one Mr. Fairfield spoke of," said Abigail thoughtfully. "And she had books in Arabic? Not to mention volumes like the *Vies des Dames Galantes?*"

"Mrs. Seckar said they had probably been her great-grandfather's," explained the Indian. "I bought two texts in chemistry, though they're fearfully out of date—the most recent was Willis's *Pharmaceutice Rationalis*, 1674—and what I think was someone's journal, which contained tables of astronomical observations and several pages of various methods of calculating sidereal time. One passage was translated from al-Farghani—an Arabic scholar nearly a thousand years ago—and I think in the chemical sections there were translations from al-Jildaki, who was one of the early Mohammedan scholars of the discipline."

"The four I bought weren't anywhere near that erudite,"

admitted Horace. "I had an edition of the Alexander Legend, Ibn-Battuta's travel narratives, a commentary on the Koran, and a book about horse-doctoring."

"So obviously, Mrs. Seckar's ancestor was the last Arabic scholar in this colony . . . How long ago? Fifty years? Sixty years?"

"Longer," said Weyountah. "Mrs. Seckar must be in her seventies. The Reverend Seckar was eighty-five, but up to the day he died he'd walk from their house on the Watertown Road to the chapel"—he nodded in the direction of the Common and the college—"to supervise prayers."

"To make sure nobody strayed from the Master's doctrines by so much as an inch, you mean," put in Horace, devouring his fifth corn-cake. "Please don't get me wrong, Aunt Abigail," he added earnestly. "I understand the need for correct understanding of the Will of God, and I know that disregard of intellectual distinctions can result in some quite frightful misunderstandings of our own unworthiness to have received salvation that lies beyond our desserts . . . but I also think that no sin lies in sweetening the lesson."

"You're saying he was a trifle dry?" She hid her smile.

"Horace is saying the Reverend Seckar was long-winded, doctrinaire, and intrusive into matters that seemed to me no part of the Church's business."

"That was his point," said Horace apologetically. "That everything in life is God's business, in that it glorifies or affronts God. He abused poor Ryland like a pickpocket at the merest hint of Arminianism—"

"Is Mr. Ryland an Arminian?" Somehow she could believe it of that grave young man, that he could not endure the belief that a man's good deeds would not suffice to bend the will of an angry God.

"He claims not to be. Of course, the Reverend Seckar would say—"

"I think his quarrel with Ryland," put in the Indian, "was as much about Ryland taking a stipend from the Governor to support him here as it was about Free Will. Seckar never forgave Governor Hutchinson for being descended from a heretic. And the fact that Mrs. Seckar had four books in Arabic in her great-grandfather's collection doesn't mean that the other books she sold at the same time contained something that could have gotten the Governor of Jamaica hanged for treason, Arabic or not . . ."

"No," admitted Abigail. "But the coincidence of a murder, an attempted murder, and the disappearance of antique books from the murdered man's rooms all within a week makes me extremely curious to have a few words with Mrs. Seckar about what other books Great-Grandpa's collection might have contained."

From Mrs. Squills, Abigail borrowed pen and paper, and wrote a note to Mrs. Seckar in Medfield ("She's gone to live with cousins, poor lady, the Barlows, at Rock Farm out nearer Stonton than Medfield . . ." Mrs. Squills provided), asking the favor of an interview at her earliest convenience. After a moment's thought, she composed another, to Governor Hutchinson, and a third note, more brief than the others, she sent by way of Mrs. Squills's niece to a Mr. Metcalfe, who lived in Cambridge and whose most recent fines for infractions of the Navigation Acts John had been instrumental in having dismissed. Had she not done so, she feared that Weyountah and Horace would beggar themselves of candle-and-food money to rent her a chaise to return to Boston in.

While waiting for Mr. Metcalfe's reply—he had assured John on the occasion of their last meeting that *any help I can be, to you or any of yours*—Abigail walked from the Golden

Stair to the town jail, only to be told by Sheriff Congreve that Diomede, still half-stupefied, had slipped back into a heavy sleep. She gave the sheriff most of her slender pocket money to provide food for the prisoner and, returning to the inn, made arrangements with Mrs. Squills to send bread, cheese, and cider to him over the course of the following days.

"Last night you spoke of poor Mr. Fairfield meeting a young friend out near the college barns," she said, when these negotiations were satisfactorily concluded. "You wouldn't happen to know her name, would you?"

And Mrs. Squills laughed. "Lord love you, Mrs. Adams, that's like putting a name on one of those butterflies out there." She gestured toward the kitchen door, beyond which lay her vegetable garden and a rather weedy border of penstemon, buttercups, and wild roses just coming into bloom. "Poor Mr. George had a dozen of them, for all he was practically engaged to Miss Sally Woodleigh. I think my Ginny broke her heart for him," she added, in a quieter voice, "not that I'd ever let her go meeting him or any man living out behind the college hay-barn . . . But it goes to show."

The tiny landlady shook her head sadly. "He hadn't an ounce of vice in him, you know, Mrs. Adams. Please don't think so. And he'd never have harmed a soul. But he was like a walking sprig of catnip, and that's the truth."

"Had he enemies?" In addition to the marketing basket she'd arrived with, Abigail now carried a small satchel belonging to Horace, into which they had crammed the papers, bills, and letters that had cluttered the hidden compartment of George Fairfield's desk. "Barring the sweethearts of his lady friends, that is." Dozens of the letters in the satchel were love-notes in a score of different hands, and in the pocket of George's gold-laced gray coat—which had lain, tossed down with his ruffled shirt and his breeches, on the floor where he'd dropped them—she had found a small packet of them, along with a note in a delicate hand saying, *As you love me, be behind the barn at midnight . . .*

"Well—" Mrs. Squills frowned, as if speaking against her will. "He was a Tory, when all's said—though I like to think it was just a boy's fancy, because he was raised that way, you know. He'd have gotten over it." She sighed, and Abigail guessed that the local beauties weren't the only ones who'd fallen for George Fairfield's easy charm. "But most of the men at the college, they're all for our liberties and will be slaves to no man, nor no King either. And yes, sometimes there was bad feeling over that, and once or twice I understand it came to blows, though never here. I stand for nothing like that in my place." (There was a Mr. Squills, stout and ox-eyed, fussing about in the kitchen, but Abigail was under no illusions about whose *place* the Golden Stair was.)

"But that sort of thing, 'tisn't the sort of thing one kills over."

Isn't it? Mr. Metcalfe's chaise drew up before the door, and Horace and Weyountah—appearing in their college gowns with a bulky parcel for her—helped Mr. Metcalfe's young groom fasten satchel and parcel onto the back. Promises were exchanged to lose no time in searching the countryside round for the house to which Horace had been taken, for a dark-haired woman of respectable appearance, for anyone who might have been called George's enemy . . . Promises to visit Diomede and make sure he had food and a blanket, to write to Mr. Fairfield protesting his innocence . . .

'Tisn't the sort of thing one kills over, reflected Abigail, as the chaise pulled away.

Only wasn't the formation of the King's Own Volunteers—a fighting-force of the young men of the district loyal to the King—preparation to do exactly that?

Kill all men who would take up arms against the King in defense of their own liberties?

Was there not every chance that the King's ship, when it made landfall in Boston, would be carrying troops with precisely that mandate? To arrest—and kill if necessary—those whose politics differed from those of the King? *Including Cousin Sam,* she thought, her heartbeat quickening unpleasantly. *And maybe John . . .*

No. She thrust the thought aside. John had never involved himself with the Sons of Liberty—not much, anyway. She leaned back in the seat, and thought about the paper-wrapped parcel the boys had given her, and Horace's worn satchel with its muddle of love-notes and who-knows-what that George hadn't wanted prying eyes to see. *A personable young gentleman . . . widely known from here to Medford . . . always invited to this house or that . . .*

Politics, passion, and mysterious ciphers written in Arabic . . .

And none of them, reflected Abigail—gazing out between the horse's ears at the bright dapple of sunshine on the shaded road, the peaceful countryside of stone walls, prosperous farmhouses, hay, and corn—none of them sufficient reason to save a man's life from those who had decided beforehand that he must be guilty.

Abigail's uncle Isaac Smith dwelled on Milk Street in a house that wouldn't have looked out of place in London. He was one of the wealthiest shipowners in the colony, and his dwelling had its own stables, half-a-dozen apple trees, and gardens stretching back to join the open fields of the Summer Street Ward. Charley and Tommy—held severely to their good manners by Aunt Eliza and Pattie—were ushered into the parlor in a scrubbed and polite condition that made Abigail's heart glow with pride. "I am covered in abnegation," she said, stretching out her hand to her aunt. "And to you, Pattie, I owe you a thousand apologies. What must you think of me——?"

"I think you're a good lady who got talking too much to her nephew in Cambridge," retorted Aunt Eliza good-naturedly, "and ended up standing on the wharf watching the ferry pull away, like nobody ever has in the history of the world——"

"I promise you, Aunt, the horse picked up a stone——"

"Oh, aye, and there was an earthquake and an Indian attack . . ."

All three women laughed. "They were honestly no trouble," said Pattie, with a slightly nervous glance at Aunt Eliza, who was, after all, a well-off lady and might take exception to a servant entering into a conversation uninvited.

"Lord, no," chuckled Elizabeth Smith. "Johnny and Nabby went off to school this morning, good as gold. I'll send them on to you when they come back, unless you'd care to stay for dinner . . . You're sure? Let me at least have Cuffee carry that package of yours, then——"

Cuffee was one of the Smith household slaves. Virginians—and the sons of West Indian merchants like Mr. Pugh—weren't the only ones in the Americas to hold black men in servitude.

"'Tis only a few books, not a bale of hay!"

It was, in fact, seven books: rather large, heavy, and old, their thick leather covers smelling of mildew and smoke. As Weyountah had remarked, there was no reason for Abigail to think that George Fairfield's murder had had the slightest thing to do with the books he'd bought from Narcissa Seckar—there were plenty of other reasons someone might have wanted to make away with a young Tory captain of militia who had apparently tupped every woman in Middle-sex County. Considering the content of the missing volumes and the presence of young men like St-John Pugh in the vicinity, their disappearance last night from George Fair-field's room might have had nothing to do with their new owner's murder.

And the fact that part of the original collection had been in Arabic only coincidence.

But she had felt better, knowing that the books would not be in Horace's room that night.

Seven

Midmorning Thursday brought a note from Governor Hutchinson.

My dear Mrs. Adams,

I well remember our brief meeting and the kindly concern that you showed for an unfortunate stranger whom Fate had brought beneath my roof. Please do attend me this afternoon following dinner, and I will do what I can for you. If as you say the matter is 'not one of politics,' it will be a most welcome relief at the present moment.

Sincerely,
Thos. Hutchinson

Abigail suspected that had she not included, in her request for a few minutes of Hutchinson's time, the reassurance that her visit was not a political one, the reply would have been merely, *Send a petition to my secretary* . . .

And so it might prove, she reflected, glancing through the kitchen windows at the angle of sunlight in the little yard. Pattie was emptying the mop-water into the gutter of the little alley that connected the yard with Queen Street—it was shocking how quickly street-dust and the general griminess of town living accumulated in a house, even with only two days of not being mopped. Abigail ticked off tasks in her mind as she tucked the note behind the household tablet on the big oak sideboard: butter to be churned—thank Heavens Their Majesties Cleopatra and Semiramis were producing milk again after the winter's drought!—lamps to be cleaned and set ready for evening, dinner to be started, mending . . . And all before she could justify to herself even touching that satchel full of young Mr. Fairfield's papers.

The "worthies" of Boston ate their dinners later than workingmen and the wives of peripatetic lawyers, so probably she could walk to Marlborough Street at six and find His Excellency back in his office . . .

Oh, drat it, the bread needs to be got up . . .

My dear Mrs. Adams sounded promising, however. From a drawer in the sideboard, Abigail pulled out a piece of paper, then—considering its rough yellow surface—replaced it. When Pattie—fourteen years old, brisk, and pretty, the dark-haired daughter of one of their neighbors on the farm back in Braintree had lived almost as a daughter in the Adams household for over a year— came back in and hung the mop-bucket in its place by the back door, Abigail said, "Would you scald the dasher and the churn for me, dear? But do *not* get the butter started—I won't have you doing my work for me; you've enough to do on your own . . . Yes, my darling," she added as Charley—just a few weeks short of four years old and filled with resentment that he no longer had Uncle Isaac's garden to play in—"I'm sorry you can't go back to Aunt Eliza's, but you can't." She lifted Tommy as the younger boy held out his arms. Twenty months old, he had recently figured out how to untie his leading-strings from whatever piece of furniture he'd been fixed to and was running everywhere now with happy abandon and was going to get himself killed, Abigail reflected, before he reached his second birthday . . .

"I will be out in exactly two minutes— Yes, Charley, you can come with me . . ."

With the boys tugging at her skirts and at each other's, she went down the hall to John's study, sat the boys firmly on the chairs there (*For all the good that's like to do* . . .) and, on the fine smooth English legal paper from John's desk, wrote a quick précis of the events of Tuesday evening and yesterday: that George Fairfield, a scholar at Harvard, had been murdered in his room by person or persons unknown; that all evidence showed that his slave Diomede had been drugged; that items were missing from Fairfield's rooms that a robber could have taken; but that the Reverend Dr. Langdon (whom Abigail knew was no friend to Hutchinson) was stubbornly insisting that Diomede must be the culprit because as a slave he must have hated his master enough to do murder, despite all evidence to the contrary.

Without your assistance in the matter, the unfortunate Diomede will be returned to his master's father in Virginia and will surely suffer the extreme penalty for a crime of which he is almost certainly innocent. In the name of justice, sir, please consider either taking the necessary steps to have the case tried in the courts of Massachusetts, or at the very least, stay this unhappy man's deportation until some enquiry can be made into the actual circumstances of the event, for he surely can expect no justice once he leaves these shores. Yours sincerely, A. Adams.

And a blot, because Tommy, overwhelmed with the endless weight of enforced stillness, was moved to pull Charley's hair, setting off a train of circumstance that precipitated both boys against their mother's chair.

One day I am going to run off to the Maine Assizes myself and let John stay here and make butter . . .

Petition in hand and, for the sake of propriety (a convention she privately considered silly), escorted by her daughter Nabby, Abigail walked the quarter mile along Cornhill to Marlborough Street at six and presented the Governor's note to the Governor's butler at the handsome three-story brick mansion allotted by the colony to the representative of the Crown. *Just as well*, she thought, *that John IS away at the Assizes* . . . To her assertion a few months ago that she had never found His Excellency to be other than polite and considerate, John had simply roared, *And I suppose you'd think well of a WHOREMASTER who was polite to you?*

If he were not passionate, about politics as well as all other things, she supposed, he would not be John . . .

But it was best that she, and not he, was in charge of this particular portion of the effort to save an innocent man from death.

A dozen men—most of them well-off merchants, to judge by the quality of their clothing and wigs—occupied the chairs of the handsome tapestried parlor to which the butler showed her; the Governor's son-in-law Mr. Oliver got quickly to his feet and offered Abigail his chair, and a man whom she recognized as one of Uncle Isaac's extremely wealthy merchant rivals brought his own seat over for Nabby, who curtseyed her thanks in some confusion. At not quite nine, the plump, quiet girl was curious and a little proud to be taken out into company, but invariably shy once among strangers, and sat with hands folded in silence, wide blue eyes taking in the old-fashioned, elegant hangings and carved wainscot of the room. Abigail sent in her petition and took note of the men whom the Governor called in before her with abstract curiosity. She rated, evidently, below the merchants—who were probably relations of the Governor— but above the two she guessed were ship-captains.

Given that no one in Boston had the slightest idea what the King was going to rule appropriate punishment for the colony and the town, it was not surprising that His Excellency was being inundated with requests for audience, favors, and assurance of protection.

From her satchel she took the small packet of love-letters that had been in George Fairfield's pocket and glanced over them while she waited, as she would on another occasion have brought a book. Delicate and rather rounded handwriting, thin expensive French paper, passionate sentiments, a faint scent of attar of roses, and no signature. But obviously some wealthy man's daughter who had been taught, at least, to handle a pen.

"Mrs. Adams?" said the secretary from the inner door.

Governor Hutchinson—whom John habitually described as a *pusillanimous traitor*—was on his feet when Abigail came into his study, and himself held the chair for her when she sat.

"This sounds like a most serious matter, Mrs. Adams," he said in his soft voice, seating himself and touching the petition that lay before him on his desk. "And one in which there is certain to be some question from Governor Dunmore of Virginia, regarding the legality of distraining a man's property here in Massachusetts, should Mr. Fairfield, Senior, demand the slave Diomede's immediate return. Are you sure of what you contend, that the man was drugged and not merely drunk?"

"Two students who entered the room and—as young men will—drank off the rest of the rum in the carafe were rendered unconscious within minutes. Two others—I presume juniors who were only able to get a lesser share—were groggy and stumbling. No rum remained in the carafe, but I found the inference compelling."

"And the items removed from the room—?"

"Two old volumes, only recently acquired by Mr. Fairfield from a Mrs. Seckar."

The Governor's narrow face lightened: "Not old Professor Seckar's widow? Dear Heavens, if ever there was a man who would cut you to pieces over whether God's predetermination of the saved and the reprobate was active or passive—I remember that thundering lecture of his on infralapsarianism and the precise timing of the Fall of the Angels that went two hours over into the dinner hour, and all of us ready to tear apart the youngest freshman in the room and eat him, we were so hungry. Which I suppose," he added with a smile, "was proof in his eyes that we were none of us saved and all doomed to the eternal fires. But I thought he left the whole of his library to the college when he died?"

"I believe these volumes had come down to Mrs. Seckar from her grandfather."

"I wonder that—" He visibly bit back some epithet applicable to the Reverend Dr. Langdon, and continued, "I wonder that Dr. Langdon didn't insist on their inclusion in the bequest. That wouldn't be Barthelmy Whitehead, would it? By all accounts the man was practically illiterate, but with a heart like a counting-frame—one of the last men in the colony to attempt to sell Indians as slaves to the West Indies and one of the first to enter the Negro trade."

Abigail guessed that having written a history of the colony—his own troublesome ancestress having played no small part in it—the Governor was intimately acquainted with the affairs of every family from Cape Cod to Halifax.

"Perhaps Dr. Langdon did not consider them appropriate for inclusion in the College library," she replied. "I understand from my nephew—whom I was visiting in Cambridge on Tuesday night, when the crime took place—that they were of an *improper* nature."

"Ah." Hutchinson frowned. "Young men being what they are, that might account for their theft but surely not for murder being done over them."

"Among normal men, no, sir. But I'm sure Your Excellency is aware that where darkness corrodes a man's heart, even matters of insignificance become reasonable grounds for murder."

He shot her a sidelong glance—clearly thinking of Wily Cousin Sam—and murmured, "Just so."

"The circumstance of their theft so soon after their acquisition, and of poor Diomede—Mr. Fairfield's man—being drugged to prevent his waking during the theft, seem to me sufficient grounds to merit investigation, and intervention on your part to have the matter tried here in Massachusetts, where witnesses in the man's defense can be brought forward. Objectionable as the condition of slavery is, I do *not* see it as ipso facto proof of a slave's guilt in his master's murder when there are circumstances that so clearly point to another cause."

"I quite agree, Mrs. Adams. And yet, the law is established to defend a man's rights to his property, and I cannot subvert it—"

"The law is established, Your Excellency, to defend a man's *life*. And the slave Diomede's life will surely be forfeit if he is taken back to Virginia, for whatever witnesses can be found as to another motive for the murder will most likely not follow him there. In their absence, I very much fear that the courts—if a slave is even entitled to a hearing before Virginia courts—"

"He is," put in the Governor drily.

"I am thrilled to hear it," she returned. "But do you trust them? Do you trust them even to read the affidavits? Do you trust them not to take the simplest reading of the matter and avoid putting themselves to the inconvenience of delving for the truth? Would you wish to rely on such a court to defend your own life? Or the life of one of your sons?"

His thin lips pressed together—annoyed at her vehemence, she suspected, yet unable to refute her words. "I see what you mean, Mrs. Adams," he said at length. "Yet your position is based upon supposition, and your assumption of what a certain body of men *may* do or *might* do. Mine is based upon the law. It is beyond my power, as Governor of this colony, to abrogate the rights of property, particularly the rights of a citizen of another colony—and it is moreover quite properly beyond my power. Heaven forfend that a man should take a legal action based upon suspicion of what *might* be in another man's mind. Yet I shall certainly write to Mr. Congreve," he added, as Abigail opened her mouth to object, "that he is not to release this Negro man into the custody of Mr. Fairfield, Senior's, agents until he has communicated with me. I assume"—his voice thinned a little, like one forcing himself to be absolutely just—"that your husband will take it upon himself to defend this unfortunate valet?"

"He will."

"Then your best course of action—and his—will be to ascertain the facts of the case as quickly as possible, before communication from Virginia forces the issue one way or another. It will be at least two weeks, perhaps more, before Mr. Fairfield, Senior, arrives on these shores. With concrete evidence of a third person involved, I shall have more leverage against the law of property. Without it, I must yield. I hope you understand my position, madame?"

"I do." Abigail rose, and held out her hand. Her whole Christian soul revolted against what the Governor had said, and yet, as a lawyer's wife, she understood the principle from which he spoke. She forced back her temper, and said with an assumption of warmth that she barely felt, "And I thank you for what you can do, sir, and for what you are willing to do in this poor man's defense."

The Governor's slim fingers—cool and dry as a snake's back—closed around hers, and he led her to the door. "Mr. Oliver—?"

His secretary materialized, bowing, to conduct her out.

"M rs. Adams!" Joseph Ryland got to his feet in surprise as she came back into the parlor, which was—despite the dimming of the daylight from the windows—more crowded than before. Nabby—to Abigail's approval—who had been about to leap to her feet and scamper to her mother's side, yielded at once to the dictum that the affairs of adults took precedence over the discomfort of eight-year-old girls abandoned in roomfuls of strangers, and settled back in her chair, grateful at least that her mother was in the range of her sight.

"Mr. Ryland." Abigail held out her hand, over which the young bachelor-fellow bowed. "Are you here also to speak to His Excellency on behalf of poor Diomede?"

He looked momentarily nonplussed. "Of course, I shall speak as to his innocence—"

"Not necessary," she assured him, a little drily. "Governor Hutchinson has agreed to intervene, insofar as the laws of *property* permit, to at least give us time to find the true culprit."

"I would have expected nothing less of the man." Ryland's shoulders relaxed, as if relieved of the weight of a water-yoke. "I know that your husband finds his politics objectionable." He spoke diffidently, but who in the colony wasn't aware—Abigail reflected—of the diatribes John had had printed, under his own name and pseudonyms like Novanglus and Mrs. Country Goodheart? "But in truth, m'am—as I'm sure you have learned, in even the briefest of encounters with him—that his nature is not only just, but generous and noble. Will your husband indeed take on poor Diomede's cause?"

"I shall see to it he does. But I did mean to ask you—"

He glanced around as another young man, trim and elegant in a suit of plum-colored velveteen, was shown into the parlor. "Mr. Ryland," the newcomer greeted him affably, casually handing off his hat to the secretary, and Ryland bowed.

"Mr. Heywood."

"Shocking business about poor old George, isn't it? So much for La Woodleigh's schemes to snabble his acres for her daughter—"

Abigail tardily identified La Woodleigh as the wife of Montgomery Woodleigh, who lived in Cambridge and owned five ships and considerable property in Boston.

"Anyone know if she's heard?"

"I myself informed Mrs. Woodleigh this morning." Spots of color appeared on Ryland's cheeks, and Mr. Heywood grinned.

"Not wasting a moment, are you, old boy? Going to get your bid in with the beautiful Sally?" But he laughed as he said it, as if he'd asked, did Mr. Ryland have plans to be crowned King of England in the near future? An absurdity, to think that a young Fellow of the College whose out-of-date coat was worn threadbare at the elbows and whose stockings showed neat mends above the re-dyed backs of his shoes would offer for the hand of a Woodleigh. Abigail felt a flush of anger rise along her neck, at his look of carefully controlled chagrin.

"More to the point," spoke up another young gentleman seated nearby—Abigail half recognized him as one of the younger Apthorps, whom she'd seen with his extremely wealthy parents at the Brattle Square Meeting-House—"d'you know when the Volunteers will be meeting, to select a new captain? I mean, we'll miss old George terribly and all that, but trouble could break out at any moment, you know. We can't be caught leaderless when it starts if we're to get any kind of preferment when the King sends in his regular troops."

"You sound very sure that he'll be sending troops, sir," said Abigail, and the young Apthorp rose to bow to her, Mr. Heywood acknowledging her with a deep salute as well.

"Mrs. Adams," introduced Ryland in a colorless voice. "Mr. Heywood, Mr. Apthorp."

She saw the glance that passed between them at her name.

"*Lieutenant* Apthorp, of the King's Own Volunteers . . ."

"If you'll excuse my saying so, m'am," replied Mr. Heywood politely, "the King can hardly do anything *but* send troops, you know. I mean, whatever is finally decided about colonists' rights and all that"—his gesture dismissed the question as if it were one of how many beads to pass along to the Indians—"Parliament isn't going to let itself be dictated to by a gang of hooligans dressed up as Mohawks. If you ask me, m'am, your husband and his friends did themselves a great disservice, resorting to violence that way. They're never going to get away with it."

"I'm not sure who you think my husband is," responded Abigail, "as there are a great many Adamses in Massachusetts—but if violence is not the answer, as you say, I don't

entirely see how sending armed men into the situation is
going to calm it. Surely——"

Young Mr. Oliver appeared in the doorway of the inner
study. "Mr. Heywood?"

Mr. Apthorp went in with his friend; the secretary raised
no objection. Nor, evidently, did the Governor, because the
door remained closed.

Ryland turned back to his chair but waited until Abigail
took the seat next to his before sitting down himself.

"And is Mr. Heywood a *lieutenant* also?"

A small sigh escaped his lips. "I had hoped——" he began,
and then was silent.

Abigail said nothing, and in time, Ryland went on, with
suppressed exasperation, "I shouldn't mind it, you know, if
either of them had the slightest experience of arms or
command—other than telling their grooms to saddle their
horses, that is. George served in the Virginia militia; for my
sins I volunteered, like the idiot boy I was, to join the King's
forces when Pontiac and his Indians attacked in the west of
Pennsylvania. I've *had* experience in war. And, His Excellency knows me. For six years I've worked in his library . . ."

He stopped himself again, and simply finished, "Well."

*And you still ask why men in this colony find fault with Crown
Governors who give positions of advantage only to those whose wealth
will help them or to friends of the King?* She didn't say it, but
Ryland, looking at her face, must have seen the words there,
for he sighed again, and said, *"Dura lex, sed lex . . ."*

"The law is harsh, but it is the law," repeated Abigail softly.

"And things as they are, are harsh," said Ryland. "But the
alternative—turning the country over to men who think the
answer to a legal problem is the destruction of other men's
property—is, I think, a solution worse than the problem."

He folded his hands and sat for a time looking at them. The Governor's butler came in with yet another petitioner and, as he passed Ryland's chair, nodded to the young man in a friendly way. She remembered someone saying yesterday— Weyountah?—that Mr. Ryland was one of the several young men whom Governor Hutchinson was sponsoring into Harvard, supporting not only the cost of their tuition and books, but in cases providing clothing and fuel in the cold New England winters as well. His faded green coat, with its old-fashioned, too-full skirts and threadbare cuffs, was of expensive wool and might well have belonged to the Governor himself ten or fifteen years ago. It was nothing a young man would buy for himself, even if he had the two or three pounds that such a garment would cost new.

At length he said, "I'm sorry, Mrs. Adams. There was something you wanted to ask of me, and I've let myself become distracted—"

"No, 'tis no matter." She put a hand briefly on his sleeve, and he raised his head a little, brown eyes meeting hers, then moving to the blue twilight beyond the windows. A servant came in with a taper and proceeded to light the candles in their holders all around the walls: beeswax and bayberry, not tallow, and all of them new. Abigail wondered what the Governor paid for lighting this great house, first and last, and if his half-burnt candles were passed along to his protégé?

"It is, though," he said. "And I see your very faithful and patient daughter is hoping that all of this will be over soon." He smiled at Nabby, which made Abigail smile in her turn.

"And so it will," said Abigail. "I wished only to ask you, Mr. Ryland . . . How difficult would it have been for someone to drug Diomede? To get into Mr. Fairfield's room, and to put laudanum into his rum? I think it must have been someone in the college, someone who knew the doors have no locks, who knew that Diomede was in the habit of sneaking his master's rum when Mr. Fairfield was out at night. Was Diomede generally in his master's rooms when his master was at lecture or in the library?"

Or meeting with "friends" behind the college barn—a practice which seems to have been common knowledge.

"Either there or close by," replied the young man. "Or Horace was there—doing George's work as well as his own, I fear." Disapproval deepened the lines at the corner of his mouth. "Two years ago—not long after the Volunteers were formed—Fairfield's rooms were vandalized: books torn up, clothing and bedding defiled. No one was ever punished for it."

Given Dr. Langdon's political views, this didn't surprise Abigail, but something inside her cringed. Though in principle she understood it when Sam said that the King and his minions would not pay attention to mere words, still she sensed that this kind of random violence did their cause no good, particularly with men such as Joseph Ryland.

"Surely students—" she began.

"It wouldn't have to be a student," said Ryland. "Laundresses, scullions, the cooks who work in the Hall . . . everyone knows everything in Cambridge. I daresay the Sons of Liberty know which staircase George lived on, and when he came and went." Bitterness tightened his voice like alum, and it occurred to Abigail to wonder what challenges and indignities this young man had encountered, both as a freshman and later, in a college population three-quarters or more given to the cause of the colonists. Every man in Harvard, practically, had been reading the broadsides John and Sam and Josiah Quincy had written denouncing his patron's venality and pigheadedness: who was it who had said that old Professor Seckar had abused him more for being Hutchinson's protégé than for his own—admittedly variant—views on a mere man's ability to alter by any human deed the abiding judgment of the Lord?

"Surely you don't think it was the Sons of Liberty who killed him?"

"Can you doubt it?"

"I've never heard that they sink to murder—"

"Have you ever seen a man who has been tarred and feathered, m'am?" The young man's voice dropped and his glance touched Nabby—engaged in a shy conversation about her schooling with a stout and fatherly merchant—then passed to his patron's shut office door. "Have you ever been there the next day, when his family and his doctor are trying to pull cold tar off his skin? Or the day after that, when the raw flesh suppurates? The mob covers their victim in feathers to make him look ridiculous, so that the onlookers don't fully realize what is being done in the name of this 'liberty' they're proclaiming . . . So those who hear about it think the object is to make a man look foolish, rather than to kill him in great agony and to terrorize the onlookers into acquiescence."

Abigail was silent, knowing what he said to be true. Then after a time she replied, "But the actions of the mob in no way alter the question of whether Englishmen here deserve the same rights that Englishmen deserve of Parliament and King."

"Perhaps they do not," replied Ryland. "Yet 'tis said, *He who sups with the Devil needs a long spoon.* However Mr. Sam Adams, and men like Josiah Quincy and Dr. Warren, may defend the question of their rights, they'll find themselves treated like savages if they employ savages to frighten those who oppose them. And, I think, rightly so, for there is no way of knowing when those savages may choose to take matters into their own hands."

Behind him, the study door opened and Messrs Heywood

and Apthorp emerged, joking and waving behind them to Governor Hutchinson. Mr. Oliver said, "Mr. Brattle——" and the stout merchant who had been talking with Nabby bade her a courteous farewell and went in. Abigail rose, tucked the collection of love-letters back into her satchel, and found a silver bit in her pocket to tip the footman who had taken charge of her lantern—congratulating herself on her fore-thought as to how long she might have to wait for an interview—and Ryland stood also, to shake her hand.

"Mrs. Adams, please forgive me if I've spoken too vehemently——"

"You have said nothing untrue," she responded. Certainly the men who'd gutted and looted the Governor's house nine years ago—destroying much of his precious collection of manuscripts—had acted far beyond Sam's intention. "And no fault lies in vehemence of sentiment. 'Tis our actions by which we are judged." She added, "Good luck, in the matter of the Volunteers."

He managed a wooden grin. "Thank you for your good wishes, m'am. I expect I shall continue as company sergeant—the position I held under Captain Fairfield—and I can do a great deal there in making sure that the Volunteers are fit to fight. Because you were quite right in your observation to Mr. Heywood: the infusion of armed men into a situation that has already turned violent will beget still more violence. And it is our duty, as subjects of the King, to keep matters from degenerating to such a pass that the French or the Spanish think themselves safe to come in and take over these colonies for themselves in the chaos that will follow."

The butler entered again and in the hallway handed Abigail her lantern, the candle lighted already and shedding a wan glow barely stronger than that of a couple of fireflies. Abigail was glad that the way home led through familiar streets and wasn't a long one. As the servant showed mother and daughter from the room, Abigail looked back over her shoulder to see Mr. Ryland patiently waiting, while Mr. Brattle emerged from the Governor's study and another wealthy merchant in a bottle green coat was shown in, in his stead.

Eight

W hat did you make of the books, Sam?" inquired Abigail, when Surry—the slave-woman who was the sole remnant, along with the ramshackle old house itself, of the modest fortune old Deacon Adams had passed along to his son Sam—showed her into Sam's book-room the following morning.

Sam Adams looked as if he might have protested that he would never have been so impertinent as to pry into volumes left in his charge by his cousin's wife, then grinned, held Abigail's chair for her, and went to the secret panel to get the books. Upon her arrival in Boston from Cambridge late on Wednesday afternoon, Abigail had taken the seven volumes straight to Sam's old yellow house on Purchase Street. Though John's clerk—Horace's and Abigail's cousin—Thaxter had been for some months now living under the Adams roof, Abigail still felt sufficiently uneasy about George Fairfield's murder to want to get the volumes out of her own hands as quickly as possible.

Ryland might say what he chose about the Sons of Liberty—and might indeed, she reflected uneasily, be right—but the coincidence of there being *two* sources of Arabic documents in the colony within the past two weeks was a trifle difficult to swallow.

Besides, Sam was the only person she knew positively had secret panels in his house. Cellar to attic, there was probably enough treasonable material cached here and there—books, pamphlets, correspondence with the Crown's opponents in other colonies, and the true names of a hundred authors of sedition—to blow the roof off the Houses of Parliament. She guessed the hidden compartment beside the mantel in his book-room was one of a dozen.

"Not a solitary thing." Sam set the books carefully on the desk between them: a folio edition, four quarto-sized volumes, and two octavos, their leather bindings cracked, age-dark, and bearing signs of having been gnawed by mice. "Three of the Arabic volumes bear the imprint of the Medici Press in Rome. I had no idea typefaces existed in Arabic—I assume for the benefit of Christians in the Turkish Empire. We would have to have Dr. Warren"—he named a mutual friend and fellow member of the Sons of Liberty—"pass judgment on the chemistry and astronomy texts, but they must be shockingly outdated."

He passed his big, square hand gently over the cover of the folio, and Abigail remembered that in his youth, Sam Adams had also been a student at Harvard and had acquired there—along with a taste for fiery politics and the Rights of Man—the fascination with books shared by so many questing minds.

"Where did you come by them?"

"My nephew Horace purchased the Arabic texts from a woman named Narcissa Seckar," began Abigail.

"Good lord, not old Malachi Seckar's wife? I can't imagine

the old boy letting his wife sell so much as the kitchen drip-
pings without his permission—"

"He didn't." Abigail gingerly opened one of the quartos,
studied the curious loops and squiggles that surrounded a
woodcut of a horse's backside, elaborately detailed. Presumably
not the legend of Alexander. "She sold these upon his death—I
understand, in order to get money to live on, her husband having bequeathed everything else he owned to the College."

"That sounds like the old—er—gentleman. Everything?"
Sam's square, friendly face clouded. "She should have sued.
John would have pried a living out of the College for her—"

"Indeed he would have. Just as well he knew nothing of it,
for we'd probably have had to send Johnny to Princeton
rather than Harvard as a result. In any case, these were hers—
or rather, her grandfather's—"

"Wasn't he a pirate or something?"

It was Abigail's turn to startle. "Not to my knowledge.
According to Governor Hutchinson—whom I called upon last
night for a perfectly legitimate reason," she added, as Sam's
frown returned in earnest at the name, "Barthelmy Whitehead
was a slave-trader and a merchant, but a pirate I hadn't heard.
Why," she inquired thoughtfully, "did you say pirate?"

"Oh, 'twas a great joke when I was at Harvard. That for all
Seckar's thunderings in chapel about how nine-tenths of us
were going straight to Hell, not for anything we'd done or
resisted, but because God in his infinite wisdom had positively determined that we should do so, before the beginning
of time for His Own Ineffable Purposes—and there was some
frightful argument about whether this decision was active or
passive and whether it had taken place before or after the Fall
of the Angels—for all his condemnation of *us*, the Reverend
Log-In-Thine-Own-Eye Seckar's wife was descended from a
pirate. We used to think it a huge jest to chalk a skull and

crossbones on the door of his study, just to hear him curse at the servants."

"And he probably went home and took his rage out on his wife. 'Tis odd," Abigail continued, "that you should speak of a pirate in connection with the books. Because there's a very strange story attached to them."

She hesitated, studying Sam's face—already lined, the gray eyes watchful but bearing no trace of sleeplessness, for all the waiting dread that had settled on the city. *If he was anything like John*, she reflected wearily, *he could probably sleep through the Lisbon earthquake . . .*

"Are you familiar," she asked slowly, "with a young gentleman named George Fairfield?"

"That young Tory jackanapes who's got up a troop of mounted militia?"

"The same."

Sam's eyes narrowed. "He was killed Tuesday night, wasn't he?"

"He was."

She saw his expression change as he realized the direction of her question.: "Oh, for God's sake, Nab—!"

"'Tis what they're saying."

"'Tis what *who's* saying? We're not the Assassins, Nab. I promise you, masked patriots don't lie in wait for every young imbecile who takes it into his head to get himself a King's Commission by raising a troop of horse that'll likely schism itself into insignificance the next time the father of one of them cheats the father of another over a land-deal. The countryside is full of them."

He made a movement to pick up the folio, then set it down, regarding her with troubled eyes. "What evidence do they have?"

"None that I know of. Yet the man they've arrested for the deed—the dead boy's servant—is to my mind as innocent as my son Johnny. And there is something most curious going on." And, a trifle hesitantly—one never knew what Sam was going to do with any piece of information one gave him—she related what Horace had told her about Mrs. Lake's disgraceful document, about the events of Tuesday night, and the sudden indisposition of four Harvard students on Wednesday morning. "Does it not seem to you that *not* having found what she sought—or all of what she sought—in the account of Captain Morgan's and Mistress Pitts's embezzlement of Crown funds, this Mrs. Lake or her scar-faced henchmen are now in quest of other volumes from the same source? I have written Narcissa Seckar—she lives in Medfield—asking for the favor of an interview, to ascertain that Mrs. Lake's Arabic document was indeed connected with the only other source of texts in that language that we know of in the colony: I hope to receive a reply tomorrow."

"And you think that this Mrs. Lake—or one of her henchmen—knew only that young Fairfield had gotten books from the same source, not knowing what they might be." Abigail could almost see the flash and flicker of thought passing through his eyes. "Who's Mrs. Lake?"

"I'd hoped you might know someone of that name."

He shook his head and opened the folio. "Geof. Whitehead," he read the large, rather crooked signature that sprawled, in faded ink, across the title page of *The Sceptical Chymist*. "Sixteen eighty-two. The name isn't familiar—Mrs. Lake's, I mean—and probably isn't her own—"

"I'd thought of that, yes."

"But I'll make enquiries. Embezzlement of the Crown treasury of Jamaica—"

"Horace is recopying what he can remember of the document," said Abigail. Having paged completely through the quarto on horse-doctoring, she opened its front cover and ran her hand over the rather mildewed marbled paper of its inner binding, but she found no evidence that anything had been hidden beneath it. Nor had anything been written on it or on any of the blank pages that made up the ends of the last signature. "His memory is excellent—"

"There are notes in the back of the Paracelsus," provided Sam, who had evidently gone over the volumes with some care. "In English, Latin, Spanish, and what I think is Algonquian, which the writer—I presume Geof. Whitehead, whoever he was—seems to use interchangeably. And that thin quarto with the red cover is all notes—mostly about chemical experiments, the position of stars as they progress through the ecliptic, where he goes to harvest witch hazel, and how long it takes cranberries to progress from first leaf to jam on his breakfast table. Nothing about pirate treasure . . ."

But there was a soft thoughtfulness in the way he said those last words, and when Abigail looked up sharply at him, she saw a distant glimmer in his eyes.

"Did you have a look about young Fairfield's rooms?"

"I did. And found naught but a great quantity of tailors' and bootmakers' bills—which I shall pass along to Mr. Fairfield, Senior, when he arrives next month—and love-notes from about a dozen young ladies." The drawer had also contained several drafts on Boston moneylenders, a huge quantity of gaming-vowels, three promissory notes that young Fairfield had signed—hair-raisingly, for other men's debts, including one for Joseph Ryland—and two letters from his father, decrying his spendthrift ways in terms that gave Abigail little hope for liberality or pity where Diomede was concerned. But these were not Sam's business.

Nor were the love-letters that had been in Fairfield's pocket when he'd died—nor the note in the same dainty hand begging for an assignation behind the barn.

"You didn't tell Hutchinson any of what you've told me, did you?" Sam asked at length. "The man's a serpent; he couldn't crawl straight if he wanted to . . . *and* he knows everything there is to know about who did what in this colony ninety years ago. He'll know who Geof Whitehead was, and if he was burying pirate treasure . . ."

"I didn't tell him that there were other books, no. I had to tell him of those in Mr. Fairfield's room. As the slave Diomede stands in peril of his life, I didn't think it proper to withhold evidence. I left him with the impression that they had not been included in the Harvard bequest because of their nature, which I understand to have been eyeball-scorchingly obscene."

"The man's a trustee of Harvard. Belike he's already got his hands on the rest."

"He said nothing of it . . ."

"Good Lord, woman, d'you think he'd mention it to you if he sees you poking about on the trail of the stolen books? The man's a snake, I tell you. There's every chance 'twas he who hired Mrs. Lake in the first place, *and* the man who put laudanum in young Mr. Fairfield's rum."

"Now, that's ridiculous!" said Abigail. "I know you and John hate the man like poison, but even his enemies allow him to be a man of justice—"

"God save us," retorted Sam, "from a good man with a bad idea—though I reserve my judgment about our dear Governor Hutchinson's goodness. He's a merchant and a pedant who convinced the King to appoint him, first to the chief justiceship of the colony, despite the fact that he has exactly as much legal training as the kitchen cat, then to the governorship—on the grounds of his loyalty to the idea that the colony exists solely for what money can be wrung out of it and handed to the King's friends. And he's kept there by his adherence to the principle that any means are legitimate to keep its people in bondage to the merchants of London who support the King. If he so much as suspects that money embezzled from the Jamaica treasury a hundred years ago is floating about in 'undeserving' hands——"

"I think you're confusing the man with Cesare Borgia," replied Abigail resolutely.

"And I think you're confusing him with Solon the Good, Lawgiver of Athens . . . who had a few weaknesses of his own that they've kept out of the history books. Will you show me this 'reconstructed' treasure-key, when your nephew finishes with it?"

"So far as I know it isn't the 'key' to any 'treasure' . . ."

"Someone seems to think it is."

"I know," retorted Abigail. "I'm looking at him."

"Don't mock me, Nab." Sam's voice fell suddenly quiet. "And don't play hide-and-seek. The matter is serious."

"Of course 'tis serious! A man's life——"

Sam brushed aside the issue of Diomede's guilt or innocence with a wave of one square, blunt-fingered hand. "We need that treasure. If it's there, we need to be the ones who find it. Not this Mrs. Lake or whoever is behind her. In a week, maybe in a day, there'll be British troops landing in Boston——"

"How can you know——?"

"For God's sake, Nab, what else can the King do? He's not going to content himself with some watered-down Royal Commission as everyone seems to expect. We destroyed his tea, he'll send troops, and the whole colony will rise in rebellion. Everyone who's been sitting on the fence dithering about which side they'll hop down onto, will see that there *is* no middle course anymore: the choice is between rebellion and slavery. No, I'm not going to make a speech at you, Nab, don't look that way," he added. "You've heard it all before."

He spread his hands out over the covers of the books and leaned toward her. He was bulky and powerful in his gray coat, and compelling, for all Abigail's distrust of his alliance with every man who liked his politics simple and violent; for all the whiff of boiling tar, burnt feathers, and charred flesh that seemed to her, for a moment, to cling about him, like sulfur on the sleeves of a man who's had supper with the Devil.

"We need money," he repeated. "Every farmer in New England possesses a gun, but when those farmers come into Boston to work on the wharves or in the grist-mills, they leave their guns at home. And every gun needs powder and ball, flints and cartridge-paper—things we're forbidden to manufacture here and must purchase . . . and the King tells us, we can only purchase them from England. We need guns for those who have not the money to buy them, but only the willingness to shed their blood for their rights to choose where and how they'll spend their money *and* their blood. Will you help us, Nab? Will you tell us what you find? This could be a Godsend, if and when it comes to shooting . . . which it will very soon. When do you go out to Medfield to find this Mrs. Seckar?"

"Monday, I hope," she replied unwillingly. "If I hear from her tomorrow. John should be back—"

"If he isn't, I'll send a man with you," promised Sam. "Did you speak to this slave Diomede about his master's books?"

"I tried," said Abigail. "On Wednesday he was still too stupefied yet from the laudanum—and were he not, I should think he would have been too shocked and grieved at the death of a master he loved . . . for all what that imbecile Langdon said!"

"If I sent a man with you tomorrow—someone respect-able," he added, as Abigail opened her mouth to make a comment on the waterfront ruffians who were usually most at liberty to run Sam's errands for him. "Would you go?"

"Thank you. And if I could prevail on you to carry a message for me there this afternoon, with some food for that unfortunate slave, I would most appreciate it." As long as Sam was eager to make himself her partner in the enterprise, reflected Abigail, she might as well take advantage of the facilities he offered, even if those consisted of assistance from every scoundrel, idler, and illegal importer of French contraband from here to Halifax. "And whatever else you may learn of Seckar and pirates and Geof Whitehead . . . I must be circumspect," she added, gathering her shawl about her shoulders again. "Else John will divorce me, I shall be forced to enter a convent, and there will be no treasure for anyone."

Sam bowed. "I should be much entertained," he said, "to see what havoc you would make of a convent, m'am. There'll be a man by at noon to take your message, and a wagon to get you to Cambridge first thing in the morning. But you watch out for Hutchinson," he added. "I understand you wanting his help in getting that poor slave out of danger . . . but the Governor is a powerful enemy. The more so because he seems so *nice*."

> *Cambridge*
> *Thursday evening*
>
> *28 April 1774*

Mrs. Adams,

Mr. Thaxter and I have spent this afternoon (following lecture and study) in making enquiries in and about Cambridge concerning either Mrs. Lake or the house in which Mr. Thaxter performed his translations. Though we have found no one of that name hereabouts, I believe that we have located the house. As it lies at several miles' distance from the town, we propose to investigate it on our half-holiday Saturday and will write you of our findings.

Moreover, young Mr. Pinkstone, who "fags" under the protection of Mr. Pugh, tells me that Messrs Pugh, Blossom, and Lowth were playing at cards Tuesday evening in Mr. Pugh's rooms, which face across from the staircase occupied by Mr. Thaxter, Mr. Fairfield, and myself, and that Mr. Pugh—clean against his custom—broke up the party at midnight and went out; this despite threats from Pugh that should Mr. Pinkstone reveal this fact he would have him killed and eaten by Pedro and Eusebius, Pugh's two African grooms.

Diomede is in good health, and Mr. Thaxter, Mr. Ryland, and I have endeavored to take food and clean linen to him at the gaol, and to see to his comfort and cheer.

Yrs respctfly,
Enoch Wylie

"Midnight," muttered Abigail to herself, turning Weyountah's note over in her fingers even as she shed her shawl and donned an apron. "A curious time to break up an evening of cards: I wonder if the Black Dog cheats? I see an interview with Mr. Pinkstone is in order—"

She glanced at the late-morning sunlight through the kitchen window, estimating the time before John would be home against the chores undone: Pattie's wooden clogs thudded on the floor overhead (doing the sweeping, by the sound of it) . . . Beds to be made, lamps to be cleaned and filled, and then the ironing of those wash-damaged linens mended yesterday . . .

At her feet, beside the heavy sideboard, Tommy played

contentedly with four walnut shells and two of Charley's toy soldiers and *where was Charley???*

His blocks were by the hearth, but her middle son was distinctly missing. Nor could his scurrying steps be heard upstairs, following Pattie from bedroom to bedroom impeding her work. Abigail's first thought—*The stable*—was succeeded by a more frightening one, *The street . . .*

Two steps took her to the back door, caught between her usual anxious spurt of panic about her increasingly adventuresome son making his way down the little alley to the street, and preparation for a stern talking-to if he was found digging around in the clean—but probably none too sanitary—straw in Their Majesties' stalls . . . And as she opened it, Charley swung into sight from behind it, clearly in disguise in the raggedy old coat that John wore to clean out the cowshed, and a knitted cap acquired from Heaven only knew where, into whose hem straw had been thrust to approximate a bandit's long, untidy hair.

"Stand and deliver, m'am!" the boy croaked throatily, brandishing a crooked stick. "For I'm a robber on the King's Highway."

"Gracious me!" Abigail flung up her hands in mock terror. "Have mercy . . ."

She broke off and took a closer look at the boy. "And just who are you supposed to be?"

"I'm Mr. Scar-Eye," replied Charley cheerfully. "I saw him, and I bet he's a robber and a villain."

He had made for himself, as a part of his disguise, out of wax and mud and Heaven only knew what, a V-shaped scar down his left eye and cheek . . .

Precisely as Horace had described.

Nine

And of course, the first thing John wanted to know of when he returned that night—just as Abigail was sweeping the coals from the lid of the Dutch oven, and Johnny and Nabby were setting the table for dinner—was about what everyone in town was saying about the King and whether the ship from London had been sighted?

This was understandable, Abigail knew, considering the possibility—remote but not unthinkable—that John himself might be included on a list of suspected persons as Sam's cousin . . . and as someone who had written any number of inflammatory letters and pamphlets concerning Governor Hutchinson. "The countryside is in arms already," he said, when Abigail had outlined what she knew on this subject, which was—as with everyone else in Boston—merely a collection of speculation and rumor. "From here to the Kennebec, every village and town has formed militia, elected officers . . . They've spoken of reestablishing the minutemen, as a first defense against an alarm, and are stockpiling powder and muskets in Concord and a dozen other places. What good that will do against trained troops—"

He shook his head, his round face grave. "What frightens me more, Portia—"

She smiled a little, at his use of the old nickname from their courting-days.

"—is that the Tories are arming as well. If war breaks out, 'twill be civil war, with every local squabble about land-boundaries and who-cheated-who-out-of-Grandpa's-inheritance dragged into it, to confuse and embitter the quarrel. Sam has threatened the King: *If you don't give us our rights, we'll open the gates of Hell in this country* . . . But I think Sam has deeply misjudged what will emerge from those gates."

He who would sup with the Devil . . .

Abigail was silent, sitting beside the spent dishes—dinner over, Nabby and Johnny quietly clearing off and (thank Heavens!) fending aside Charley and Tommy as they clamored for their parents' attention . . . "How much danger are you in?" she asked at last.

"Not much, I don't think. I'm Sam's cousin, not Sam." John finished his cider, handed the empty cup to his daughter, who—Abigail feared—was listening more than was probably good for the little girl's peace. "I've done what it's within the rights of every Englishman to do: spoken for our rights as Englishmen. I've broken no windows, boiled no tar, hamstrung no man's horse—"

"What if they don't care?" asked Abigail softly. "What if the Crown gives Hutchinson extraordinary powers to disregard the rights of habeus corpus, to suppress disorders here as and how he pleases, and sends him the troops to do it with? You've marked yourself his enemy—"

"If the Crown has given its Governor the power to punish a man's thoughts and words," returned John, "it will have made me its enemy indeed . . . and every man of the colony as well. Now leave over the clearing-up for a time, and tell me of your endeavors these two weeks, dearest friend." He gathered her onto his knee. "And tell me how it happens that you left our children with Uncle Isaac and Aunt Eliza for a night while you went gallivanting about the countryside—"

"Gallivanting, is it, sir?" Abigail raised her brows. "Take the log from thine own eye, Lysander, before you go looking for specks in mine . . ."

He pressed his knuckles to his breast and inclined his head in penitence, with an expression so humble that Abigail couldn't keep herself from pushing back his wig a little to kiss the smooth skin of his forehead.

Then she rose, and while she helped Pattie and the children clear up and do the dishes ("Sit down, John, you've a dispensation for today . . ."), she recounted the tale of Horace's adventure and its increasingly disquieting chain of sequels. She did not speak of Charley's encounter (*HAD it been an actual encounter?*) with Mr. Scar-Eye until she had returned to John's side, on the settle by the fire, and the children were occupied with their studies or their play, but when she did, she saw how his face flushed with anger.

"How would such a man have known of you? Of our house?"

She shook her head. "As Mr. Ryland said, in some ways Cambridge is very like a village. Word gets about very swiftly, from servants at the college overhearing the conversations of their masters belike: it doesn't seem very difficult for Weyountah to have learned from the unfortunate Mr. Pinkstone what he was sworn not to tell under threat of being eaten by cannibals."

"And anything you happened to speak of to Ryland," remarked John, leaning to the fire to tong up a coal for his long-stemmed Dutch pipe, "has now gone straight to His Excellency—if he didn't know it already."

Mrs. Lake's note he turned over in his fingers and held to the strengthening light of the kitchen hearth: "It's a man's hand, anyway, so we can assume Mrs. Lake is a cat's-paw—"

"Or had the wits to guess that her intended victim might wonder why a Boston lawyer's handwriting was so girlish?"

John made the gesture with his pipe, of a fencer acknowledging a hit. He'd taken off his wig, and without its neat frame of snuff brown waves his round face seemed more relaxed: the at-home John, the evening-John who seemed to her like lover and brother and best friend in one.

"Is the hand anything like Hutchinson's? Do you have a letter of his?"

"In his own hand and not a clerk's? I doubt it. As I recall it, Narcissa Seckar's father was Emmanuel Whitehead, who held the Vassall Chair of Theology before Seckar did. I never heard anything about a pirate in the family—"

"I should imagine 'twas the sort of thing they'd hush up. Particularly after Sam making a jest of it."

"Well, 'tis nothing you'd think of, looking at Old Whitehead. The man was dry and cold as the Original Snake in the Garden. You'd never have caught him giving his books to a college. He left everything he owned to Seckar, who was his student—house, property, the very dishes in the kitchen—rather than turn any of it over to a member of the sex that was responsible for human perdition, he said—"

"Wretch. I take it Mrs. Seckar was his only child."

"I think there was another daughter who ran off with a horse coper or something. 'Twas all a very long time ago. I believe his father was a merchant—"

"And a slave-dealer, His Excellency said. Myself, I had

rather have a good, honest pirate than the pack of hypocrites I've heard about—"

"That's only," said John quietly, "because you've never found yourself in the hands of one."

"And in any case," went on Abigail, "there must have been a genuine pirate somewhere in the family, because from what I gather of the two books that are missing, they're nothing that would have been purchased by a man who held the Vassall Chair of Theology . . . unless he was a thoroughgoing hypocrite indeed. I've found nothing out of the ordinary about the papers in Mr. Fairfield's desk and will return them there tomorrow for old Mr. Fairfield to deal with; the love-letters I shall burn. Weyountah writes me that they think they've found the farmhouse where Mrs. Lake lured Horace, so we shall see what the place can tell us—"

"Not much, I daresay. Ten to one you'll find 'tis the house of a Tory family that lives in town these days and rents out the land—and if Hutchinson's behind it, they'll not even have asked why he wanted to borrow the key to the place. And don't burn the love-letters just yet." He took from the settle beside them the packet of letters that had been in Fairfield's pocket, unfolded one of them in the flickering hearth-light. "French paper, expensive scent, a hand that shouts 'governess'—would there be any chance that these were sent by the Woodleigh girl?

"Montgomery Woodleigh's fortune is sufficient temptation, given the right circumstances, for a man to want to kill a rival, and given the nature of the missing books, they may in fact have nothing to do with the murder. Ask Diomede about whose hopes these letters"—he gestured with the scented packet—"might have crushed. And be careful, Nab."

He took her hand. Abigail was about to disavow any danger in dealing with possible minions of the scholarly gentleman to whom she'd spoken the evening before . . .

And then glanced across the hearth at Charley progressing through the alphabet at Pattie's side. She had, of course, scrubbed off the V-shaped "scar" that afternoon the moment the boy had come into the house, and Charley denied that Mr. Scar-Eye had spoken to him or even attempted to do so . . . and later, that he'd even existed.

And yet, for a moment, it seemed to her that she saw the mark on her son's face still.

When Abigail returned from her marketing on the following morning, she found Sam's promised minion waiting for her, a grim old codger in his sixties who was reassuring John—as Abigail came down the passway into the yard—that he would treat and treasure Mrs. Adams as if she were the Queen of England, and the more so because it stood to reason the bastard King wouldn't marry any but a whore . . .

And for the hour and a half that it took for old Mr. Creel's wagon and team to reach Cambridge, Abigail was obliged to listen to that gentleman's opinions as to what ought to be done to those who were conspiring with the King to enslave the men of Massachusetts—as well as to the New Hampshire sons of whores who were trying to cheat the colony of the best of its lands, the heretic bastards in Rhode Island who were siding with the Indians in a conspiracy to massacre women and children because they (the heretic bastards) were in the pay of the French, and all Pennsylvania merchants who were all born cowards and thieves. Abigail made several attempts at rebuttal to his more outrageous statements ("Them praying-Indians they talk about got no more prayer in 'em than cats: they worship the Devil 'cause they're Devils themselves . . ."), but the old man was almost stone-deaf and violently obstinate, and by the time they'd crossed the narrow neck of land that joined Boston to the mainland, she gave up and sat fuming. The man was, after all, giving her a ride in his wagon for seven rather weary miles, and she realized she had the choice of shouting her objections to him at the top of her lungs—objections to which he wouldn't listen even if he could hear them accurately—or walking.

Even attempts to turn the subject availed little: his neighbors were all Tory traitors also, apparently. And heretics. "Served 'em right that their horses was blinded and hamstrung by the Committee—that'll show 'em not to go speaking against Mr. Sam Adams and Mr. Hancock— We took an' strung up Cal Lechmere's dog, hung it right in front of his door with a sign on its neck, *This'll be You* . . ."

"And what did the dog ever do to harm you?" demanded Abigail. "Or the poor horses, either?"

Which was a mistake, resulting in a long catalog of the late dog's transgressions—which seemed to consist merely in doing its loyal duty to drive off intruders—and the observation that a) Tory beasts deserved what they got and b) women didn't understand these things and should keep their noses out of men's doings.

Abigail was frothing with wrath by the time she was set down outside the gates of Harvard College, and the first thing she did was to take from her pocket Sam's letter of introduction to one Lazarus Dowdall—of Perking Hill Farm—asking him to oblige Mrs. Adams by returning her to Boston that afternoon, and tear it up. The man was probably the local sheep-thief anyway.

A man in shirtsleeves pulling weeds around the single great tree in the court informed Abigail that Mr. Thaxter was carrying a note from Mr. Pugh to Mr. Beecham in town and would be back any time; Abigail watched through the window of the parlor of Massachusetts Hall where she was seated until she saw Horace come through the gate carrying a package. When she intercepted him, he greeted her with obvious relief—"I've been carrying notes back and forth between Pugh and Jasmine half the morning, just to be bloody-minded . . ." She walked with him up the end staircase of Harvard Hall, when he went to knock on Mr. Pugh's door.

The door was opened by a very young-looking fair-haired boy in a short freshman's gown, over whose shoulder Pugh's voice called out, "Oh, is that you, Thaxter? Did you get the coffee? Good lad! Now I've one more errand, if you would be so kind—"

"I beg you'll excuse my nephew," said Abigail, and the baby-faced freshman stepped quickly aside out of the door-way as Pugh set aside the enormous white Persian cat from his knee and rose from the chair beside the window: the study reeked of beer fumes and stale smoke, and Abigail had the impression, looking in, of rather old-fashioned furniture—opulent and tapestried—and not a book in sight. "I've come from town this morning to visit him."

"Madame, I abase myself in shame." Pugh made a surprisingly graceful leg for a man that corpulent, sweeping aside the skirts of the brocaded banyan he wore over his shirt-sleeves as if it had been a court-coat at the Palace of St. James. From the mantle of the fireplace a black cat blinked down, like Satan surveying the world beneath his feet; a long-furred gray tortoiseshell was washing itself in the windowsill. "Had I known our Horace was expecting company, I would never have taken him from his morning tasks. Don't just stand there, Pinky, put the coffee away—"

The freshman hastened to relieve Horace of his package.

"Will you have some tea, Mrs. Adams? No? My heart shall never recover. Yes, yes, Horace, it is well, run along—Pinky, dearest, I fancy you'd better take this note on to

Jasmine's room—" He scooped up the tortoiseshell cat as it moved to wind itself around Abigail's skirts.

"That's Mr. Pinkstone?" asked Abigail softly, as they descended to the courtyard again.

Horace nodded as he took Abigail's basket. "Is that gingerbread?" he asked, sniffing the air rather wistfully—since gingerbread was one of the many things that brought on his hives.

"I brought it for Weyountah," she explained, "and some honey for yourself—"

The gratitude and delight in his face were almost painful to see. Honey was one of the few treats that her nephew could consume with impunity.

"—and a little extra gingerbread, for purposes of corruption. I take it Mr. Blossom lives in Massachusetts Hall?" Though Horace would have turned right toward the main door of Harvard as they emerged from Pugh's staircase, Abigail set out briskly across the courtyard for the hall opposite.

"How did you know?"

"I assume Mr. Pugh would not have been sending you back and forth with notes to someone who didn't live in the building farthest from Harvard Hall . . . I think the walk will do us good, both to unload the honey, which is rather heavy, and to lie in wait for Mr. Pinkstone, who—threats of cannibalism aside—seems ripe to do his master a disservice. Upon which staircase does Mr. Blossom reside?"

After lying in wait for a very few minutes within the entry of the hall that led to the various staircases, Abigail and Horace were rewarded by the sight of young Mr. Pinkstone emerging from Harvard Hall and scurrying across the open court as if pursued. The clock on the chapel chimed noon as he came, and from the doors of the hall a great number of students began to pour forth, gowns bright against the Indian red of the brickwork and the green of the new grass.

Abigail rather feared that Mr. Pinkstone would turn back or engage himself in conversation with one of them, but in fact he quickened his steps—probably fearing to be intercepted by some student more senior to Mr. Pugh and sent on some yet more tiresome errand.

He checked his steps as he approached the door, but Horace called out, "I wanted quick word with you, Pinky, where the Black Dog couldn't see—and I'm sorry you got caught up in all his bloody-minded note-carrying. Here," he said, and took Abigail's basket from her. "My aunt brought Weyountah some gingerbread, but I think he doesn't need all of it."

The young man took what Horace handed him and began immediately to devour it, like a small dog who expects his bone to be seized by a larger dog. "That's decent of you," he said, and after the first bite, "Lord, that's good, m'am! Did you make it?"

"Catch me palming off someone else's gingerbread on my nephew's friends," said Abigail. And then, to Horace, as if they'd arranged the matter beforehand, "Ask him about the marzipan tea I'd sent you that was in poor Mr. Fairfield's rooms."

"What? Oh, yes." Horace looked momentarily startled, then nodded. "I've been thinking what you said about the Black Dog breaking up the card game early Tuesday night—You don't think he came across to poor George's room then, by any chance, do you? It's just that my aunt had sent me some marzipan tea, and I had it in the room with me when I was studying there—"

"'Twas in a Japan-ware caddy," corroborated Abigail, "that belongs to my grandmother. I'm afraid it sounds like a terrible thing to be concerned with, but she'll be very upset if it's lost. And while I wouldn't wish to accuse anyone of thievery, the tea is the sort of thing that someone might help themselves to, and you can't carry it off in your pockets, you know. And I only wonder—"

"Well, m'am, I wouldn't put it past Pugh." The boy rubbed his eyes tiredly. "I haven't seen anything like a tea caddy in his room— What color was it?"

Abigail described her Grandma Quincy's Japan-ware tea caddy, which was in fact safely on a shelf in Aunt Eliza's kitchen. "It just occurred to me when Horace mentioned the matter, that midnight is a tremendously early hour for a man like Mr. Pugh to be breaking up a promising game."

"He was winning, too," said Pinkstone. "Not that that's anything new—the fellow cheats like Iscariot. He'd heard Shallop from over in Hollis Hall had just got money in from his family, and was physicking him of it when he said, of a sudden, that he had a headache, and we were all to get out. I knew that was all stuff—Pugh wouldn't have a headache if you gave him a hundred pounds to do it and wouldn't stop a game if there was an ax sticking out of his skull . . . Myself, I thought he'd got a signal."

"A signal?"

"Through the window," said the boy. "He'd sat himself where he could see it, instead of where he usually sits in the corner by the fireplace. I thought later—when I was talking to Horace—that he might have been meeting a girl. He wouldn't have come across to speak to George anyway, because George's window was dark."

"Hmm," said Abigail. "Well, another theory gone west. Would George have been asleep at midnight, Horace? It sounds a trifle early for him."

"I don't think so," said Horace, and she saw the shadow of grief darken his eyes. "He—Weyountah and I stayed up until nearly ten thirty, at work on a—a *translation*—which I have yet to finish," he added, seeing that she understood that he meant his reconstruction of Mrs. Lake's naughty document.

"George hadn't come back from when he left me after we spoke to you at the Stair . . ."

"There was a light in his room earlier," provided Mr. Pinkstone. "But that would have been old Dio waiting up for him like a mother hen." He grinned sadly. "I say, that was all stuff about Dio murdering him, wasn't it? Old Dio wouldn't hurt a fly, and the way he quizzed George when he'd been out, and waited up for him when he was off with some girl or other, and tried to find fellows to do his work for him—that's a damned shame, what they're saying. But when Pugh broke up the card game, George's window was dark, because he looked out—Pugh did—and I was standing behind him, and him with one of those nasty cats sitting on his shoulder like a parrot. Besides," added the boy, "the Black Dog wouldn't have come across to speak to George anyway—they couldn't stand one another."

"Really?" said Abigail. "Whyever not? Mr. Pugh wasn't in favor of colonial rights, was he?"

"Not that I ever heard." The boy glanced up the stair, then back across the courtyard toward the window of the man of whom they spoke, as if Mr. Pugh might be standing in it, watching for his return. "No, the thing is, m'am, old George had cut him out with Sally Woodleigh, and had drawn his cork over it but two days before. So there'd be precious little that he'd have wanted to say to George at midnight or any other time."

"Did he, indeed?" murmured Abigail, as she and Horace made their way up Horace's own stairway to deposit the honey— and Weyountah's rather depleted stock of gingerbread—behind the books in Horace's room. "Did you know that?"

Horace shook his head. "I knew George and the Black Dog were at odds, but I thought . . . George never could stand a bully," he said. "I think even before Pugh started plaguing me, it raised George's dander. He was like that." He was silent a moment as they returned down the stair. Then, carefully controlling his voice, he added, "But I can't see even Pugh poisoning Dio in order to lie in wait for George . . ."

"No, of course not. Yet if George surprised him in the act of stealing from his rooms—an act that might end Pugh's career at Harvard and would certainly end any chance of his winning back the fair Mistress Woodleigh—it might be enough to make a man lose his head in anger or in fear. 'Tis only a theory," she added.

"One that takes no account of Mrs. Lake," pointed out the boy diffidently.

"On the contrary: the Black Dog might have been watching George's window, waiting for the candle to wink out, demonstrating that Diomede was well and truly asleep. 'Tis far more likely that he went across on account of Mrs. Lake's business than that of Mistress Woodleigh; what matters would be that he was in the room when George returned. 'Twill be something to bear in mind when we drive out to see this house that you and Weyountah have discovered."

Ten

Diomede bore out Horace's account of relations between George Fairfield and St-John Pugh, and to it added an eyewitness account of the combat that had taken place between them the preceding Saturday afternoon. "It was nothing much, m'am." The servant leaned forward on the bench in the sheriff's little watch room, his elbows on his knees. Abigail was pleased to see that Mrs. Squills had kept her word about seeing to it that Diomede had at least clean linen and food to eat in the jail. And the small brick jail in Cambridge—though it could never have been called comfortable—was at least habitable, unlike the "Hell on Earth," as it was described, of Boston's.

Through the window that opened onto Church Street, the sound of drums drifted from the Common, where the militia of Cambridge were beginning their drill. Mr. Congreve, slouched in a wooden chair (he had given Abigail his good one) by the door, moved his head now and then as if following the sound with his ears, though whether this was because he thought he should be among them bearing a musket or because he was waiting for the sound of a fight beginning, Abigail couldn't tell.

Diomede looked haggard, and—Abigail was distressed to see—older than he had only four days ago when he'd joked with her as they'd walked back to Cambridge in the twilight, leading the limping Sassy by the bridle.

"They'd always rubbed each other the wrong way, from the time Mr. Pugh was a junior ordering around Mr. George as a freshman—not that Mr. George would take any nonsense from him or any man, no matter what these college customs say. First day he was a sophomore, Mr. George thrashed Mr. Pugh, and him five years younger than Pugh and nowhere near his weight. Miss Woodleigh, I can't say she favored Pugh much over any of the others that courted her—if you'll excuse me saying so, m'am, she's a bit of a butterfly—"

"She's a damned little flirt," put in Congreve from the doorway, "and her father'll be the happiest man in the colony when she finally settles . . . and her new husband the most miserable."

"Well," said the slave carefully, "it's not my place to say, of course."

Not about a white girl, at any rate, reflected Abigail. "What happened?"

"What you'd expect, m'am. Mr. George and a dozen of the Volunteers rode over to Mr. Woodleigh's house on the Lexington Road after they were done with their drill; I think Mr. Woodleigh had invited them all for a bowl of punch. He—and Mrs. Woodleigh especially—had great hopes for Miss Woodleigh and Mr. George, and of course from the moment Miss Woodleigh saw George in his uniform, she'd had eyes for no one else. Myself," he added with a wry half smile, "I think the uniform might have had a great deal to do with it, for he did look mighty splendid. Mr. Pugh's nose was out of joint over it, as you'd expect."

"Everyone's was," put in Horace, glancing up from surreptitiously counting his own pulse. *"Varium et mutabile semper femina* . . . at least, she was variable and mutable to those wealthy enough for her to notice in the first place. She's above *our* touch, but every senior and bachelor-fellow who isn't a candidate for the ministry is courting her, and half the professors are as well."

"And the prettiest little thing under a bonnet in Suffolk County." Diomede smiled.

"The best-educated little thing under a bonnet in Suffolk County," added Weyountah thoughtfully. "Or at least the most comprehensively tutored. Entirely free of charge, I might add. They fall over one another to instruct her—Latin, history, theology, not that she'd know a sacrament from a syllogism. I taught her astronomy for about three months when it was first fashionable, but I made her father pay me, since there wasn't a hope he'd have let me court her if I'd wanted to. She burned off Ryland's eyebrows during a chemistry lesson, but he's still tutoring her, I think: he'll be lucky if she doesn't blow him to bits. She's clever, though . . ."

"She's clever enough to pick the handsome ones as tutors," grunted Congreve. "Makes the rest jealous. And who was it who said, there's no such thing as an ugly heiress?"

"Well, be all that as it may," continued Diomede, "Mr. Pugh was there when the Volunteers rode up. Of course Miss Woodleigh went into ecstasy over Mr. George. She always spoke of him as her affianced, but there was nothing formal to it, and to my mind he never favored her above the common run."

"I just don't think it ever crossed her mind that the man she adored wouldn't adore her in return," Horace opined. He coughed and cleared his throat and wiped his lips with one of the half-dozen clean white handkerchiefs he habitually carried in his pockets. "I know he didn't speak of her when they were apart—well, not more than any of the others."

"Which I expect is what fascinated Miss Woodleigh the most," remarked Abigail. "No wonder she pursued him."

"That I wouldn't know, m'am," said the servant. "But Saturday she leaped up from where she was sitting beside Pugh and cried out that she counted the days 'til she and Mr. George could be wed, and Mr. Pugh got pretty red in his face and said as how Miss Woodleigh would favor Pedro—that's one of his own grooms, m'am, a savage straight from Africa—if he was to dress up in a red coat, or a monkey for that matter, and added that to get Mr. George's notice she'd have to stand in line behind half the tavern-maids in the countryside. Mr. George flung himself straight off Sassy's back onto Mr. Pugh and threw him down the porch steps, then leaped down after him and beat him to the ground. Made him look no-how, and sent him off with a blooded nose and a lesson about bandying a woman's name in front of a troop of cavalry. He was like that," he added quietly, his voice altering. "No, she wasn't his affianced—and it rubbed him, I think, to hear her go on about it—but he wouldn't hear her slandered, not if she was a scullery-maid."

In the stillness that followed, a sharp-shouted command could be heard from the Common, followed by the ragged thunder of musket-fire. It was only the men drilling, Abigail knew, yet the sound made her shiver.

From here to the Kennebec, every village and town has formed militia . . .

Stockpiling powder and muskets in Concord . . . What good that will do against trained troops . . .

Civil war. The words filled her with dread, echoing the bloody chaos that had brought down the Republic of Rome.

She remembered Joseph Ryland's grave face as he watched men less competent than he step ahead of him to take George Fairfield's place in command.

It is our duty, as subjects of the King, to keep it from degenerating to such a pass that the French or the Spanish think themselves safe to come in and take over these colonies for themselves . . .

And young George Fairfield, riding here and there through Massachusetts, raising *a company of gentlemen loyal to the King . . .*

She forced her mind back to the man before her. *One thing at a time . . .*

"And nothing further came of it?"

"No, m'am. Mr. George was a little more careful after that about hiding—well, hiding things that might get him into trouble if it should come to Dr. Langdon's ears that he had them in his room—"

"Like his rum?" asked Abigail. And then, sinking her voice to a whisper—though Congreve's attention had been drawn to a confusion of angry shouting from the direction of the nearby tavern on Church Street—"Or his books?"

"You know about his books, m'am?" Diomede's voice lowered to match hers, and behind Abigail, Horace coughed again and fished for another clean handkerchief.

"I know he had them."

The servant sighed, and his face creased with vexation. "I told him— Well, they were mighty tempting books. But I did warn him, after he wouldn't sell them to Mr. Pugh, that Mr. Pugh would turn around and use them to get him into trouble—report him to Dr. Langdon and get him sent down. Dr. Langdon being a great Whig and always crying out for the colony's liberties. Everyone in the college knew he was just looking for a reason to get Mr. George turned out . . ."

"Mr. Pugh tried to buy those books?"

"Yes, m'am." Diomede looked apologetic. "Right after Mr. George bought them from poor Mrs. Seckar, almost three weeks ago now it was. Knowing Mr. Pugh and half thinking the offer might just be a way of learning if Mr. George had them, so he could report him to the provosts, Mr. George refused to admit he had them. But the day after this to-do at Mr. Woodleigh's, the Sunday evening, Pugh sent Eusebius, that other black African of his, to me with five pounds, m'am—five pounds!—for me to steal them and get them to him—"

"How did he know of them in the first place?"

The slave shook his head. "That I don't know, m'am."

Abigail was silent, thinking about the young man who'd come striding breezily out onto the landing, crying, *Good Lord, get that woman out of here!*

About the handsome young face lying so still on the pillow in the instant before Dr. Perry had twitched the sheet over it.

It seemed impossible that she'd known him for less than twelve hours.

"Does Mr. Pugh have any white hangers-on?" she asked quietly. "A dark-haired gentlewoman whose name may or may not be Mrs. Lake? Or a man with a scar like this"—she made a V of her fingers and pressed it to the left side of her face—"over his eye? Have you ever seen a man with a scar like this in Cambridge? Or in the countryside round about?"

Diomede turned the matter over in his mind. "No, m'am. I wish—" He looked aside, his features twisting with the effort to control them. "This is my fault, m'am, and I know it's my fault—"

"'Tis nothing of the kind," said Abigail firmly.

"If I hadn't been drunk—"

"Then whoever did this would have found some other way

of drugging you. The drug was meant for him as well as you, Diomede . . ."

"But they knew! They knew I have this weakness—"

"Pish-tush! There isn't a servant on Earth who doesn't drink his master's rum when his master isn't looking. 'Twas only chance that Mr. Fairfield woke when the intruder came in, and cried out—"

"No," whispered Diomede, and clasped his hands together, pressing the knuckles for a moment to his lips. "I swear to you, m'am, when I woke up—when I heard what had happened . . . It was my fault, the same as if I *had* got up and used that knife myself—"

"Stop it!" ordered Abigail. "What you're saying does no one any good and will only confuse the search for Mr. Fairfield's real killer." But her heart sank within her, for she guessed that was precisely what Charles Fairfield was going to say when he came north from Virginia to collect his son's body . . . and to avenge himself on those responsible for his son's death. "Can you write, Diomede?"

"Yes, m'am. Mr. Charles's father—*old* Mr. George—he didn't hold with servants being ignorant. I was made to do lessons alongside Mr. Charles and his sisters."

"Could you write out what you've told me? About the fight with Mr. Pugh and his attempts to bribe you, and about Mr. George's books that he bought from Mrs. Seckar? Write it in your own words, everything that you can remember. Mr. Congreve, do you have any objection to that? Weyountah, if you could see to it that Diomede has pen and paper—"

The Indian—who at Horace's nervous insistence had been listening to Horace's heartbeat—nodded, and Congreve said, "For all the good it's like to do you, m'am. I tell you, I've met these Virginia planters—"

"Which is exactly why every effort should be made to get the case heard here in Massachusetts— Yes, Horace, I'm sure you're *quite* all right; your coloring looks just as it should. With sworn statements in hand, I think my husband will have a better chance of at least getting a trial here—"

The slave closed his eyes for a moment, his face immobile; then he whispered, "Thank you, m'am," in the voice of one who knows perfectly well that miracles do not happen. "I'll do as you ask and have it for you if you should come here again. But if you would, m'am—could I trouble you, if I were also to write out a letter to my wife and to our daughters back in Virginia? Would you see that it's sent to them?"

"Of course." Then another thought occurred to her, and she dug in her pocket for the elegant love-letters. Lowering her voice to exclude the sheriff—who might not approve of a young lady's letters being viewed by a slave—she asked, "Does this handwriting look familiar to you, Diomede?"

He responded immediately, "Yes, m'am." And—taking the letters, with his own swift glance toward Congreve, who seemed to be preoccupied with the shouting from the Common—he whispered, "It's Miss Woodleigh's, m'am."

"Let me see those—" Horace held up his hand to stay her from tucking them away, as he, Abigail, and Weyountah stepped into the sunlight of Church Street.

"Is he right?" Abigail glanced up at Weyountah, who was looking around Horace's shoulder. "You tutored her—"

"That's her hand, yes."

"Yes, but this—" Horace held up the note. *As you love me, be behind the barn at midnight . . .* "This isn't her paper. It isn't the same as the letters, look—"

Which was quite true. The note was stiffer and thicker, and of a warmer hue than the thin, slightly crinkly sheets on which Sally Woodleigh had poured out effusions of love.

From the pocket of his hand-me-down coat, Horace took an identical sheet—folded in the same fashion as the note, in quarters, rather than the longer letters, which had been folded rather elaborately and sealed.

Startled, Abigail asked, "How did you come—?"

"This one's not from Miss Woodleigh." Horace unfolded it. "It's the one St-John Pugh gave me to deliver this morning to his bootmaker. You can see the paper—and the ink, too, look"—he held both notes to the sunlight—"are exactly the same."

"Pugh," said Weyountah. They came onto the Common again, headed for Brattle Street and the College. "Pugh sent him a note in Sally's hand . . ."

"To get him out of his room at midnight." Behind his thick spectacles, Horace's gray eyes seemed to glow with somber eagerness, his fancied ailment forgotten. "Pinkstone said he was watching for something . . ."

Before them, men formed up uneven lines, officers—that is, the men they'd elected as their own officers—dashing back and forth among the would-be soldiers like distracted sheepdogs, shouting commands to load and fire. Light powder, Abigail calculated, and no bullets: Sam had not been exaggerating when he'd said how short the militia was of such supplies. Most lead had to be imported—illegally—from France.

"But if he'd got George out of his rooms. . . ." said Weyountah doubtfully.

The Indian's face was still soot-smudged. Abigail and Horace had found him that morning in one of the laboratory rooms in Harvard Hall, trying to focus beams of sunlight with mirrors through a choking cloud of sulfurous smoke ("This is nothing, m'am—last fall Ryland nearly suffocated everyone in the Hall with some phosphorous compound he was working on . . ."). Horace had been coughing and check-ing his pulse ever since.

"He must have returned sooner than expected."

"Yes, but he was on his way to meet someone just at dusk when he parted from me. Would he have met—I mean . . ." Horace blushed again at the thought that his hero would have dallied with one girl from eight 'til midnight to pass the time before a second tryst.

"Diomede said he'd no deep fondness for Miss Wood-leigh," recalled Abigail thoughtfully. "Contrary to what Miss Woodleigh was obviously telling Mr. Pugh. Obviously, the Black Dog thought that a lover so gallant as George would wait at least an hour for his lady fair before coming back to his room. George must have returned and caught him."

"How do we prove this?" Weyountah's voice was grim. "'Tis all very well to guess at what the man did, but I doubt a Virginia jury will free a slave accused of killing his master on the strength of two sheets of paper. Particularly not to convict a white man in his place."

"Even searching his rooms might not help us," said Abi-gail, "without other proofs in hand. Though we shall cer-tainly have to try it. They are—as everyone keeps pointing out—volumes that any young man might easily wish to steal without also murdering their rightful owner; though by Hor-ace's own testimony, they were in his desk that morning. Where is George, by the way?" she added in a quieter voice. "I mean, where has his body been bestowed to await his father's arrival?"

"In the holding crypt behind Christ Church." Weyoun-tah's lips settled for a moment into a hard line of grief. "Would you like to go there?"

"When we return," she said. "If there's time."

"Sally Woodleigh has been there three times to leave

flowers," Weyountah went on drily. "In full mourning—and always with some solicitous gentleman offering her his shoulder upon which to weep. That night I heard George cry out." He had said this to her before, but it was as if he were driven to repeat the words, to understand what they meant and what they could not mean. "I thought it was only him angry at Dio for getting drunk—"

"Do you know what time that was?"

The Indian shook his head. After a moment he went on, "I heard nothing further."

I went back to sleep . . . I let my friend die . . .

"And George would not have thanked you," Abigail pointed out gently, "had you gone charging across the staircase while he was dressing down Diomede for stealing his liquor."

"No, m'am." The Indian's voice was nearly inaudible.

They had reached the quadrangle between Harvard Hall, Massachusetts, and Stoughton College. Most of the students— and a certain proportion of the younger masters—being on the Common, comparing cartridge-boxes and arguing about the merits of French over English powder, the only scholarly gown visible was Mr. Pugh, strolling in the direction of Harvard Hall with one of his "cut-faced savages" at his heels. This man—small, wiry, and black as ink—appeared so barbaric, with his head shaved, his face crisscrossed with tribal scars, and plugs of sharpened bone thrust through the septum of his nose and the lobes of his ears, that Abigail suspected his master of playing up his African customs to impress and intimidate others.

"I'll hitch up Sassy," said Weyountah. "Dr. Langdon lets me take her out. If you're to be back in Boston by sunset, we'd best start now to show you Mrs. Lake's farmhouse—"

"Then we shall linger only long enough to return Mr. Fairfield's bills to his own room." Abigail patted her satchel.

"Provided my going up there won't get you boys thrown out of the College."

"What, for an *aunt*?" Horace looked grateful—Abigail suspected that if she'd gone into the parlor and left her nephew to carry the bundle of papers up alone, he ran the risk of being sent to the other side of town on some foolish errand by Mr. Pugh.

Pugh himself bowed as they passed him. "Not going out to march with the traitors, Mr. Wylie?"

The Indian returned the bow. "No, I thought I should stay in today with the cowards."

Smiling to herself, Abigail followed Horace into Massachusetts Hall and up the middle staircase. "You said Dr. Langdon was taking charge of George's things," she said as they climbed. "Is the room kept closed up, or can anyone come and go?"

"Anyone can," said Horace. "It's just that—" His voice tailed off as they reached the landing and saw that the door to Fairfield's room indeed stood open. Horace's lips pursed and behind the heavy spectacle-lenses, his gray eyes hardened. *Of course*, thought Abigail, *the one day the building is certain to be empty—*

The boy strode ahead of her into the empty study, Abigail at his heels, and through it to the bedchamber beyond. "Who's in here?" he called out, in a hard voice completely unlike his usual mild tones. "And what are you— Oh!"

He stopped in the doorway, blocking Abigail's view.

Beyond him, a young woman's voice demanded, "And who are *you*, frog-eyes? I have every right to be here, I guess—"

Abigail looked around her tall nephew's shoulder and saw, standing beside the desk, a girl of seventeen or so—"well-set-up," John would have described her lush figure—in a short petticoat and coarse skirt of striped linen, tucked up to show off slim brown ankles, and a brown linen jacket, much patched. Wisps of black hair, straight and heavy as an Indian's, floated free from her cap, and so sun-browned was her face that were it not for the morning glory blue of her eyes, she might have been mistaken for one of Weyountah's relatives.

She nodded toward the bed, stripped of bedding and mattress. "Has his Pa come for him, then?"

"Not yet," Horace stammered.

"Then where is he?"

"Christ's Church."

Her eyes narrowed beneath butterfly-wing brows: "Doing what? They're not making him marry that Woodleigh cow, are they? Because if she—"

Abigail said quietly, "You have not heard, mistress? George Fairfield was killed Tuesday night." The girl pressed her hand quickly to her lips, and though her expression didn't change, she went sheet white under her tan. It was as if she'd been struck but would not acknowledge the pain of the blow. Then she whispered, in a small despairing voice, "Oh, George."

"And you are—?"

The girl said softly, "I'm his wife."

Eleven

George said he'd keep the license." Katy Pegg—as she had said her name was—sat on the edge of the naked bedframe, brown hands folded in her lap. "There's no place at home I could put it that it'd be safe from my step-pa. We married in December, before George left for Virginia."

Abigail glanced at the desk beside the window. It had not been opened. Among all the tailors' bills, all the gambling-markers, all the love-letters she'd taken out Wednesday morning, there had been no marriage license.

"We rode down to Providence together. I don't know what he told Diomede—the man his Pa wished on him, to keep him from meddling with girls, George said. Tuesday night—" Tears flooded her eyes, and she almost slapped them away with impatient fingers. "I was with him—"

"He was killed by an intruder," said Abigail gently, "late on Tuesday night after he came back here to his rooms. A thief."

The girl closed her eyes, her face like a defiant child's, who'll take a whipping rather than ask a parent to stop.

"What time did you part?"

"Midnight. He said he was meeting friends, and the—the men I'd rid out here with would be leaving soon. My step-pa would skin me if he knew—"

She took a deep breath, some of the terrible tension going out of her slim shoulders, her oval face. "My step-pa hated him. He said he was a damned Tory and would break my heart for me, *and* leave me caught with a baby . . . which is what *he* was after himself, the—"

She stopped herself, looked down at her square, boyish hands, folded tight in her lap. "George said he'd come for me on Wednesday night. That's the night Mr. Deems—my step-pa—goes out with the Watertown militia. I wrote Thursday . . ." She raised her hands quickly to press against her lips again, then lowered them almost at once. "So I got a lift this morning from one of the farmers that was coming in for the militia. I knew George's Pa wouldn't stand for it, for George and me, I mean. But he said—George said—that marrying me made it all right, and they couldn't stop us if we were wed."

Abigail rolled her eyes heavenward. Carmody—the worst of her brother's ne'er-do-well friends—had boasted to William once when he didn't realize Abigail was in earshot of having "wedded" a girl who couldn't be persuaded and was too cagy to let herself get into a situation where she could be raped with impunity ("Well, they always cry rape afterwards," Carmody had shrugged . . .)

And the young scoundrel with Sally Woodleigh's love-letters in his pocket—! She felt sick with disappointment, as if she herself had been betrayed.

"What happened?"

"Mrs. Adams—" Weyountah's light tread sounded in the study. "If we don't leave now . . ."

He halted in the doorway, startled to see Abigail not alone.

"Mr. Wylie," Abigail introduced, "Mistress Pegg. Or, as she claims is the truth, so far as she knows it, Mrs. Fairfield."

Weyountah's jaw dropped for less than a second. He shut his mouth and bowed. "I'm very sorry, m'am," he said. "Mrs. Adams must have——"

"She did." Katy stood, her shoulders straight. "And as for, *so far as I know it* . . . It is the truth. We brought proofs of my age and that my parents were dead, and the county clerk in Providence made us out a license and a certificate, and married us——"

"In the courthouse?" asked Weyountah.

Katy shook her head. "In the back room of a tavern about a mile outside of the town. George's father has many friends in Providence, merchants who do business with him. George made this arrangement, so that we wouldn't . . ." She broke off, looking from Abigail's face to those of the two students, and her own cheeks reddened. Her chin came up. "And no, it wasn't as it looks—as I can see you're thinking. The man was genuinely the county clerk, and George gave him ten shillings to put it in his book at the courthouse that we'd been married there, though there's nothing in the laws of Providence nor of Massachusetts, either, that says a marriage isn't valid if it's not performed in some certain magical place."

"But it is the reason, m'am," said the Indian gently, "that they want witnesses and the presence of the families, to make sure the girl isn't being lied to——"

"Oh, and wouldn't my step-pa just *love* to see his girl married to a Tory? George didn't lie to me. He said he'd keep the license——"

"It wasn't in his desk."

"Look in his books," said Katy, in a small, steady voice. "He was always putting things he wanted to keep in the backs of his books . . ."

"That's true," said Horace. Abigail's heart went out to him, at the expression of wretchedness on his face, that his hero would have played so despicable a trick on a girl.

"But I did see it when 'twas signed, m'am," said Katy. "And the clerk did sign it after he'd read the service over us. And he truly was the county clerk."

"Be that as it may," said Weyountah firmly. "The chaise is at the door, m'am, and further delay will prevent Mrs. Adams from getting back to Boston, either by the ferry or through the town gates. Moreover, Mrs. Adams is Horace's aunt, and you—Mrs. Fairfield—are nothing of the kind, and we could all of us be in serious trouble if some mean-spirited bachelor-fellow were to happen along and report the lot of us to Dr. Langdon."

"Like that wretch Ryland? He'd do it—Mrs. *Adams*?" The name finally seemed to register, and her blue eyes stretched wide. "Not . . . Not *Samuel* Adams?"

"I am Mrs. *John* Adams," said Abigail. "Are you staying in Cambridge, Mrs. Fairfield? Or can we leave you somewhere?"

"Looks like I've been left somewhere as it is." Katy turned and picked up the small bundle she had left, almost out of sight by the end of the bed. "John Adams—that wouldn't be he who writes as Novanglus, would it? And those other letters he's done . . . You'll be Weyountah, won't you?" she added, turning back toward the Indian. "You'd never get the four of us into that little chaise of George's."

"It's why I borrowed Millard's old post chaise and Benton's horse. If Horace has no objection to riding on the back—"

"And if Horace does?" protested Horace.

"Then *I'll* ride on the back," said Katy, with a sudden flicker of a grin. "I've always wanted to, seeing the gentlemen coming into the tavern yard—" She followed Abigail down the stair, halting obediently at Weyountah's signal so that the Indian could step out first and make sure that the corridor was clear. They hastened to the door, where the dwarfish Mr. Beaverbrook was holding the heads of Sassy and the tallest, boniest black gelding Abigail had ever seen. As Abigail handed Mr. Beaverbrook a quarter of a silver doubloon and touched her finger to her lips for silence, Horace climbed rather gingerly onto the footman's stand on the back of the little vehicle. "I suffer from vertigo," he warned. "And sometimes even scotodinia . . ."

"Where do you go?" Abigail asked Katy, as Weyountah helped them into the four-wheeled post chaise and then went to mount Sassy, the harness permitting a rider.

"Home, it looks like." Abigail heard in the girl's voice the effort to keep it steady. "Mr. Deems is the head hostler at the Yellow Cow, if you know where that is?" She leaned from the door of the chaise to address this last to Weyountah, who was preparing to put the whole equipage into motion. "Where the road forks to go to Watertown—"

"Never tell me you walked!" protested the scholar. "That's almost to Concord!"

"Lord, you think I couldn't get a ride?" retorted the girl, with a quick flash of a grin. But as she settled back into the worn leather of the seat and Weyountah touched his heels to Sassy's sides, Katy admitted wanly, "But to be honest, I'm just as glad to have the ride, if go back I must. I'd hoped . . ."

She broke off her words and sat for a time, looking out at the handsome houses as they passed along Brattle Street and out toward the countryside beyond the town. The drumming of the militia faded behind them, the ragged crackling of rifle-fire like very distant lightning. Katy began to say, "George—" She stopped herself. Whatever George was or could have been, it was over now.

"What about Diomede?" she asked after a time, returning

her attention to Abigail. "I only ever saw him at a distance, but George told me about him, and I feel like I know him— just as I feel like I know Weyountah and . . . It is Horace, isn't it? Was Dio drunk when this thief came in? I know he drank," she added. "But according to George—I'm sorry, I can't seem to stop bringing up his name, like a grandmother . . . George said Diomede seldom got so fogbound he couldn't pull himself together and wake up at need. Diomede's a terrible mother hen, George said. Well, he had to be; it was his job, like those old Roman he-nannies they used to have—"

"Pedagogues," said Abigail, smiling.

"Yes . . . and about time the men found out what it was like, having to chase around after a child all day long. Not that they aren't sweet," she added, with a secret smile of her own and a small movement, to lay her hand on her belly, that made Abigail moan inwardly—*And the young blackguard made her pregnant as well!* "I know all this is bad for me, but the poor man must be devastated! To look after someone all those years . . . Is Diomede all right?"

"I fear not," Abigail said. "Diomede is being accused of the murder."

The girl's eyes flared with horror, and when Abigail sketched the circumstances—saying nothing of what was stolen, only that the rum had been drugged—Katy cried again, "Oh, *NO!* How *awful*—"

"Is there anyone you know of," Abigail asked curiously, "who might hate George enough to harm him?"

"Bruck Travers," replied the girl at once. "He's captain of the Watertown militia. He's also on the Committee of Correspondence. Mr. Deems—my step-pa—says Bruck is the greatest patriot in the county, and so he is. Twice he had the boys out to ambush George and Diomede when they were coming back from drilling with the Volunteers."

The heartfelt approval in her voice made Abigail raise her brows. "I thought you were a Tory?"

"What on earth gave you that idea?" Katy looked genuinely surprised. "I listened very carefully to the clerk when he read the marriage service, and I didn't hear a single thing about a woman having to cleave to her husband's politics if her husband's idiot enough to believe the Governor's Tory lies. George can take care of himself and whip a dozen of Bruck Travers. That is—"

Her voice stammered a little, and she looked aside again, fixing her attention on the open cornfields that lay beyond the tree-shaded road, the grazing cattle and the black circling shapes of crows. After a moment she went on, "Just because George let a bunch of lying Tory merchants talk him into believing a King who wants to put us all in chains, doesn't mean I don't . . . I didn't . . ."

She took a few breaths, her body swaying a little with the motion of the chaise. "If your husband were a raving Tory, m'am, would you cease to love him?"

"No," said Abigail, smiling. "No, I suppose not."

About ten miles along the Concord Road, Weyountah reined the team up a side-trace that ran through a woodlot, across a very rickety bridge, and past what looked like, in previous years, had been corn fields, now given over to pasturage of a herd of black-and-white cows. Twisting in her seat to lean out the window and holding perilously to her sunbonnet, Katy said, "It's the Chamberville place, isn't it?"

"Is it?"

"Of course." She returned to a normal posture and looked at Abigail as if surprised she hadn't heard the whole tale. "Lemuel Chamberville was the magistrate at Waterford when the King tried to force the Stamp Act down our throats, and Boam Travers—Bruck's father—and his boys hamstrung Chamberville's cattle and horses, and burned his barn, and half killed his coachman, and eventually Chamberville went to live in Boston and rents out his land to the Harters, who're Tories, too, but have about five sons and hold the debts on nearly everyone in the township. The house has been empty for years."

And through the window, Abigail heard Horace cry excitedly, "That's the house! I know it!"

Score one for John.

Weyountah tied up the horses as Horace—pale with mal de mer—sprang down from his tall perch and ran across the drive (which could have stood a few wagonloads of gravel, in Abigail's opinion) to the shuttered windows. "These were open," he said at once. "When we drove up, there were lamps burning inside."

"They show no sign of having been forced," remarked Abigail, bracing her feet on the foundation bricks and raising herself up a little to examine the wood. "Either that, or whoever did it was very skilled—I myself have no practical experience in the forcing-open of window-shutters." She led the way to the front door, and knelt on the single shallow step to examine the wood around the doorknob. "No fresh scratches here—"

"And we're far enough back from the road that there's no reason they'd have chosen the back door over the front," added Weyountah. But they went round to the back in any case, checking every shutter en route, and found the kitchen door likewise innocent of fresh evidence of a break-in. The stable was also closed up, but horses had certainly stood in the yard, and the droppings left there looked no more than a week old—

"And look here," called out Katy, emerging from around

the corner of the stable with her short skirts tucked up even shorter under her belt. "Someone's eaten an apple and smoked a couple of pipes of tobacco here by the corner—"

"That would be *Oculus Cicatricosus.*" Horace turned back to look at the house. "I don't think the parlor I was in over-looked the stable-yard . . ."

"No, but Mrs. Lake left you, as you recall, to fetch you poisoned bread and coffee," pointed out Abigail. "And this corner lies in clear sight of the kitchen door."

"Were you here?" Katy hunkered like a child to prod at the nasty little wads of tobacco with a twig, where they lay all but hidden in the unscythed grass. "Did someone try to break into the house?"

"We think Horace—Mr. Thaxter—was lured to this house," explained Abigail, "by people who almost certainly were not the Chambervilles . . . On the other hand," she added thoughtfully, "they might well have been."

"Chamberville is a Tory of the deepest dye." Katy straightened up and tucked back into her cap—under the shading brim of her straw sunbonnet—the long wisps of Indian-black hair that seemed to have a tendency to stray everywhere. "A close friend of the Governor's and ripe to turn his hand to any villainy in the King's name. What happened?" She looked sharply from Abigail to Horace, then back toward the house . . . which certainly could have been easily opened, Abigail reflected, by someone who had simply been able to get the key from its owner, as John had said.

"And is there anyone that you know of," she asked, "whose face is scarred in a *V* over his left eye—" She demonstrated again the mark that Charley had so carefully duplicated in mud on his own pink countenance.

"Blue eyes," said Horace eagerly. "Very light blue, under

black brows—the one brow whitened where the scar goes through."

Katy frowned thoughtfully and shook her head. She trailed Abigail and the two young men as they circled the stable, all four studying the ground without any clear idea of what they sought or might find. "He doesn't sound like the sort of person Mr. Chamberville would employ," she guessed, which, Abigail reflected, was probably true.

"I daresay not. And I daresay he and his spiritual brethren could be hired for a penny a day on the wharves, by whoever knows Chamberville well enough to beg his key off him for a night, with the throat-cutting thrown in gratis."

"Were they going to cut your throat?" The girl regarded Horace's tall, bespectacled form with renewed interest.

"I don't know," said Horace uncomfortably. "It seemed so to me last Friday night, stopped in the darkness of the woods with these people . . . Now, I'm not so sure."

"You must be sure," pointed out the girl. "'Tis when you have doubts and hesitate that you become their victim—whether highway robbers or the Governor's men spreading lies to keep the people from acting for their rights. Only in certainty lies the attack, and only in the attack lies salvation and freedom."

"*Some craven scruple,*" quoted Weyountah, shaking his head, "*of thinking too precisely on the event.*"

Horace replied, from the same play, "*But I am pigeon-livered, and lack gall.*"

"Well, you can't be all *that* pigeon-livered," reasoned Katy, "if the Tories want to kill you—"

"We cannot be sure they were Tories," said Abigail. "For the simple reason that it appears—at least at the moment—that they were also the ones who killed Mr. Fairfield."

The girl stopped still, thinking about that. Abigail saw

the tears rise to Katy's eyes, only to be pushed aside with a shake of her head. "Who are they, then?" she whispered.

"That's what we're trying to learn. Did you leave your stepfather a note?" she added, as they approached the chaise again. "When you set out to find George this morning?"

The girl nodded, her eyes bleak. "I told him . . . well." She gestured helplessly, letting the thought go. "I've wanted to leave him," she went on. "And I'll not say it wasn't in my mind, when George proposed marriage to me, that even if he later cast me off—which, mind you, I wouldn't put it past that pa of his making him do, in the end . . . But George wasn't the man to behave scaly to a girl. I know he wasn't. And I know it shocks you to hear it, m'am, and I really did marry him before a clerk of the county . . . Anything was better than staying with Mr. Deems."

She looked aside, and color crept up again to her cheeks.

"Did you tell him you weren't coming back?"

A slight move of the head that might have been a nod.

"Will he come after you?"

"He might. Because of Bruck," she added. "He had it all fixed up with Bruck that Bruck was going to marry me and take Mr. Deems in to work for him at his livery, because Mr. Deems never did like Mrs. Cousins who owns the Yellow Cow—Mrs. Cousins is my aunt."

Abigail nodded. Life was such that many people of her acquaintance ended up raising other peoples' children simply because they were thrown onto the world suddenly parentless. She knew, too, that stepsons and stepdaughters were often looked upon as a kind of bounty from Heaven, a cheap source of labor that didn't have to be paid or—frequently— fed with any regularity.

"That is, her first husband and my mother were brother

and sister, but she's never had much use for me, nor for Mr. Deems, not that I can blame her for that."

"Can you cook?" asked Abigail as they reached the chaise, wondering if she'd regret this. "And clean? And mend?"

Katy was nodding, her eyes suddenly huge with hope. She seized Abigail's arm. "M'am, I swear—"

Abigail held up her hand. "Can you take orders?" she went on. "'Twould be from a girl younger than yourself . . ." She was aware that not only Katy, but Horace and Weyountah were looking at her like overboard mariners gazing at a drifting plank. *John is going to kill me—*

"It cannot be permanent," she added firmly. "Yet I daresay you can remain in my house until we find another place for you—"

"Oh, m'am—" began Katy, and then—wholly to Abigail's surprise—the girl burst into tears.

When Abigail, startled, said, "Here—" and moved to take her hand, the girl pulled away, shook her head, made a gesture of denial.

"I'll be all right, m'am. It's just—I really didn't want to go back . . . But I can't—"

"You can." Abigail possessed herself of Katy's hand. "And the rest we can talk about in private. Now get in the chaise," she added, "because that's three o'clock I hear striking—is that the Concord church?—and if I find myself stranded in Cambridge once again Mr. Adams really *will* kill me."

Their speedy departure notwithstanding, Weyountah thought it better to take the land route back to Boston, swinging south through Cambridge at a smart clip and down through the sunny fields and scattered woodlands to

Brookline, and so across the salt marsh, shallows, and mud-flats in the lengthening spring sunset, then over the Neck to the town gate. "If we tried for the ferry and missed," reasoned Abigail, when Katy pointed out that from Cambridge the way was slightly shorter to the ferry, "then we'd have twice the distance to reach the Neck overland and might find the gate shut against us. This way, though 'tis a trifle longer, we'll be certain of getting home."

Katy looked askance at the red-coated guards, as Wey-ountah drew rein before the three brick archways and Horace sprang down to open the chaise door, and at the sight of them Abigail felt herself shiver again: *Has anything happened while I was away—?*

And yet when they'd passed through Brookline, though militia had been drilling on the Common there, there had been no uproar. In Roxbury, at the land end of the Boston Neck, the local volunteers had been clustered companionably around the door of the Sun.

All is well. I'll return to find the house as it always has been, the boys well—

She pushed from her thoughts Charley's counterfeit scar and vague assurances that he'd only seen Mr. Scar-Eye yesterday or the day before, he didn't know where . . .

—John safe . . .

"Are you able for the walk of a mile and a half?" she asked Katy, as she kissed Horace, shook hands with Weyountah, made a hasty exchange of promises to keep one another abreast of whatever might be found while the guards glared at them, and pointedly pulled the leaves of the gate half to. "The house lies on Queen Street; 'tis some little distance."

"I'm well, m'am." The girl glanced sidelong at the soldiers again as they passed through, the last of the day's traffic. The gate-guards shut the three great archways behind them as the last light flashed on the shallow waters, a hundred yards off across the rough field that was all that the Neck contained, and shot the bars. A number of men—rough-coated and jesting with one another—were also coming in on foot from Roxbury: Abigail guessed they'd gone across to drill with the militia. Darkness outlined the hills and trees beyond the river where it flowed into the bay. As the fields along Orange Street gave place to the brick houses of the wealthy, set in their own orchards and gardens, lights were coming up in the windows, a guilt-inducing reminder of those good housewives who had *not* spent the day gallivanting about with undergraduates in the countryside around Cambridge looking for villains, Tory plots, and pirate treasure.

Those Marthas of the world, who had prudently cooked the meals for the Lord's Day tomorrow instead of hastily giving instructions to servant-girls who were really too young to have the whole of those duties thrust upon them—though Pattie was *perfectly* capable of putting together chickens to roast and beans to bake . . .

And so it proved. When Abigail and Katy reached the house, the kitchen was redolent with the scents of tomorrow's dinner and filled like a jewel box with the amber warmth of firelight and lamps. John was, of course, still out at the Green Dragon—Abigail knew that it wasn't the ale in the place that kept him, but the conferences going on all day in its long upstairs room with the Sons of Liberty—and Charley and Tommy flung themselves on her with the frantic abandon of children who sense themselves set aside, however necessarily, in favor of matters that they cannot understand.

Katy was introduced, and when Abigail came downstairs from showing her the small attic room in which she would sleep (with no little relief that she was at least enough of a housewife to have extra sheets clean, ironed, and on hand),

Pattie handed Abigail a letter. "This came this afternoon, m'am. Will Mistress Fairfield be having her bath here in the kitchen, when the rest of us do?"

"If she does," said Abigail, "she'll go after you—I brought her in to help you as much as because she needed a place to stay. But she may not, tonight," she added, remembering that the girl had heard only that morning that her lover was dead.

She broke the seals.

> *Rock Farm*
> *Medfield*
>
> *28 April 1774*

Mrs. Adams,

Thank you for your kind favor, which I have received today. How extraordinary, that strange matters seem to follow my great-grandfather's books! It is as if one of the old man's own curses has clung to them, and though I am indeed sorry to learn that one of these curses has cost a young man his life, still I yearn to hear more of the matter.

Indeed I would be delighted to receive you at your soonest convenience. Rock Farm lies four miles beyond Medfield, down the second lane that branches to the left from the road that continues on toward Stonton. It is a fearful drive from Boston, and I shall speak to my niece to prepare a bed for you here.

So retired is my state here that your visit would be attended with eagerness, even were it not in connection with that wicked old pirate's evil doings!

Sincerely,
Narcissa Seckar

Twelve

The reflection that the books were indeed connected with a wicked old pirate's evil doings—not to speak of a possible curse—made it no easier for Abigail to keep her thoughts focused the following day upon the Reverend Cooper's sermons. As usual, these ostensibly concerned the doings of ancient Hebrew kings but showed a marked tendency to drift toward Parliamentary injustices and the modern misbehavior of monarchs whose deeds rivalled those of Ahab and Herod; Katy seemed to enjoy both morning and after-dinner discourses hugely.

To Abigail, this was a great relief. From the sound of it, Mr. Deems at the Yellow Cow—not to speak of his associates in the patriot militia—left much to be desired as a moral preceptor, and at intervals during the family baths in the kitchen on the previous night, she had experienced qualms about her generosity in offering roof and bed to a girl whose existence she hadn't even been aware of that morning—and pregnant to boot! But while Pattie was bathing Charley and Tommy,

Abigail had gone up to the attic to offer the facilities of kitchen, towels, hot water, and a screen before the fire to her new guest, and had found Katy, by the light of her single candle, on her knees beside the little pallet bed, weeping—as she had not let herself weep while anyone could see—for George Fairfield. It had led to a long talk, and by the time Katy had descended to take her turn at the end of the bath-line, Abigail had no more doubt that she might not have done the right thing.

"Which is fortunate," said John, when—Saturday night, clean and damp and smelling of soap—he had yanked shut the bed-curtains and tumbled in beside her, "since Sam's been pestering me to ride down to Providence to meet with the Committee of Correspondence there Monday. As you are deserting me again, you wayward woman, I had thought to see if Uncle Isaac and Aunt Eliza might be prevailed upon to look after the children once more. Heaven knows I've heard nothing all evening but about how they'd like to go back. You can send both girls along with them without fearing for Eliza's silverware. Alone at last!"

He sighed, and in the darkness filled his hands with her hair—which, though hidden all day beneath a very proper cap, was in its unbound state like a black silk cloak. "I would bless you a thousand times, my dearest friend, only for not snoring—unlike every traveler I've shared a bed with these past two endless weeks . . ."

She kissed him, those lips so surprisingly soft against hers, and stroked the shorn velvet of his hair. "Bless me, then, dearest friend."

It was good to have John home.

Thus it came to pass that on Monday morning, after helping John and Johnny with the cowshed and dispatching the older children to school, young Mr. Thaxter—John's clerk—

harnessed a horse borrowed from the neighbors to the very old Adams chaise. The prospect of three days in Aunt Eliza's garden had reconciled the boys—and almost reconciled Nabby—to their mother's absence; sitting between the younger boys as they drove slowly back to Milk Street with Thaxter, Pattie, and Katy pacing along beside the vehicle like the aldermen of London escorting the King in procession, Abigail heard all about Charley's plans to implement Johnny's design for a bird-trap, and Tommy's intention to dig a hole clear to China.

"I trust you'll see that he doesn't," said Abigail to Pattie, and both girls nodded. "At least not among Aunt Eliza's roses. Katy, I must beg your forgiveness for saddling you with these two ruffians while Pattie helps Johnny and Nabby with their lessons—"

"Never fear it, m'am," said Katy stoutly. "I'll teach 'em their rifle-drill, and march 'em up and down the garden 'til they faint with fatigue—"

"I'll faint before you do!" Tommy challenged Charley. To judge by their expressions, neither boy found the slightest objection to this program. All four children had taken to Katy with the aplomb learned early by those in large New England families, where unmarried cousins, maiden aunts, and hired girls came and went in farm households like birds of passage. Her ability to whistle, play cat's cradle, and whittle toys won her the loyalty of the younger boys, and her curiosity and eagerness to be instructed in Latin by Johnny sparked his immediate approval. The boy loved to instruct anyone in anything and was well on his way, Abigail reflected with a sigh, to being as much of a prig at that age as Horace had been.

Katy's hard life—harder, Abigail guessed, than the girl

would admit—had left her willing and happy to fit herself into any environment, and Abigail sensed that beneath her sauciness lay great reserves of strength and loyalty. And John, of course, had fluffed up like a pouter-pigeon at the news that she had read his patriotic essays and thoroughly understood and approved.

After kisses, embraces, admonitions, and promises in Aunt Eliza's kitchen, Thaxter helped Abigail into the chaise again, and minutes later they were passing beneath the central archway of the Boston town gates and into open country.

"Don't you worry, m'am," said the clerk, as Abigail turned in the seat to look behind her at the tall jumble of roofs visible beyond the curve of the harbor, at the black masts and hulls clustered along the wharves, the violet green islands floating in the water beyond. "Uncle Isaac will keep them safe, even if . . . well, even if the King's message arrives and there should be trouble. And—well . . ." The young man coughed apologetically. "If you'll excuse my saying so, m'am, but if there's trouble, it's just as well Mr. Adams is out of it."

"Mr. Adams is *not* a member of the Sons of Liberty," retorted Abigail acerbically—a little tired of her neighbors' assumption that just because he shared a great-grandfather with Sam Adams he was naturally hand in glove with his cousin's more nefarious deeds. "He has no more to fear from the King's edict than the Reverend Cooper would . . ."

"No, m'am," agreed the clerk, a stolid young man whom Abigail had known since his school-days. Their mothers had been sisters, and they were both part of a wide-flung family network that stretched over most of the eastern part of the colony. "All the same," he added with a fleeting grin, "if the edict should happen to mention Mr. Adams, it's probably best that he's out of Boston just now—and the children out of the house."

* * *

Medfield lay at a day's drive along the wide bend of the Charles, and was a cluster of brown, peak-roofed houses set among stony fields and woods that stood untouched since the days when the Indians had had them to themselves. A harsh country, Abigail knew, and in places, appallingly primitive. Beyond the town's fields the woods stood thick, a dark roof of oak and hickory shading ancient deadfalls and centuries of fallen leaves. Most of the houses in Medfield boasted two rooms plus whatever loft-space could be used beneath the steep slant of the roofs; more than one, she could see, had the enormous old-fashioned chimneys that spanned the whole of one wall, like the one in Sam Adams's ancient house on Purchase Street, that you could sit inside in perfect comfort while Bess cooked dinner. In the winter, even the village would be isolated for weeks at a time by snow—as her childhood home of Weymouth still was, and John's village of Braintree also—and she shivered at the thought of those outlying farms they passed. Only a hundred years ago, half the town had been burned by Indians, and only a few days' distance to the west, she knew, some of the tribes still lived . . .

Lived, and watched with festering anger the advance of the white farmers, whose cattle destroyed their village fields of corn and pumpkins, and whose craving for land ate away at the hunting-grounds that for the Indian's substituted for livestock as white men understood it.

Ten years ago the French had armed the Indians as part of their war with England, and the King, Abigail knew, was anxious to keep the tribes on his side because of the enormous profits the Crown reaped from the trade in furs. If it came to fighting—and if the King landed troops, she knew that it would—would the King arm the Indians? Would he turn them loose upon those he perceived as rebels against his authority?

The thought was deeply unsettling. The more so, Abigail realized, because she recalled not only a hundred details of massacre-stories and farm-burnings, but the equal outrages done by the whites against the Wampanoag and the Abenaki, the Pequot and the Nipmuc . . . the summons to peace-conferences that had ended in slaughter of the Indian delegates, the burning of villages and crops. The tribes would side with the King, both in revenge and because the King guaranteed them their rights against the settlers, who bitterly resented the fact that they could not farm wherever they wished.

They can't reach Boston, she told herself. *As John said, every militia in the state is drilling . . .*

And may be off fighting British troops in the east if an uprising comes.

The thought that she'd left her children in the town—though how she herself would defend them in the event of riot, invasion, or Indian uprising she couldn't imagine—pierced her heart like a knife, and she barely heard Thaxter's humorous observation on a very young child attempting to drive a herd of geese across the town's unpaved street.

Rock Farm lay four miles beyond Medfield at the end of nearly a further mile of lane, and it was nearly dark when Thaxter finally guided the tired horse into the yard. A lantern hung over the door of the farmhouse—small, old, and crude-looking beyond belief—and a couple of men were just crossing from the barn to the lean-to with pails of milk on their neck-yokes. The oldest of them, bearded and grim-looking except when he smiled, set down his pails and strode to the chaise, holding out his hand and beaming, a huge yellow dog trotting at his heels.

"You'll be Mrs. Adams, I expect? Seth Barlow—my son Eben, our cousin Jehu. Tilly, go tell your mother and auntie Mrs. Adams is here—" A girl in faded hand-me-downs darted from the woodpile into the house. "Mr. Thaxter? Pleased to meet you— Down, Rex! Sit, sir . . . Thad, help Mr. Thaxter with the horse— Methusaleh, take Mrs. Adams's things—" Mr. Barlow seemed to have an infinite number of children and young adults on-call, some of the boys no older than Horace but clearly men who did men's work. "I can't tell you how much Aunt Sissy looks forward to your visit, m'am." He held out a hand like a pickled cutting-board to assist Abigail down. "Tell me if you will—and just yes or no, I've no intention to tire you after that drive!—what's the news from Boston? Has the King's edict come?"

"It has not," said Abigail, marveling at the reach of the Boston newspapers. She hadn't seen a coffeehouse or anything resembling one in Medfield—presumably the newspapers were left at the local tavern, though she hadn't seen one of those either. Sam would be pleased. "The town waits daily, and—I am told—every militia from the Kennebec to Martha's Vineyard is readying for trouble."

"And out to Springfield as well." Mr. Barlow named one of the westernmost of the colony's settlements as they crossed the yard to the house, where in the open doorway two women stood framed. One was stout and rosy even in the fading daylight, in a much-mended apron and a dress worn colorless by age and sun—Mrs. Barlow, Abigail guessed even before her bearded husband kissed her. The other, fragile and white-haired, held out her hand with a welcoming smile.

"Mrs. Adams? I'm so pleased you could come. I am Narcissa Seckar—and I knew that old sinner would cause trouble, though he's been in his grave for close to eighty years now! My husband said there was a curse on those books— Do you mind a bed in the kitchen tonight? Hannah and I are quiet as mice when we start the fires up in the morning, I promise you . . . I would say I'm pleased he was right—my husband, I mean— save that it's brought death and grief to innocent men. Girls, this is Mrs. Adams, she'll be staying tonight."

Abigail was introduced to Tilly, Hagar, Zilpah, Dinah, and Susanna, all engaged in putting up their after-dinner tasks of mending, knitting, weaving—a loom took up most of one end of the sand-floored "keeping room" that combined the functions of kitchen, parlor, dining room, wash room, and nursery. They hurried about in a rustle of hand-me-down skirts, setting the long table for a modest supper of bread, molasses, and milk. Hot water was fetched for Abigail, and her portmanteau set near the box-bed beside the fireplace where, Abigail guessed, old Mrs. Seckar herself usually slept: Thaxter would bed down in the loft with the boys. The younger Barlows—and those of the company who were cous- ins or hired help or both—stood behind the benches of the adults to serve, and to eat their meal standing in the old way; one of them (*Hagar? Susanna?*) brought close a lamp, so that Mr. Barlow could read a chapter of the Bible before the meal. (Second Peter, and a very proper warning to the righteous to avoid conversation with the unrighteous lest they be cor- rupted as the Children of Israel were corrupted by long asso- ciation with Egypt.)

He quizzed the younger children on what he'd read, prayed an extensive prayer that included thanks for Abigail's safe journey and a blessing—rather surprisingly—on Rex the Dog, the horses, cows, pigs, and cats in the barn, and pro- ceeded, finally, to supper. After a day of travel, Abigail had never encountered bread, milk, and molasses that tasted so good.

A conscientious guest, Abigail helped the women and girls of the family clean up, while Thaxter went out to give the boys a hand bedding down the stock. When the young clerk sat down with Mr. Barlow, Eben, Jehu, Methusaleh, Josiah, and Cry-Out-at-the-Coming-of-the-Lord to discuss the latest news from Boston, Abigail was taken aside to the corner beside the enormous hearth to share a little tisane with old Mrs. Seckar and to talk of pirates and curses.

He was my great-grandfather." The tiniest trace of admiration flickered in Mrs. Seckar's voice. "And a fearful old sinner he must have been, by all accounts. In addition to commanding a fleet of four vessels—with a flagship whose name was so scandalous my father wouldn't even tell me what it was—old Geoffrey Whitehead was said to be a sorcerer, able to call the storms or flatten the waves at will, and to turn common rocks into gold, though if that were in fact the case I'm sure he would not have spent so long on the high seas plundering Spanish ships. Old Beelzebub, they called him, and the Nipmucs worshipped him as a god."

"What on earth was he doing in Massachusetts?" By the light of the fire—and a branch of work-candles—Abigail was helping her hostess mend sheets that were so worn she herself would have converted them to dish-cloths . . . having the luxury of one of the busiest lawyers in the colony for a husband. "Spanish ships being rare in these waters, even a hundred years ago."

"I gather he'd hide here when he made things too hot for himself in the Caribbean." Narcissa deftly turned the heel of the sock she was making, her knitting-needles long darts of reflected gold. "He'd repaint his ship and change her sails, and come ashore pretending to be a Dutch merchant—he spoke over a dozen languages with ease, and could pass himself off as anything from an Arab to an Indian. It also turns out he had at least three wives that anyone knows about, in different colonies. The Massachusetts one was my great-grandmother, the daughter of a Boston merchant who didn't see anything odd in her sea-captain husband being gone for a year at a time . . . nor apparently questioned why he would return from his voyages so *very* rich. In addition to her, he was said to have married a Nipmuc chief's daughter and built a castle in the backcountry somewhere, where he'd retreat when his Boston in-laws got on his nerves . . . as I imagine they must have," she added, giving her ball of yarn a twitch, which immediately brought it under attack from two of the kittens whose brothers and sisters were virtuously asleep in the basket beside the hearth. "If they were anything like grandfather Barthelmy, whom they raised."

"A heart like a counting-frame, was how I've heard him described," Abigail remarked.

"I suppose I should be charitable toward him," sighed Mrs. Seckar. "Given that he, his mother, and his sister were deserted when he was small, and he was raised among her family as a poor relation—no wonder the man was grasping. Oh, I don't mean all poor relations are treated ill," she added, with a smile and an affectionate glance across at the group on the other side of the hearth. "The whole family here is poor, by Boston standards, and I could not be better treated if I were their grandmother rather than just their mother's aunt. But Mr. Seckar's mother and sisters lived with us, and when Mr. Seckar died, there was talk of me going—with my surviving sister-in-law—to Mr. Seckar's brother near Concord. I would . . ." She seemed for a moment to grope for a polite way of describing him, and Abigail's mind returned to Katy Pegg and the way her glance had dodged aside when she'd spoken of her stepfather. Abigail remembered, too, some of the tales her parson father told of how children—and the incapacitated elderly—within his own flock were sometimes treated by those obliged to take them unwillingly in.

"Then it seemed Providential," Narcissa went on tactfully, "that I *did* have great-grandfather's books to sell, so that I could contribute a little toward my own keep here—in spite of what my husband's family insisted: that the books, by coming into my possession, were in fact *his* and should go on to Harvard with the rest. I was grateful, too, that I could find buyers for them all so quickly—though mind you, I was not at all surprised that the indecent ones went first!"

She sank her voice, though the girls were chatting happily among themselves as they sewed and the men were totally preoccupied in slandering the King. "I was almost tempted to keep those. I'd had no *idea* . . ."

Among the deep lines of laughter and age, a dimple touched her cheek, and Abigail saw how pretty she must have been as a girl. "Such an amazing thing, is the human imagination!" Mrs. Seckar went on. "But of course, Mr. Seckar—my husband—was the first to cry out that they should be burnt, for if anything bore Beelzebub's curse, 'twas those. And alas," she added, raising troubled eyes, "that it seems to be so. No ill has come of the others, has it? The Arab texts—which I believe you said your nephew purchased?—and those that the Governor bought . . ."

"The Governor?" said Abigail, startled.

"Governor Hutchinson." Mrs. Seckar regarded her in some surprise. "He purchased the bulk of them. Fifty-four books, not counting those I sold to your nephew and his friends."

"He never spoke of them—"

"Perhaps the subject did not arise," said Mrs. Seckar, in her comforting, grandmotherly tone. "He might have thought—"

"No, we were speaking of the books," objected Abigail impulsively. "He's the one who told me about your grandfather's grasping heart, and said he was surprised your grandfather had owned books at all. The whole question of the slave Diomede's guilt or innocence is hinged to the theft of the books. Yet he didn't mention them at all."

Thirteen

"That is most curious." Mrs. Seckar's hands stilled on her knitting; she regarded Abigail for a time in the dim flicker of the fire. Mrs. Barlow was nursing the baby for the last time that night; the younger children had already scrambled up the ladder to the loft and bed. "He paid me twenty-five pounds for the lot of them, hard currency, which was extremely generous. I am sorry to say, the transaction annoyed Mr. Seckar's sister Reuel beyond speaking." Her lips twitched, but she put the un-Christian smile quickly away.

"How did the books come into your hand?"

"Now that," said Mrs. Seckar, shaking her head, "was entirely my doing. For years, I had asked my husband if 'twere possible for us to enlarge the rear wing of the house, which was used as a laundry. He argued I had done quite well there for the whole of my life, and 'twas only vanity that sought more room for ironing and primping . . . though an ill-ironed shirt was enough to justify the cancellation of supper—"

"For a *shirt*?"

The old woman looked for a moment as if she might have made some comment about her husband, but again, she mastered herself and put the thought away, this time without a smile. "He was as he was," she said at last. "I daresay it taught me care in my work—"

"He would cancel his *wife's* supper? 'Tis not the maid we're talking of?"

"We had no maid," Narcissa replied calmly. "He said, 'twas against the will of the Lord to bind another to servitude—"

"He seems to have felt no compunction about binding *you* to servitude."

"A good wife is given unto man for his comfort." Again that small silence, as she looked back over the years spent with Malachi Seckar, infinite tiredness in those surprisingly bright blue eyes. Then she repeated, "He was as he was. My father, while he lived, thought it no great matter, and worth an occasional missed meal himself, to school me, as he said. And I had old Mrs. Seckar, who lived into her nineties, and my husband's sisters Reuel and Rachel to share in the work, though toward the end, in that last ten years, there was only Reuel and myself."

Narcissa Seckar looked to be in her seventies, white-haired and rather fragile in appearance, and Abigail felt herself flush with anger at that selfish old man who had decreed that his wife could do the tasks of hauling water and wood, cooking and cleaning, with her only help a woman who was probably as old as herself.

Before Abigail could snap ungracious words about the dead, however, Narcissa forestalled her. "In any event, I did at last prevail after quite literally decades of asking. And when the workmen broke down the wall of the laundry, lo and behold, they found a sort of little chamber hidden between it and the newer portion of the house. The whole end of the room had been bricked across and plastered, and in the space behind the bricks were two shelves of books."

"Good gracious!" Abigail—a bit reluctantly—put aside the subject of this woman's father, who hadn't even protected his daughter against a domestic tyrant, in contemplation of a treasure trove more valuable, to her mind, than gold. "I take it the house had been in your family? Was it your father's house? I know the Reverend Seckar willed it to the college when he died—"

"The house was built by old Beelzebub." Again there was that trace of pride in Narcissa's voice as she spoke her ancestor's name. "By *Captain Whitehead*, as my father insisted upon calling him. Father pretended to the end of his days that his grandfather had been no more than a sea-captain in the West Indies and had not even sold slaves, much less stolen them from the Spanish and sacked towns in passing. One cannot really blame him, considering the position he held, in the college and in the Church."

"And Beelzebub was—?"

"My father's grandfather, Geoffrey Whitehead. Of course he hushed the matter up, and I think 'twas one reason my father pushed me so hard to wed Mr. Seckar, who was his favorite student and his amanuensis after Father had his stroke. He edited Father's sermons, and acted as his secretary in all his business with the college and with the other churches in the colony. He was the son Father had always wished he'd had, the more so after Phoebe—my sister—wed a man who danced and played the fiddle and spent all his little money on fine horses . . . which he bred, to a fair profit, though Father would never hear of that. Father told me when I was seventeen that he was leaving the house to Mr. Seckar, who came of poor family and needed property. Better that a man of Godliness and worth should have it, he said, than a girl who would only marry it away to one of the Damned. I could marry Mr. Seckar, he said, and continue to live there, or leave it upon Father's death."

"Was your father—" Abigail had to bite back the words *right in the head?* stifling her anger—the man was after all great-grandfather to Tilly and Hagar and Zilpah and at least some of the others . . .

Narcissa only regarded her, with slightly raised white brows. "I was—a defiant girl," she said matter-of-factly. "Rebellious of Father's authority and scornful of the Fifth Commandment. I'm sure had I been the boy Father wanted, I would have kicked up all sorts of riot and rumpus, a fact which he ignored completely when he bemoaned the fact that God had inexplicably saddled him with the wrong sex of children. My sister was younger, and very sweet and meek, until she ran away at age fifteen with Mr. Wellman, who was Sarah's father." And she traded an affectionate glance with Mrs. Barlow. "Mr. Seckar was modest of bearing, right in thought and deed, saw clearly the will of the Lord—in Father's words—"

"Meaning saw clearly the will of your father."

"That, too, though perhaps he did clearly see the Will of God. I have no way of knowing. He was always ready to smite the unrighteous, Father said—meaning spiteful to those who didn't agree with him—and upright to those who look to him for guidance, meaning cruelly harsh to his mother and sisters when he brought them in to live with us. And if he was as filled with pride as a toad is with poison, where Father could not see, and sometimes used the rod as well as the word to smite and guide . . . I'm sure Father would have allowed that some latitude is to be given for one so filled with the zeal of the Lord."

She returned to her knitting, and the gray kitten stood on its hinder legs and snatched at the moving needle-heads with its white-tipped paws. The farmhouse had no glass to its windows, and outside the tight-barred shutters, Abigail heard the hooting of an owl and the noise of some larger creature, moving about in the woods.

"I'm afraid I've wandered rather far afield," apologized the old lady after a moment. "But indeed, the house was the one I had grown up in, and the rear wing—the laundry and the kitchen—had once, I think, been the main part of the house. 'Tis made of stone, and very long and narrow, and the floors only dirt. I believe 'twas my grandfather, the despicable Barthelmy, who had the main house built in 1683, and old Beelzebub went on living in his old stone wing until his death nearly ten years after that."

"I wonder what the good citizens of Cambridge made of him?" Abigail couldn't keep the amusement from her voice, at the thought of a pirate and sorcerer—and sometime collector of naughty volumes—retiring for his declining years to that quiet town of divinity students and Tory worthies. "Or he of them, for that matter. And what of his castle in the backcountry where Indians worshipped him as a god?"

"From what Father said—though he was quite capable of making it up—toward the end of his life, Old Beelzebub repented of his sins, gave up alchemy—"

"He was an alchemist?"

"Oh, good Heavens, yes. In his quest for the ancient formula for Greek Fire he is reported to have burned down half an Indian village. In addition to which he summoned the Devil, invented a flying machine, and, of course, turned common rocks into gold. His repentance, Father never hesitated to point out, would not have done him the slightest good, as he was clearly destined for Hell, and he—Father—became thoroughly incensed when I asked, *Should we then not trouble to encourage thieves and slave-traders to abandon their evil ways?* and told me not to be impertinent, though I thought it a perfectly reasonable question . . ."

"My son asked me that, too," sighed Abigail. "I told him that only God knows whether a man is ultimately destined for damnation or salvation, and that we must encourage the unrighteous to abandon evil, because it might be—but we do not know—that we are God's chosen tools in another's path toward righteousness, like the ass that bore Saul of Tarsus toward Damascus."

"Well, that explanation would involve my Father not knowing something." Narcissa finished off the top of the sock, clipped the yarn, and slipped it neatly into her basket, as if all the long years she spoke of had happened to someone else. "So it could not be true. In any case, according to my aunt Serafina—Grandfather Barthelmy's sister, who lived with us for some years while I was a child—her father, Old Beelzebub, built the stone house in Cambridge just after King Philip's War, so it might have been he was simply driven out of the backcountry by the Indians and felt himself too old to make a new start there. The newer portion of the house lies at right-angles to the old, in such a way that it was not at all obvious that about eighteen inches of its northern end had been bricked and plastered over, to hide the two shelves of books. Only when the eastern wall was broken out—how long ago it seems! But 'twas not even a month!—to make the enlargement was this secret space found and, in it, my great-grandfather's books."

Thoughtfully, Abigail said, "Which the Governor then bought." She frowned. "But you said your husband ordered the work done—"

"He died," said Narcissa, "not a week after the workmen broke down the wall."

"Will you ladies stay up and make a night of it?" Seth Barlow grinned good-naturedly as he crossed the keeping room to their corner. Thaxter and the older boys came back in from having a final piss and disappeared up the loft-ladder;

the yellow dog turned around a time or two where the benches and chairs had been. The farmer put the tin lamp he carried on the table beside his aunt-in-law's chair and felt the side of the red teapot. Mrs. Barlow and the baby had disappeared into the bedroom some time previously. The house had grown deeply still.

Abigail said apologetically "I should——" and Narcissa waved her small, work-rough hands.

"Don't worry for me, Mrs. Adams, if you're wanting to sit up a little longer. If you're not too tired after your journey——"

"Heavens, no! I only worry that you——"

"Well," said Barlow, kneeling beside them to bank the hearth-fire under a careful mound of ashes, "while you two ladies are arguing out which of you is being polite, I'm for bed. Are you warm enough? 'Tis a mild evening——" He got to his feet, dusted his hands, and brought shawls from the great, clumsy sideboard, one of the few pieces of furniture in the room. "The pallet's made up for you in the bedroom, Sissy——" He bent to kiss the old lady's wrinkled cheek. "Mrs. Adams"—— he grasped her hand—"my wife promises she'll be silent as a mouse in the morning. And don't mind old Rex. He snores."

"Anyone who promises mouselike silence," remarked Abigail ruefully, when the bedroom door shut behind him, "has never heard the ones we get in our attic. Five minutes," she promised, "and then I shall let you go to bed."

"Five minutes." Narcissa hobbled to the cupboard, took out a small pot, and from it dripped a spoon of honey into her tisane. "Will you have—No?—Where were we? Oh, yes, selling the books to the Governor."

'Twas true, Abigail reflected, there had been no real NEED for Hutchinson to tell her he'd bought Mrs. Seckar's books . . .

But they had been discussing the books, and Barthelmy

Whitehead, and old Emmanuel Seckar. They had been speaking of Diomede, whose life hung in the balance depending on the events of the evening when two of those books had disappeared.

Only a dullard would not have exclaimed, *But here, I have the rest of those books right here in my study . . .*

And whatever else John and Sam liked to claim, His Excellency Thomas Hutchinson was not a dullard.

"How did that come about? I take it your husband was not ill then——?"

"Heavens, no. That is, Mr. Seckar's health was fragile by then—he was in his eighties—but he never really ailed. He always walked to the college. And he would not hear of selling the books. In fact he spoke of burning them."

"Did he have offers?" Abigail wrapped her shawl around her shoulders, though in fact, as her host had said, the night was a pleasant one. Outside the tiny glow of the betty lamp, the big keeping room was like a friendly cave. The gleam picked up for a moment the round gold reflection of Rex's eyes before that faithful retainer dropped his nose back to his paws, sighed, and returned to his well-earned sleep. He did indeed snore.

"Three," said Mrs. Seckar. "The first was from a West Indian bachelor-fellow named Pugh—who naturally enough offered for the disgraceful books, of which there were about five, as I recall—I think he offered for three or four other volumes as well. Mr. Seckar refused and swore he'd burn them before he'd sell them to the likes of Mr. Pugh."

"I have met Mr. Pugh," said Abigail. "I should like to think myself spiritually fit enough that I would sell him a map were he lost in a desert without water, but I am not sure of it——"

"Well, he's the one who thought it a hilarious jest," said Mrs. Seckar, "to stand up and ask at Mr. Seckar's lectures, was it true that a member of his family had once kept a

harem of Berber dancing-girls, and how was the state of their
salvation affected by being tupped by a Christian man?
Father had managed to completely scotch the rumor about
his grandfather," she added. "But Mr. Pugh's great-grandfather
had done business with Old Beelzebub in Jamaica. Threats to
have him sent down served to keep him from spreading these
tales—yet he made the mistake of offering to blackmail Mr.
Seckar on the subject when Mr. Seckar would not sell. Of
course this only rendered Mr. Seckar quarrelsome. Not," she
added drily, "that it took much to render Mr. Seckar quarrelsome."

"And of course the one he quarrelled with was you."

"One did one's best." Narcissa sighed, and her arthritis-
crippled fingers stilled on the looped yarn of a new-started
sock. "And one did one's best not to be pulled down by his
ways. At any rate I did. Poor Reuel was forever trying to
please her brother—and her mother, while she lived, who
was in many ways worse." She shook her head and went back
to setting stitches onto the needles. "I think one of the other
offers was from a relative of yours—you said your Mr. Thaxter was your cousin? This young man's name was Thaxter as
well, a nice boy with spectacles. He said he had heard that
Mr. Seckar might have some books in Arabic to sell, only by
that time Mr. Seckar had made up his mind that he would
burn the books. That was because of Mrs. Lake."

"Mrs. Lake?"

"If that was her name." Narcissa's tone made Abigail's
eyebrows—elevated already—ascend further. "A well-dressed
woman who came in her own carriage and offered twenty
pounds for the lot. Only Mr. Seckar took one look at the cut
of her dress and the cost of her lace—for a man who claimed
that God had no use for furbelows he was a sharp judge of
them—and the quantity of white lead and cochineal she had

plastered from bosom to hairline, and declared her to be the blood-sister of the Whore that Sitteth upon the Waters . . . A remark he made to her face, unfortunately. This provoked a response from her, and the conversation rapidly lost whatever dignity it had begun with. He called her a Babylonian harlot, and I do not even know the meaning of the terms she applied to him, but the interview ended with Mr. Seckar screaming at her to get out of his house and Mrs. Lake threatening to call in her footmen—her *boys*, I believe she termed them— and have him thrashed."

"Footmen?" said Abigail thoughtfully.

"Two of them, as well as a coachman who would not have looked out of place on the gun deck of great-grandfather's flagship—"

"Had he a scar on his face?"

The old woman nodded at once and held up her two fingers in a *V* before her left eye. "A frightful one, just here . . . He and one of the footmen came up as far as the front door as she opened it to go out. I was in the hall at the time and could smell them—rum and dirty linen. After that of course, your poor nephew—who arrived only hours later with his offer—received short shrift, accompanied by an accusation that he was in That Harlot's pay. Mr. Seckar worked himself into a terrible passion." Her lovely brows tugged down into a frown. "Such things left him exhausted as mere walking did not, and he still felt a heaviness in his limbs, he said, on the following day. And on the following night he died."

She fell silent, gazing past the tiny gleam of the betty lamp into the silent gloom. The cat woke in her basket and padded out through the hinged flap in the door to hunt; the kittens tussled a little among themselves, then returned to sleep. Rex turned upon his side with a profound sigh. Though it was nearly too dark to see anything, Abigail could hear in

the other woman's voice, despite the outrageous conduct of
the man who had been her master for nearly three-quarters of
her life, a break of regret, of grief.

It had, Abigail reminded herself, only been a few weeks—
after how many years? One might hate the husband who
crushed and oppressed and bound one's life, but he had been,
when all was said, Narcissa's nearest company for almost fifty
years.

"How did he die?"

Narcissa shook her head. "I think in his rage, he had
strained his heart," she said. "Then we all three came down
ill that evening—Mr. Seckar, Reuel, and I. One of his students had given him a frumenty, a dish of which he was very
fond, and I suspect that under all the spices it might have
been a little unwholesome. The doctor, when he was called,
bled us and said 'twas likely an influenza, but neither I nor
Reuel had a fever, though all the next day I had a headache,
and felt stupid and not myself, though that," she added,
"might have been the bleeding. In a way I am grateful, for I
don't even recall feeling shock when I woke—halfway through
the morning and the sun high in the sky—and found him
lying dead at my side. I staggered to the door wrapped in a
quilt, and managed to get it unlatched and to call out to
some boys in the lane to fetch a doctor. Beyond that I recall
little of the day. They tell me they found me curled up asleep
in the quilt on the floor of the hall when the doctor arrived."

She fell silent again, a little like Weyountah, Abigail
thought, repeating his memory of last Tuesday night as if to
fix it in his mind. To make it something which had once happened to him, rather than a gnawing and present pain.

After long silence, Abigail asked, "And were any of the
books gone the next day?"

The older woman looked up from her contemplation of

the dark pit of the hearth, startled. "Why, I have no idea," she said. And then, "Good Heavens, Mrs. Adams, you do not mean to suggest that my husband and I were *poisoned*? So that someone could get at the books?"

"I don't know what I mean to suggest," said Abigail. "You say your husband was frail?"

"He was active," she said. "And alert. But his heart was not good, and after preaching or lecturing, he would often come home and sleep for hours."

"Then a drug administered to put the household to sleep might easily have been too strong for him."

"Good Heavens," she murmured again, her hands still upon her knitting, her bright blue eyes gazing for a moment into the darkness, as if through it she could see the face of the horrid old man who had forbidden her supper if his shirt was not ironed as he liked it, and who would not have in a servant to help two old women whose strength was nearly gone.

Then her gaze returned to Abigail. "On the other hand," she said, "if someone knew of his infirmities, 'twould be just as easy to poison him—you must inquire as to the source of that frumenty, Mrs. Adams, the moment you return to Cambridge!—knowing that I would sell the books afterwards . . . would it not?"

"You, Mrs. Seckar," said Abigail, "are too clever by half. No wonder your husband wanted to keep you a slave."

Fourteen

Firebells ringing. In the kitchen Abigail heard them, and panic seized her: four-fifths of the houses in Boston were timber, and of those, most were crowded in these dense neighborhoods around Brattle Street and Brattle Square, where flames could leap from roof to roof. Though the cold March evening was still (*March?* she thought cloudily, 'tis *the second of May* . . .), if the fire was close, it wouldn't save their house . . .

(*We left that house, didn't we? We went back to Braintree because of John's chest-pains . . . Tommy was born in Braintree . . .*)

She ran down the corridor from the kitchen of the house on Brattle Street, tiny Nabby and tinier Johnny clinging to her skirts. Her movements clumsy (*Because of the baby? Or because I'm dreaming* . . .), pregnant with the child who became Charley, she flung open the front door, the cold smiting her, snow on the ground.

Voices shouting all around her in the twilight as her neighbors came rushing to their doors. Men raced to pump water from frozen pumps, to form up the lines that every neighbor-hood knew by instinct to form, buckets passed hand-to-hand . . .

Only there was no smoke in the air. Just shouting from the direction of King Street, men's voices with a savage note in them that raised the hair on her nape. In her dream she knew what was going to happen and turned, shouted over her shoulder at her children, "Stay inside—"

A single shot cracked out in the icy twilight—going over it, dozens of times, with John later, she never forgot that sequence: a single shot. Then a volley of gunfire, like ragged thunder.

John had been out that evening at his club in South Boston, and her heart was in her throat that he might have been in King Street—she knew exactly what had happened. For weeks the citizens of the town—the prentice-boys, the layabouts, the Sons of Liberty, the children—had been hectoring and cursing and threatening the British troops that Governor Hutchinson had asked the King to send, to help him keep order in the town that hated both Governor and King. For weeks she'd seen the redcoats walking about the icy streets armed with their muskets, primed with the Governor's accounts of riots and dis-orders, and confronted every day with handbills and broadsides decrying the troops as slave-masters who must be cast out.

Even in those dark days, pregnant and ill and sick with grief at the loss of the tiny daughter who had died the month before, Abigail knew that it would come to shooting.

She reached King Street while the powder-smoke still hung thick in the darkening air, the sharp smell of it overrid-ing the characteristic stink of fresh-spilled blood. Bodies lay in the snow: a young boy in a pool of blood at the mouth of Quaker Lane, a black man and a white sailor sprawled in the rucked and muddy slush close by the little knot of British soldiers whose coats seemed dark in the twilight, like the blood spilled all over the snow.

* * *.

H er eyes opened with a snap: *Where am I?* Unfamiliar smells, the close air seeming to press on her . . .

She put out her hand and instantly touched a wall, like the side of a coffin . . .

Her other hand, flailing, met curtain.

Rock Farm.

The clink and scurry of tiny paws beyond the heavy cloth.

Those dratted kittens . . .

A bigail slept again.

Firebells ringing in the cold March twilight, only this time she saw the kitchen of her own house in Queen Street. The house was burning, and she heard gunfire in the street; Nabby, Johnny, Charley, Tommy fled out the back door, Abigail calling after them in a voice that had no sound to it . . . *Why are they alone? Why is no one else in the house?*

The cowhouse was in flame, and so was the house next door. Johnny led the way down the smoke-wreathed alleyway that led toward the street, clinging tight to Nabby's hand on his left, to Charley's on his right, smoke-blind, terrified, stumbling.

Charley was holding Tommy's hand, and when Tommy stumbled, tripping on his long leading-strings on the sides of his dress, Charley's hand slipped from his.

Tommy screaming, shrill voice tiny against the roar of the flame, trying to get to his feet in the snow as his sister and brothers fled down the aisle of smoke and burning. Fled away from him, unaware that they'd left him behind . . .

Gunfire somewhere close. Men shouting as the city burned.

Tommy screaming . . .

* * *

Abigail jerked awake, ill with panic, heart hammering. In the kitchen beyond the bed-curtain something fell with a small clatter. More dashing little feet.

I will catch those kittens and dunk them up and down in the water-bucket by their little tails.

Then half-grasped fragments of a dream, of distant gunfire and distant burning, very far-off now and visible in the darkness through the window of Governor Hutchinson's tapestried study. The Governor raised his head a little where he sat beside the cozy hearth, listened. Then touched the rim of his reading-glasses to settle them and went back to his perusal of the book in Arabic that lay upon his knee.

Did Mrs. Lake come back to buy the books after your husband's death?" Abigail took the breakfast plates from Tilly, Hagar, Zilpah, et al., and arranged them on a towel-draped corner of the table where the basin was brought for washing. Mrs. Barlow had already gone out to feed the chickens—at the wooden counter, two of the girls helped each other, dumping boiling water into the churn to scald it for butter, while two others gathered up straw sun-hats to start on the garden work. In the country, there was always something that needed doing. Abigail helped Narcissa and the youngest girl with the dishes, the stillness of the spring morning broken only by the crack of axes in the woods, where Thaxter obligingly lent a hand with the endless summer task of cutting winter fuel. When Seth Barlow had asked them last night, *Would they remain a day?* Abigail had assented, despite her uneasiness about leaving her children.

To return to Boston would entail a drive of all the daylight hours. She knew there were things that she had forgotten to ask last night.

"She did not." Narcissa paused, frowning, a rag daubed with soap in her hand. "Drat it, there goes my theory that the murder was done without robbery. I wish I could remember how many of those books there were, hidden behind the wall and what they were about."

"You said, fifty-four."

"'Twas only what I sold to the Governor." The older woman rubbed briskly at the pewter, went to the counter to cadge the last of the boiling water to add to the basin. "And the list of them that Mr. Seckar made went with them. Once I had said that they were mine to sell or to keep—this was after your nephew's first attempt to purchase and Mrs. Lake's visit—Mr. Seckar took them away and hid them in his study."

"Hid them literally? Not just shut the door and turned the key?"

"Hid them," said Narcissa firmly. "He said he would not put it past me to try to steal one or two, to sell them, and to blame his sister for the theft . . ."

"Why would you do that?"

"To make up household money that I had overspent. 'Twas ever his fear," she explained, "that I would spend too much at market and that I would sell something of his to make up the difference. His mother and sister were both fearful pinchpennies, and I could not throw out so much as a torn napkin without accounting of it to them."

No wonder this primitive farmstead where she was obliged to sleep in the kitchen seemed to fill the old woman with such happiness. It did not include any of the Seckar family.

"So a thief who came in when the family was drugged might not have got them all," said Abigail. "He—or she—would not have known where to find them. Was there any who knew the house well, besides yourself and your sister-in-law?" Abigail settled the dripping plates on the towel—only six of them, which had probably come across from England with the original settlers: the children ate off trenchers made of the dried heels of bread-loaves and shared a cup among them.

"Nary a soul," the old lady replied promptly. "You must understand, Mrs. Adams," she added with a rueful smile, "there was not a man of the faculty—and I think every single one of the Fellows—that my husband wasn't in a quarrel with, over everything from the Nature of Time as it existed *before* God created the Heavens and the Earth, to whether women should be permitted to learn to read and write . . . which my husband said were not necessary to a woman's salvation and were in fact a detriment, for with our limited understanding we would only come to hurt in using such things."

She stepped aside to let one of the little girls—Hagar or Susanna—sweep the sanded floor around her feet. "And then, there were a number of men in the college who felt that my father had been completely wrong in leaving the house to Mr. Seckar, and this, too, was a fruitful cause of backbiting. As a farmer's son, Mr. Seckar was considered by some to be undeserving of the Vassall Chair—though he was a great scholar and well deserved the honors accorded him. He felt everyone was in league against him."

"Did anyone come to try to purchase the books the day after your husband died?"

"That evening young Mr. Fairfield came with food from the College Hall—Heaven only knows who he bribed to get it!—and to make sure we had all we needed. We were both, Reuel and I, still very weak from being bled—and poisoned into the bargain! 'Twas then I asked him, was he interested in purchasing any of the books? Perhaps I'm as wicked as Mr. Seckar and his mother were always saying," she added, and though she kept her tone light, Abigail heard in her voice that it was something she had indeed believed from time to time. "And it may come from being the great-granddaughter of a pirate, but 'twas already in my mind that Mr. Seckar's brother would be taking us in—Reuel and I. I thought that I had rather have a little money of my own . . . and the books *were* my own, as Old Beelzebub's heiress, even if the house had been left to the college. In any case, I suspected Mr. Fairfield would be interested in those volumes that Mr. Pugh had found so congenial, and I was right. I think he at once told your nephew that I would sell, for young Mr. Thaxter and his Indian friend appeared the next morning to buy what they could afford, and later in the day the Governor sent a man to purchase the rest from under the noses of the College Board of Governors. Mrs. Lake herself never came back."

"Curious," said Abigail softly. "Curious."

Through the long spring day, Abigail helped the girls and Narcissa in the garden, took her turn minding Baby Mary, listened to Tilly, Methuseleh, and Josiah recite their lessons, and in general gave herself over to the peaceful rhythms of the deep countryside. In such a place, it was impossible to know what was happening in Boston and thus necessary to trust entirely in the mercy of God. The family kept insisting that she was here as Aunt Sissy's guest, and they were glad of it for they feared Aunt would miss the town life, and it wasn't necessary for her or Thaxter to do a thing . . .

And yet, Abigail missed the vegetable-rows back in Braintree almost as much as her children delighted in the open spaces of Aunt Eliza's garden, and she revelled in the smell of the earth as she pulled weeds in a borrowed sun-hat. In the forenoon she helped Sarah Barlow prepare dinner for when the men came in from the woods and the field, and looked over the stitches of the younger girls, and now and then sat with

Narcissa and came back to the subject of alchemical books and pirate treasure . . .

"How did you know your great-grandfather was a pirate?" she asked at one point. "If your father worked to keep the matter hushed, and his father as well . . ."

"Aunt Serafina told us." Narcissa deftly untied the strings of Baby Mary's clout, took the washrag Abigail handed her. "She was, as I said, Grandpa Barthelmy's younger sister and lived with us when I was a very little girl. She remembered Old Beelzebub—her father—very well. She said he looked like the Devil would have, if the Devil were ever to sit in a corner of the kitchen and play the fiddle. This was after he had changed his way of life, of course, so she never saw him in his glory, with a cutlass in his teeth and burning cannon-fuses braided in his beard. But she said he was very tall, with long gray hair thick as a horse's mane, and had a long mustache whose ends he braided, and that he was missing two fingers of his right hand so that he held the fiddle-bow strangely. She swore us to secrecy, Phoebe and I, and at night when Father had put out the lights, Aunt whispered to us about the Indians worshipping him and how he burned down half their village and summoned the Devil and all the rest of it—"

"Did she ever speak of him hiding a treasure?" Abigail handed her a clean baby-clout and made finger-waggles at Baby Mary, laid on the keeping room table, who caught at Abigail's fingers and threshed her tiny legs.

Narcissa frowned as she tied the clout in place. "In a general sort of way," she said after a time. "Though that may have been only something Phoebe and I made up later, because pirates are supposed to have buried treasures. Certainly I recall nothing being said of one buried in Massachusetts. And even if there had been, I can't see that it would have gotten past Grandpa."

"Did your grandfather ever search for one?"

"If he had, 'twould have been an admission that his father was a pirate." Narcissa picked up the infant and carried her toward the door, Abigail following with a blanket. "Not that it would have stopped the old scoundrel. I'm a little surprised he hadn't had all the walls of Beelzebub's original stone house sounded the minute the old man died. Perhaps he thought that in repairing his way of life, his father had given the money to charity . . . something it never sounded like the old sinner would have done, either after his reformation or before it, according to Aunt Sera."

Abigail spread out the blanket in the sun, shaded her eyes to catch a glimpse of those three little straw-bonnets bent dutifully over the garden rows. "Why did he reform?" she asked. "Did your aunt tell you that?"

"No." Narcissa's forehead puckered as she considered the matter, putting together old tales half recalled, which might— Abigail reflected—have been hearsay anyway . . . "Yet it must have taken some great event, don't you think? For a man given heart and body to the ways of sin—not only sins of the flesh, as all pirates do, but the sort of intellectual dabbling in alchemy and demonology that can be twice as fascinating to an intelligent man. For such a man to reverse his steps and try to walk back uphill to the Light. Particularly," she added, "when everyone around him is telling him, as they must have if he was living in Massachusetts, that 'twould not have done him any good anyway."

"Exactly." Abigail adjusted a portion of worn sheet over a long billet of firewood to make a sort of lean-to above the baby's head. "So why would he have done that?"

"Does it make a difference?"

"I don't know. But 'tis odd—one of many odd things about this whole adventure. Is his castle still standing? The treasure would be there if anywhere."

"I've never heard of a castle anywhere in the backcountry." Narcissa fished last night's sock from her workbasket. "It might only have been a sort of *palisado*, such as soldiers build of logs in enemy country, in which case, 'twould have been occupied by the Indians when he left it and certainly destroyed during the fighting with France, if not before. And it may not even have existed at all. If he'd ever had any claim to land in the backcountry, it's been long sold. For again, Grandpa Barthelmy would have got hold of it, had it still been in the family, and I can't imagine he'd have sold a square foot of his father's land without searching it for buried treasure."

"'Twould serve Grandpa Barthelmy right, and your father, too," retorted Abigail, "had there been land with treasure buried on it, and they sold it . . . *Was* Old Beelzebub in Jamaica when Henry Morgan was Lieutenant Governor there?"

"Oh, I should think so." Narcissa grinned cheerily. "Nearly every pirate on the Spanish Main passed through Port Royal at one time or another, did they not? If he'd wanted to blackmail Morgan for his congress with Jezebel Pitts, he'd have had plenty of opportunity to do so."

Fifteen

Abigail's sense of well-being—of a job well accomplished, and of new friends made—lasted her about a hundred yards down the lane toward the Boston Road.

Thaxter hitched up the chaise shortly after first light Wednesday morning, and they were sent off with much hand-shaking and the gift of fresh-baked bread, new butter, and several slabs of soft cheese ("The landlady at the Anchor on the road back to Boston hasn't washed a dish in twenty years . . ."). Mr. Barlow bade her tell Mr. Adams that he and all the men hereabouts stood ready to defend the colony's liberties (he obviously thought she was married to the *other* Mr. Adams).

But no sooner had the house disappeared among the trees behind them than the enormity of having been gone from Boston—and her children—for three days settled upon Abigail like the fall of night, and her dreams of the Massacre, of fire and peril, of Tommy left behind crying in the snow returned and tormented her like a persistent gadfly for the remainder of the day.

The reflection that Cousin Sam would have sent out riders to Medfield and every other town posthaste in the event of any real trouble gave her only momentary comfort. "If the British have not yet arrived, the whole household has come down with the smallpox," she sighed ruefully, as the chaise turned onto the main road. "Or the house has burned to the ground."

"I'm sure all is well, m'am," replied Thaxter soothingly, which caused Abigail to smile despite her anxiety. In his months of association with herself and John, her young cousin had yet to pick up their sense of humor. John would have immediately set himself to cap her visions of disaster: *I think a lightning-strike, rather than the smallpox . . . If the harbor hasn't risen in flood . . . No, wait, we've entirely forgotten the earthquake . . .*

Instead, for the next several miles, the clerk set himself earnestly to assuaging her fears with assurances of how secure and happy the four children would be at the home of Eliza and Isaac Smith . . . something of which Abigail was herself already aware. Yet he meant well, and she knew that to summarily silence him would hurt his feelings. So she settled herself to listen and to sort in her mind what she'd learned, like a card-player arranging clubs and spades, hearts and diamonds.

A frumenty was exactly the sort of thing a solicitous student might bring to an elderly professor about whose health he was concerned—and the old man was probably vain enough to believe assurances of concern even from a man with whom he'd quarrelled. But it pointed back yet again to the college: to someone he knew. And from Abigail's experience with the dish, the dried fruit and assorted spices that customarily flavored the meaty porridge could easily conceal the bitter flavor of opium.

Mrs. Lake presumably had access to a kitchen, but 'twas certain Seckar wouldn't have taken a cup of water from her hand if he were dying.

Did they make frumenty for the students in the Hall?

There are two of them in it, she thought. *Mrs. Lake—whose name almost certainly isn't Lake—and someone connected with the college. Someone who knows Old Beelzebub was a pirate. Someone who knew about—or learned very quickly about—the books.*

All of which would amply describe St-John Pugh . . .

Were it not for the curious fact that the Governor had not mentioned to her, Abigail, that he'd bought Mrs. Seckar's books, and the ease with which Mrs. Lake could have gotten the key to the Chamberville house from the Governor's hand.

Mr. Pugh had forged the note designed to keep George Fairfield from his rooms past midnight, when he could feel safe in searching for the books . . . Had he searched for them before, in the Seckar house, while its owner lay dying at the side of his sleeping wife? Would a young and dissolute man need to believe a copy of Aretino's *I Modi*—complete with illustrations—might conceal a pirate's treasure-map, to move Heaven and Earth to take possession of it?

And would St-John Pugh—the son of a West India merchant who was almost certainly a smuggler—enter into alliance with the Governor? And if George Fairfield had come back from his tryst to find Pugh in his room, would he not have been slain in his clothing rather than his nightshirt? Had he come in before midnight and gone to bed?

"Why would the Governor have to use subterfuge, drugs, and burglary to enter George Fairfield's rooms in the first place?" asked Thaxter, when Abigail spoke of the matter just east of Dedham. "I realize he can't simply detain the Vassall Professor of Theology for twenty-four hours while having the sheriff search his house, but an undergraduate? He could have simply had Horace and the servant arrested."

"With a King's Commissioner due to arrive within the week, I should be careful—were I the Governor—about going on public record as having jailed the son of a Virginia planter who is moreover the captain of a troop of Loyalist light cavalry. Particularly if I had no intention of turning over to the King any treasure that I might find."

Thaxter said, "You think Cousin Sam is right, then? That there is treasure?"

"I think that *they* think so," replied Abigail grimly. "Whoever *they* are, they consider what they're looking for worth three men's lives . . . so far. That's what concerns me."

They passed through Dedham and through the wooded farming country along the Charles. Eschewing the slandered Anchor, they had a picnic-lunch in the overgrown ruin of what had once been a farmstead. "It must have been quite a fire," remarked Thaxter, after tethering the horse near the crumble of anciently charred timbers that marked where the barn had been. "To have jumped that distance, from barn to house—"

"I should say rather that the two fires were started separately." Abigail rose from spreading a blanket on the bare stones of the foundation and peeked behind a tangle of gooseberry at the old smoke-blackening of the walls. "To judge by the growth of the trees in the dooryard, I'd say 'twas King Philip's Indians that destroyed this place, a hundred years ago."

"Philip—" Thaxter frowned, counting back in his mind. "Was he King of France . . . after Louis? The old King Louis, the present King's . . . grandfather? Great-grandfather?"

"Great-grandfather," said Abigail. "And no, Philip wasn't King of France. He was a chief of the Wampanoags who united the tribes against us . . . for all the good it did them," she added sadly. "They might have chased us out of their hunting-grounds hereabouts when first we set foot in this land, but they didn't. Like Virginia and the Carolinas and Connecticut—and Massachusetts—each tribe of Indians saw itself as a separate nation: Nipmuc and Wampanoag and

Pocassett. They would not unite with their enemy tribes, and so all fell to a greater foe."

This led to talk, over bread and Mrs. Barlow's excellent cider and cheese, of the excesses of Virginia's Governor—every bit as arbitrary as Hutchinson, but at least Hutchinson had never stirred up war with the Indians on the frontier as a means of distracting the men of the colony from complaints for their rights, as Dunmore was said to be doing.

"Were the King to send troops to occupy Boston in consequence of the dumping of the tea," said Abigail, "I doubt the Virginians or the New Yorkers would raise a peep over it. They seem to think we should apologize for protesting against the King's tyranny *and* pay for the tea that we wouldn't pay for when we were commanded to buy it and none other—even Mr. Franklin"—she named the Pennsylvania philosopher whom many considered the intellectual head of the movement toward the colonies' rights—"has advised we do so . . . presumably so he will not be put in the position of speaking in favor of hooligans."

As they gathered up their much-depleted supplies and corked the remains of the cider, the young man looked around him at the ruined farmstead again and commented—with a town boy's ignorance—"I wonder they never rebuilt this place."

"The land's dreadful." Abigail nodded toward the shaggy remains of what had been an orchard. "'Tis all rocks among the trees, and I see no well here. And it may be the land was taken over by some wealthier farmer in the district, the records having been burnt with the burning of the town. All the good land is west of here, in the valley of the Connecticut. The whites took that from the Pequots long before King Philip raised his forces—killed them all, my father told me, by selling them blankets taken from men who'd died of the smallpox."

"Is that true?"

"Having met some of the merchants in Boston," replied Abigail drily, "can you doubt it? I wonder myself if Old Beelzebub did not change his way of living—move to Cambridge and build his house there—because the Indians no longer worshipped him, but drove him out."

"And he left his treasure behind?" The clerk's eyes brightened as he slipped the bit into the horse's mouth again, hooked the harness to the traces once more. "Then it might still be there! All we'd need to do is check the county land-records in the State House . . ."

"And discover that Old Beelzebub lived on in Cambridge a good fifteen years past King Philip's War and maybe more, and had plenty of time to return in perfect safety and dig his treasure up himself. Or, in the years since his death, if he indeed owned land, his clutchfisted son would have done so."

"But if he did not find it? If the treasure were cleverly hidden, in a cave or a pit, and the direction coded to look like a disgraceful account of an assignation by a pirate queen and a government official who should have known better—"

"Then it might indeed," said Abigail, as the chaise pulled out of the weed-thick dooryard and down the dim trace back to the road, "be worth three men's lives . . . to somebody."

As had been the case a week ago, Abigail and her escort reached the Neck of Boston just as the sun was touching the distant hills. Coming through Roxbury, acquaintances had waved to them as they passed the Common, and no one had run out to them shouting, *Turn back, turn back, the streets of Boston run red with blood!* . . . Nevertheless, Abigail was conscious of deep relief not to see the smoke-plume of a burning town rising before them. Thaxter put the tired horse into a smart trot, and they jolted along the track between the shining and fishy-reeking shallows, with the red-coated soldiers standing waiting—again—for them in the half-closed portal.

The Common lay as it always had, a great ragged pasture sloping upward toward Beacon Hill, fading into the twilight. The tinny toot of the herd-boys' horns as they gathered up the cows mingled with the clatter of wheels on the cobbled street. The familiar mix of fish, woodsmoke, and latrines seemed to welcome her as they rattled up Orange Street, and Aunt Eliza and Uncle Isaac greeted her with embraces and laughter and offers of supper. Even her self-important cousin Young Isaac—a clergyman who seemed to regard Abigail's marriage into the Adamses as the worst mésalliance since Persephone's nuptials with Pluto—forebore to chide her about John's associates. Nabby clung silently—as if she suspected that her mother preferred jauntering over the countryside hunting pirate treasure to remaining hearth-bound and cleaning lamps—while Johnny brimmed over with an account of how profoundly he had impressed his Latin master that day. Charley wanted to know why they couldn't have a garden on Queen Street, and Tommy was missing altogether—they had to go out into the garden and hunt for the boy among the beanpoles.

"We've taken turns going over to the house to milk the girls," said Pattie, as she and Katy herded the children to the Smith kitchen to get cleaned up for the return home. "Mrs. Butler offered to do it, but 'tis no trouble. We take Charley and Tommy with us—"

"We're due there now," added Katy. "I can hear the boys bringing the herd in."

The Butlers, and the Hansons on the other side, had offered to look after Cleopatra and Semiramis in the absence of the Adamses and to have their prentices clean the stalls in return for a dozen small favors John had done them over the past few years.

"We've put the milk in the coldest corner of the pantry, so there'll be a fair deal of butter to be made . . ."

"I went out to Cambridge yesterday," added Katy, a little shyly, "to see Diomede in the jail, as you said I might—"

"I did indeed," said Abigail, "and I'm glad you thought to do so. Really, Eliza," she added with a smile, "there's no need—"

"Nonsense, nonsense," declared her aunt, as the maid brought to the kitchen table a tray laden with Dutch coffee, bread and butter, marmalade, and cold meats, "after a journey like that you must be famished—"

"*I'm* famished," said Charley hopefully, looking at the marmalade.

It was well and truly dark, and Tommy and Charley were sound asleep on the seat of the chaise when the little party returned along Queen Street by lantern-light. The lamps in the houses they passed, even, were being quenched on the lower floors, leaving only the very dim squares of illumination higher on the brick walls, where bedroom candles flickered over the pages of Bibles or novels, while men took off their wigs and scratched their heads, and women brushed out their long hair. Eliza had handed Abigail a letter from John, who had been delayed in Providence—*Another night bedding down with snoring strangers, poor lamb,* reflected Abigail ruefully. *Just as well, I can get the house in order again before he arrives.*

The children crowding around her while Thaxter unharnessed Tom Butler's horse, she handed her lantern to Katy, unlocked the kitchen door, and banged her ankle very smartly against something hard that lay almost on the threshold as she stepped in.

She began to say, "Good Heavens, Pattie, we didn't acci-
dentally leave Messalina indoors——?" but the smell of spilled
vinegar smote her, and the faint sickliness of spoiled milk.

She held the lantern up to further throw its light.

She'd nearly tripped over a crock of butter—not broken,
but lying on its side where it had . . . *Fallen? How could it?*
Even had the cat been somehow trapped indoors, she could
never have——

Slowly, the light penetrated through the kitchen and pantry, showing Abigail an appalling shambles. Chairs had been
pushed about, every drawer of the big sideboard stood open,
cupboards agape. Beside her, Johnny said, "Ma——" and Nabby's hand, cold and frightened, gripped suddenly at hers.

And Charley, delighted as all three-year-olds are with
chaos: "Was it bears did this?" He darted forward and Abigail grabbed him by the shoulder, pulled him back, and
backed out of the pantry, out of the house.

"Katy," she said, "hold on to the children—Nabby, run
next door and get Mr. Butler and his boys. Pattie, go with
her," she added, seeing the little girl hesitate in fear.

"You don't think there's anyone——" began Pattie hesitantly, and then, as if exonerating herself, "I was inside yesterday,
to make sure all was well, and it was. Pfew, that vinegar is
strong! What happened?" She looked back toward the stable,
from which Thaxter emerged, bearing the other lantern.
"Who would do this?"

Happily, Charley opined, "I bet it was Mr. Scar-Eye!"

Sixteen

While Katy and Pattie took the children next door to the Butlers', Abigail, Thaxter, Tom Butler, and the cooper's two apprentices went through the house armed with kindling-axes, barrel-mallets, and every lantern that could be borrowed up and down the street. They found no human foe on the premises, but the house had been ransacked from cellar to attic. Even Katy's pallet bed had been shoved away from the wall and its mattress torn open, hay strewn everywhere in the room.

Abigail and the children went back to Uncle Isaac's to sleep, leaving Thaxter to guard the premises until morning. She dreamed of being locked in the house while it was being searched, hearing the scrape of Mr. Scar-Eye's boots as he groped toward her in the dark.

When she returned in the morning, it was to find Sam Adams in the kitchen, with his wife Bess, his daughter, Hannah, and their maid Surry all engaged in mopping up the spilled vinegar from the broken kitchen cask and scrubbing everything in sight. Abigail groaned inwardly—it was John's unvarying contention that the scene of any crime contained at least some piece of information about the criminal. Though she had a strong suspicion that Charley had been right about the culprit being Mr. Scar-Eye, she had hoped to find something that might tell her where to look for this sinister gentleman and who might be his employer.

Yet she was far too grateful at the prospect of not having to clean up the entire house herself to quibble, only assigning to Sam and Thaxter the task of straightening the tumbled library (*John will never be able to find anything on his shelves ever again!*) while she made a careful tour of the upstairs.

It told her nothing she hadn't known before. It had been too dark to see much by lantern-light last night, and their only object had been to make sure there was no one still lurking in the house, so the tracks of the reconnaissance party—herself, Tom Butler, et al—did not penetrate beyond the doorway of any room. Morning light showed Abigail that there had been three burglars, men in rough boots . . . something she could have guessed, she reflected wryly, from Horace's account of the sinister coachman and his henchmen. She also knew they were sized Small, Medium, and Large from Horace's account, information borne out by their tracks, which were just barely visible in the bedroom she shared with John. The merest modicum of guesswork would also have been sufficient for her to tell from Horace's story that they were men used to burgling places—there wasn't a nook in the house that they hadn't plundered, a fact that made her very glad she'd left the household money and her pearls at Aunt Eliza's with the children.

Beyond those obvious indicators, the visitors had been annoyingly fastidious. No one had dropped so much as a button, let alone a dagger that might match the wound in George

Fairfield's side or a letter from Mrs. Lake bearing instructions to murder Horace. No bloody handprints (*thank goodness!*); no mysterious documents in Arabic or any other language.

But, Abigail reflected as she came downstairs, she'd had to look. If they'd left any of these things in the kitchen, well, Bess, Hannah, and Surry had taken care of them and there was nothing that she, Abigail, could do about it now. The best she could accomplish at the moment was to assign various tasks to clean up, and herself go to the market—which, though it was now late in the morning and nothing would be available but picked-over leavings, was a matter of critical importance, particularly if John was due back tomorrow or Saturday . . .

"And we need to get up laundry tonight," she added to Thaxter, as she passed the study door. "I will *not* have anyone in this house spend a moment on sheets those villains have pawed—"

A familiar voice called from the kitchen, "Is she in? Aunt Abigail—!"

Then Weyountah's, deeper and steadier, "Is there something we can help with—?"

"Yes." Abigail entered the big room, dusting her hands. "Horace, get my marketing basket from behind the pantry door, please. Weyountah, would you be able to stay and assist Mr. Adams in straightening up the study? Oh, thank goodness, Arabella," she added, as her next-door neighbor knocked at the back door with a plate of smoking-hot griddle cakes and a jug of molasses, "you are a choir of angels and all the saints in Heaven rolled into one! Speedy help is double help . . ."

"*Amicus certus in re incerta cernitur,*" quoted Horace automatically, and then, thin face flushing with excitement, "Aunt Abigail, I've seen him! I know who he is! Mrs. Lake's coachman! Dubber Grimes!"

Abigail set her marketing basket on the corner of the

table, cast a glance at the angle of sunlight in the yard—*There will be NOTHING left in the market* . . . !—and said, "Bess, would you and Bella do the honors? I *beg* you will excuse me, but if I don't get to the market now—"

"We'll save you griddle cakes," promised Arabella Butler with a smile, and playfully shoved Abigail toward the door.

"And coffee," added Bess, "if we can keep Sam from drinking it all . . ."

Abigail seized Horace by the elbow and thrust the market basket into his hands as she was pushed out the door.

"Tell me," she commanded, as she and the young man hurried their steps down Queen Street toward the big market square.

"'Twas entirely by accident," said Horace, and shoved his spectacles more firmly onto the bridge of his nose. *"Res hominum fragiles alit et regit—"*

"Yes, yes, I know the fragile affairs of men are guided by chance," said Abigail impatiently. "Where did you see him?"

"At the Crowned Pig. The seniors were ragging poor Yeovil again and I followed him to give him a hand, and when I walked into the tap-room, there was Grimes—the scar-eyed coachman—dicing in the corner with Black Dog Pugh! I ducked back out at once and asked one of the—er—young ladies who work there, who was that man with Mr. Pugh? And she said his name was Dubber Grimes, and he is from Charles Town, and the men with him—there were two others at the table besides Pugh—were Newgate Hicks and the Cornishman, and they all worked as bullyboys at a . . . a house of ill-fame in Charles Town called Avalon. While the girl was getting the ale for Yeovil, I watched them; they weren't only dicing, but talking with Pugh. He gave them money!"

"Only to be expected if they were dicing. Still . . . Avalon," said Abigail thoughtfully. "Well, well—someone has a sense of humor. In the tales of King Arthur," she explained, seeing her nephew look blank, "Avalon is the location of the lake, which has in it the Lady who gives Arthur his sword, if I remember aright . . . Your aunt Elizabeth"—she named her mother—"never considered fanciful tales proper for us children, but Aunt Eliza has a book of them and would read to us when we'd visit. Though I never thought to find the reference useful—"

"Mrs. *Lake?*"

"When you think of it," said Abigail, as they turned from Cornhill into the square before the great market-hall, "what other sort of woman might a man know that he could hire as a cat's-paw, to look respectable enough that a young man like yourself would get into a carriage with her? Would you have gone with Dubber Grimes on his own? Or with gentlemen named Newgate or—er—the Cornishman? Or even Pugh himself, for that matter?"

Horace seemed to be digesting the information that he'd ridden in a carriage with a bona fide Scarlet Woman while Abigail made her way to the stalls of the farmers whose chickens, rabbits, and lambs she knew to be freshest and most plump, and who picked their vegetables in the dark of early morning and not the afternoon before. And since everyone else in Boston knew who those farmers were also, she found, as she had feared, no lettuces left, no peas (*DRAT "Dubber" and his henchmen!*), and the only asparagus remaining was thick and tough as tree-trunks.

With a basket full of beets and carrots, some elderly lamb, an assortment of very small fish wrapped in rushes, some strawberries, and a huge quantity of rather raggedy spinach, she turned her steps back toward home. John would just have to make the best of it. "When was this?" she asked.

"Yesterday afternoon. 'Twas too late to come to you then—

we'd never have made it to the ferry before sunset—and Wey-ountah was at a demonstration of vacuum-pumps, which he would not forgo . . . But what is a vacuum? Nothing! What can we do?"

"I think the time has come," said Abigail, "for a search of Mr. Pugh's rooms. Those grooms of his are generally there, aren't they?"

"Either the grooms or Pinky."

"Not surprising, if he's in the habit of keeping indecent books about—not to speak of treasure-maps. John won't be home until tomorrow evening or Saturday morning, and thank Heavens there's not a great deal of laundry to be done, bar the sheets and assuming the weather stays fine. Our Black Dog had mortally offended the Reverend, but 'twould have been easy enough to send him a frumenty by the hand of one of his minions. Do the cooks at the Hall make frumenties?"

"Sometimes," said Horace, a trifle startled at this conversational detour—frumenties were utter poison to him, and it clearly wasn't something he'd ever considered. "I know he gets custards and syllabubs from them—and pays them extremely well not to speak of making him things, since he could be sent down for it, and *they* could be sacked for selling the College provisions that way."

"I see." Abigail paused at the corner of Cornhill to let pass a group of men: laborers from the ropewalks that abounded in Boston, rough-looking men talking heatedly, and she heard among them the words *God-damned lobsterbacks* and *bloody bleedin' Parliament* . . . "So our best course would be to attack the problem from the other end—which will entail a visit to the farm of the Reverend Seckar's brother."

"He has a brother? It's like hearing there was a fourth Gorgon." Horace shook his head. "I always thought the Reverend Seckar was spontaneously generated from a vat of sour lemons."

"My only hope is that his family does actually live in Concord and not out in somewhere like Haverhill or Springfield. If I have to chase off for another three days to speak to the sister about who drugged the family, Heaven only knows what I'd return here to find."

Over a nuncheon of Arabella Butler's griddle cakes ("Now, we must save a few for Nabby and Johnny when they get home—"), Abigail thought to ask Sam, who as a longtime rabble-rouser knew everyone in the Boston area, about Genesis Seckar. As she'd suspected, Sam knew all about him.

"His farm lies about seven miles the other side of town." Sam poured out coffee for Abigail, Pattie, and Katy—who had brought the younger boys back from the Smiths'—as they settled around the much-battered table in a kitchen now spotlessly clean (Abigail could have kissed Sam's womenfolk for sparing her the appalling task). "Your husband," he added, "likes to chide that two-thirds of the men in the colonies either enjoy being the King's slaves or don't care whose slaves they are so long as they're able to cheat the poor out of their rightful money—"

"That is *not* what John says!"

Sam waved away the objection. "Well, Genesis Seckar belongs in the category of men who wouldn't care if they were slaves of the Grand Turk, since everyone around them is going straight to Hell anyway, so how they or anyone else lives on the Earth doesn't matter, because they've no proof that the world won't evaporate in flames tomorrow, so there! He lets the militia drill on his pasture—the place is well away from prying eyes—because it doesn't matter to him whether there's going to be fighting or not. Bruck Travers with the Watertown militia tells me Old Man Seckar comes out and preaches during drill at the top of his lungs."

"Oh, *him*." Katy made a face. "He's down to two cows these days and doesn't take care of either of 'em, poor beasts. You're not thinking of going out there, Mrs. Adams?" She turned on the bench to regard Abigail worriedly. "He's about a hundred and fifty years old, and proof, I always thought, that his way of life is holy—"

"How's that?" asked Sam, hugely amused.

"Oh, because if it wasn't, God would have let him die years ago, only He knows that if he did, the old wretch would be in Heaven, and God just can't stand the idea of putting up with him."

"You don't think he knows where your treasure-map is hid, do you?" Sam's gray glance cut sharply across at Abigail. "Or the sister? Is that why you're going?"

"It is not," she retorted. "I'm not entirely convinced that there *is* a treasure or a map to find it with. But I'm not trying to find a treasure; I'm trying to prevent an innocent man from being hanged for a murder he didn't commit. And since it's nearly impossible to prove a negative, we are reduced to finding who actually *did* kill poor Mr. Fairfield . . ."

"Does it matter?" His voice was suddenly hard.

Horace and Weyountah, on the other side of the table, looked at one another uneasily, and Bess said, "Now, Sam . . ."

"I'm sure it matters to Diomede," replied Abigail evenly.

Sam waved as if chasing away inconvenient flies. "Let me take care of Diomede, then. What we need of you, Nab— what Massachusetts and all free men in it need of you—is that you find that treasure-map of this Mrs. Lake, and that you find it before that British ship lands . . . or before whoever the damned Governor is paying to do his dirty-work for him decodes the cipher and scoops the money that *we* desperately need."

"Which reminds me," began Horace, reaching for his coat-pocket, "I have—" And Abigail, guessing what he was about to produce, kicked him hard under the table.

"You don't really think the Governor is behind the man who killed George, do you, sir?" Weyountah sounded worried. "George was loyal to the King—"

"You think that would matter to any red-blooded Tory merchant?" retorted Sam. "Old Hutchinson'll be falling over himself trying to figure out what the cipher is so he can get the gold out of there before the British land as well, lest he be accountable for it. I'll send a man out to Concord to talk to Old Seckar—"

Abigail remembered old Mr. Creel and his spite-filled diatribes; thought about the unshaven rope-workers, with their hickory clubs and angry voices and dirty hands, she had passed on the way home. "That's quite all right, Sam."

"And I'll send someone out with you to Cambridge to find this map or cipher, and the books it's hid in—I can probably get you someone to burgle the Governor's house for you—"

"That's *quite* all right."

Sam was silent a minute—his expression reminded Abigail of Johnny's when the boy had verbally given away something he was planning and was trying to think how to cover his tracks. But at last he said, quietly, "I don't think you realize how important it is that we find that gold, Nab. And find it soon."

Around the table, Bess and Hannah, Katy and Pattie, Charley and Tommy, Weyountah and Horace had all fallen silent, as if they had ceased to exist . . .

And they HAD ceased to exist, reflected Abigail, *for Sam.*

As Diomede had ceased to exist.

Because Seth Barlow had been right, the other evening out in the isolated darkness beyond Dedham, when he read the evening portion of scripture . . . Violent men spread violence like a contagion, and greed in a good cause was still greed. When you supped with the Devil, even the longest spoon would not keep his whispering out of your ears, long after you had thanked him for his hospitality and scurried out the door.

Sam and his patriots, just like the rest.

"'Tis worth more than finding who killed some Tory or who gets accused of it," Sam said. "'Tis worth more than my life or yours—" His glance flicked across the table to the two young men. "The offices of friendship are one thing, boys, and I can see you're shocked at my saying so. But I tell you this. Once the British land—once fat old King George lands his troops here, the first thing he'll do is either close the courts or put his own men in charge of them, which amounts to the same thing. Then it isn't going to matter a split grass-blade who killed your friend or why, because the only thing that *will* matter anymore is who the King's friends are . . . or who gains the favor of the Governor. To fight that, we need money: money for guns, money for powder, money for food for the men who'll have the manhood to take up arms. And beside that, nothing is important."

He stood and went to the sideboard for his hat. "The wind's inshore," he said. "That ship can be only days away. We must do what we can, while we can, and let all else go by the wayside. Nab," he added, returning to the table to kiss her cheek, "thank you for your hospitality—"

"No," she said, rising, "thank you—and Bess, Hannah, Surry . . ."

The tension of the moment was lost amid handshakes, embraces, farewells.

But it wasn't until Sam and his family were out of the

house, that Abigail asked softly, "Do you have your recon-struction of the cipher, Horace?"

"I do. I meant to tell you, but with everyone here—and seeing Dubber put it from my mind—"

She gripped his arm, shook her head, "'Tis well."

"Is it true what he said?" asked Weyountah, deeply trou-bled. "That the King will close the courts?"

"The truth is that I don't know," said Abigail. "And nei-ther does Sam. But the truth is also that when a man starts saying that the cause of defending our liberties is more important than justice or truth or saving the life of a man who has no rights before the courts of law, then I start to wonder what he *would* stop at. And a man who'll stop at nothing . . ."

"Becomes very difficult to distinguish from a robber," con-cluded the Indian. "Come into the study, and let's have a look at Horace's paper."

Seventeen

When Abigail had finished reading the two pages of Horace's sprawling, uneven scrawl, she said, inadequately, "Goodness." Although, quite patently, none of the recorded proceedings had anything to do with goodness.

The language was stilted and old-fashioned and used a great number of plain English words not generally encountered in polite conversation. At least her nephew hadn't translated these passages into Latin, as any number of Abigail's male acquaintances would have, under the impression that a mere woman wouldn't understand what *futuo* meant. Between the farmers around her childhood village discussing their stock, and her younger brother's raids on the higher shelf of their father's classical library, there was very little that Abigail had not at least heard about.

Horace, who had gone to gaze out the study window while she was reading, turned around and tried to pretend he wasn't breaking out in hives with embarrassment.

Weyountah said matter-of-factly—since his friend was quite clearly incapable of speech—"It's as close as Horace could make it to the original wording, but of course it isn't word-for-word. I don't see how we could decipher it, if it is a cipher, without knowing that."

"No, we couldn't." Abigail turned the sheets over in her hands, trying not to remember that these were what the two young men had been working on the night George had been killed. "And yet—Horace, you said that it was English written in Arabic characters, as if the Arabic was itself a cipher. Did the prose itself seem labored or . . . or *odd*? Given the subject matter," she added drily. "And the fact that 'twas written a hundred years ago.

"What I mean is," she went on, when her nephew merely looked uncomprehending, "did you ever write one of those every-other-letter or every-third-word codes to your friends when you were a child? Your uncle William was forever getting me to do so when he was trying to slip information to those good-for-nothing friends of his that he didn't want Papa to see. He was terrible at it," she explained. "They always sounded hideously labored, and words like *gambling-debts* and *liquor* are nearly impossible to conceal, if you're supposed to be writing about the new shirt your mother is making for you. And writing the operative words in Latin didn't do any good because Papa reads Latin as if it were English . . . considerably better than William or his friends."

"So if 'twere every third word or something like that," said Katy, perusing the disgraceful account with interest from her perch on the corner of John's desk, "you'd expect there would be words like *tree* and *dig* and *paces* somewhere in it, wouldn't you? And there aren't. Except where Mrs. Pitts refers to a 'mighty oak . . .' "

"And letter-ciphers were even more of a nuisance," agreed Abigail. "I always had to go fishing about for words that had a *q* or a *y* in just the right place, until I was astonished that Papa couldn't tell at a glance that William's notes to his friends were ciphers, they read so clumsily."

Horace still looked a little puzzled, but Weyountah nodded. "I see what you mean, m'am. I expect one needs imagination to . . . to feel that there's something amiss like that. Is your father an imaginative man?"

Abigail smiled at the recollection of that kind and steady old scholar back in Weymouth. "He's an excellent man," she said, "and a compassionate man—which requires a certain type of imagination, and one that is in short supply generally in the world. But he's not fanciful. He can write a very fine sermon, but when he reads a text, the only thing that he sees is its meaning, not . . . not what might be implied about the writer by its form. What I'm saying is that the paper Mrs. Lake gave to Horace to translate might not have been a cipher at all."

"Then what was it?" asked the Indian in surprise.

"And why have me translate it?"

"She didn't *know* it wasn't a cipher, goose," said Katy, leaning forward to pluck the paper from Horace's hand again.

"I don't think she knew quite what it was," said Abigail. "'Tis why she—and whoever hired her—needed it translated . . . and didn't trust her, by the way: you said that the original had been copied by someone who didn't know that Arabic is written right to left . . ."

"Which should let out the Governor," put in Horace, taking the paper back. "Whatever Mr. Adams says of him, he's an educated man and knows that much."

"Might *she* have copied it, though?" Katy leaned around

his arm to look at it. "Got at it at the Governor's, I mean, and made her own copy to beat him to the treasure?"

"What I think happened," went on Abigail, "is this: whoever broke into the Reverend Seckar's house found *some* of the books, one of which had what *appeared* to him—or her—to be a cipher or secret writing in it. The sheets were probably either written on a flyleaf or tucked in loose, as you say Mr. Fairfield tucked papers into his books. He—or she—took it, and only after 'twas translated, realized that it was no cipher at all but merely notes for blackmail that were never used."

"And that's when he started looking for the other books!" said Horace excitedly. "He must have known about Old Beelzebub's treasure from the Governor, if it's not His Excellency himself we're talking about—Poor George! If he hadn't waked when he did . . ."

"Then it might have been you the following night," said Katy softly. "Or Weyountah the night after. And one of you *would* have waked—I can't imagine how anyone would poison you, Horry, you don't eat anything but vegetables and clabbered milk—and seen someone in his room that he knew . . ." She looked over at Abigail. "'Twas why he was killed, wasn't he? Because he recognized whoever it was he saw."

"I think so, yes."

"If 'twas someone working for or with the Governor," said Weyountah, "'twould stand to reason that George would have known him from the Volunteers, wouldn't it?"

Abigail nodded. "I don't say it couldn't have been someone like Bruck Travers—did Bruck and the others in the Watertown Committee of Public Safety know where George's room was, Katy?"

"Of course. There's dozens of the college men in the Sons or the militia, and that's not counting the college servants. But for one thing Bruck wouldn't know one book from another, and for another, I met Seph Nuttall from the militia in the market day before yesterday and asked him about where Bruck was that evening, and he was drilling with the militia in Watertown. Two hundred men saw him. Are you truly going to desert poor Diomede?"

"What, because Sam Adams told me to?" Abigail sniffed. "But to remain on his good side—because we may very well need his help before all's done—I think 'twere best we go to Charles Town tomorrow, and at least have a look at this Avalon, and see what its weaknesses are and if we can catch a glimpse of its proprietress. And in the meantime—"

"She didn't . . . She was quite modestly dressed," protested Horace. "She didn't have the air of a—er—*meretrix* . . ."

"Obviously she knew enough not to dress like a bird of paradise," said Abigail, "for fear of frightening her own bird away. You'd never have gotten into the carriage with her," she explained, to Horace's inarticulate protest that he wasn't *that* much of a shrinking violet, "if she'd been tricked-out and tire'd up and painted to her eyes like Jezebel at her window. I claim no knowledge of ladies of ill fame," she went on thoughtfully, "but it sounds to me—does it not to you?—that she's more than the answer to some sailor's prayer. She could steal a key, but a carriage and pair is another matter, even for the madame of a house of accommodation. Would you know her again?"

"Of course."

"If she were dressed differently, I mean, and painted up?"

He blushed. "I think so. Her hair was her own; I'm not sure I'd know her in a wig."

"Then let us make a pilgrimage tomorrow," said Abigail. "I can do that in the morning before John gets home—and see what we can see before Sam takes matters into his own hands.

For when a man will truly stop at nothing, there is no telling who may be hurt."

She asked the boys to stay for dinner, and prepared the lamb (only she would have gone bail that it was actually mutton) dressed with spinach, and put up a pan of potatoes beneath the hearth-coals to roast and some corn-and-milk for Horace. Johnny and Nabby came home from school, and Abigail let them thoroughly explore the cleaned and tidied house before starting them on their chores. Though the spring evenings were long, she guessed that once darkness fell, the children would be uneasy in a house that had been entered and ransacked by strangers, had they not had the chance to patrol it by daylight and see with their own eyes that all was safe. The boys departed immediately after dinner with a basket of provisions for themselves and another to be delivered to Diomede in the Cambridge jail—and Weyountah returned fifteen minutes later with Charley, whom Abigail had not even missed in the confusion of good-bys and who had managed to follow Horace and Weyountah nearly to Summer Street.

Since the handsome Indian didn't return a second time she assumed he did, in fact, make it through the town gate by sunset, though he and Horace—unless they found a friendly farmer with a wagon—would beyond all doubt be walking the last mile back to Cambridge in the dark.

Between dinner and supper, she and the girls put up laundry to soak—Abigail's housewifely instincts revolted at not having spare sheets clean and ready at all times—and as she at last led her little household in Bible reading and evening prayer, she reflected that few Israelites in Pharoah's brick-pits had put in a more strenuous day than her own.

* * *

Friday morning was, fortunately, a mild one. While Katy and Nabby milked the cows ('twas miraculous what one more pair of hands would do for the household), starting the moment it was light enough to see, Abigail and Pattie beat and rinsed, beat and rinsed the lye-smelling oceans of laundry, and had sheets, shifts, shirts, and clouts flying like flags from the maze of clotheslines in the yard by noon. By one (Charley had disappeared again, to be rescued by Katy from almost beneath the hooves of a dray on Cornhill), Abigail and Katy were crossing the Charles Town ferry.

"No sign of them yet." Katy folded up the brass spyglass she had drawn from her pocket to look out past the steep promontory of Copp's Hill toward the bay. No need to specify who *they* were.

From here Abigail could see the brick walls of the British camp on Castle Island and thought with deep regret of her friend Lieutenant Jeremy Coldstone, the assistant to the Provost Marshal and a young man, she sensed, who might greatly assist her in the unraveling of this tangle of codes and books and treasure that seemed to appear and disappear. But with tensions rising every day in Boston, it would be impossible these days for Coldstone to enter the town unmolested— particularly if Sam got word of his presence.

And in any case, reflected Abigail, the young lieutenant undoubtedly had enough to deal with these days. But she wondered what the men in the castle fort were doing to pass the time while *they* waited for word from the King to come.

"Do you think there will be fighting when they come ashore, m'am?"

Abigail sniffed. "I think there'll be fighting the first time the Royal Commissioner's bodyguard attempts to get a drink in a tavern. 'Tis all the prediction I feel can be made with certainty. As for Sam's contention that we'll face a flotilla and an invasion-force, I can scarcely see where the King is likely to find, at short notice, soldiers enough to hold a city the size of Boston. My guess is that he'll send a Royal Commissioner, not an invading general, with orders to the colony to pay for the tea. 'Tis an understandable request but not worth battle in the streets."

"To Mr. Deems, 'twould be. And Bruck Travers and his father. And George, I'm afraid," the girl added sadly. "Just the thought that patriot militia would have the temerity to form in defiance of the King's rule had him red in the face. Joseph Ryland had to talk him out of taking the Volunteers on Saturdays to attack the militias while they drilled."

"That's all we would need." Abigail folded her shawl around her shoulders at the chill of the sea-wind.

"'Twouldn't have been much of a battle," pointed out Katy practically. "They're barely a handful, and half of them not mounted, nor armed. They'd only come to the drills to cheer the others on and wear the uniforms and drink punch. At least our men have guns."

"And massacring them would solve something? Besides giving Parliament a far better reason than a little saltwater tea to send in a few regiments to keep order?"

Katy was silent for a moment, considering this, tucking the trailing streamers of her black hair back beneath her cap. In a somewhat smaller voice she said, "Well, howsoever, Ryland talked George out of it. He's got a great deal of sense and is a fine soldier, even if he does look at me as if I'd just crawled up out of a drain."

"Because you're a patriot?" Abigail had heard the slight break in her young companion's voice.

"I daresay it's what he tells people—and himself. But me, I think 'tis because he's been writing love-poems to Sally

SUP WITH THE DEVIL

Woodleigh and sending her flowers, and she won't so much as turn her head to say hello in the street but makes—made"—she corrected herself—"sheep's eyes at George." She was silent for a time; the brass tube of the spyglass forgotten in her hand, she looked out across the violet chop of the bay toward Charles Town, rising on the slopes of its hills.

"I saw her Tuesday when I went to Cambridge," the girl continued after a time. "I went to the King's Chapel, to—not to *see* George, because of course the door's locked, but to . . . I don't know. He's dead—'tis only his body in there . . . cold clay. But 'tis the body I held in my arms. The mouth I kissed; the fingers that would braid my hair. His hair was so soft, like silk . . . I know he's not in there, but . . ."

She shook her head, looked away across the bay again, her eyes clouded with grief. "And Sally was there. All in black, with a veil on her bonnet, as if she'd lost a husband, instead of a man she'd talked herself into thinking wanted her. I don't think she even saw me there. She had her maid with her, and Mr. Heywood from the Volunteers. She was taken faint and leaned on his arm."

The Charles Town wharf was drawing near. Young Mr. Peasley, the ferry's captain, shouted himself crimson while the two deck-boys swung the yard this way and that, trying to catch sea-wind against the inshore gusts that blew off the hills behind the town. Abigail clung resolutely to the edge of the bench where she sat and fixed her eyes on the tall green summit of Bunker Hill.

"He didn't lead her on to think it of him, did he?" she asked, and remembered the young man's careless smile. The Sally Woodleighs of the world, at least, were not to be caught with faked marriage ceremonies . . . but even if she had not truly sent the message, asking for a meeting behind the barn, George Fairfield at least had believed that she *would* have.

"No!" retorted Katy. "At least—I don't think he did."

"Did she favor one above another, of the others?" Abigail asked. "The Black Dog, for instance?"

"Oh, you heard about the fight that Saturday, did you?" Katy managed a pale and crooked grin. "'Tis funny, in spite of the things Mr. Ryland called me—he and George got into a *tremendous* quarrel about me—I could almost feel sorry for the poor man. Teaching her chemistry and writing love-poems—he really does write his own, you know . . . Mr. Apthorp pays Beaverbrook to write his—'tis like watching some poor mouse in a trap, running round and round against the wires, and you know he's never going to get out. Look, there's Weyountah!" She pointed, her face breaking into a brilliant smile. "And Horace, there on the wharf! What are you going to say to this Mrs. Lake when you find her?"

"It depends," replied Abigail, as the ferry at long last was drawn up alongside the wet, dark bollards, "upon how we find her and where."

Though it had been the original capital of the colony, Charles Town was barely more than a bustling little village these days, built on the footslopes of two tall hills at the mouth of the Mystic River and slightly less than three-quarters of a mile end to end along the shore. The house known as Avalon stood a few hundred yards from the ferry landing, east of the town proper, in a discreet grove of trees just where the gentle slope of Breed's Hill began to steepen. Abigail wouldn't have guessed it was a place of ill repute, save that Weyountah and Horace had inquired at two alehouses and had received the same directions from both. Avalon certainly bore no resemblance to the slatternly taverns along the Boston waterfront. It was built in the old style, partly of timber and partly of brick, with tall gables and an upper story that overhung the lower.

The sign above its door depicted—not much to Abigail's surprise—a woman's arm emerging from the waters of a lake, caressing rather than brandishing the upright sword.

"'Tis known in town as an alehouse," said Weyountah, as the little party walked along the road that curved toward the brick kiln at the foot of Moulton's Hill some half mile ahead. "Though the man in the taproom at the Peacock gave me a wink when I asked after the place—by which I assume that it is indeed what we're looking for."

"With a nice, sheltered approach on the other side of the hill," murmured Abigail, as they reached the place where the road curved northwest again toward Bunker Hill. "Invisible if you're coming in from Cambridge or Medford in the dusk, I daresay." She looked back toward the Avalon. "I don't see anyone about, do you? Though I don't imagine there's much activity here 'til nightfall. Still, one would expect servants at least and some sign of smoke in the kitchen chimney . . . and grooms about the stables. Best you stay out of sight, Horace. Shall I knock on the front door and see if I can at least get a look at this Mrs. Lake?"

Horace looked shocked, but Weyountah only said, "Lend Horace your spyglass, Katy; the trees across the road here ought to be close enough. Can you see the door clearly, Horace? No, turn it—that way. Good. Mrs. Adams?" He offered her his arm, and Katy drew her cloak-hood up over her head and did her best to look like a respectable servant-girl as she trailed Abigail and the Indian back toward the front door. With the trees thick with spring leaf, the whole dooryard of the house called Avalon was rather gloomy, and close-up the shabbiness of the place was more evident: the dooryard muddy, the path needing gravel, the backhouses quite obviously in need of cleaning. The diamond-paned windows had not been washed recently, and the house had an air of uneasy quiet. Abigail felt herself reminded of a woman who has been struck and waits to see what will happen next.

She knocked at the door and assumed the expression of a righteous matron drawing aside her skirts to wade through garbage in a holy cause.

The footsteps inside approached the door at a near run.

The young woman who opened the door—plump, freckled, and matter-of-fact in the rather faded print dress of a servant—looked both wary and scared. And, when she saw Abigail, taken aback—

Who is she expecting?

"Please pardon this intrusion." Abigail inclined her head. "My name is Mrs. Percy. I was told I might find a woman here who calls herself Mrs. Lake, though that might not be her right name. Dark-haired, about my height"—this was a guess, from the fact that Horace hadn't noted either tallness or shortness—"a lady, I suppose you would call her . . ."

Something altered in the young woman's stance: shoulders slumped, mouth tightened, eyes . . . not grieved, but the eagerness died from her face and was replaced by anxiety.

"Is she not here?" asked Abigail. "I was told—"

"She's gone," said the girl. "She's been gone two days. I hoped you had word of her, for God's honest truth, there's not one of us that knows what to do."

Eighteen

H ave you spoken to the constable?"
Abigail's tone of genuine concern seemed to have its
effect, for the girl's guardedness faded, and wry resentment
took its place. "Oh, aye, *that* did us a world of good! 'Run off
with some other man,' was all *he'd* say—and so he wrote to
Mr . . . to Mrs. Morgan's friend, who was good enough to buy
her this house."

"I daresay," remarked Abigail, "if Mrs.—Morgan, is it? It
would be. If Mrs. Morgan's friend had ever instructed some
one of the Town Council to quash objections by Mr. Munn"—
she named the Charles Town constable, a member in good
standing of the Sons of Liberty—"concerning Mrs. Morgan's
way of life, he might well turn spiteful—"

"*Him?*" The girl sniffed. "Spite's old Munn's middle name,
right after Hypocrisy, carrying on the way he does with his
wife's own sister. And what's it to him anyway if Mr. Chamberville wants a little comfort from time to time and a woman
who'll let him know he's welcome in her bed? When I was a

little girl," the servant added, shaking her curly head, "and I'd cry 'cause we weren't rich, my auntie would always say, 'If we were Quality, you'd have to marry some old merchant whether you wanted to or not, old enough to be your da.' I didn't understand then, but Lord, hearing about when people marry for ships and lands and warehouses, I understand now. There," she added. "I've spoke too free, m'am, but it just makes me mad as fire—"

"You probably ought not to have," said Abigail encouragingly, "since you've your position to think of. But, though I've always counted myself a Christian woman, I'm afraid I agree with you—" She let the end of the sentence hang with an unspoken question.

The servant said, "Dassie. Dassie Mitchell. Please do come in, m'am; it won't do you any good if you're seen standing outside this house, the way folk around here talk as if they hadn't anything better to do with their days. Belinda!" she called out, as she closed the door behind Abigail and her party. "Nancy! No word," she said, to the two young ladies who appeared in an inner doorway, a blonde and a brunette clothed, like Dassie, as maidservants, but in dresses far newer and more stylish.

Abigail guessed it was Dassie who did the actual work in the house.

"This is Mrs. Percy. She came— Who was it who told you to come, m'am?"

As they crossed through the beautifully furnished parlor and proceeded to the kitchen, Abigail spun her story—freely lifted from events that had befallen one of her father's parishioners some fourteen years ago—of the daughter of a fictitious elder brother who had been lured into a pretend marriage with a Frenchman, who had (she said) abandoned poor Pamela in Boston. A friend of the family had recommended Abigail inquire of the proprietress of the Avalon in Charles Town, Pamela being young and very pretty—"That frightful mother of hers seems to feel that sin is sin and that the Avalon is no better than some of those . . . those *kennels* down along the Boston wharves—"

"Your sister-in-law must be related to half the women in Charles Town, then," remarked the dark-haired Nancy drily, as she poured out her mistress's tea. "And to my stepmother and aunts as well. It's not like this is a sailors' knocking-shop, begging your pardon m'am for speaking so free—"

It was in fact, Abigail gathered, what John (and several English novelists) referred to as a House of Accommodation: a venue where those who could afford it could bring their mistresses for a few hours' congress. Mrs. Morgan provided for the rental of clean, youthful temporary mistresses along with the rooms more as a sideline than a principal business—

"Though mind you, m'am," said Dassie earnestly, "you'd think those sniffy mamas in this town would be glad the girls are here, when you think that if those boys over at the college didn't have a place to come visit—as boys will—"

Blonde Belinda winked at Weyountah, who inclined his head to her politely and passed her the plate of slightly stale cakes.

"Why, think what trouble they'd get into with the respectable girls in the town! Like your poor niece!"

Abigail's mind—always ill-regulated concerning points of doctrine and morality—momentarily scouted the question of whether this was more or less sinful than an out-and-out house of prostitution: it actively encouraged double adultery rather than simple fornication. Then she glanced sidelong at Katy, who was looking around the kitchen with great curiosity and obviously didn't connect any of this tale of falsified marriage-vows and wheedling seducers with herself. Did she really believe that the young heir to five thousand acres of

Virginia tobacco would genuinely marry the daughter of the head hostler at the Yellow Cow?

And if she did, what then? That he'd take her home to the master and mistress of a plantation and present her to them as their daughter-in-law?

And a dyed-in-the-wool patriot to boot?

Gradually—by dint of interest, sympathy, and letting the three confused and worried servant-girls simply talk—the story emerged. Wednesday afternoon—May fourth—Mrs. Morgan had gone for a walk, as she generally did before dinner . . . dinner being served at the fashionable hour of five, rather than at three or four as working-folk did. The girls didn't think much of it when she didn't return for dinner. It happened—not frequently—that Mrs. Morgan's particular friend would cross over from Boston where he lived, and they would meet to go driving. Only when night fell—the moon being on the wane— did they begin to worry, but there was a gentleman scheduled to come calling Wednesday night with a lady friend, and with one thing and another, none of the three of them—Nancy, Dassie, nor Belinda—quite knew what steps to take.

"And did not Mr. Grimes or Mr. Hicks have anything to suggest?" inquired Weyountah, which caused the girls to look at one another worriedly. "It is Mr. Grimes who has charge of Mrs. Morgan's stables, is it not?" he asked, as if the matter were common knowledge, and Nancy nodded.

"They said not to worry, that she'd most likely met Mr.— met her friend—and would be back late." With her long face and wide, rather mannish shoulders, Nancy was nowhere near as pretty as Katy or Pattie, Abigail judged, but she had a smooth briskness to her and a lovely velvet voice. *She probably has half the boys in the college in love with her. And is certainly more obtainable than Sally Woodleigh.*

"Might she have gone to Mr. Chamberville's house near

Concord with him?" asked Abigail smoothly. "I believe you said she had a key—"

Again the girls traded frowns, not remembering whether one or the other of them had mentioned Mr. Chamberville's name and, if they had, whether they'd also mentioned the Concord house or whether or not Mrs. Morgan had the key to it. It was Dassie who said, "I don't think she'd have gone there, m'am. Not with rebels all over those parts, as they are, and every sort of rumor flying about. Mr. Chamberville hasn't been next or nigh Concord in months."

"And did *you* write to Mr. Chamberville about this? Or is Mr. Munn the only one he's heard from?"

"M'am, to tell you the truth we haven't the least idea what it's best we do," replied Nancy. "'Twould be different if any of the three of us had family, or a friend who'd so much as acknowledge us in the street—not that a one of 'em would recognize our *faces*! Begging your pardon, m'am," she added. "The household money's gone—that's the first thing we checked, unless she moved where it's hid again—and 'tis only a matter of time before Mr. C takes his house back. And Mr. Grimes—"

"Here he comes!" Belinda, who'd been sitting near the window, sprang to her feet.

"Grimes—?"

"Cornishman."

"Hide us," commanded Abigail sharply, and Nancy flung open the door of the backstairs, then caught Weyountah's arm as Abigail and Katy darted up the narrow, boxed-in flight.

"You stay. He knows someone's here—"

The door shut. Much as she wanted to get a look at one of the men whom she strongly suspected of breaking into her house, Abigail knew how these narrow, concealed kitchen flights carried the sound of ascending footfalls. If she stayed for a look through the door-crack, she couldn't later flee

upward if the Cornishman had enough imagination to disbe-
lieve the girls and checked the backstairs. Pushing Katy
ahead of her, she ascended in almost complete darkness, thrust
open the door at the top, and emerged into a hall furnished—
as the parlor was downstairs—with the newest style of straight-
legged chairs, a small marble-topped table, and a painting by
an inferior artist of Venus putting on her makeup.

Abigail signed Katy sharply to stay where she was, then
moved with all the silent care of which she was capable—and
having grown up with William for a younger brother, there was
little she hadn't learned about sneaking in silence—from one
door to the other of the four rooms that opened from the hall.

Two bore the appearance of guest-rooms—beds with French
hangings of brocaded silk—one was a parlor with a large mirror on the ceiling, and one, Abigail guessed, belonged to Mrs.
Morgan—the Lady of the Lake—herself. She signed to Katy
again—*Wait*—and slipped inside, stepping carefully on the
worn oak planks. The dressing table bore silver combs and
brushes—putting paid, reflected Abigail wryly, to Mr. Munn's
theory that Mrs. Morgan had run off with another man—and
investigation of the highboy showed that she hadn't taken any
chemises or petticoats, either . . . or at least that she hadn't
taken so many that it showed.

Abigail checked all the drawers of the highboy and between
the mattresses of the bed—no book, no notes, no mysterious
manuscripts in Arabic, and no household money. She crossed,
stepping carefully, to the dressing table, examined its drawers,
and found only an astonishing quantity of white lead, carmine,
pomade, rice-powder, and kohl. *Drat the woman . . .*

And in a corner of the dressing table, an ink-bottle.

Half empty.

And a used quill. Much used, in fact, its tip was whittled
down nearly to the feather.

Abigail gathered her skirts about her, knelt carefully, and reexamined the marble surface of the dressing table itself.

Ink-stains. Granny Quincy had owned a marble-topped table, and Abigail knew exactly what happened if you didn't wait until the ink was absolutely dry before you turned the sheet over to write on the back—you ended up having to rub and polish with solutions of oxgall and wood-sorrel and chalk, listening to Granny Quincy's lectures on cleaning all the while.

So what had Mrs. Morgan been writing up here that she wouldn't write at her very pretty gilt secretaire in the parlor downstairs?

Gently, Abigail removed every drawer from the dressing table in turn and found the papers tacked to the back side of the lower left-hand one. Four pages torn out of what looked like a housekeeping book; two bearing a laborious, crooked-lettered copy of Arabic writing; and two written over with the now-familiar dialog (and descriptive prose) between Lt. Governor Morgan and Mistress Pitts in a woman's strong hand.

Footsteps in the backstairs—Abigail knew she'd been correct, they vibrated all over the house—and a voice calling softly, "Mrs. Percy—!"

Abigail shoved the papers into her pocket, wiggled the drawer back onto its runners, and darted to the window in time to see a huge, hulking man in a corduroy coat crossing back to the stables: the Cornishman. His head was cropped so closely it might almost have been shaved, and he carried it thrust forward, rather like an animal that has only recently learned the trick of walking on its hind legs . . .

"He's gone," said Nancy, as she and Katy entered the bed-room together.

Abigail heaved a convincing sigh—not entirely feigned—and put a hand to her chest: "What did he want? I vow, I was ready to go under the bed—"

"And you'd have done well to," replied the dark-haired girl. "He's a foul one to cross, and the more so when Dubber's not around, for he hasn't the brains on his own to know when it would pay him to hold on to his temper. Your redskin friend's got a ready tongue in his head," she added, with her sidelong, triangular grin. "I was afraid he'd get himself into trouble when the Cornishman demanded what he was doing there—he'd seen there was someone at the house—but Lord! The excuses and the whining, and letting the Cornishman bully two shillings out of him before he slunk out of the house with his tail between his legs—our boy never even thought there might have been someone else here. But," she added, "it's best you go. He's a nasty piece of work, and you were right to hide. He wouldn't think twice of telling your husband you were here, and getting money to keep quiet about it . . . and maybe worse, for your girl here."

She put a brief arm around Katy's shoulders.

"Is the coast clear?" asked Abigail. "Dassie said there were three of them . . ."

Nancy smiled—very briefly—at her use of the smuggler's slang, but only said, "Grimes and Hicks went off to town this morning. Hicks and the Cornishman are straight off the boat this year, but Grimes has friends in town. And to tell the truth," she added, as she led Abigail down the main stair to the front parlor downstairs, "that has me worried, for I wouldn't put it past Grimes to sell us—Belinda and me—to one of those waterfront kens your sister-in-law spoke of . . ."

"*Sell* you?" Abigail stopped in the doorway.

Nancy regarded her with a dark eye full of wry amusement. "You truly are an innocent, aren't you, m'am? Girls with no family, no one to speak for us and—God knows—no way of making a living, save what she and I have done since we were thirteen . . ."

She put an arm around Belinda's shoulders, as she had Katy a few moments before, and hugged her, all the beauty leaving her face for an instant, shadow in her wry and tired eyes. "I could probably sew a straight seam for twelve inches if the salvation of humankind depended on me doing so, but Belinda would need six months' teaching by St. Martha herself to learn to sweep a floor. Don't you worry, m'am," she added, seeing Abigail's face. "I've saved a little and so has Dassie, and if Mrs. Morgan isn't back by morning, we'll be out of here. What was your niece's name, m'am? The girl you're looking for? Pamela, yes—Pamela what? Not that she'll use her right name . . . If I see her, m'am, I shall tell her you're looking for her and will help her . . ."

"Thank you," said Abigail, with difficulty retrieving her appearance of concern over that fictitious damsel's plight in the face of this tall young woman's genuine fears.

"And confusion to your nasty old sister," added Nancy with her tight-lipped grin. "And to my nasty old aunt as well, and Belinda's ma, and all them others . . . Well. Now best you be gone. Last thing any of us would need is for Dubber and Newgate to come strolling up and see you here . . . Ah, there's your chief, I see him in the trees. Good luck to you, m'am."

And with a smiling wave at Weyountah, Nancy closed the door, leaving Abigail with a good deal to think about as she and Katy crossed the road.

Nineteen

"That isn't my hand," protested Horace at once, when Abigail showed him the paper she'd taken from Mrs. Morgan's dressing table. "'Tis a fair copy, though, of what I wrote . . ."

"At a guess, I'd say Mrs. Morgan copied it for herself the moment you were out the door." Abigail handed him the other sheets, which he turned over in puzzlement. "Not the same ones you translated from? But the same text, no?"

"Yes. Copied left to right by rote again—"

"Precisely. Mrs. Morgan is working for someone: possibly the Governor, possibly—dare I breathe a sullying word upon a reputation so spotless?—Black Dog Pugh—"

"Catch me," remarked Katy, "ere I faint with shock." They lengthened their steps as they came near to the first houses of Charles Town, and the bright sharp breeze from the harbor flapped at the women's cloaks.

"Do you see a rash on my neck?" asked Horace of Katy, as they dropped behind a little. "I think one of those trees was a poisonous sumac . . . And I was bitten to pieces by gnats . . ."

"Goose, the only mark there is where you've scratched yourself . . ."

"I thought Miss Belinda looked like the sort of—er—young person who might attract Pugh's attention," said Weyountah. "If he isn't corrupting some presumed-virtuous young matron in Cambridge instead. What have you there?"

"Letters purporting to be from my husband," said Abigail, "and my great-uncle, Justice Mercer from Haverhill . . . Look at the paper. And the ink." She held them against Mrs. Morgan's copies of both text and translation. "Not that 'tis proof—we couldn't take it before a court and hope to impress anyone with the existence of conspiracy—but it confirms what I've thought."

"Yet the hand on the forged letters is a man's." Weyountah paused in his steps, held the two forgeries that had brought Horace into the business up to the light as he had done not quite two weeks ago at the Golden Stair.

"Is it anything like Pugh's? It's disguised, I know," Abigail added, as the Indian opened his mouth to point out that very fact. "But is there any similarity?"

"I can see none, but that means nothing. Horace would know his writing—we've both seen it on enough notes we've been sent with—and we know he's a fairly pretty forger from his imitation of Mistress Woodleigh's."

"I wonder if she wrote him love-letters as she did to George?" Abigail frowned, thinking of those wholly conventional outpourings of passion that George had been carrying in his pocket on the night he died . . . on the night Pugh had lured him out of his room . . . *Why carry Mistress Woodleigh's love-letters when the rest were all chucked into his desk?* "Are you returning to Cambridge?" she asked, as they turned along the street toward the ferry landing.

"We were, yes," Horace replied, still rubbing uneasily at the completely invisible spots and rashes on his neck. "Ryland

is holding a sort of seminar in his rooms on translation of
Plato, and with examinations coming up, nobody wants to
miss it. One has to arrive early to obtain a seat."

"Would Mr. Pugh also attend?"

"He has in the past," said Weyountah. "He's clever—
always passing his examinations by just enough not to be
sent down."

"Then I think the time has come," said Abigail, "to make a
search of Mr. Pugh's chambers and see if there is more there
than expensive coffee and brandy smuggled from France."

There was a certain amount of discussion in the ordinary
of the Peacock Inn—where Weyountah had left Sassy
and George's chaise—about who should ride back to Cambridge and who should walk. "I'm not going to abandon Mrs.
Fairfield by the side of the road for a four-mile walk back to
the college," stated Weyountah, as the hostler went off to harness up the little vehicle, which would take three people at a
very crowded pinch.

"Don't be silly," Katy retorted. "You need Horace to get
Mrs. Adams into the Black Dog's room to do the searching,
and you to stand guard. If old Ryland sees me anywhere in
the vicinity of the college I'll be shown off the grounds and
like as not everyone will start asking questions. I'll walk—
and I'll meet you at the jail, where I'll go to cheer up poor
Diomede and let him know he's not been abandoned and
everyone is doing all they can."

Since Abigail had repeatedly contended that an American
woman—even one as young and pretty as Katy—could go
anywhere afoot in the colony without fear of the kind of
insult that by all accounts lurked everywhere in crime-ridden
Britain, there wasn't much that she could say against the

plan. Horace provided several moving little homilies in Latin on the subject of self-sacrifice before Weyountah heaved him up into the chaise . . . The afternoon was, in fact, getting on. The Indian whipped up Sassy, and they bowled away down the tree-lined road for Cambridge.

"Did George speak much of his father?" asked Abigail, as they passed the old cemetery, and left the town behind. "Of what sort of a man he is and how he's likely to react to news that Diomede killed his son?"

"He called him 'stern,'" reported Weyountah, after a little time of thought. "And I understand their relationship was stormy, though George loved his father very much."

"More than once he spoke of how his father and his friends were forever uneasy about the idea of a slave uprising," said Horace, lowering Mrs. Morgan's copy of his translation, which he was comparing with his later reconstruction. "Like the Romans, the men of Virginia have become *servos servorum eorum*—an attitude that outraged George, I might add. But he was forever quoting his father on the subject of this trusted mammy of some friend, who had smothered the babies under her charge, or that trusted cook who'd put Jamestown weed into the family ragout. The most their cook ever did, George said, was, when she was angry with the master, spit in the coffee before bringing it to table . . . something he never told his father, because, he said, she was a very good cook and didn't get angry very often."

Abigail said, "Remind me never to breakfast with a Virginian in his home."

"But it doesn't bode well," concluded Weyountah, "for Diomede's chances of a fair hearing."

Nor did it bode well, reflected Abigail, as the little vehicle passed along the Charles Town Neck toward the mainland, for the chances that Mr. Charles Fairfield would welcome a pregnant tavern-girl with open arms, prospective grandchild or no . . .

And she was acutely conscious that at this point there was little she or anyone could do, save marshal evidence for John to use when Diomede's owner arrived . . . if Mr. Fairfield would even consent to see John or to listen to some Massachusetts lawyer explaining that George had been killed in the course of a hunt for buried pirate treasure . . . *No, we cannot prove by whom* . . .

Too easily she could hear the man simply shout, *He's my property, and he's coming back with me* . . .

Her fists tightened where they lay in her lap. *The law is established to defend a man's rights to his property* . . .

Horace handed her the paper, and as the chaise passed along between stone walls, quiet fields, and shading elm trees, she read over her nephew's translation, which, as he had said, was so close to his later reconstruction as to give little encouragement to any alternate reading. At no point did it mention paces, yards, directions, digging, or trees (beyond the single reference to a *towering oak* in a context that was clearly metaphorical), or in fact any words that could be construed as being part of a simple cipher. Nor, to Abigail's practiced eye, did it have the style of the labored cadence of words that have been selected because their fifth letter was *q*.

The only cipher involved was that Old Beelzebub had written his blackmailing account in Arabic letters to protect it from prying eyes until he should have call to spring it on Lieutenant Governor Morgan and demand hush-money. She wondered if he'd ever done so. Or was it only one more scheme he'd tucked away in the back of his alchemy books and carried north with him when he'd left the Caribbean for good?

He looked like the Devil would have, if the Devil were ever to sit in a corner of the kitchen and play the fiddle . . .

She frowned in thought, eyes narrowed against the sprinkling of the sunlight through the trees.

Yet someone at least was fairly certain that there *was* a treasure.

Well, hundreds of thousands of people in New Spain are fairly certain that all Protestants are inevitably bound for Hell, which certainly doesn't make them right.

Why did her mind hark back to the question of what had made old Beelzebub turn his back on his past? Walk away from the man he had been?

What man HAD he been?

As the chaise swung around toward the gates of the college, Abigail's glance strayed toward the King's Chapel by the Common, and a flash of black, like a crow against the green of the grass, caught her eye. A young woman in black—extremely fashionable black. Even at this distance, Abigail could tell the sable skirts gathered into the latest style of polonaise, the elbow-length sleeves festooned with sable lace and bedight with inky ribbons. Even the maidservant who followed her was in deep mourning, and the lapdog borne in the maid's arms wore a sable bow on his neck.

Weyountah said at the same moment, "Good Lord, it's Mistress Woodleigh! And there's the Black Dog coming to greet her! And comfort her, I dare—"

Abigail estimated the approach of that massive yellow-robed figure—trailed likewise by a black servant . . . "Which servant is that?" she asked as the chaise rounded the corner toward the college stables. "He has two—"

"Pedro." Horace twisted his body around in the chaise to look back. "He'll have left Eusebius in his room—"

"Let me out here," said Abigail, and dug in her pocket for pencil and her commonplace-book. Quickly she wrote:

Mr. Pugh,

'Twould be to your *GREAT ADVANTAGE to meet me at four o'clock*—a glance at the clock above the King's Chapel showed that it wanted but ten minutes of the hour—*at the Crowned Pig. Wait for me there, as I cannot linger long; this matter concerns certain BOOKS that I understand you seek.*

Althea Mainwaring

"Who's Althea—?" began Horace, and Weyountah chuckled.

"Very good, m'am! And if Mr. Pinkstone is there studying, I'm to send him on an errand to fetch a hair from the Great Cham's beard?"

"Something like that." She sprang down from the chaise and handed Weyountah the note. "Do you know anything about this Eusebius? Anything at all that I can use to keep him talking when he gets here?"

"He has a wife in the West Indies named Violetta and is courting one of the maidservants at Mr. Vassall's house," provided Weyountah. "He was brought from Africa as a youth and was trained there by the local witch doctor—"

"Was he, indeed?" asked Abigail sharply, and the Indian's eyebrows went up thoughtfully.

"So far as I know, the only thing he's used his training on in this country is making up embrocations for the Black Dog's horses and cats."

"Ah," said Abigail contentedly. "I had forgotten the cats. While Weyountah is searching Pugh's room, Horace, perhaps—

to make sure we've covered all possibilities—you have a look through Mr. Ryland's, just to see if the Governor is in the habit of sending him on errands. It occurs to me that as His Excellency's pensioner, Mr. Ryland may well have been the one who undertook the purchase of the books and can testify that indeed the Governor took possession. Now, go—"

"*I go, I go, look how I go . . .*"

"*Aquilis velociores; leonibus fortiores!*"

St-John Pugh was still deep in conversation with Mistress Sally Woodleigh as Abigail came around the corner of Massachusetts Hall and crossed the road toward the chapel. Like a good servant, the man Pedro stood impassive, his scarred face expressionless, looking around him with dark uninterested eyes. Abigail called out, "Mr. Pugh!" and was greeted with a deep bow and an off-swept cap, and introduced to Sally Woodleigh.

"I am terribly, terribly sorry to hear of your loss," said Abigail, taking the two fingers offered her in the British fashion, and Mistress Woodleigh immediately began to shed tears, silently, tragically, and without any accompanying sobs that might have rendered her lovely nose red.

"Thank you," the girl whispered—she must have been sixteen or seventeen, Katy's age, Abigail guessed—and wiped her eye with a handkerchief, trimmed in Brussels lace a handspan deep, that her handmaiden stepped forward to offer her. "Everyone has been so good . . ."

Pugh took her other hand in his and pressed it expressively; Abigail noticed the squeeze of gratitude that Mistress Woodleigh returned.

"I was never more shocked," said Abigail warmly, "as when I heard the news. I did not know Mr. Fairfield well, though my nephew thought the world of him."

"All loved him," replied the girl simply. "And I—I never understood what the poet meant, when he spoke of one's heart being in the grave. But it is, m'am. My heart is back there in that chapel—" She turned and gestured, a trifle too much like Juliet in an amateur theatrical performance. "I only go to visit it . . . and him."

"Say not so." Pugh patted the small gloved hand still in his. "Leave those of us who loved him—and others yet on this earth—still with the blossom of hope."

Sally Woodleigh, Abigail reflected, watching the dewy smile she gave him, though she had the air of one who has talked herself into believing in a grief that made her the center of attention, was clearly in actual pain; the glint in Mr. Pugh's eye could not be described as anything but amused at the scene. It was just as well that the slave Eusebius appeared at that moment, calling out, "Michie Pugh, sir! Michie Pugh! Got a message here; he say it important for you!"

Abigail watched St-John Pugh's face as he read the note she had written five minutes previously and was gratified to see how his eyes narrowed. "Thank you, Eusebius," he said. "Who delivered this—?"

"Michie Thaxter, sir. He say a woman give it to him, out by the stable; say she couldn't come into the stair."

Good for you, Horace!

The Black Dog looked as if he might have cursed, had he not been still standing next to Mistress Woodleigh. Abigail guessed he had a Rabelaisian turn of phrase. He glanced toward the Chapel tower, then turned back to the girl, and bowed deeply over her hand. "Please pardon my haste, *bellissima*; a matter of great urgency."

Certainly more urgent than Mr. Ryland's opinions on translating Plato or your own upcoming examinations, reflected Abigail, as the clock struck four.

In a sweetly pouting voice, Mistress Woodleigh chided,

"And who is this lady you're running off to see the instant she beckons?"

"A withered old trout who's done business with my father," replied Pugh at once, though Abigail had made up the name Althea Mainwaring out of thin air. "'Tis tedious, beautiful nymph, but she carries tales, and I wouldn't have my father's ill-will for worlds." He bent to kiss her hand. "I know 'tis an effort for you to shake off your grief, but for the sake of those of us who—who are deeply concerned for your feelings, will you permit me to call on you tomorrow and take you walking with me on the Common? You must have a care for your health."

"You are too kind . . ."

Abigail was afraid Pugh would prolong the scene and send Eusebius back to his room again, but evidently both men knew that Mr. Pinkstone had been left in the chamber; in any case, Pugh, after another bow and a further reverent salute on the hand of his beloved, set off at a smart pace for the far end of Cambridge, trailed by Pedro, and Abigail turned just as Eusebius was walking away.

"Eusebius," she said, as if trying to remember something about the name—and, well-trained slave that he was, the African came back. One did not walk away from a white woman who spoke to you . . . "My nephew tells me you know something of the ailments of cats?"

To her surprise the ferocious face, with its tribal scars, relaxed into a gentle smile. "Oh, pretty ones," he said in a deep bass voice, and made a gesture as if cradling a cat in his arms.

"Could you spare just a moment?" asked Abigail. "I know it sounds fond and foolish of me, but my poor cat has begun scratching at herself, constantly, poor thing . . ."

She described at considerable length symptoms displayed by Granny Quincy's sour old Black Witch the previous summer, and Eusebius listened gravely, asking questions now and then—What was m'aum chatte's age, did she have rough bumps of the skin beneath her fur, was she lose fur on her backside? Since poor Black Witch had suffered with precisely these symptoms through the past three summers, Abigail took notes of what Eusebius prescribed—putting garlic in her food, braiding herbs into a collar for her if she would take it, washing her ("She no like, so you make her do anyway, m'aum") in a solution of mild aromatics.

With luck, she reflected, handing the servant half a Spanish reale, Mr. Pinkstone would have time to return from whatever errand Weyountah had sent him on before Eusebius got back to the rooms, sparing them both anxiety about what to tell Michie Pugh . . .

She had to remind herself, as she walked round to the lane by the college stables where Weyountah and Horace waited for her with Katy—flushed and cheerful and not a penny the worse for her long walk—that Eusebius's obvious expertise with the ailments of cats was a sword that cut both ways . . . and he would have known exactly how much to dose a frumenty to guarantee that it would transform an entire household into Sleeping Beauty's castle.

"We both went in to look," said Weyountah, as Horace helped Abigail and Katy up into the chaise and the vehicle set off at a smart pace—as the sun was, yet again, sinking toward the hills and threatening to catch Abigail on the wrong side of the Boston town gates. Katy turned around to wave back at Horace, then clung to the rail of the little wicker seat, smiling into the breeze that whipped back her long black hair. "So there would be no doubt about who found what, where—"

"And did you find anything?" demanded Abigail, hearing already in his voice that they had.

"We found both George's books—the *I Modi* and the *Vies des Dames Gallantes*—in Pugh's room . . . along with considerable other literature from other sources, but along the same lines."

"And they won't tell me what the others were," added Katy. "Well, I'm a married woman," she added, as Abigail frowned at her.

"And in Mr. Ryland's room," Weyountah's voice cut inexorably over Katy's protests, "we found . . . all the rest of Beelzebub's books, save only for the ones Horace and I gave to you."

Twenty

"Hidden at the bottom of his clothes-chest, in every drawer of his desk, and four-deep beneath his mattress, Weyountah says," Abigail reported to John, who had been listening to Nabby's history lesson when—tired and famished—Abigail and Katy came into the lamplight of the kitchen after the mile-and-a-quarter walk from the town gates in the deepening dusk. Weyountah had—yet again—barely reached the gates in time, and there had been no question but that he was obliged to leave her and Katy there, and turn back for Cambridge by the thin light of the wasting moon.

"And he was certain they were Old Beelzebub's?"

"Well, aside from the question of what other fifty-four books the Governor's protégé would be concealing under his mattress . . . Please, no, I'm quite all right—" she added, when John forced her into the settle beside the kitchen hearth and went to the pantry.

"You're not," he called back over his shoulder, handing bread, butter, and slices of cold sausage and cheese back to

Nabby, who had hastened after him with plates. "Did you have any dinner at all? Or you, either, Katy? I didn't think so—"

Johnny came hurrying back to the fire with mugs of cider, followed closely by his sister and father, bearing food. Abigail had to reach up over the heads of Charley and Tommy to get her plate, both the smaller boys having flung themselves ecstatically into her lap. "Mr. Adams, really you shouldn't—!" Katy protested, and then tucked into the sausage and cheese like a starving cannibal.

"In fact," Abigail went on as John brought her small sewing-table close to the fire, "Weyountah recognized a number of them from Mrs. Seckar's house. Others had Geoffrey White-head's name written in them and dates ranging from 1630 to 1693, which was the year he died." Pattie carried lamps from where she'd been sewing and hung them on the wall near Abi-gail's head. "There were also exactly fifty-four of them, which was how many the Governor's 'man'—obviously Ryland—took away with him—"

"Only to learn that nine had been sold elsewhere." John had shaved and washed his face, but he looked deeply weary from two days on the road. Yet the fact that he had shaved told Abigail that he was going out again to meet with the Sons of Liberty at the Green Dragon while yet it was possible to do so.

"I can't really see Mr. Ryland stabbing his captain over them, even if they *had* quarrelled."

"Can't you?" He settled with his own cider on the settle at her side. "Friends stab friends every night in this colony, Por-tia, and for the stupidest possible reasons or no reason at all: drunkenness, politics, anger at someone else. Then they panic and blame someone else. You'd like to think 'twas Black Dog Pugh because he's a slaveholder and personally obnoxious—"

"And you'd like to think 'twas the Governor because he was appointed Chief Justice of the colony in 1760 with no other qualification than that he was a good friend to the Board of Trade. And we don't either of us seem," she added, spreading the soft pale cheese on the crusty bread, "to be much closer to the answer. Pugh definitely—or as definitely as we can ascertain from the paper of the note—forged Sally Woodleigh's hand to a note to get George out of his room at midnight. But whether George then lingered behind the barn in hopes of meeting the girl . . ."

"I think he did," said John. And when Abigail frowned and Katy looked aside, he went on, "Why else would he have taken the girl's love-letters, if not to return them? If not to honor-ably inform her"—he glanced at Katy—"that he had married another woman—even if he *had* bribed the quite-genuine clerk of the Providence county court to perform the ceremony in a tavern instead of the courthouse. 'Twas still a legal marriage. Easy there, girl," he added, as Katy flung her arms around his neck and kissed him, "I'm just the messenger—"

But he beamed upon the girl as she embraced and kissed Abigail as well. John was as faithful a husband as could be found in the compass of the world, but Abigail knew he had the same soft spot in his heart for pretty girls as she had for good-looking young men.

"Therefore, he could have waited—who knows how long?— for the girl to put in an appearance, and returned, disap-pointed, to his chambers and gone to bed . . . to be wakened in the dead of night by an intruder whom he recognized, an intruder who had thought him drugged and had, therefore, taken no precaution to keep silent while he searched for books that were already gone."

"It still doesn't mean 'twas Mr. Ryland."

"No," said John. "But there's a simple way to find out."

Abigail sighed, and said, "Drat. 'Tis a day's drive to Concord, so we'll not leave 'til Monday—are you away tonight, dearest friend?" She put her hand on his.

"I must." He glanced across the room to where Pattie was seating the children in a small halo of lamplight, ready for evening prayers. "In truth, Portia, none of us has the slightest idea how many nights we have left to meet freely and make plans—nor what conditions will prevail once the King's Commissioner lands."

"You won't—" She kept her hold upon his hand as he rose, and went with him to the sideboard to fetch the Bible. "There is not the possibility that *you'll* be arrested?"

"Governor Hutchinson hates me as I hate him," said John grimly. "If friends stab friends under the impulse of momentary fears, how much more will a frightened man be tempted to stab his enemy if someone puts a knife into his hand?"

Yet he went to the table smiling and asked among his children whose turn it was to pick a portion from the Holy Writ (it was Charley, so they got Samson trouncing the Philistines—with John's observations that 'twas only God's love for Samson that strengthened the hero's arm to defend the weak). Sitting at his side with the fire's warmth shining on her back, Abigail listened to her husband's voice and reflected that this man had far greater matters to deal with than one lonely and frightened black man sitting in the Cambridge jail.

That he would take up his cudgel and fight like that ancient Israelite hero for a slave's life she didn't doubt—if she pressed him to do so. He would always take on one more task, one more responsibility, one more foe, for justice's sake or his country's—until, facing an army of assailants, he went down before them in defeat.

Diomede's freedom was her battle.

Enslaved, as Samson had been enslaved (and with far less foolishness, in her opinion), and helpless . . .

Across the table she saw Katy startle, and in her wide blue eyes Abigail read sudden enlightenment, something realized that she had not guessed before . . .

When the children had been kissed and herded upstairs, and John was adjusting his wig and putting on his greatcoat, Katy came up to them, and whispered, "Can you prove my marriage to George, Mr. Adams? Weyountah looked in the back of both of George's books and found no trace of the license."

"I took notes of the date and the circumstances and the name of the clerk," said John. "I'll write them out for you if you wish—"

"Belike that scoundrel Pugh took the license to blackmail George with," sniffed Abigail, as she brought paper and pencil from the sideboard drawer. "Or to blackmail Charles Fairfield when he arrives next week. If you like, Katy, we can speak to the man—"

"Yes, later," she said breathlessly. "But if Mr. Adams will be so good as to write out at least proof that I *am* George's legal wife—and lend me Thaxter and the chaise tomorrow— then I'll go out to Cambridge and tell the sheriff that Diomede is to be tried here in Massachusetts after all. Don't you see?" She looked from Abigail's face to John's, her eyes shining with triumph. "If Diomede was George's property, then he's *mine* now, and I can arrange his trial where I please!"

Neither John nor Abigail thought this would actually work, "But you might as well give it a try," said John. Abigail had intended to send Thaxter—*who surely has enough to do just keeping up with John's legal copying so the lot of us don't starve!*—to the State House in the morning and look up if, in fact, Old Beelzebub Whitehead had owned land in the colony, with or without a stone castle and a tribe of worshipful Indians, and if so, where this had lain. But she agreed that the journey to Cambridge took precedence.

It would be another week, she calculated—as she went about her marketing, did the long-delayed mending, and prepared the usual Saturday double meals in anticipation of the following day's enforced rest and meditation—before Charles Fairfield arrived in Boston: he did not sound like the kind of man to welcome even a legitimate grandson whose mother was a tavern-maid. Having her claiming to own a valuable slave would not endear her to him nor help her cause—nor that of the slave. As she and Pattie dumped snowy mountains of ironing from their baskets to the towel-draped table (a task that should have been done yesterday, she reflected guiltily)—she mentally marshalled various schemes to help either Katy or Diomede should Fairfield prove intransigent . . . in between forays into the yard and once into Queen Street when Charley's silence indicated that he'd gone exploring again.

"At least, thanks to the Committees of Correspondence, we now know the names of Virginia lawyers to whom Katy can go," she remarked, as she sprinkled water from the bowl at her side over the first of John's shirts.

"But what if the King closes all the courts?" asked Pattie worriedly. "In Virginia as well as here."

"What?" Abigail rested the heavy iron's butt on the table-edge. "What has Virginia got to do with Sa—with *Persons Unknown*," she corrected herself, "destroying tea in Boston?"

"They're both colonies," reasoned Pattie. "You know how everyone talks about 'the Indians,' when Weyountah speaks of the Narragansetts and the Wampanoags and the Nipmucs all being completely different peoples—some of them sided with the French during the war and some with the English, and some just tried to keep out of things as best they could. What if the King and Parliament—who are farther away from us than we are from the Narragansett villages—just think of everyone over here as 'the colonies,' the way my father thinks of 'the Indians,' and think to punish us all alike?"

"It isn't the same," protested Abigail. "Each colony is a separate entity with its own government and its own agents in London. You'd have to be a fool to mix up someone from Massachusetts, for instance, with a Carolinian . . . or a Carolinian from the coast with the sort of savages they have in the northern mountains. Even the—oh, drat the boy!" she added, looking quickly around the kitchen as Tommy—fastened as usual to the leg of the massive sideboard by his leading-strings—set up a protesting wail that indicated that his interest in his toys had flagged and his elder brother was nowhere to be found.

"You, sir," she informed her errant middle son, when she finally located him in the loft above the cowshed, "are far too old to wear leading-strings, which means you are old enough to obey your mother. Where is it that you are allowed to play by yourself?"

"The house and the yard," replied Charley obediently.

"And is the cowshed part of the yard?"

"It's *by* the yard."

Abigail led Charley firmly back across the narrow expanse of bricks as Pattie reemerged from the alleyway to the street that she'd just checked—

And behind her, Thaxter and Katy, leading Balthazar.

"What happened?" Abigail let go of her son's hand, and he immediately darted to hug Katy and put himself in danger of being trodden on by the horse. "We didn't expect you back 'til near dark—"

Thaxter shook his head, and Katy flung up her hands: "'Tis all solved," she said, and beamed happily as she lifted Charley into her arms. "Diomede was broken out of the Cambridge jail last night—and old Sheriff Congreve is mad as fire."

O f course it was Sam. Even John thought so when Abigail took the news to him in his study, where he had been immured all day, sorting out depositions and writing case notes—neither the colonial courts nor the natural litigiousness of New Englanders having come to a halt just because the King might be irate over some spilled tea.

"Drat the man." John looked up from the drifts of papers on his desk. "He might at least have waited 'til we'd *seen* Fairfield—"

"He might just as well have taken out advertisements in the *Gazette* in Diomede's name saying, *I AM GUILTY*! Not to speak of making it impossible for him to ever see his wife and family again—"

"Do you think that the slave stood the slightest chance of having his innocence even considered in his master's home country? Either way, his wife and daughters would lose him, and he them. At least as things are he lives—"

"And I'll wager Sam did this," went on Abigail wrathfully, "just to get my mind off saving an innocent man's life and onto finding a treasure for him to spend on gunpowder. Beyond doubt, he didn't even ask poor Diomede if he *wished* to be saved!"

"If he didn't wish it, he's a fool." John wiped his pen carefully, set it down beside the sheet he was fair-copying—a task that was generally left to Thaxter, if that young man hadn't been halfway to Cambridge with Katy in the neighbors' borrowed chaise. "You know as well as I how difficult it is to prove a negative—even had the true murderer not cast the blame on the nearest convincing suspect. Do you truly think the father will seek truth when vengeance is right before him? Nine men out of ten will settle for the ease of heart that vengeance gives rather than press on for the more astringent taste of facts."

"Robbing Diomede of his good name, his wife, his family, his home, and all his friends . . . so that Sam can hurry me into the quest for treasure—"

"Before he himself has to flee the city?" John raised his eyebrows. "I could wish Sam would have waited to see if there were need for Diomede to flee—or be dragged—into hiding, but once Diomede's owner is present, it might have been far less simple to free him out of hand, you know. And as I have said, tomorrow or the next day or the next might have been too late for anyone to do anything."

Abigail's shoulders relaxed, and her head lowered. "You are right," she said quietly. "'Tis just . . ."

He reached across the desk and took her hand. As always his fingers felt very warm on hers, and strong. "Sufficient unto the day is the trouble thereof," he said. "Monday we'll speak to Sam and have a word with Diomede if we can. Or—" He hesitated, glancing at the mountain of work before him, clearly trying to calculate when on Monday he would have ten minutes to spare . . .

"I'll speak to Sam," said Abigail. "You needn't come with me."

"Sam is my cousin," returned John. "Thus it is incumbent upon me to keep him from being murdered in his own house—so I think 'tis best I come with you."

Abigail laughed, and returned to the kitchen and the ironing and the task of tracking down the errant Charley, who had managed to make it all the way down the alley and out onto Queen Street . . .

* * *

On Monday she and John did indeed speak to Sam, but by Monday, Diomede and his fate had been removed, suddenly and terrifyingly, from their minds.

In general Abigail had little trouble keeping her mind focused on the Reverend Cooper's sermons, for the man was a good speaker, and his arguments—if sometimes more political than theological—were well thought-out and proceeded in good order. But on Sunday, as she sat next to John for the morning sermon, she found her thoughts straying to Diomede, to the wife he had left behind him in Virginia, to the daughters he had begged to be able to write to. By breaking out of the Cambridge jail, he had virtually guaranteed that he would never be able to go home—for who would believe him when he had fled from justice?

And yet, she thought, Sam had not been obliged to do anything at all for the man. Diomede was nothing to him, save an obstacle preoccupying Abigail's thoughts and preventing her from concentrating on what Sam wanted her to do. And it was true, she reflected—as she listened to the long elaboration upon the adventures of King David and his men hiding out in the wilderness from the King whom the Prophet Samuel had deprived of his crown—that there was every chance that Sam had saved Diomede's life . . .

And how could I tell?

How can any of us tell what lies down the road we do not take?

Dr. Cooper's second sermon—after eating a cold Sabbath dinner, and reading a little to the younger children, and hearing Johnny and Nabby give their summaries of the earlier sermon to make sure they understood the matter—concerned such martial prophets as Gideon and Deborah: *Hear, o ye kings, give ear o ye princes; I, even I, will sing unto the Lord . . .*

One of the oldest songs in all the Holy Writ, her father had said: how the small nation had risen against those that would oppress it, and how the stars in their courses joined battle on the side that was right. *So let all thine enemies perish, o Lord; but let them that love him be as the sun when he goeth forth in his might.*

Sisera was coming—the King's Commissioner or whoever the King was going to send.

With who knew how great an army in his train? With who could tell what weapon in his hand?

And by what would that Commissioner be met?

Abigail walked home quietly through the beautiful light of the early evening, listening to Pattie and Katy's soft chatter behind her: the girls had remained at home in the morning to look after the smaller boys—Thaxter invariably spent Sundays with his mother, so John and Abigail took turns missing the afternoon sermon to mind the children so that the girls could attend. *If I speak to Sam just after the marketing is done tomorrow, 'twill give me time to go with him out to Cambridge or to wherever they've hidden Diomede. And if he DARE bring up the subject of Old Beelzebub's treasure, I really will strike him with a broom-handle . . .*

She turned from Brattle into Queen Street and saw, rather to her surprise—for Boston streets were quiet as a rule on the Sabbath—John. John hastening along with no hat on his head, looking right and left about him . . .

She quickened her stride in the same moment that he saw her. What she saw in his face shocked and chilled her; she gathered up her skirts and ran.

Before she could even ask him what was wrong he said, "Charley's gone."

Twenty-one

They didn't get the note until morning.

Before darkness fell Sunday evening, the whole of the neighborhood had been called into service: Tom Butler the cooper and his two sturdy apprentices, Ehud Hanson the shoemaker, Uzziah Begbie and his wife, Gower the blacksmith down the street . . .

No one had seen a sturdy fair-haired little boy, not even quite four weeks from his fourth birthday . . .

Please, dear God, Abigail prayed soundlessly as she walked along Cornhill toward Milk Street, *please let him see his fourth birthday. Let us all see his fourth birthday . . .*

The streets were Sabbath-quiet—*Thank you, God!*—without the carriages and cart traffic of the weekdays, without the cattle being herded along and the barrows, drays, flocks of chickens and geese that rendered the cobbled, crisscrossing ways so confusing for a tiny child. *He'll have set off for Aunt Eliza's*, Abigail told herself as she walked, *and gotten distracted by something else*—the handsome lawn of the Governor's house or horses being harnessed to take some fashionable "worthy" to church. In this part of Boston, at least, if a stray child was found wandering—even one of the ragged little urchins from the North End waterfront—someone would take him or her in, would ask, "Where do you live, dearie?" and if no answer was forthcoming would keep an eye on the street for a distrait dark-haired woman in her blue go-to-church gown looking up every alleyway, around every tree . . .

Eliza and Isaac Smith were horrified. Eliza and Abigail searched the garden, and Young Isaac—for all his usual talk about not profaning the Sabbath—instantly put on his hat and went out to search in the streets round about, returning only when darkness was settling over the town to offer to walk Abigail home. "Of course we'll send and let you know . . . We'll have Cuffee outside in the street watching for him . . ."

"And poor Johnny thinks 'tis his fault," said Abigail, as she and Young Isaac—still so-called though he was twenty-five years old and had his own church and congregation—made their way along Cornhill arm in arm. "Nabby was watching the younger boys and Johnny got into some kind of quarrel with her—as children do, with their rivalries over books and toys and slate-pencils. John came out of the front of the house and adjudicated the conflict, and by the time anyone looked round, Charley was gone."

"He can't have got far," opined Isaac firmly, despite the fact that his mother's house on Milk Street was far from Queen Street by anyone's stretch of the imagination and no one seemed to think that Charley had any other destination. And then—giving himself the lie—"Would he have found his way to the Common?"

Abigail looked up. Dark had fallen, and above the black jumble of rooflines, stars shone clear and glittering, like diamonds. The moon was in its last dwindle toward darkness. "*Why?*" she asked. "Your mother's house is nearer—"

"Would he have known that?" reasoned the young parson. "He could simply have gotten lost. And if he grew frightened, it could easily be that he'd hesitate to speak to a stranger . . . and there are few about the streets of a Sunday between dinner and dark."

"True," said Abigail, as they passed the tall brick tower of the Old Meeting-House and turned up Queen Street. "But Charley isn't the least shy of strangers. When he gets hungry, he'll turn to the first friendly looking stranger he meets to ask him to lead him home. And he knows he lives in—"

She broke off, seeing the men moving about the alleyway that led to the back of the house. She quickened her steps, almost snatching up her skirts to run. When she got close, she saw that in addition to her neighbors, there were four or five of the North End roughnecks whose assistance Sam could habitually call on if so be he needed a Tory's shopwindow broken or—for instance—a mob to storm the Governor's house . . .

Paul Revere was in the kitchen, talking to John. "—almost certain, 'twas the same woman," he was saying. "I'll tell Sam to get his men out onto the Common, though I cannot imagine Charley wouldn't walk up to the door of the first house he came to and knock on it, asking to be taken home— or given part of their dinner on the spot, more like—"

"You've heard nothing, then?" Abigail's glance went from her husband to her friend. "Did Sam send you?"

And saw the look that passed between the two men, that turned her blood to water in her veins. "I came on another matter," Revere said. "Sam heard today that the corpse of a woman whom he believes might be this Mrs. Lake you spoke of—the one who kidnapped your cousin Horace—"

"She didn't precisely—" Abigail hesitated on the denial, realizing that, effectively, that was exactly what had happened. And then, as the silversmith's words sank in, "Corpse?"

"A couple of boatmen"—by which Abigail knew he meant *smugglers*—"found her washed up on the rocks of Bird Island, where the river's current sets around with the tide. She was well-dressed, they said, and dark-haired. They said they'd heard from Munn in Charles Town that a woman thereabouts had disappeared."

"Mrs. Morgan," said Abigail softly. "The owner of—"

"Good Lord, not La Fata Morgana?" Revere almost laughed—he clearly knew what Mrs. Morgan was known to be—but sobered at once. "Well, I'll be . . . She's William Chamberville's mistress, isn't she? One of our dear Governor's in-laws—"

"Was she drowned?" Abigail recalled uneasily the glimmer of the river through the trees past the foot of Moulton's Hill. "The house isn't far from the river—"

John shot her a sharp glance; Revere barely raised an eyebrow. But he only said, "No, not drowned. Her throat was cut."

Whyever Revere had come to the house, he wasted no time in sending one of his men to fetch Sam, and by midnight—when Abigail finally went to bed—every smuggler, rope-beater, and out-of-work apprentice in the Sons of Liberty was moving about the streets of Boston, lantern in hand, searching for Charley. Katy went out with them. Pattie remained with Abigail to comfort Nabby's guilty tears and Johnny's even more excruciating stoic wretchedness: "'Twas only his way, my Hercules," whispered Abigail, gathering her eldest son against her side as they sat together on the settle and stroking his baby-fine fair hair. "You know how he is. If it hadn't been you and your sister, he'd have gone for the door next time one or the other of you buckled your shoe or went to the backhouse—" She said it to make them giggle, which they did. "'Tis just how Charley is right now, always wanting to be off exploring. You remember how you were, Johnny. How you had to follow Ben Clayford and his brother when they went fishing, and you climbed out the window of your room to do it—"

"I was a baby then," protested the six-year-old. "All the more, I should have been watching Charley, and not giving in to my ill-temper and sinfulness."

Nabby, on her other side, clung to Abigail's arm and began to cry softly again. "If something hasn't happened to him," she whispered, "they'd have found him by now."

This, Abigail knew, was perfectly true.

And it was also perfectly true that there were a thousand places within a quarter mile of Queen Street where a well-meaning, inquisitive boy of only-just-three-weeks-short-of-four could come to terrible and irrevocable grief.

The Long Wharf. Endlessly fascinating, and extending close to a half mile out to sea: ships, boxes, coils of rope. Wet boards slippery and slanting. Mysterious ladders extending down to the cold beryl black chop of the water.

Merchant Street, every shop and warehouse shut up and secretive-looking on the late Sabbath afternoon: cellar-doors, stacks of barrels, piles of crates that could easily fall unheard by any, pinning a little boy underneath.

In the other direction the Common, whose grassy open spaces might tempt the boy to explore further. Yet if he'd gone to the Common, what harm could he come to—?

In her mind she saw the men, nevertheless, traversing the dark rise of the ground toward Beacon Street, where the lamps of Mr. Hancock's elegant house shone against the slope of the hill.

The Mill Pond—

Abigail closed her eyes in prayer that she couldn't even phrase. Then she said, "Come. 'Twill do you no good, nor Charley either, to have you sitting up and making yourselves sick just because he's been goose enough to get himself lost. The moment he's brought back—and you know he'll be brought back and have his hide well tanned by his father for worrying us all!—I shall wake you and fetch you down."

"Might Johnny sleep in with me and Tommy," whispered Nabby, "'til Charley comes back?"

Pattie carried the sleeping Tommy up to the small room at the end of the hall, and Johnny and Nabby snuggled in together in the girl's narrow bed, like two doleful little ghosts in their white nightrails. Abigail held them and sang to them and reassured them, though neither felt much like hearing a story. When she left them, by the light of her single candle she still saw the glimmer of their open eyes.

If something hasn't happened to him, they'd have found him by now.

She leaned her head back against the hard wood of the fireside settle, staring into the silky whispers of light as they played over the embers.

He didn't start his running away until I left him at Eliza's, she thought. *Because 'twas only then that he was old enough and strong enough to get far? Because 'twas only then that he realized that a world of delight existed in her garden, which our pokey little yard could not approach in wonderment?*

Because 'twas only then that his mother would leave him with Pattie and Katy while she swanned off to Cambridge in quest of mysteries and justice?

Admit it, Portia, she told herself, knowing it for the truth of her heart and hating herself. *YOU have supped with the Devil in meddling with justice that is John's work—a man's work. You revel in "seeing through the riddles of criminal conduct," in being "a veritable Alexander . . ."*

She closed her eyes.

And this is what has come of trying to take a man's part. Her whole soul cried out in anger at this view, repeated to her throughout her childhood by her mother and aunts. She knew herself capable of more than just bearing children and washing baby-clouts . . . *It CAN'T be God's intent . . .*

Where your treasure is, there shall your heart be also, the Scripture said.

Your treasure should be here, in this house, with your children.

She could almost hear her mother saying it. And in her heart of hearts, she knew that the house was not where her treasure lay.

I am what I am! God made me what I am!

A woman, her mother's voice replied. *God made you a woman, with a woman's lesser part to play.*

"*Who can find a virtuous woman?*" the Psalmist asked, "*for her price is far above rubies.*"

Who can find her indeed, if she's left for Cambridge for the day to look for pirate gold?

"*The heart of her husband doth safely trust in her . . .*"

. . . and should be able to have faith that she won't mislay his children.

"*She will do him good and not evil, all the days of her life.*"

Abigail could almost see her mother, a tall stern woman and extraordinarily beautiful, despite the tightly pinned daycap on her raven hair and the trim dark simple dress of a minister's wife. Long hands like a queen's, roughened and reddened by laundry diligently done each Tuesday and not pushed off until some later date, by dishes washed, by floors swept. A beautiful alto voice reading the verses of Proverbs to her three too-intelligent daughters: *She worketh willingly with her hands . . . She riseth while it is yet night, and giveth meat to her household . . . She considereth a field, and buyeth it: with the fruit of her hands she planteth a vinyard . . .*

Abigail's heart protested furiously, *A man's life is at stake . . . A dozen mens', or a hundred, depending on that wretched Commissioner or whoever the King is sending that keeps John up all the night planning and organizing what can be done . . .*

But that is not your business, Abigail. She could almost hear her mother saying it.

The Scripture might proclaim, *She stretcheth out her hand to the poor; yea, she reacheth forth her hands to the needy—*

But her mother would say—and she was right, Abigail reflected in agony—that the first duty of a woman was to her children, and her second to her husband, whose children she must guard while he went and had all the peril . . .

And the excitement and the intellectual sharpening that went with it.

She felt the guilt like a physical pain, an ache in her side where Charley would curl himself up against her when, worn out with the mischiefs of a three-year-old, he would come back to her, cling to her, knowing she would keep him safe.

And she hadn't.

She woke up cold, her neck aching where her head had tipped sideways, the kitchen dark around her. The faintest glow of the unbanked hearth rimmed the pans on their hooks, the queens-ware dishes on their shelves, made copper mirrors of Messalina's wide, demented eyes. She had dreamed of arguing with John—shouting at him through iron bars that separated them, *You left them! You left them, and you left me!* knowing he would be taken away to Halifax, tried by a military court, and hanged for treason. Knowing that it was somehow her fault.

For a time she listened in the stillness, wondering what it was that had waked her. Then she rose slowly, stiffly, to stir up the fire again. Not long after that John and Thaxter came in, their voices muffled in the yard, calling out to others, thanking them . . . arranging a meeting by the Mill Pond as soon as it grew light.

"You didn't find him," she whispered, when the men came in, and John gathered her in his arms. She clung to him, trembling, trying to shove away the last stains of her dream out of her mind. Feeling in the rhythm of his breath the degree of his own dread and pain.

"We will," he said. "We will, Nab. 'Tis dark as pitch; we could have walked within a yard of him on the Common and not seen him. If he'd knocked himself senseless—falling out of a tree or off the back of a dray trying to hook a ride . . ."

He turned his head sharply at the sound of someone knocking at the front door. Thaxter, already in the hall, reached it—Abigail guessed—in two strides, for she heard the bolt clack, the hinge creak almost before the sound of the first salvo died. She and John were in the doorway of the hall an instant after that and saw by the light of the lantern the clerk still held that it was Revere and Dr. Warren in the aperture, Revere in the act of handing a piece of paper to Thaxter.

"This was on the door," he said.

GIV US THE BUKS
WE GOT YR BOY

Twenty-two

A day passed before the second note reached them, nerve-racking hours that brought Abigail close to unforgivable words with Sam, with Sam's wife Bess, with John himself. Last night she had silently cursed her mother's iron insistence upon the role of womanhood. Now, in her calmer moments—when, from long practice in forbearance and patience, she was able to take a deep breath and hold her always-unruly tongue at Sam's suggestion that they bring in Horace for an all-out attempt to find the treasure-code in the seven books before they had to be surrendered—she blessed her mother for not causing her to break irretrievably with every Adams on the planet . . . not to speak of murdering Sam.

She only said, "Bring the books here, Sam. They're going to be handed over the moment someone tells us where and when."

He looked like the words *Try to stall them* were upon his lips, but to his credit he didn't utter them. He said, "Of course. You'll have them tonight."

That had been during last night's conference in the small

hours when Sam was called back to see the note, and Abigail forbade them—any of them—to do a single thing, even call on the constables, until Charley had been returned safe. As the men were leaving, only an hour before dawn, she had caught Paul Revere by the sleeve: "Will you go out to Mrs. Morgan's house in Charles Town? You, yourself, without any others and without telling Sam— Go out and see if her scar-faced coachman and the two grooms are still there? Don't go near the place—if they have Charley there . . ."

She bit back the words, not even daring to think them.

Revere's dark eyes narrowed, but he nodded. "I won't be seen."

Unable to utter a word, Abigail squeezed his hand.

Throughout Monday, it took all her self-command not to speak of the note to the other three children or to Pattie—whose self-control she did not trust as she instinctively trusted Katy's. With the bred-in discipline of one who has spent her life taking care of animals, Katy made sure that the milking was done before the town herd-boys drove the cattle down the street to the Common in the first pink twilight of morning; Pattie saw to it that Nabby and Johnny were clean and fed and off to school. But it was Abigail who sat down with her older children before their departure, and told them that 'twas best they go to school as ever and keep their minds from Charley, whom they could not help. "The men will search the Common again today," she said, "and the fields on the other side of Beacon Hill." She repeated John's argument of last night about how impossible it was to find anything as small as a three-year-old boy in the open fields on a moonless night.

While she was comforting them, a knock sounded at the front door, and Pattie came into the kitchen a moment later with the news that Mr. Ryland, the Governor's young man, was here . . .

"You had best go," she said, and kissed the two children,

aware that her efforts at control had robbed those kisses of anything but perfunctory motion. "Pattie, will you walk with them to the school?" Both children opened their mouths in protest—being escorted by an adult was the ultimate of babyishness—but Abigail was already out of the kitchen, with barely more than a glance at the small mirror in the hall to make sure that her cap was straight and her eyes those of a Roman matron and not a wild woman.

Yet when she opened the door and saw Joseph Ryland sitting beside the parlor's cold hearth, for that first instant it took everything she had in her not to walk straight up to him and seize him by the hair: *What has the Governor to do with this . . . ?*

Then he stood and faced her, white with shock and distress. "Mrs. Adams, I beg your forgiveness, for coming to you at a time like this—"

What are you doing with Beelzebub Whitehead's books in your chamber?

She took a deep breath. "No—" She hoped her gesture would convey this forgiveness to him. "'Tis well."

Did you hire Dubber Grimes to kidnap my son? The question shattered, dissolved against the haggard suspicion in his face, the sickened expression of someone who is trying very hard not to see something that's under his nose. Faced with Ryland's honest integrity, she could no more ask that than she could ask, *Did you tell Dubber Grimes to murder Horace and leave his body by the side of the Concord Road?*

It was absurd on the face of it.

"They have found nothing?" he asked.

She shook her head wordlessly.

"His Excellency asked me—I have been at his house yesterday and today . . . He said, he has had his quarrels with Mr. Adams, but 'tis all politics; this is another matter entirely.

Have— Pray forgive me asking this, m'am . . . Have arrangements been made to drag the Mill Pond?"

"I believe so, yes."

He made haste to add, "Of course 'tis absurd to think—"

"He is only three," said Abigail quietly. "Boys that age
have neither the judgment to keep away from places of danger, nor the strength to swim or climb or scramble to safety."

Silence stood between them, and Abigail's jaw ached with
the effort not to shout at him: *What do you know? What do you
suspect? What has Hutchinson said? What has he done?* In the
young man's brown eyes she saw the agony of surmises that
he was trying his best to thrust away. And how not, when
Hutchinson was not only the man who had gotten him into
a college he could never have afforded to enter, but *who was
keeping him there now* and upon whose continued goodwill he
depended for everything?

To the marrow of her bones she knew that if she spoke of
her suspicions, his honesty would drive him back to Hutchinson: *Mrs. Adams says this of her son's disappearance—is it true?*
Too clearly in her mind she heard Paul Revere's voice saying,
Her throat was cut, of the woman whose discreet house she had
been in Friday . . .

Rage and tears and dread fought within her; the Lord only
knew, she thought, what he was seeing of this in her face.
And he would, thank goodness, attribute it simply to anxiety
for her son . . .

At length the young man said, "His Excellency—Please do
not hesitate, or let political enmities prevent either you or Mr.
Adams, from calling upon His Excellency for any assistance
whatsoever: men, authority, vessels, Writs of Assistance, whatever you require. As a father, an uncle, and a grandfather, he is
utterly at your disposal, and that of your husband. As am I."

She managed to say, "Thank you," and made herself repeat

for the third time John's argument about the moonless night and the possibility that Charley had been lying stunned somewhere, and she saw relief flood into Ryland's sensitive face. "You're quite right," he exclaimed, with an eagerness to believe that told its own tale. "And a sturdy and well-grown boy—especially of that age—could well have missed his direction to your aunt's garden, if that's what he was seeking, and finding himself in open country . . ."

Some of the awful tension left his shoulders, and his face relaxed a little and grew sad. "My mother lived in Germantown but a little distance from Philadelphia," he said. "When I was apprenticed in the city, I ran away—three or four times—only wanting to be back where the streets weren't brick, and the houses weren't tall, and there was space to walk alone among the trees and smell the earth and the river. 'Twould have been easy, I think, for your son to let himself run too far."

She met his eyes then, and asked—with a softness that surprised herself—"And is that what you think happened to him?"

And his glance ducked away, but not before she saw the pain at the back of his eyes. "I don't—"

The rear door opened and Katy came in, a pail of milk in either hand. She stopped on the threshold and regarded Ryland warily; his brow clouded as he recognized her, and his glance went sharply to Abigail's face. Abigail said, "Mr. Ryland? I believe you know Mrs. Fairfield."

His lips tightened and a dusky flush crept up over his skin, that she would give the name of his captain to the daughter of a stableman. "Servant, m'am." His bow was a vocabulary of obligation, scorn, and restraint.

Katy set down one pail and offered him two fingers, as the Tory ladies did. They were stained, where Semiramis (as she so often did) had dunged her tail.

"M'am." His bow deepened by a degree and a half from the upright over her hand. Then he was gone.

Only an hour after that, Paul Revere arrived with the news that the house called Avalon was closed up tight: shuttered, locked, the barns closed and the horses and carriage gone.

When the cows came home that night, the head herd-boy beat with his fist on the back door and handed Abigail a paper. "'Twere tied 'round Cleo's horn, m'am," he explained, "when we gathered 'em up, like."

LEAV EM DED CENNER OF Y YARD WTH LANNRN
BURNINNG MIDNIT TOMORO WEN LANRN GOES
OUT YR BOYLL BEE THER TRY AN STOP US AN
HEL BEE THER DED

Should Dr. Langdon or Sheriff Congreve be informed?" Joseph Warren handed the note back to Revere and looked inquiringly toward Sam, John, and Abigail in the lamplight.

"I don't know Congreve well enough to know whether he can be trusted to keep his hands out of the matter." Paul Revere turned the paper over in his hands, letting the gleam of the parlor fire fall upon it. Examining the writing, the ink, the quality of the paper itself, as it was, Abigail knew, his habit to study everything that came his way. "Langdon would try to interfere," he added.

"Langdon would try to interfere if he got news of a war between the Chinese and the Hottentots," remarked Sam bitterly. "He cannot be kept from interfering . . ."

"And can *you* be trusted?" With a queer, cold sense of

being someone other than herself, Abigail turned her glance to Sam. Darkness had fallen by the time the men had reassembled in the parlor; by the low gleam of the lamps on the table his face had a slightly sinister look. He made a gesture of surrender.

"John and I will go," Abigail said, without even a glance at her husband. "Mr. Revere, would you be so good as to accompany us? For the rest of you, Sam, Dr. Warren . . . I forbid you to be part of this. Any of you. My son's life is at stake, and I *will not* have interference in doing exactly as these men demand."

Revere began gently, "Mrs. Adams—"

"*No.* We will do as the note asks and nothing else. I defy any one of you to explain to me why the filthy gold collected by some pirate, no matter what noble purpose you intend to put it to, is more important to me than my child's life."

She waited for a few moments. The unruly portion of her soul—the portion that her mother had always deplored, that wondered things like how exactly HAD Jesus managed to multiply five loaves and seven fishes (*What kind of fishes?*) to feed five thousand people: had each fish regenerated its head or tail when pulled in half?—*that* portion of her soul wondered if Sam actually *would* try to argue for her putting in an effort to find the treasure in the time remaining. And wondered if she would be able to keep herself from clawing his face if he did.

But Sam clearly sensed that if Abigail didn't kill him for such an attempt, his cousin John would, and only said, "If you need any help, please—"

Abigail forced herself not to say, *You've helped enough, Sam,* and repeated what her mother had always told her: *When there is nothing to say that will help a situation, say, Thank you.* "Thank you," she said. "But we are well." In a slightly more natural tone she went on, "And I must thank you also, John says, for removing the man Diomede from harm's way—"

"Had we waited," said Sam, "we might have lost our chance completely. John—"

Sam rose from his chair, and John—who had stood unwontedly silent (for John) beside Abigail's hearthside seat—stepped forward to shake his hand.

"'Tisn't that we have no trust in you, Sam," he said, "as I hope I've no need to tell you. But not all the men you command have so complete a command of themselves as one would wish."

Sam looked on the point of saying something else—Abigail could read it in his eyes when they met John's—and she knew that what he wanted to say was, *We have no guarantee that the boy isn't already dead . . .*

And John's answered, as clearly as speech, *Don't say it, Sam. It doesn't matter.*

There were times when Abigail felt that John was the best and wisest man on the face of the planet.

In the hallway Sam turned to her, and said quietly, "If I've harmed or offended you, Nab, in any of this, I am more sorry than I can say—particularly now. I had meant to tell you earlier . . . I've spent the afternoon at the State House. 'Tis why I haven't those wretched books about me, that I said I'd return to you. I've been looking through every record and transaction recorded by the colony, hoping to circumvent our friends' quest for the cipher by finding Old Beelzebub's stone castle and the remains of his Indian village . . . For where a man's heart is, there will his treasure be also."

He cocked a wry eyebrow.

"And?" said John, and Sam shook his head.

"Nothing," he said. "Barring the Cambridge town-lot and three lots in Boston, no Whitehead in this colony owned land before 1693—the year after Old Beelzebub died."

"You mean," said Abigail slowly, "that there *is* no treasure?"

"There may well have been." Sam picked up his lantern from the bench in the hall. "Geoffrey Whitehead could have buried or concealed some kind of treasure in Massachusetts, either Spanish gold—if he really was a pirate—or whatever coin he had, if he happened to be staying in an area that was overrun by King Philip's warriors in '75. But 'twould have been a cache hidden away in haste and gone back for, I think, the moment the Indians were driven off."

"Which our Governor," said John grimly, "seems to wish to conveniently forget. You're sure there's no record of his owning land in the west?"

"Nothing." Sam flipped open the lantern's door, held it steady while John lit the candle within it from his own. "Which has never stopped Hutchinson from going after something he thinks is there for the taking. Well, I wish the man joy of those books, cracking his so-called scholarly attainments against Arabic chemistry texts and alchemical discussions of how to make gold out of lead . . . Believe me, I've been over all seven of them with a magnifier and calipers, and haven't found anything in them that looks like a cipher to me. Fear not," he added, and bent over Abigail's hand. "All will be well."

He turned to where Revere and Warren waited for him on the doorstep. Abigail folded her arms beneath her shawl and watched from the doorway as those three bobbing blurs of yellow light disappeared down Queen Street. Far off, the crier's voice could be heard in the still night, *Nine o'clock of a clear night, and all is well . . .*

Twenty-three

True to his word, Sam sent the seven books, made up in a package thickly bound with string and crusted with blots of sealing wax, via Paul Revere. The silversmith arrived in Queen Street midmorning, driving his own light chaise with his quick-stepping little mare Ginny tethered and saddled behind. Johnny and Nabby had been sent off to school with instructions to go to Aunt Eliza's in Milk Street when they were done: Pattie had taken Tommy there as soon as the house was tidied and the marketing done for Thaxter, who would remain in the house. Neither Johnny nor Nabby had been much comforted by John's explanation that he and their mother were going across to the mainland to widen the search ("How would he have got over there, sir?" had been only the least acute of Johnny's questions), and it cut Abigail like a knife to see the confusion and suspicion in her son's eyes as he understood that he was being kept outside of the truth.

She tormented herself on the drive by conjuring visions of some independent scheme of Johnny's to discover the truth of his brother's whereabouts for himself. Nabby, silent, had simply nodded, her blue eyes a world of wretchedness—as if she, too, understood that something was appallingly wrong beyond what was being said—and Tommy had only cried.

They crossed the Neck to Roxbury, Katy riding pillion behind Revere, and reached Cambridge a little after noon. Weyountah and Horace were horrified at Abigail's news and offered a) to immediately try to decode whatever might be in their books and b) to stand watch with as many of their classmen as required, all around Harvard Yard, that night at midnight, to apprehend the villains when they came to the appointed meeting-place. Abigail firmly quashed both suggestions.

"What I will ask of you," she said, "is that in the meantime you show us old Reverend Seckar's house, that was Emmanuel Whitehead's."

Revere went off in search of Sheriff Congreve—he seemed to know everyone in the colony—and returned with the keys to the Seckar house, which had been closed up upon the quarrelsome old professor's death, pending disposal by the College.

"'Tis the closest we'll come, I presume," added John, as they crossed the Common from the Golden Stair and made their way along the road that eventually led toward Waterford, "to this stone castle Old Beelzebub was supposed to have built."

"He *must* have had property somewhere," said Abigail stubbornly. "Mrs. Seckar was quite clear that he did built a fortress of some kind . . ."

"Stories get conflated, Nab," returned John patiently. "Especially family stories. You remember Tilda Farren back in Braintree? The one who's convinced her parents fled England because her mother was the true heir of King James—the daughter for whom the baby Prince James was substituted for political reasons in 1688."

Abigail privately suspected that their neighbor back in Braintree was far too partial to the medicine she took for her so-called rheumatics and back pains, but was too distracted with dread to reply. Part of her prayed that there was something at the Seckar house that would solve the entire question—some hidden map or cipher that Grimes and his cohorts were actually looking for that could be handed over to them . . .

Another part of her was despairingly aware that if a map of the colony had been drawn on one of the bedroom walls complete with large red letters saying, HERE LIETH THE TREASURE, such was her mental state that she would be incapable of realizing what it was.

Dear God, keep him safe, she prayed . . . Did the sun never move? Would sunset never come, let alone midnight? And that detached and disrespectful part of herself, looking at her prayer as through a pane of glass, wondered how she had ever thought herself a woman of faith, when nothing—NOTHING—as precious to her as her son's life had ever hung in the balance like this before.

Mr. Scar-Eye . . . Dubber Grimes . . .

God, keep my boy safe.

The Seckar house turned out to be one she'd seen a hundred times in passing through Cambridge, its newer portion—facing the Waterford Road—built of brick and timber in the '80s of the previous century, tall and old-fashioned like Sam's house on Purchase Street, with most of the lower floor taken up by a great keeping room and a fireplace at one end that a family of four could have set up housekeeping in. The older portion of the house was hid from the road, lying perpendicular to the new, and had been built of a combination of stone and "nogging"—clay mixed with twigs and horsehair—a single story with a loft over part of it.

"This must have been the original keeping room," surmised John, as Congreve led them through its ancient door and into the chamber that had—for as long as anyone recalled—been the laundry. The big coopered tubs had been moved, and its northern wall knocked out and rudely patched over with boards. The eastern wall—what had been the gable end of the original house—joined to that of the newer structure but had never been pierced with a door: one entered the old wing from the yard, with no communication between the old part of the house and the new. *Old Beelzebub's idea to keep his son at a distance?* About twenty inches in from the original eastern wall a second wall had been built of bricks, plastered and whitewashed to match the rest of the room. Between the two walls a couple of shelves still remained, smelling of whitewash and dust.

Is Charley frightened? Have they hurt him?

He is in the hands of God . . .

Abigail stood back while John—who must, she knew, be in as great an agony as herself—methodically examined the space and the shelves. She herself looked around the old laundry-room, toward the great fireplace at its other end, where the copper and the racks of irons still stood . . .

He looked like the Devil would have—she heard Narcissa Seckar's thin old voice in her mind, passing along the words of Beelzebub's daughter—*if the Devil were ever to sit in a corner of the kitchen and play the fiddle . . .*

Here in this long, narrow chamber, the whole tangled knot of circumstance had begun: at the great old table, worn marble-smooth and so big it could not have fit through the doors, Old Beelzebub had undoubtedly copied out his original notes about the Governor of Jamaica into script unreadable by anyone in the colony and shoved it for safekeeping into one of his books.

This was the room where he—or perhaps his sanctimonious son—had walled his books away.

Where he had turned his back on his studies, thought Abigail. Why?

A man who'd sailed the seas, burned Spanish towns for their gold, studied the writings of the Mahometans, practiced sorcery, chatted with Satan, been worshipped as a god?

Deeper than ever did plummet sound I'll drown my book, swears Prospero in *The Tempest* when he forgives the men who wronged him and returns to the human world again. *I'll break my staff . . .*

Why?

He was missing two fingers of his right hand, so that he held the fiddle-bow strangely . . .

For a moment in her fancy she saw him, with his long gray hair like a horse's tail, and the ends of his silvered mustache braided and tied with green ribbons.

Playing the fiddle strangely with his mutilated hand. Looking straight into her eyes with a gaze black as coal and smiling mockingly. Had he, too, supped with the Devil and afterwards found that he had started chains of circumstance that he could not call back?

The Devil carried off children, she thought.

No. The Devil puts it into the hearts of MEN to carry them off.

She had been taught from tiniest childhood by her father never even to think, *May God curse this or that person.* But she thought it now.

May God curse Dubber Grimes and his henchmen, and may they die.

"Aunt?"

Shadows darkened the old door into the yard: Horace, Weyountah, Joseph Ryland.

"Have they found aught?" Horace stepped inside, gazing

around him with deep interest at the smoke-stained plaster and the high, steep rafters of the ceiling.

And Weyountah: "Dr. Langdon had men in two weeks ago to take away the books in the Reverend Seckar's regular library in the main part of the house. About half of those had been bought originally by Emmanuel Whitehead, though a few must have belonged to Barthelmy."

"Mrs. Adams." Ryland bowed deeply over her hand. "Mrs. Squills at the Golden Stair said that you could be found here. His Excellency has authorized me to offer a reward toward which he will contribute. He is most distressed and most anxious to show your husband—and indeed all the citizens of Boston—that he bears no ill-will. If there is anything that he can do—if there is anything that *I* can do—"

"Yes," said Abigail softly, "there is." And taking Ryland by the shoulder, she guided the young man into the corner near the great fireplace and lowered her voice still further. "You can tell me what you were doing with fifty-four of Beelzebub Whitehead's books in your chambers."

Ryland looked aside, flecks of color slowly rose to mottle his colorless cheeks. "Please, Mrs. Adams—" He glanced toward Revere and John, still poking about before the hidden cache on the east wall. "I beg of you, tell no one—"

"Not His Excellency?"

He put his hands briefly to his face. "I don't know how you can know this—"

Horace opened his mouth to make the obvious remark that they'd searched his room, but Abigail cut in ahead of him with, "Mrs. Seckar told me that you'd purchased them."

"His Excellency—" began Ryland, and stopped. Then he let his breath out in a sigh. "His Excellency has never been poor," he said, in a tone of weary defeat. "He heard that Old

Beelzebub's books had been found and mentioned that the old man had been a pirate. I-I thought, I hoped, that there would be some mention . . . pirates hid gold along these coasts as far north as Philadelphia, I know." His voice faltered as he spoke, as if he could not easily find words. "He asked me to enquire and I—'twas the act of an ingrate, but I can only plead that I was poor. I purchased the books of Mrs. Seckar with the Governor's money and told him that they had all been sold to others before I came with my offer. I thought—if there was a map or a cipher in one of them . . ."

"You didn't try to buy them through someone else?"

He looked at her blankly. "Someone else?"

"A Mrs. Lake?"

He frowned a little, fishing through his memory for the name, then shook his head. "I mean only to hold them until I've had a chance to go through them—"

"You have not done so yet?"

"No, m'am. I—since the books came to my hand, I've been in Boston more than I've been here, helping His Excellency. The only times I've come to Cambridge have been to help my students prepare for the examinations, to drill with the Volunteers . . . and to"—he stammered just slightly on the words—"to be of service to a . . . a private pupil who has suffered a great loss . . ."

Sally Woodleigh. Who is in elaborate mourning for George Fairfield and fainting in the arms of any wealthy man who'll stand still for it.

And if you were wealthy, she reflected, looking into those deep-set brown eyes, *she would be fainting in YOUR arms . . .*

"Please." Ryland swallowed hard. "Please tell no one of what I did. I will make the money good . . . There's treasure out there somewhere, I know there is. His Excellency's records of the colony speak of—of old Whitehead . . . I know he must have left some . . ."

"And do they speak," asked Abigail, "of this stone fortress of his? Or of where he might have held land?"

Ryland shook his head. "He held none, m'am. I've looked through all His Excellency's records. He had a sort of stronghold on the coast up above Lynn, but that was all, and 'twas burned by the Navy in King William's War. 'Twas thought the old man's books were all destroyed then—he was well known as a scholar. So I was surprised to hear that they'd survived here."

"As indeed you might be. Does anyone know you have these other books?"

"Not that I know of, m'am."

"Then keep it that way," she said softly. "And if any man approaches you about them, deny it, or invent a tale that you've passed them along to the Governor. Mrs. Seckar spoke of them as cursed," she finished. "And 'tis true; ill things have befallen those who've had them in keeping. And I only hope and trust," she murmured, as with a deep bow Mr. Ryland took his leave, "that you survive the possession of them once our friends discover nothing in those books of ours but chemical formulae and notes concerning the treatment of horses' piles."

They set forth quietly from the Golden Stair at half-past eleven that night: John and Abigail, Revere and Katy, crossing the Common on its northern side by the slitted glimmer of a single dark-lantern held low. The new moon had set early. By wan starlight the world was formless, trees like black thunderheads and the fine brick houses of the village's worthies no more than dim cutouts of dark against darkness. Abigail carried the wrapped package of books in her arms. *Accursed things*, she thought . . .

Was it only that *love of money is the root of all evil*? Mr. Joseph Ryland had, from the moment she had met him, impressed her with his integrity: even his devotion to the King's cause sprang not from place-seeking, but from dread of civil war. The fact that he would embezzle money from his benefactor, lie to him, then take advantage of his collection of the colony's old documents to hunt for the location of the treasure, only for money . . .

For money and love?

Sally Woodleigh's lovely face floated for a moment in Abigail's thoughts.

Going to get your bid in with the beautiful Sally, haha?

She burned off Ryland's eyebrows during a chemistry lesson, but he's still tutoring her . . .

He is young. And beneath that steady exterior, she sensed in the young bachelor-fellow the capacity for passion—for Sally as for the cause of his King.

The dark bulk of the college buildings rose to their right as they moved on into the open field of the Harvard Yard, where the young men ran their footraces on bright spring days and played at ball, and where the hay was harvested in June. A single lamp glimmered, high in some uncurtained room, like a dim gold star in the blackness, and a stirring of night-breeze brought the smell of the college stables. Revere had brought a long, forked stick with its straight end sharpened; this he drove into the ground in the center of the yard, then hung one of the lanterns on it, above the level of the tops of the long grasses that in some places grew thigh-high. At the foot of this, Abigail laid the wrapped package of the books.

Please, God, let all be well . . .

She was trembling as John took her hand in his, and

together they retreated back toward the college, her cloak and skirts flapping around her ankles, the yellow smudge of the closed-down lantern-beam bobbing on the ground before them in the dark. Her thoughts seemed to have narrowed, running in a blind circle of fear and hope and agony.

Charley. Dear God, keep him safe.

Stillness and the watching sparkle of the distant stars. John shut the lantern-slide and they stood in the darkness among the trees along the wall of the college barn, where Fairfield had met with goodness only knew how many young ladies in his short career. Nothing below the level of the sky was visible, save that single light out in the midst of the Yard. John's breath was a steady whisper beside her, and his arm circled her waist, his strength surprising. Katy's hand stole into Abigail's free one, chilled in the night. A bird cried somewhere in the trees.

Then silence.

The distant light went out.

Abigail's breath caught. She started forward; John's arm tightened around her: "Give them a moment to get away from him."

But she knew if Charley had the freedom of his own limbs he'd immediately start looking for them, would get lost in the long grass . . .

Then a rifle-shot cracked, like thunder in the darkness. Then another and another. Abigail gasped as if cold water had doused her—somewhere a man cried out . . .

Sam. Dear God. Dear God—

She tore the lantern out of John's hand and the two of them were running, running toward where the light had been. John shouted, "Nab—!" and his hand caught hers in the darkness, and then, *"Charley!"*

Don't be an idiot, John, he'll try to run toward us and get lost—

"Charley!" she screamed. "Charley, we're here—!"

Shouting ahead of them, in the direction of the Sever orchards, and another gun fired, and then, thready in the blackness, a child's wail, "Ma!"

"Stay where you are!" shouted John. "Stay where you are and GET DOWN!"

I'm going to kill Sam. I'm going to kill him—

"Ma!"

How she found her way in the whole blackness of the Harvard Yard she didn't know, but the jolting lantern-beam showed her Revere's forked stick, the quenched lantern, and Charley huddled down next to the stick—not in fear, but trying to untie the short piece of rope that fastened him by one ankle to the upright wood. Somewhere in the darkness men were shouting, a confusion of sounds—*Get him! Hold him! Tory bastard!* The child stood up at the sight of their lantern, held out his arms, and Abigail and John both fell to their knees, catching him tight—

"Are you all right?" gasped Abigail. "Are you—"

The soft skin pressed her cheek, miraculously, blindingly.

"I wasn't scared," said the boy cheerfully. "I knew you'd get me."

In the blackness behind them, two more shots rang out.

I'm going to kill Sam.

At John's insistence—obeying his direct order was one of the most difficult tasks in their relationship so far—Abigail remained in their room at the Golden Stair, lying beside the sleeping Charley while John waited in the common room downstairs for Sam to put in an appearance. On the walk back to the inn, Paul Revere swore with such soft-voiced fury at his fellow Son of Liberty that Abigail was inclined to believe that he hadn't been in on the plot, but cold rage at them all nearly stifled her.

"How dared he?" she began, when she and John carried their son up to the chamber, "How *DARED* he—?"

John stroked Charley's head—the boy had fallen asleep in Abigail's arms before they'd even reached the Common—and breathed, "Later, Nab. Look to the boy."

Do what you should have been doing all this time . . .

Look to your child. Let men do men's work.

Sick rage filled her: at herself, at them, at the world. At the Sons of Liberty. At Sam.

Listening—for their room at the Golden Stair was close to the staircase that led down to the common room—she heard when the Sons of Liberty came in: the sarcastic voice of Mrs. Squills asking, would Mr. Congreve care for some assistance in arresting them all for breaking the curfew?, and then the low-voiced rumble of explanations, arguments, accounts. Twice Abigail almost fell asleep only to jolt awake again from dreams of panic, dreams in which she reached the lantern-staff in the middle of Harvard Yard and there was no child sitting beneath it, or dreams in which the child beneath it—

She shook her head, forcing the image away in panic. *He's well. He's truly all right. He wasn't even frightened, he says . . .* Oddly, she believed him. His body bore no signs of mistreatment, just a little bruising on his wrists where he'd been tied—no worse, so far as she could tell by the candle-glow, than he got from some of his rougher games with Johnny. (Despite the strictest orders all the children had not to play any game that involved tying each other up . . .)

If Dubber Grimes and his minions hadn't been shot out of hand by the Sons of Liberty, she supposed she owed them a plea of clemency for that.

The voices faded.

John's tread on the stair.

His dim shape in the light of the candle in his hand as he

opened the door. She could see he carried the package of books beneath one arm.

"Did they take them?"

He set the light down on the small table beside the bed, barely large enough for the candlestick and the package he bore. It was still wrapped all around in string, the big red globs of sealing wax uncracked. "Two of them," he said. "The scar-faced man—Grimes, I think his name was—and the man they called Newgate Hicks. Both are dead, shot in the scuffle—"

"And I suppose Sam didn't give a thought to the fact that we might want to ask these gentlemen who was paying them for their services? Whether it was the Governor or Mr. Pugh or—"

"Sam is furious. Of course he wanted to know who the true culprit is."

"You astound me." Abigail heard the shrewish shrillness that cracked her voice but couldn't help herself. "I didn't think Sam had a thought in his mind except finding this accursed treasure, if there is a treasure, no matter what it costs . . . just like whoever it is who is behind this attempt. And will be behind the next one."

She was aware that she was trembling, almost sick with reaction to shock, with anger. She reached out, ran her hand over the package of books—

Then looked up at John and said, knowing it for the truth, "Were the books even in this package?"

"No." He sat on the bed at her side, and when she threw his hands off her—furious with him as with the others—and ripped at the thick paper, the heavy seals, he persisted and took from her the half-revealed copies of some of Sam's old Greek textbooks. Drew her against him, held her close. "'Tis all right," he said softly. "'Tis all right, Portia. 'Tis done."

"It isn't," she whispered, and leaned her head on his shoulder.

"It is for tonight."

Twenty-four

Abigail was calmer when she and John descended to breakfast the following morning, but the anger she felt, though colder, was no less real. Years of milking cows and doing farm-chores had made of them both early risers; they were halfway through Mrs. Squills's porridge, eggs, and coffee before Revere joined them.

While she and John were still alone, Abigail inquired, "Does Sam have the true books here with him? Or was he so sure he could get away with his trick that he didn't even bring them?"

"He has them," said John. "He's staying at the Indian's Head—"

"For fear I may have glimpsed him yester'even and guessed what he was about?" She poured a dollop of cream from the pitcher into her coffee, a drink of which she was not truly fond, but Mrs. Squills would serve no tea.

"For fear you'd stab him in his sleep afterwards, I think." John spoke lightly, but Abigail could see him watching her sidelong. He knew she was still very angry indeed.

Stab him as George was stabbed . . .

Revere felt it, too, she could tell, when he descended the stair and greeted her, and—though happily married to his lovely Rachel—flirted a little with Mrs. Squills as she brought out hot bread and more coffee. "Is the boy well?" he asked, and John nodded.

"He slept soundly—sleeps still. Katy's up there now with him."

"I want to thank you," said Abigail, holding out her hand to her friend. "More than I can say."

The silversmith shook his head. "All's well that ends well. I could have murdered Sam—"

"Yes," said Abigail. "Sam. All's well that ends well, as you say . . . But if you would, Mr. Revere, when you're done with breakfast, would you be good enough to go to the Indian's Head and tell Sam I want the thinnest of the quarto volumes—the handwritten one with the red cover that contains the astronomy tables and the chemical experiments and the accounts of what flowers bloomed when. Katy and I will be going on to Concord—"

"Nab, I can't leave Boston now!" cried John. "The King's ship—"

"I didn't ask you to come with me. I know what you need to do in Boston—and you, too, Mr. Revere. All's well that ends well—but the matter isn't ended. Horace and Weyountah will come with us to have a few words with Reuel Seckar about who it was who handed her vile brother that poisoned frumenty. Is Diomede still in the vicinity, by the way? Or has he been smuggled clear out of Massachusetts?"

"He's at a place called Phips's Farm," said John, his brow furrowed with uneasiness at her words. "Travers—the man who actually carried out the jail deliverance—tried to talk him into flight to New York or Philadelphia, but Diomede says, he will not leave this area until one or another of us has spoken with his master, when he arrives, that Diomede may learn in how much peril he actually stands. He is loathe to utterly separate himself from all chance of seeing his wife and children again—"

"Oh, the foolish, foolish man," said Abigail sarcastically, and dabbed butter on her bread. "Loathe to brand himself utterly a murderer by breaking jail and fleeing? Now who ever would have supposed a man could be so silly?"

"A man would consider the course a good deal less silly when he has a noose about his neck," returned John. "There are men in Concord who have said they will take him in and claim him as a servant of theirs—"

"Can he be sent for here?" Abigail glanced at the slow-graying darkness of the window. "To be honest, I could do with another outrider—"

"You could do with half a dozen," said John bluntly. "Sam has half a score of men at call who can bear you escort—"

"The men Sam would give me as escort," retorted Abigail, "if the local Sons of Liberty bear any resemblance to those of Boston, would be as dangerous to Katy and myself as Messrs Grimes, Hicks, and the Cornishman. At least they would who haven't any business in their lives more pressing than hunting pirate treasure, rather than starting to cut their hay or make silver teapots or organize the defense of our liberties or pursue their livings like honest men. Do you think," she added, when John opened his mouth to protest, "that ruffians like Bruck Travers and smugglers like Ezra Logan whom Sam gets to fetch and carry for him would stick at carrying off treasure if they could? Do you think Sam would stick at it if I spoke of doing a thing with the gold—if there *is* gold— besides handing it over at once to the Sons of Liberty?

"I trust Horace, John," she went on more gently. "I trust Weyountah. And I must do this now, soon—ere the King's ship lands and the Governor acquires more strength, as you know he'll do, whatever else the King's Commission decides. And if it isn't the Governor, but only Black Dog Pugh, do you think *his* strength will be less if the Crown's is greater?"

"You sound as if, having found the true culprit in Fairfield's murder, you intend to go on from Concord to seek this mythical treasure."

"I do, John," said Abigail. "I must. Whoever is behind the attempt to kidnap Charley—whether 'tis the Governor or Pugh or someone else we've no notion of—do you think his failure will make him shrug his shoulders and give the matter up? If this treasure is not accounted for and *seen* to be accounted for, one way or the other, these men will try again, to force me or Horace or someone else close to us to aid in its discovery. We might not be so lucky next time. Next time you or Sam or any of our friends may be in jail or in hiding, and unable to lend a hand. It must be done now."

And she knew that—whatever her mother might say of it—this was true.

"Where do you mean to look? Sam has been through the court records, and this Mr. Ryland of yours"—she had told him of her conversation with the young Loyalist—"has seen everything the Governor has in his private collection, and both agree Whitehead had no property in the backcountry."

"If he was living in an Indian village, he wouldn't have," replied Abigail. "And if land were registered in his name, after King Philip's War I'm very certain some good Protestant congregation made sure that the records were changed, and serve him right for living with the Infidel. I shall see what Katy and Weyountah—and old Beelzebub himself—can tell us of the matter. Charley!" she added, springing to her feet as Katy came down the stair with the boy's hand in hers.

"You've had an adventure, son," said John, moving over on

the bench to make room for the child. "Will you have coffee with us?" Which meant a great deal of milk and the tiniest bit of the bitter black fluid to darken it. "So tell me, lad, did they starve you and keep you in chains?"

Thus encouraged by the lightness in his father's attitude, Charley poured forth his account of his captivity from the moment that Mr. Scar-Eye had scooped him up in the alley that led from the yard to Queen Street (only Abigail suspected that her son had actually gone out to the street). Other than being tied up and locked in an attic somewhere near the waterfront, it didn't sound as if Charley had been mistreated, and Abigail marveled a little at John's handling of what was, essentially, an interrogation: *Where were you taken? What did they do? Could you recognize the place again?* By treating it as an adventure—when Abigail knew, from the redness of John's ears, that his rage was no less than her own at the men who had kidnapped his son—he drew the fear from the event and disabled nightmares to come. "I knew you'd save me," Charley said again, hugging his father's arm and pressing his face to his coat-sleeve.

All's well that ends well. Yet aside from the fact that the deaths of the scar-faced Dubber Grimes and his associate prevented learning who had paid them, Abigail felt no pity for them and tried not to be glad that they were dead. She was burningly conscious that "all" had come very close to *not* "ending well."

"Do you think you—and Weyountah—will be able to figure out at least where Old Beelzebub's fortress might have lain from the notes in his commonplace-book?" she asked Katy quietly, when Revere returned to the inn with the volume.

"If someone can read it to me." The girl turned the pages as—at the other end of the table—Charley negotiated for a ride back to Boston on the crupper of Revere's mare instead of at his father's side in Mr. Revere's dull old chaise. "Lord if

I ever saw handwriting to beat this! It seems like the old man took careful note of where he found things and what the woods looked like and whether the dirt was clay or—is that word supposed to be *gravel*? That bog he speaks of where he'd gather his cranberries—that sounds like the one over beyond Medway—I don't know another where you'd get twelve gallons of berries in a day in mid-September. But over here he speaks of walking out to gather witch hazel, which grows on higher ground, and it doesn't sound as if it's far. And I do know there's high ground just north of there."

Horace and Weyountah arrived shortly after that, driving Sassy in George's chaise and accompanied by Diomede, who had been mounted—and armed—by the local militia. Two other saddle horses were tethered behind the chaise, from the same source, Abigail assumed, though Sam had had the good sense not to show his face anywhere near her. The prospect of riding back to Boston with Mr. Revere—and of boasting of his adventures to those of his siblings who had not been so fortunate as to be kidnapped by villainous ruffians—had reconciled Charley to his mother not coming back with them. He flung his arms around her neck and kissed her before his father tossed him up onto the back of Revere's saddle: Abigail smiled a rather crooked smile.

"Take care," whispered John, and glanced at Diomede as he handed rifles to Weyountah and Horace.

"We should be back tomorrow near sundown," said Abigail. "With at least some idea of where this treasure lies . . . if anywhere."

"And if the King's vengeance comes to Boston whilst you are gone?"

"Get the children to Isaac and Eliza's," she said. "And I shall meet you in Concord."

She kissed him then, and he helped her up into the chaise—

and gave a good-natured boost to get Horace onto the obese and mild-mannered nag that one of the local Sons had lent to the expedition. Weyountah, with a rifle on his back and another scabbarded beside his saddle, was very different from the scholarly chemist Abigail had met only a few weeks before: quiet and grim and watchful as he prepared to return to the world on which he'd turned his back. Horace, in his ill-fitting black coat and hand-me-down boots, looked considerably less heroic— he'd coated his face with an aromatic compound designed to keep mosquitoes and gnats at bay.

But when he nudged his borrowed horse over to the other side of the chaise, to exchange words with Katy, Abigail saw suddenly in her nephew's eyes the way he looked at the girl . . .

And there are heroes and heroes, she thought. *And one doesn't have to wear a crimson coat or join the Sons of Liberty to be one. Only have a willing heart.*

And for herself, like the heroines of ancient Rome she'd read about in Livy and Tacitus, it was up to her to defend her family as well as she might while her husband dealt with the greater threat to the State. She did not, however, feel tremendously Roman as she touched Sassy's flank with the end of the whip, and the innyard fell behind them as they set off into the morning's brightness.

They passed over the bridge at the village of Lexington midmorning and a little over an hour later crossed the narrow wooden span over the Concord at the town that shared the river's name. Like Cambridge, Concord had the peaceful air of well-being so often to be found in New England villages: sturdy houses of brick or clapboard surrounding a Common where cows grazed on the rather shaggy grass;

wide house-lots and tidy fences of stone and hedge surrounding the fields of the nearby farms. The farmer to whom Diomede had been sent for concealment—a colonel in the local
patriot militia—directed Abigail on to Genesis Seckar's
farm, deep in the woods at the end of a rutted track: "Though
if you're hungry for a little nuncheon, m'am, I'll get my good
wife to bring out some bread and milk for you, for you'll get
nothing from him, not if you was starving."

"If a son shall ask for bread of you, shall you give him a stone?"
Abigail quoted the Gospel, and Colonel Barrett made a
mouth of mock dismay.

"Now, m'am, that's doing the man injustice! He'd never
part with a stone that could be put to work in a fence!"

"If it's all the same with you, m'am, sir," said Diomede,
with a little half bow and a glance at Barrett, "and not wishing to treat your house as an inn—but I should feel a bit
better to go on with Mrs. Adams here, and Mrs. Fairfield, to
their destination to make sure all goes well. I'll keep well
out of sight if any tries to stay us, and won't come next or
nigh your place, if I think any would be after me—"

"Oh, Lord, man, don't worry over that!" The colonel
laughed. "Every man in the militia's heard you'll be staying
here—on the run from the Tories, I think Mr. Adams said? Bad
cess to 'em! And those who aren't in the militia can come speak
to me if they've a problem with it." He grinned. "And there's
enough of us here in the town that there won't be a problem.
Come and go as you please, man." He slapped Diomede's arm.
"And stay as long as you wish! And if you're any hand with a
musket, you'll find you'll be welcome in my company."

"Er—thank you, sir." The valet looked slightly disconcerted at the idea of joining the patriot militia so soon after
riding in his master's company with the Loyal Volunteers,
but—wisely, Abigail thought—held his peace.

"Tell me truthfully," said Abigail, once they were on the road again toward the Seckar farm. "You're the only man, among all those who're saying what you ought to do, who actually knows old Mr. Charles Fairfield: what are the chances that he'll listen to testimony that says your master was murdered by someone else? When I've spoken with Mistress Seckar, I hope to be able to put a name on the true killer—but will Mr. Fairfield listen? Out of all of this, what would *you* have?"

"What I'd *have*, of course," replied the slave slowly, "is for Mr. Charles to be so struck by your proofs that he'll take me home to where I can be with my Maggie again, and our girls . . . But to tell you the truth, Mrs. Adams, even if he said he agreed, I'd be afraid to go. Because once we'd get home, sure as grass grows in the spring, there'd be some among his friends who'd start in saying how I'd actually done it—and them not knowing a thing about it, only that they've been afraid all their lives that they'd die at the hands of one of their own slaves. And then I *couldn't* flee. Yet I know if I just run off, when he gets back to Albemarle County, Mr. Charles will sell my Maggie and our girls, and I'd never find them, not if I searched a hundred years."

"He won't," said Katy firmly. "Because when he gets here, I'm going to start proceedings—that is," she added, "if Mr. Adams is agreeable—to be recognized as George's wife with interest in you and Maggie and your daughters . . . And he can't very well sell them if there's a lawsuit going on."

Diomede grinned, a little wanly. "That's kind of you, m'am," he said. "And a good thought, for no man wants to buy a slave that might get him brought to law. Yet I think, to stand a chance of winning that suit, you're going to need all the pirate treasure we can find and more."

* * *

The Seckar farm was very much as Katy had described it: ruinous with neglect, the miles of winding lane that connected it with the Concord Road a river of potholes, while its aged owner concentrated on the salvation of his soul. Abigail and Katy both climbed down from the chaise after the first few yards, and were taken up behind Weyountah and Horace, leaving Diomede with Sassy and the vehicle. "One would think the man had little taste for company," murmured Weyountah, glancing about him at the woods that closed in around the neglected track.

"Or company had little taste for him," retorted Katy with a grin.

Reuel Seckar proved to be a gaunt giant of a woman, her untidy hair dirty beneath a dirty cap, her dress spotted with tallow and food. She and her cowed and delicately built sister-in-law—brother Genesis's wife—emerged from the house when the visitors first came clear of the woods, and Mistress Reuel strode toward them like some gaunt Titaness from an earlier phase of the world, her white hair flying like some grimy sybil's and bare feet slopping in the clayey mud. By the look of the house, Genesis either shared his brother's feelings about household help making women lazy, or more likely, he couldn't get anyone to stay. When Abigail brought up Narcissa Seckar's name, Reuel sniffed with contempt.

"The whore of Babylon," she said. "Given over to Mammon and to chasing the things of this world, and greedy as a Jew: What profit it for a man—aye, or a woman!—to gain the whole world and to lose her soul? And defiant," she added bitterly. "Sweet-mouthed as a honeycake, and a heart rotted with Satan's pride and defiance against the Lord."

Abigail—whose slender experience with Jews had exposed none noticeably more greedy than some good Congregationalist slave-traders she had encountered—bit back the urge to remind this sour-faced bissom that she'd spent thirty years of her life under a roof that belonged to that Babylonian whore, and replied merely, "What a relief for you, then, to be no longer obliged to share a home with her."

The glare that Mistress Reuel shot Abigail amply informed her that Brother Genesis—whatever his other sins—had not been pleased to take his sister in when he'd thought he'd gotten her safely palmed off on Brother Malachi. Heaven alone knew what their mutual mother had been like, God rest her soul.

"I've no time for idleness," said Mistress Seckar. But instead of turning back toward the kitchen, she snapped at the woman who waited by the kitchen door—white-haired and almost toothless, with the bludgeoned air of one who barely realizes anymore that she is human—"Get back to the stew, or Gen'll be in a passion when he gets home."

The other woman moved heavily off.

"What is it you want?" Reuel glared at Weyountah, with his long black braids and his hunting-shirt, then transferred her scornful stare to Katy, sitting *à l'Amazone* behind him, her slim brown ankles visible beneath her rucked-up skirt. "Brother Genesis don't hold with visitors, and he's his meditations to do 'fore he sits to his dinner."

Abigail wondered if this woman did meditations also, rather than clearing up the piles of husks, peelings, cores, and cobs heaped knee-high around the rear door of the house. "I took the liberty of coming to see you," she went on matter-of-factly, "because my husband is attempting to trace the books that Mrs. Seckar sold: the ones found behind the wall in the laundry-room."

"Greedy slut." Mistress Seckar's face darkened with suffusing blood. "The books were part of the house, as 'twas willed to my brother, God rest him, by Mr. Whitehead—and a good Christian man he was who had the strength to abide the Lord's law. Threatened me, she did—threatened to go to law, bare-faced as Jezebel at her window—"

Horace looked as if he were going to point out that Jezebel had not been bare-faced at her window but in fact had been comprehensively painted, but Katy—Weyountah's horse was close enough beside his for her to do so—kicked Horace in the ankle and he said, "Ow!" instead.

"For shame!" cried Abigail—of Narcissa Seckar, not of Katy—and added, "And with her husband dead beside her in her bed! I understand her poor husband had had offers for them?"

"Devil-books." The old woman's lip lifted to show bare brown gum adorned by a single canine. "Wrote by the Devil, and give to that Devil that hid 'em. There isn't but one book in the whole of the world that won't damn the soul of him that reads it, and that's the Scripture. Gen tried to tell Malachi that, and Mother . . . As stubborn and willful as she was, in his way." She shook her head, and added, with a distinctly medieval relish, "And he's burning in Hell now on the unquenchable pyre of his own books. He'd never turn loose of them, though he saw right enough that those Devil-books were evil, and burn *those* he should have, with their filthy pictures and their heathen writing. I always thought that sweet that Mr. Ryland brought us that night was to butter him up, to get him to sell them books—"

"Mr. Ryland?" Abigail tried not to raise her brows in surprise.

"Governor's lapdog." Mistress Seckar nearly spit the words.

"A lying weasel. Hutchinson is the son of witches, that's never touched nothing that didn't turn to vileness. I wouldn't put it beyond that smooth-faced hypocrite Ryland to have poisoned that frumenty to get at the books for that heretic Hutchinson. For he had 'em in the end, all but eight or ten."

"He did indeed," agreed Abigail thoughtfully. "All but eight or ten."

Twenty-five

W hat an archwife!" said Weyountah, when they were on the rutted lane once more, working their way back to the road. "I wonder she isn't poisoned by her own spit."

"*Mulier ira Jovis*," added Horace sententiously, then glanced across at Katy and blushed in confusion, though Abigail guessed that if annoyed, Katy could outdo many women in the *ira Jovis* line.

Katy murmured, "Mr. Ryland—"

"I don't believe it," said Horace, baffled. "Ryland, kill George for—for money? Or just the rumor of money? Not to mention shuffling off the blame on poor old Dio! He didn't have a bean, of course, but he would *never*—"

"Not for money, I don't think," said Abigail slowly. "For silence after George woke and saw him standing in his room— to protect his position in the college, his position with Hutchinson—"

"His Excellency would never have ordered Ryland to—"

"No," said Abigail. "In fact I think he'd have been

horrified, had he learned his protégé had broken into another student's rooms—particularly if all that could be visibly *proved* was that Ryland was trying to lay his hands on a couple of singularly disgraceful books. If Hutchinson knew *nothing*—of the treasure, of the books, of Ryland's attempts to have translated the one handwritten document that he *was* able to find at Seckar's that looked like a cipher—if Ryland was not entirely certain even that the treasure existed but hoped to present his patron with a fait accompli . . ."

"He may very well have done what he did." Weyountah spoke without taking his eyes from the dappled depths of the woods around them. "Once he'd killed a fellow student, he had to cover his tracks, even if it meant accusing an innocent man."

"And if George thought Ryland was looking for something else there," said Katy softly, and tightened her grip around the Indian's waist as the horse hopped across a little stream that had washed out the path. "They'd quarrelled over me the day before, George told me—Ryland told George he had no business meddling with tavern-wenches when Sally Woodleigh was breaking her heart over him and everybody in the Volunteers was watching. The captain must be worthy of respect in all things, he said. George told him to go soak his head. When he saw Ryland in his room—"

"He shouted," finished Weyountah. "And sprang out of bed—especially if Ryland had the desk open—"

"And of course the books weren't there," said Abigail. "Because Mr. Pugh had already been in and stolen them before George even returned."

When they reached the road where Diomede waited, Diomede listened, appalled, to what they had learned and what they surmised, but he confirmed what Katy had said. "I didn't know it was you they spoke of, m'am," he said, as the chaise moved off toward Medfield. "But it's true Mr. Ryland is in love with Miss Woodleigh, and he was angry for her sake. Angry, too, that Mr. George was 'bringing down' the Volunteers in the eyes of folks like Miss Woodleigh's father and Mr. Lechemere and Mr. Vassall. It was far from the first time Mr. Ryland had spoken to Mr. George about how he behaved."

"It must have gone to his heart," murmured Abigail, "to see the militia troop he worked for and the woman he loved, both taken so easily by someone who was behaving so unworthily—"

"That's still no reason to have Mrs. Lake and her bullyboys attempt to murder *me*."

"I'm not sure Ryland knew anything about it." Abigail glanced up at her nephew, jogging beside the chaise on his fat and amiable mare with dust sticking to the mosquito-grease on his face. "He may not have—even as elegant gentlemen like Mr. Hancock and my uncle Isaac don't *really* want to know anything about what happens to a Tory when he's tarred and feathered. Ryland would know about Old Beelzebub from the moment word got around that the books had been found in his house. And from associating with the Governor's household, Ryland would certainly have known about Mrs. Morgan and the Avalon. Perhaps he knew also about Mr. Chamberville's house. He may have thought Mrs. Morgan would bring Horace to the Avalon to do his translation . . . and he may not even have known she *had* the kind of henchmen one would expect to find, working in the stables of a house of accommodation—"

"Well, he jolly well should have known." Katy raised her head from puzzling out the pages of the notebook.

"I don't expect he had ever been to the Avalon himself, or to anyplace like it. But once Dubber Grimes got wind of the treasure—and since Mrs. Morgan made herself copies of both the original Arabic document and Horace's translation, it looks like she planned to go treasure-hunting herself almost from the start—Ryland had no more control of how the hunt was going to be conducted than Sam had when he stirred up that mob to attack Governor Hutchinson's house back nine years ago over the stamp tax. Sam doesn't want to admit it—and Ryland didn't want to admit it—but these things do get away from one."

"And all the henchmen knew," said Weyountah, "was that it was connected with a code . . . and that the code was to be found in one of the books."

"So *is* there a treasure?" Katy wanted to know. "At the end of all that?"

Abigail was silent for a time, watching the sun dapple through the trees on Sassy's dark flanks. "I think so," she said at length. "Though perhaps not the sort of treasure that Mr. Grimes and his companions thought they'd find."

It was growing dark when they reached Framingham, famished and exhausted. At the single tavern there, Abigail asked, first, after word from Boston—had any message come concerning the King's reply? When the answer came in the negative, she asked after the countryside west of Medfield, and did my good host or his good wife—or the half-dozen members of the local militia who'd come in at the end of their chores to make the same enquiry about affairs in Boston—know the whereabouts of Deckle's Farm? Her sister—"That's Mrs. Deckle," she explained earnestly—had writ her that it lay about a day's journey on from the village and that 'twas near a stone Indian ruin, or maybe 'twas the Spanish that had built it . . .

"Spanish?" The innkeeper shook his head. "Not never heard of Spanish in this district, m'am—"

"That wouldn't be the Devil's Castle, would it?" A very young militiaman looked up from his ale.

"Is it a castle, then?" exclaimed Abigail in assumed surprise. "I'd heard, 'twas built by the Indians—"

"Narh, Indians never built in stone, m'am." (Abigail already knew this.) "Never heard about the Spanish, neither. But there's supposed to be a stone ruin over near Hassanamisco Pond where there was a Nipmuc village onc't upon a time. Never seen it myself—"

Enquiries for Hassanamisco Pond elicited several sets of mutually conflicting directions, most of which began, "You take the Grafton Road . . ." and ended anywhere in the countryside. Descriptions of the countryside between Framingham and Grafton were not encouraging.

"Is there a cranberry bog nearabouts there?" asked Katy, and that brought better results. Three of the militiamen testified to the location of Shelby's Bog, but two-three miles from the Grafton Road.

"And Shelby is the name of the man who owns the land?" inquired Abigail.

"Not now it's not. 'Twas the feller who took it over after King Philip's War, after the Nipmucs was wiped out there, so I've heard—"

"Friend of the Governor in them days," put in somebody's white-haired grandfather.

And another, derisively, "Ain't it always?"

"Had the records changed, I heard, to prove 'twas always his," confided the oldster. "Didn't get no good of it. 'Tis bad, hard land."

"Good cranberries, though . . ."

Bad, hard land, as Abigail feared it would, translated to, *few farms, much woods, impassable roads, and nobody within ten square miles to ask after the whereabouts of Shelby's Bog.* Most settlement in this part of the colony had gravitated toward the easier land of the Blackstone Valley to the south. In the course of the following morning, the two farms they encountered, at the ends of overgrown lanes from the not-very-well-kept Grafton Road, appeared to have been burned out by King Philip's Whampanoag warriors a hundred years previously and not rebuilt. The track branched and branched again, the chaise wheels sinking in the clayey muck. Abigail watched the angle of the sunlight slanting through the woods, and with an acid sense of urgency, she calculated when they must turn back in order to make Boston by nightfall. *We must find the place. Find the treasure, or prove that there is nothing there.*

Else we will know no peace . . .

Ahead of the chaise, Weyountah rode imperturbably, drawing rein from time to time to listen to the woodlands that were growing steadily thicker around them, though Abigail heard nothing but the twittering of birds, the rustle of the wind. He was listening, she thought, as a hunter listens—or a warrior entangled in the endless, ancient woodland fights between tribe and tribe.

He had turned his back on that world, she thought, looking up at the tall figure in his hunting-shirt and boots. And she wondered why. A world where his family clung to the old ways; a world in which visions counted for more than the theorizing of mathematicians and the spirits of the land clung tight to the hearts of its children, holding them in corn-patch and longhouse forever.

He had made his choice and refused to be part of that past. At what cost, Abigail could only guess.

But turn away as he might, thought Abigail, the old world of the forest was in his blood nevertheless. As they moved on again down the less travelled of those forking traces, she could see him sorting out the sounds of birds, the scent of the wind in the woods. As a child he'd hunted and learned what the land should sound like if all were safe.

"Oh, thank Heavens!" exclaimed Katy. "The cranberry bog at last!"

Sunlight brightened through the trees. Bees hummed over milkweed and marsh marigold, and the heavy, peaty smell of wet ground and standing muck breathed through the sweeter scents of the woods. Abigail drew rein, and Katy produced old Beelzebub's notebook again, marked in a dozen places last night as the five of them had sat around the lamp in a corner of the ordinary of the inn at Framingham until the innkeeper had good-naturedly told them he was banking the fire and putting up the shutters for the night.

"The village should be no more than a mile or two north-west of here . . ."

"And it being noon," replied Abigail mildly, unwrapping the lunch that Mr. Buckminster at the tavern had put up for them, "if you can determine which direction *is* northwest—"

"Back that way." Weyountah pointed. "At least," he added, as he stripped the harness from Sassy and tethered her to graze, "that's where I'd put a village: up the stream that feeds the bog, on the higher ground where the soil is better. Look, you can see where the trees were cleared and have grown back. Will you stay here or come with us?"

"Stay here?" Katy stared at him as if he'd suggested she drown herself in the bog. "And miss finding the treasure?"

"And miss a hard walk of a couple of miles uphill." Horace attempted to spread the carriage-rug for her over a couple of dry tussocks, only to have her turn impatiently away.

"I'm two months with child," she pointed out. "I didn't lose a leg."

"Don't be a goose, Horace," added Abigail. "Katy will be fine."

They shared bread and cheese and cider, and proceeded up the hill.

Weyountah said, "Damn it!" and stopped where the trail steepened, holding up his hand.

Abigail followed his eyes down to the trail and saw in the soft ground the tracks of a man's boot.

Even to her totally inexperienced eye, she could tell they were fresh.

And that there was only one man.

Horace gasped, "The Cornishman . . ."

"Don't be silly." Abigail dropped her voice, knowing how sounds carried in the quiet of the woods. She nudged Weyountah, who put his foot next to the track. "The Cornishman's as big as an ox. At a guess," she said, considering the difference in length and breadth, which was barely any and that little in the Narragansett's favor, "'tis Mr. Ryland."

Horace breathed, "He must have found the location of this place in the Governor's records after all—"

"And lied to us about it?" Abigail mimed shock. "The scoundrel!"

Beside her, she was aware of the girl's eyes suddenly growing hard.

Weyountah signed Diomede to separate from them and follow through the woods some half-dozen yards to the right. Then he handed Katy his spare rifle and motioned her to do the same to the left. In this configuration—picking their every step in the brown leaf-mast—they moved up the hill to where the land flattened out a little. A century had eradicated all trace of the cornfield-patches, where beans and squash had been trained up among the stalks, and the trees seemed to Abigail no thinner or smaller than the surrounding forest. Yet she guessed that a village had been here simply from the shape of the land. There was a spring and level ground big enough for houses to be built by men and women who'd lived and died in this place, worshipping strange gods and minding their own business until the white men came.

Horace's hand closed tight around Abigail's wrist. Between the trees she saw it: stones scattered among the deadfalls and tangles of witch hazel, and a little farther on, the shape of a curved stone foundation and what had been a wall. Trees had grown up close to it, roots forcing apart the stones in places. Elsewhere what looked like shallow steps had been cut in the rock bones of the hill on which the fort had been built, and the ruins of what could have been a tower.

The Devil's Castle.

Her nephew tried to run forward, and both Abigail and Weyountah pulled him back. They moved forward slowly, Diomede and Katy edging inward from the sides. It was Diomede who reached the stone remains first, surmounted a sort of breastwork, then straightened up in an attitude of shock. He called out, "Mr. Ryland!" and scrambling over the wall, sprang down. Horace broke from them, ran toward the place at the same moment that Abigail saw Diomede lift the head of a man who had been lying on the broken foundation-stones, half hidden by the walls.

Ryland struggled a little, flailed one hand, then seemed to come to his senses and cried out, "Get away! Go back!"

And around them in the woods, half-a-dozen rifles crashed.

Twenty-six

Weyountah grabbed Abigail by the arm and nearly dragged her up behind the low walls of the ruins, thrust her down beside him, and peered over the tumbled stones. Another rifle crashed and the ball cracked against the barrier near were they lay. Abigail gasped, "Don't tell me the Governor has men out after us after all!"

Diomede dropped beside her, bleeding from where a rifle-ball had grazed his arm as he dragged Ryland to shelter beside them.

Through gritted teeth—not taking his eyes from the surrounding trees—Weyountah replied, "I'd say the Cornishman went and got some friends after Tuesday night."

"Drat the man! They're as bad as the Sons of Liberty for coming out of the woodwork—I daresay some of them *are* Sons of Liberty in their spare time . . ." Keeping crouched behind the wall as best she could, Abigail pulled open Ryland's coat and shirt; blood was welling from a fresh wound.

"He was hit just now, m'am," said Diomede. "When he sat up a little and cried for us to get back—"

A short distance away she could see a huge pool of the man's blood where he'd been lying when Diomede had found him.

"Give me your handkerchief or anything you've got . . ."

Close beside her, Katy got off a shot, then cursed vividly and added, "Horry, have you ever loaded a gun? Curse it . . . Dio, let Horry take care of Ryland, we need you to cover the other angle—"

Obediently the servant shoved his handkerchief into Abigail's hand and, catching up rifle, powder, and patch-box, sprang to the remains of the tower. "I can load." Abigail had performed that service on numerous occasions when her father or William had gone duck-hunting. "Just give me a moment . . . Horace, don't you *dare* faint—"

She dug in the pasty and staring boy's pocket, pulled out five handkerchiefs, and wadded them tight against the bleeding hole in Ryland's chest. The bullet was lodged—at least there wasn't a corresponding wound in his back—but it seemed to her for a time that the blood would never cease pumping out beneath the reddened linen, no matter how hard she pressed. Behind her she heard Katy swear again, and say, "I'd better go to loading. I can't seem to hit the whoresons—"

And another crack of gunfire from the woods.

A swift glance back across the stone foundation—it seemed to have been a rectangle some thirty feet by fifty with a tower at either end—confirmed Abigail's first, fleeting impression that there was a square hole in the flooring of the more intact of the two towers, where Diomede crouched on the high-point of the remaining wall. A broken paving-stone and a couple of pieces of wood lay next to it, the remains, presumably, of a trapdoor . . .

"Good Lord, don't tell me there really is a treasure!"

She looked back down at Ryland's face. It was wax white beneath horrible bruises. Shocked, she said, "He's been beaten!" When he reached to touch her hand, she saw the mutilated fingers, sticky with blood.

Katy dumped powder from her hand down the rifle-barrel, shoved in a patch and ball, and whacked the whole thing with the ramrod. "I thought they worked for him!"

Ryland turned his head a little and without opening his eyes managed to whisper, "Saw me. Harvard Yard."

Enlightenment flooded Abigail and she said, "Were you the one who shot Dubber and Hicks after the kidnapping?"

"Had to," breathed Ryland. "They'd seen me—Mrs. Morgan's—" His eyelids fluttered open and for a moment he looked toward Horace. "Sorry. Never meant . . ."

"And I suppose you never meant that old Professor Seckar would die, either," retorted Abigail tartly.

"*Had* to," he insisted. Pleaded. The long fingers—their ends bloodied where the nail beds had been crushed—tightened feebly on hers. "Destroy them . . . within their camps. *Defend this city, for mine own sake . . . for my servant David's sake . . .*"

"Did they take the treasure, then?" asked the girl, as Abigail sat back on her heels, shocked—and suddenly cold—at his words. "Then why the Devil are they still shooting at us?"

"Or was it gone when you got here?" Weyountah fired again, followed instantly by another shot from Diomede on the tower. "Quick—!" The Indian stretched out his hand for Katy's gun, and she pressed it into his grip and instantly reloaded, twice as fast, Abigail noticed, as William had ever managed to . . .

"Not gone—"

Softly, while Katy was reloading, Abigail said, "It wasn't gold, was it?" She understood then what the treasure was, what it had to be. Pieces falling into place . . .

Ryland shook his head. *"Defend this city . . ."*

So THAT, she thought, *is what he would have brought in triumph to Hutchinson. As vindication of whatever it had cost.*

And she had to admit, it would have brought him all the preferment, all the advancement, all the recognition he wanted and had never received.

Maybe even the hand of the lovely Sally Woodleigh.

She felt breathless with rage and horror.

On the tower, Diomede called out, "They're coming around to your downhill side—"

Weyountah nodded sharply in that direction, where the cover consisted of trees rather than the stone walls, and Katy snatched up rifle and ammunition, and darted across the open space of the foundation. "How many?" he called out to the servant.

His head on Abigail's lap, Ryland whispered, "Ten."

"And they didn't believe you," said Abigail, "did they, when you said the treasure consisted of . . . What? Other books?"

Ryland shook his head, closed his hand on hers again in a paroxysm of agony as more shots chipped the stone behind Abigail's head, fragments stinging her neck like bees. Weyountah called out, "Don't fire unless you have to! They're trying to draw our ammunition!"

"Didn't believe." Ryland's voice seemed to fumble at the words. "Followed me here . . . Excellency's papers . . . Shelby . . . records . . . Devil's Castle . . ." His eyes opened a slit under fluctuating lids, and he seemed for a moment to come back to himself. "Tried to buy them . . . The books. Excellency spoke of him . . ."

"Did you think 'twas gold you sought at first?" whispered Abigail. "Or did you know from the start it wasn't?"

". . . was a scholar, Excellency said . . . rumor of what he'd made . . ."

"Did Hutchinson know what you were doing?"

"Foolish." Ryland shook his head. "All tales. If it was real, he'd have used it. Knew it had to be here. Knew—somewhere in his books—had to be a way here. He'd write—Arabic—secrets . . ."

"And you tried to get Horace to translate," said Abigail. "Only to find you'd got hold of the wrong secrets."

Weyountah rammed home his load, swung the rifle to his shoulder, fired over the wall; a second shot immediately from Diomede told Abigail that someone had probably tried to rush them. How many shots had they left? How much powder?

And what would the Cornishmen and his friends be likely to do to two women in order to convince the wounded man—or the two other students—to tell them of the location of a treasure that didn't exist? Or didn't resemble any treasure they understood?

"And you knew George had some of Seckar's books in his rooms . . ."

"Wretched slut." The cold fingers picked anxiously at Abigail's hand. "Best—most beautiful—not worthy—untie her shoes . . ." Abigail realized he was trying to talk about Sally Woodleigh. "Loved him, and all he could see . . . some hostler's daughter . . ."

Well, reflected Abigail, *considering the nature of the missing books, 'tis no wonder he wouldn't admit having them to YOU . . .*

"Hush," she whispered. "Hush . . ."

"Had to find it." Ryland shook his head, pushing her admonition aside. "Came here—had to be here. Governor's papers . . . They followed. Cornishman . . . men with him . . . They think it's gold. Wouldn't listen . . ." He moved his head weakly, flexed his massacred hands. "Destroy the rebels. Destroy . . . utterly within their camps . . ."

Katy shouted, "Weyountah!" and a salvo of gunfire came

from the thicker trees on her side of the enclosure. Weyountah stood—Abigail had no idea where he got the courage to do it—for a better look through the trees, fired, dropped to his knees, and began loading with cool precise haste as a shot came from Diomede on the wall, and when Weyountah rose to his feet again, rifle at the ready, two more shots cracked out. He dropped behind cover again. Abigail could see blood on his coat.

"Followed me," whispered Ryland again. "Followed me here. Knew if I could get it . . . all those years of waiting and work. Knew if I could defeat them . . . kill the rebels in their camps . . . Sally . . . His Excellency . . . His Majesty . . . He'd made it. I know he'd made it. All the stories say . . . Beelzebub. He'd used it. Why he left, why he came to Cambridge . . . *I will defend this city, for mine own sake, and for my servant David's sake* . . ."

With a heart turned to ice, Abigail finished the passage from Second Kings: "*And it came to pass that night, that the angel of the Lord went out and smote in the camp of the Assyrians a hundred four-score and five thousand; and when they arose in the morning, behold, they were all dead corpses* . . ."

"*I will defend this city,*" murmured Ryland. "*I will defend this city* . . ."

And as Abigail had done, Horace whispered, "*What*?!?"

". . . *the angel of the Lord* . . ." Ryland's bleeding hand loosened in hers.

"It's what he thought was in the only handwritten Arabic document he found among Beelzebub's books," said Abigail softly, laying the back of her hand close to the unconscious man's nostrils to detect the thread of his breath. "And you have to admit, 'twould have made his fame not only among the Loyalists, but with the King as well." And as gently as she could, she began going through the pockets of his coat.

Horace turned and handed Weyountah the last of the rifle-balls, and by the way the Indian shook the lead powder-bottle, Abigail knew that was the end of the powder as well.

"Go to Katy, Horace," said Weyountah softly. "Get her rifle, cover that side of the enclosure—I should be surprised if she has shot or powder left either. Mrs. Adams, take Katy and flee up the hill into the deepest woods you can find. Go to ground as soon as you find someplace where you won't be seen; I doubt they're good enough trackers to follow. Stay there until dark—"

Abigail thrust the cracked and yellowed wad of papers she'd pulled from Ryland's pocket into her own. "We can't leave—"

"Do it. Crawl along the wall 'til you get to the woods—"

Crouching behind the ruined heaps of stone, Abigail darted and crept to where Horace and Katy knelt in the shelter of the trees, arguing in furious whispers—

"Don't be a goose, girl." Abigail caught Katy's arm.

"They need every gun—"

"And how many loads have you left? I thought so. Give it to him, and follow me—"

Abigail pulled her heavy skirts up and wrapped them tight around her hips and thighs; she dropped to the ground as close to the wall as she could. *John*, she promised, *I'll never follow my own course again in the face of your objection* . . .

And leave the possibility open, her non-Mother self whispered in her ear, *that one of those men would find those papers in Ryland's pocket and sell them to someone who DID know what to do with them* . . . ?

At the end of the wall the laurel grew thick. She and Katy slipped in among the glossy branches and crept uphill, trying to keep from thrashing the foliage too much. When they reached its end, Abigail heard behind them the thunderous crashing of rifles in the woods downslope, caught Katy's wrist in her hand, and ran. Her long skirts tangled with her legs, the uneven ground catching at her feet: deadfalls, rivulets, holes hidden beneath thick leaves. As a child she'd been swift as a sprite, but it had been a long while since she'd run full out any distance—not a thing a respectable matron was supposed to do.

A rifle crashed somewhere in the woods behind them, close enough that she could smell the powder. At the same instant a man sprang from behind a thicket: he was no taller than she but hard-looking as carved hickory, with a brown face burned by weather and the tarred pigtail of a sailor and the hardest, coldest eyes Abigail had ever seen.

He held a knife in one hand.

The two women swung around to find another man—a rough laborer of the kind that Sam routinely summoned to form his tame mobs—pointing a rifle at them at a distance of a few yards.

The man with the knife said, "An' the next shot goes right in your back, m'am."

The man Abigail recognized as the Cornishman—the hulking, heavy-browed ruffian that blonde Belinda had cried warning against at the house called Avalon—stood over the crumpled body of Weyountah in the old ring of the stone tower. One of his men held a pistol on Horace and Diomede. Others were slapping and shaking Ryland and pouring rum down his throat, with oaths fit to scandalize Satan in the Pit. Katy let out a cry of anguish and tried to run to Weyountah, and the hard little sailor laughed and grabbed her by the arm, yanked her back. A couple of the men grinned and called out, "That's the dandy, poppet!" and "Aw, 'fraid we've broke his courting-tackle?" and "'Tain't all we'll break, 'fore we're done—"

Horace lunged at them in blind fury, and the man guarding him reversed the pistol in his hand and gave Horace a crack in the head with it that dropped him to the broken pavement. The Cornishman grunted, "'Ere, none o' that," in a thick slow voice, like a semi-articulate pig's. He turned beady eyes toward Ryland, who had given a sort of faint cry that ended in coughing. Abigail could see blood trickling from his mouth mixed with the rum.

The Cornishman took Katy by the hair, dragged her over to Ryland, and pulled a knife the size of a small cutlass from his belt. "You 'ear me, Ryland?" He kicked the young man's ankle. Ryland managed to move his head. Abigail wrenched herself from the grip of the man who held her—she counted seven of them and wondered if Ryland had miscounted or if three of them were lying wounded back in the woods—and ran to Ryland's side. She dropped to her knees as one of them reached to stop her, propped the young bachelor-fellow gently against her, his head on her shoulder, instead of on the stones.

Three days ago she would have condemned the man who had put in motion Charley's kidnappers—however little he had had to do with the kidnapping itself—to the bottom-most circle of Dante's Hell without a thought. But she knew what she saw, looking at the color of his face and that dribbling line of blood. Probably the Cornishman did, too. And wanted Ryland to last at least through questioning.

The Cornishman kicked Ryland again, and when his eyes fluttered open, grunted, "Can you see, mate?" He slid the knife under Katy's bodice and sliced the cheap cloth open to the waist, jerked down the chemise beneath, and put the knife-blade against the side of her breast. "I'm only gonna ask this once," he said. "Then I starts cuttin'. Where's the gold?"

"Hutchinson has it," said Abigail.

Those piglike eyes narrowed. "Then why'd he say there wan't none?"

"Probably because Hutchinson told him there wasn't," she replied, with a dizzy sense of walking across a tightrope. "He sent him here to find what was in that pit—books and scientific implements . . . You know how His Excellency is about books."

The Cornishman blinked, thrust unexpectedly into the position—as Abigail felt she had been for weeks—of trying to prove a negative, and he was no better at it than anyone was . . .

He shoved Katy away from him, sending her sprawling to the stones. Before the other men could get to her, Horace reached her side, drew her up against him and away from the Cornishman as that hulking man stepped close to Abigail, knife extended inches from her face. "You lyin' to me, bitch? 'Cos if you are—"

Abigail never heard what he would do to her if she was, in fact, lying. In the same second, it seemed, that she heard a gunshot in the woods, the Cornishman's narrowed eyes popped wide, as if startled, and a rifle-ball exploded out of the front of his throat in a shower of gore. Abigail rolled aside, dragging Ryland with her, as the Cornishman dropped before them like a felled steer.

Two other shots cracked. The man standing nearest Horace and Katy fell, clutching his side and shrieking; with great presence of mind Katy grabbed the pistol away from him as he fell and shot the next-closest man through the body. Weyountah rolled and caught up that man's rifle, and the four remaining ruffians dropped their weapons and threw up their hands at once.

Diomede tossed one of their rifles to Katy and went around collecting the rest even as Black Dog Pugh—trailed by his two slaves, both armed to the teeth—emerged from the trees.

"Sink me, I thought I'd never find this place," Pugh exclaimed. "Wouldn't have, either, if they hadn't started shooting. And a damn good shot," he added, looking down at the Cornishman's sprawled body and the bullet-hole in the back of his neck, "if I do say so myself. Pity I can't scalp him as a trophy." He held down his hand for Abigail. "Don't you think, m'am?"

Twenty-seven

"D id you follow him?" asked Abigail, as the slave Eusebius rose from beside Joseph Ryland's body and shook
his head. Abigail knelt also, to feel the young man's wrists
and throat, though she trusted the African's judgment, and
indeed, it was clear to her that Ryland was dead.

She looked up at Pugh.

"Lord, no. And just as well," the bachelor-fellow added,
and rubbed his fat, unshaven chins. "If we'd been following
him, instead of our upstanding friend here"—he nudged the
dead Cornishman with his foot—"we'd probably have fouled
on him like two dogs on the same lead. No, the fair Nancy—
when she came to me rather the worse for wear, for having
been locked up in some sailor's trap in Boston where Grimes
had left her and the other girls—told me the Cornishman
had come in and got himself a band of tavern toughs to find
'pirate gold,' as he put it—"

"You knew about Old Beelzebub's treasure, then?"

"Lord, who in the islands didn't? Is it here, then?" He

walked to the opening in the floor and squatted to peer in. "Grimes and his bravos were boasting about looking for it down at the Pig one afternoon, so I knew there was a rumor *someone* had found it. I had five shillings with Jasmine that the thing didn't exist. I should love to find out I'm wrong, though."

Abigail looked around her a little distractedly, and Eusebius—in the process now of tying the hands of their prisoners—wordlessly stripped off his coat and handed it to her to lay over Ryland's face. As she did so, Abigail drew out the knife that Ryland wore at his belt, noting the slender blade was only barely wider than a paper knife. Precisely the width, in fact, of the wounds in poor George Fairfield's side. Whether a judge would recognize this—or even look at it as evidence—she didn't know, but she pocketed the weapon just in case before she followed the Black Dog to the trapdoor.

"The treasure that Ryland was seeking," she said carefully, "I don't think was gold at all, but rather books and formulae of chemistry—or alchemy, as Beelzebub would have thought of it . . . Did Grimes tell you that?"

"Grimes? He swore it was gold, so much it wouldn't have fit into one shipload—sort of thing one talks oneself into after the second bottle of Hollands. I was buying the Hollands." He winked one long-lashed green eye. "A small investment, considering the money I took off him as the afternoon wore on. Doesn't look far down," he added. "And stap me if I see any gold. But when Nancy and the other girls came knocking at my door Tuesday night, asking shelter and swearing the Cornishman was off after the treasure, that was enough to get me to follow along and see. Hold this for me, would you, m'am?"

He put a candle in her hand. He had taken it from his pocket along with flint and steel.

"Are they all right? Nancy and Belinda and Dassie—"

"You've met 'em, have you, m'am? Good girls, and corky

as squirrels—" He cracked flint to steel briskly, then blew on the spark where it had taken on the loop of tinder through his fingers. "Grimes took 'em off to some crimp named Manchet down by the harbor who runs a nunnery out of his backroom. Kidnap, too, by the sound of it. Nan laid old Manchet out with a pintle Tuesday night after Grimes and his bravos had left, and the three of 'em came to me. Just bring that winker over here—"

He fastidiously removed his coat, then lowered himself down the trap, holding his hand up afterwards for the light. Abigail saw the small glow bob and shift beneath her in a hole that resembled a cold cellar, perhaps six feet by eight, beneath the stone foundation of the old fortress: "Coming down, m'am? That's the dandy!" He set the candle on a shelf and held up his hands for her as Abigail wrapped her skirts tightly around her legs and slid down into his grip. "What a mess, eh? And not a gold-piece in the lot."

He held up the candle, as Abigail looked around. The few books that the old pirate had left in this little strong room had mildewed into black blocks, but the glass vessels had survived the passage of years. Abigail recognized them from Weyountah's workroom in Harvard Hall, what she'd seen of it through his poisonous smoke: crook-necked distilling-bottles, thin measuring-flasks. Two carboys showed signs of having contained fluids of some sort, now dried away to glossy dark scum on the bottom and sides. In clay pots, a number of salts and something that smelled like sulfur remained.

"Weyountah would know what all this is," she said, trying to keep her voice casual.

"Wonder if it spoils with keeping?" Pugh held the light close to the largest vessel, where the liquid had dried and crusted with time. "Does Jasmine owe me five, or do I owe him? Would have been a jolly good sport if there had been something here . . ." He picked up a telescope from the shelf, pointed it at the sky and peered through it for a moment, set it down again. "Would have guaranteed me the fair Sally's hand, anyway. So this is what poor Ryland was after?"

"I think so, yes. He told me—in the course of the affray—that he'd hoped to gain some recognition from the Governor for it."

"I expect he would. The old boy's never given up the hope of putting together a history of the colony, and a find like this—proof that old Beelzebub did really do alchemy to get the Nipmucs to worship him—would turn him pink down to the ends of his prehensile toes."

Pugh chuckled, like the great black bulldog he was called. "Ryland was just wild that old Seckar wouldn't sell him the old man's books when they were found back in April. I'm afraid I muddied the waters there a bit . . ."

"And George got the two you wanted in the end," said Abigail drily, "didn't he?"

Pugh met her eyes in the dim glow.

She raised her eyebrows, and his heavy mouth quirked sidelong. "You know about that?"

"I have a good guess. Your note to George—sorry, *Sally's* note to George—was in his pocket when he came back to his rooms that night . . . on *your* notepaper. I take it George was still away from his room when you went in—"

"Oh, Lord, yes. Bed all made up and turned down waiting for him—Dio's a born chambermaid. Glad to see the old fellow here, by the way—did you arrange a jail deliverance? Good on you. I tiptoed in just after the clock struck twelve. I was pretty sure, with George gone, Dio'd be laid out stiff as a board on the rum, though 'fore God, m'am, if I'd known how stiff I'd have gone out to the barn and warned poor George something was afoot." He stood frowning, gazing at the dulled and dirty equipment crowded on the little bench. Then, more quietly, "Ryland really killed George for *this?*"

"When one chases the Devil's treasure," said Abigail, "one pursues the illusion that Satan conjures in the mind, not the handful of sticks and dirt that are often the reality. It's not only that the heart lies close to the treasure . . . sometimes one finds that the treasure exists only in the heart."

"Silly bastard." Pugh shook his head, placed the candle on the table's edge, and held out his hands to her. "George was worth a thousand of him. Well, I always said old George didn't care about Sally one way or t'other—not that I'd say so to the fair Sally herself. That young lady upstairs—" He jerked his head toward the hole above them, "would be the girl he married, would she? Katy Pegg? Thought I recognized her."

"Was the license in one of the books?"

"Wasn't sure what to do with it." Pugh shrugged. "No need to go waving it in front of Sally, of course. D'you think the girl would go halves with me for whatever we could screw out of old man Fairfield on the strength of it? You know he'll never let it stand up in a Virginia court."

"That," said Abigail sternly, "is something you would have to discuss with Mrs. Fairfield. I believe she would settle for ownership of Diomede, and Dio's wife and children—and some sort of maintenance for her child. If you're going up," she added, as Pugh whistled sharply beneath the trap-hole for Pedro, "would you be so good as to ask Weyountah to come down? I want to see if he can salvage any of this for himself."

Pedro held down his hands for his master, and when he'd been hauled (*Pedro must be stronger than he looks!*) up through, Abigail made a swift search around the cellar for any further papers or notes that might have been left. There were none. Joseph Ryland had had sufficient time, before his erstwhile henchmen had put in their appearance, to gather them all, into the thick block of folded pages that poked Abigail in the thigh beneath her petticoats every time she moved.

"*Do* these things spoil with keeping?" she asked Weyountah, when the Indian had dropped lithely down beside her.

"The phosphorous certainly has." He hastily re-stoppered a flask in which the waxy crusts of something white clung to the sides; Abigail stepped back, repelled by the smell of it. "I'm not sure what some of this is, even. But he was doing something with sulfur, and the sulfur is still good—"

"Let's take that, then," she said, "and pass it along to Sam or Mr. Revere . . . One makes gunpowder with sulfur, no?"

"Among other things, yes. It doesn't seem like that's what Old Beelzebub was doing down here . . ."

"No," said Abigail, a little quickly. "Can I ask you something, Weyountah? We can take the sulfur, but when we depart, would you stay behind and destroy the rest of this? Destroy it so that none of it can be used again? I shall explain later," she added, as the Indian looked quickly sidelong at her. "Beelzebub's treasure is . . . not something I want anyone else to happen upon by accident. It has brought too much grief and trouble to the world already. 'Tis a secret best forgotten."

The Indian looked puzzled for a moment, then turned his head to study the chemical apparatus—the retorts and alembics, the filtering coils and small furnace, the piston air-pump and oily crusts in the vessels—and she saw something change in his dark eyes, as he guessed, perhaps not what the treasure of Beelzebub had been, but the *sort* of thing it was. Softly, he said, "You can rely on me, m'am. I shall join you in Boston tomorrow."

It was in fact late the following afternoon—Friday, the thirteenth of May—before Weyountah and Horace appeared on the Adams doorstep. Abigail—after a brief consultation with John—bade the two young men stay on for dinner with the family and to spend the night. Upon Abigail's return Thursday evening in company with St-John Pugh and his party—Katy, their various prisoners, and Joseph Ryland's body—John had listened to her account of the young Loyalist's death and her own theory about what Beelzebub's treasure had consisted of, and had agreed that it was a matter that must go no further.

From regard for their children—Charley seemed far more taken up with the equitable distribution of the wooden soldiers in the toybox than with the fact that he'd been kidnapped and held in the back-room of Mr. Manchet's tavern on Fish Street for forty-eight hours earlier in the week—the conference after dinner was held in John's study rather than the kitchen. But throughout the meal, Abigail kept glancing at Weyountah's face, reading her suspicions in the grimness of his eyes.

When John closed the door behind him and poked up the little hearth-fire—for the spring afternoon was chill—she asked, "What was it that Old Beelzebub had figured out how to make in the Devil's Castle back in 1675?"

Weyountah had spread out the notes on John's desk, a dozen folio-sized sheets, yellow with age and stained with time and mold. Notations of chemical formulae covered them, and writing both in Arabic and what Weyountah told her was Algonquian, the language spoken by many of the Massachusetts tribes. "All of this is written in Algonquian, but sometimes he'll use Roman letters for it and sometimes Arabic. No wonder people thought he was the Devil."

"But what is it?" Katy leaned from her chair at Abigail's side, tried to read past his shoulder. On the trip back to Boston, the girl had had a long, quiet conversation with Black Dog Pugh, presumably about whether half a loaf would be better than no bread once Charles Fairfield came to Cambridge. The West Indian had called again that morning, and conferred with both Katy and John. Diomede had wisely remained at Mr. Barrett's farm near Concord, under another name. "Why would anyone want a lot of chemical formulas so badly they'd kill for them?"

"Formulae," corrected Horace automatically.

"Killing is what they're about," said Abigail softly. "Isn't it?"

"I think so, yes," said the Indian. "I recognized a number of the experiments he's done. Beelzebub was working with combinations of poisonous vapors—mixtures of sulfurs and phosphorous a hundred times more deadly than the poisoned smokes the Romans used. Vapors that stuck to the skin and remained in the air for hours rather than dispersing."

"The Chinese used poison smokes, of course," said Horace. "The Persians, also—everything from balls of burning mustard to clouds of powdered antimony and chalk designed to asphyxiate the enemy . . . beastly. It sounds as if Old Beelzebub took a more scientific approach to produce clouds that would hang for hours in the air after they were shot by means of hollowed cannon-shells into enemy villages."

"Enemy?" said Thaxter, puzzled. "Who—?"

Weyountah held up the smallest of the sheets of paper, which contained not formulae, but simply writing in a firm, faded hand.

"*Evil Heart,*" he read slowly, translating as he went. "*We the fathers of the Abooksiqun village have smoked over the offer you have made to us to deal with the white men who come against us, who have tried to take our land. We have talked and we have prayed to the spirits that guide us. You say that you can kill the white soldiers who will come to our villages before they can reach us; that you can rub them out before they can see a single warrior of the Nipmuc tribe; that you can stretch them dead upon the ground miles from us and destroy their villages without a single warrior of the Nipmuck ever having to enter there. This you will do, you say, out of thanks to us, for taking you in when your own people had turned their faces from you."*

Weyountah turned the paper over, his strong-boned young face grave and sad in the lamplight.

"This we do not want and will not have. We the fathers of the Abooksiqun village understand the greatness of this gift of death that you offer to us, and thank you that we are in your heart and your thought. Yet we find this gift that you offer us an abomination. This is not what we wish to do or what we wish to become or how we wish our sons to speak of us after we are gone. When we are gone, we want our sons to say, Our Fathers were warriors, not, Our Fathers were cowards who poisoned their enemies from afar."

"He couldn't have done it," said Thaxter after a time. "Could he?"

Horace regarded him in surprise. "Of course he could have. 'Twas only a century ago that poisoned vapors were outlawed, when the French would use them against the Germans during the wars of religion . . ."

"And he had the materials," said Weyountah. "And notes for the making of phosphorous and other ingredients . . . He had made the vapor in a small quantity already. 'Twas devilish stuff, cleaving to the skin, both outside the body and inside the nostrils and throat. It would blind and blister where it did not kill, and apparently it rendered at least some of its subjects permanently paralyzed. Moreover, it sounds as if he were working on means to make it in quantity, and cheaply, and to lay it down everywhere in the forests where the militia would come to attack the Indian villages."

"And that's what Ryland wanted?" asked Katy, both shocked and sad. "Not gold, but a weapon to use on those who stand against the King?"

"Worth a thousand times as much as gold," John said,

from his chair by the little hearth-fire, "if one side has it and the other doesn't. As Ryland would know. 'Twould be a guarantee of advancement, more so than mere money, in the eyes of the Governor and the King."

"And the elders of the village decided they'd rather die," said Katy, a little wonderingly, "before they'd use it. Before they'd let themselves turn into people who would use it."

"People like Beelzebub," said Horace. "No wonder he left the village when they told him that."

"Because he couldn't bear to see them killed, as he must have known they would be?"

"Or because," said Weyountah, "he couldn't bear to see himself through their eyes. We found no evidence, by the way," he added, looking across at John and Abigail, "that His Excellency had sent anyone to follow Ryland. I'm inclined to think Hutchinson really didn't know." He shuffled the deadly papers together, passed them back to Abigail. "He was out in Cambridge this morning—Hutchinson was—and they say he seemed deeply distressed to see Ryland's body, but he didn't ask about the books or make any attempt to see his rooms—"

"Which is just as well," added Horace, "since we'd already moved the books to *my* room."

"You can have a look through them," offered the Indian. "They're just perfectly ordinary old books, you know. We had a look through them this morning when we got back—here's the list of them—" He withdrew a handwritten sheet from his jacket pocket and held it out to John. "The cover-papers had all been slit with a paper knife, and to judge by the smudges everywhere, Ryland had searched through them pretty well."

"That may have been before he got word back from Mrs. Morgan that what he'd hoped was the formula for a poisonous gas was just some old notes for blackmail," surmised Abigail. "Since afterwards, he certainly didn't waste any time trying to get his hands on the other books. Which is just as well," she said slowly, "because even if he had not intended the deaths of Seckar and George, having encompassed them, he would have to cover his guilt . . . in any fashion that he could until he had the formulae and equipment in hand. I don't imagine—"

Sharp knocking sounded on the front door, making them all look around. John rose and opened the study door as Pattie's swift footfalls passed in the hall. An instant later a familiar voice called, "John, it's Sam—"

Sam Adams strode into the study, greatcoat flapping open and a small portmanteau in his hand. "I've just come from the harbor," he said. "The *Duke William*'s been sighted coming past Calf Island—from London. She'll be docking at Castle Island before dark."

"Anyone go out to it?" asked John, with an eye on the portmanteau.

"The harbor pilot. And some traders with water and rum." Sam's voice was grim. "General Thomas Gage is aboard—the commander in chief of the British armies here up 'til last year . . ."

"They've sent him back?" asked Thaxter, a little apprehensively.

"They've sent him back," replied Sam. "Not *only* as commander in chief . . . He's now Governor of Massachusetts as well."

"Governor—" began Abigail, shocked.

John's voice was hard and strange. "They've put a *military commander* as our *Governor*?"

"Has he troops?" asked Weyountah.

Sam's mouth twisted, and he picked up his portmanteau. "Some. And you can bet your Sunday hat there are more on the way. From Halifax, from Ireland . . . And that's only the beginning. The King has signed something called the Boston Port Bill; it goes into effect in June. They're closing down the port of Boston: no shipping, no trade, no vessels of any kind to land at all until we knuckle under and give them money for their damned tea. Justices in the Colony Courts are henceforth to be appointed by the Crown. Juries selected by the Crown. All town governments in the colony—not just Boston—are to be disbanded . . . There are other provisions, but I'm not waiting here to learn of them. John—" He clasped his cousin's hand. "Can I rely on you for messages? John Hancock and I are bound for Concord. The militia's already starting a weapons depot there, where a British warship can't shell us—"

"Won't they be watching the gates?" asked Horace, and Sam grinned.

"We'll make a patriot of you yet, my boy. Hancock's got a couple of lads who're taking us across before the warships turn up in the harbor in earnest. Nab—" He turned to Abigail, bowed over her hand. "Barrett in Concord tells me you had sent on from Framingham about thirty pounds of sulfur you'd found in old Whitehead's fortress. You didn't happen to find anything of that mythical treasure there as well?"

He spoke lightly, but as the dying fire set up a little spurt of light, it seemed to find reflection in his eyes: anxiety, fighting-spirit, a mind that was already sorting a thousand things at once and racing ahead. Mentally rallying his troops and readying his response . . .

Troops coming into Boston.

The British military commander made Governor of the colony . . . and of how many other colonies, she wondered, besides? Town governments disbanded—to be replaced by what? The Crown controlling the courts. She was aware of John watching her, of the rough, worn texture of the papers beneath her fingertips on the table. British troops converging on Boston, and how long before they were marching out into the countryside? To Lexington where the militia was drilling. To Concord where the weapons would be hidden . . .

She took a deep breath, gathered the papers together, and said in her lightest voice, "I fear that a myth is all that it was, Sam. Myth and rumor that reached the degree of obsession, to the point that men would kill for what might only be a myth in their dreams." She crossed to the hearth, with the air of a woman tidying up the last household details before starting her mending, and dropped the papers into the flames.

"If there was treasure there," she said, "'tis gone now. We will do what we can, within the bounds of honor, to defend ourselves against the British."

"And more than that," added John, and in the new, sharp flare of light from the burning paper, he caught her eye and nodded his agreement, "more than that, we cannot do."